Christian Reid

The Man of the Family

A Novel

Christian Reid

The Man of the Family
A Novel

ISBN/EAN: 9783337001865

Printed in Europe, USA, Canada, Australia, Japan

Cover: Foto ©Andreas Hilbeck / pixelio.de

More available books at **www.hansebooks.com**

THE MAN OF THE FAMILY

A NOVEL

BY

CHRISTIAN REID

Author of "A Woman of Fortune," "Armine," "Philip's
Restitution," "The Child of Mary," "Heart of
Steel," "The Land of the Sun," etc.

G. P. PUTNAM'S SONS
NEW YORK & LONDON
The Knickerbocker Press
1897

The Knickerbocker Press, New York

THE MAN OF THE FAMILY.

THE MAN OF THE FAMILY.

PART I.

CHAPTER I.

No one who has seen the beautiful Bayou Tèche country of Louisiana—the land where the exiled Acadians found a second and fairer home—can ever forget its charming and picturesque aspects : the broad stretches of its verdant levels ; its fields luxuriant with cane or green with rice ; its pastoral expanses of meadow and plain ; above all, its spacious, old-fashioned homes, which, with their broad roof-trees and wide galleries, stand beneath the spreading shade of giant live-oaks, gazing out upon the wide, silvery reaches of the river.

At the landing in front of one of these residences, the steamboat which plies up and down the Bayou dropped one day a visitor—a man of middle age and business-like appearance—who walked towards the house, which stood a hundred or so yards distant from the stream, under the shade of its great trees. No one was to be perceived in or around it ; and an air of slumberous quiet seemed to pervade the whole place, although the doors and windows were all open to the golden sunshine of the autumn day. As the visitor approached he paused now and then to survey comprehensively the mansion in the midst of its lawn, the tangled garden in its rear, and the level green country, a very Arcadia of fertility and beauty, which spread on each side as far as the eye could reach ; while the smoke from the chimneys of the various sugar-mills in sight rose into the exquisite atmosphere, a token that it was the height of the sugar-making season.

"A fine plantation," observed the new-comer to himself, as his glance passed over the fields of cane in the immediate neighborhood ; "and well kept up, considering that it is in the hands of a woman. Hum-hum ! The money will not be badly invested. Interest for ten years, and at last—this ! But who comes here ?"

The figure on which his eye had suddenly fallen was advancing towards the house from the direction of the sugar-mill, which stood at one side, perhaps a quarter of a mile distant—a slim, straight feminine figure, dressed in a dark skirt and light shirt-waist, with an immensely broad-brimmed shade hat, such as the laborers throughout the country wore. Under this hat, as its wearer drew nearer, he perceived the delicate-featured face of a girl, whose dark eyes regarded him with anything but a look of welcome. They met in the middle of the lawn, and he lifted his hat in salutation.

"How do you do, Miss Yvonne ?" he said, with an ease of manner for which there seemed scant warrant. "I see that you are busy, as usual, overlooking things. Quite the 'man of the family '—ha, ha ! I've often said that your business qualities are most remarkable—for a young lady. I hope your mother is well ?"

"Is my mother expecting you ?" asked the young lady.

"N—o," with a little hesitation. "I have taken the liberty of coming without notifying her. Business called me to Bayou Tèche at this time, and I decided that it was a good opportunity to have a personal interview with Madame Prévost. Letters are apt to be—ah—unsatisfactory, and things can be better arranged sometimes by talking them over."

"If you will come in," said the girl, ignoring this as she had ignored his other remark, "I will let my mother know that you are here."

They had now reached the steps which led down from the pillared front of the dwelling to the lawn ; and, ascending them together, crossed the gallery to the door, which stood hospitably wide open, displaying a spacious hall that rose to the second story, and extended throughout the house. Leading the way, Yvonne ushered the self-invited guest across this hall and into a large, lofty room of fine proportions.

"My mother will no doubt see you in a few minutes," she said ; and then, closing the door, left him alone.

He stood where she had left him, taking in the aspect of this apartment, so different from any to which he was accustomed, and so full of the subtle aroma of the past that it was able to impress even his dull soul with a sense of something apart from the intrinsic value of the objects at which he looked. There was not a trace of the modern world perceptible in this stately *salon*, with its lofty ceiling panelled in fine stucco relief. Every article of furniture which it contained was clearly an importation from France, and at least a century old. To one who could appreciate such associations, how many suggestions of the Paris over which Marie Antoinette reigned gayly as the fair young Dauphiness, and of the romantic days of colonial New France, dwelt in these tables with their curving legs, the inlaid cabinets, the gilt-framed mirrors, the chairs with harmoniously faded wreaths of flowers upon the ivory satin which covered their cushions, all reflected in a floor polished until it shone like a sheet of ice.

Strangely incongruous amid such surroundings was the figure of the man gazing upon them—typical of the least admirable of modern conditions. No hint of anything derived from or owing to ancestry was to be discerned in those blunt plebeian features, sharpened only by an expression of shrewd, hard cupidity. "A man of business," he would have defined himself with pride; and a man of business, in the narrowest sense of that abused term he was, one for whom the word "business" covered not only stern bargains ruthlessly driven, all advantage of others' necessities taken, and every possible amount of usury that could be exacted, but also all transactions, however dishonest, which the letter of the law did not declare illegal. And yet this man now stood as virtual master in a house where men of another order had upheld in all the acts of their lives the highest code of a fine and delicate honor, and, when the necessity arose, had counted life and life's best possessions as nothing for the sake of principle and a cause.

It was not long before, shaking off the influence which had momentarily touched him, and which was chiefly due to certain recollections of his youth connected with this house, he walked with heavy tread across the floor, greeting with a glance of recognition one or two portraits as he passed them; and, as if fearing to trust his weight to any of the slim-legged chairs, stood by one of the windows, looking out once more over the fair, level country. But he was not at this instant thinking so much of the rich acres before his gaze as of the unwise disdain that he had read in a girl's dark eyes.

"In any case, whether my offer is accepted or not, your

reign is nearly over, my young lady," he was thinking, with a sense of triumph. " D——n your cursed aristocratic pride ! I am glad that *you* are not the one who is to stay here !"

The girl whom he thus addressed in his thoughts had meanwhile crossed the hall and entered a smaller apartment, the windows of which overlooked the green vistas of the garden. It was the sitting-room of Madame Prévost. She was seated now before an open escritoire of finely carved ebony, so old, so quaint, so charming that it would have delighted an antiquarian ; and was engaged in writing a letter, from which she did not lift her eyes when Yvonne entered.

So it was that for a minute the girl stood looking at her silently, with an expression of infinitely wistful compassion. In truth her heart was wrung with that sense of unavailing pity which is one of the most painful of human emotions. It was an emotion which even a stranger might, in some degree, have felt for Madame Prévost, so plainly were the marks of corroding care set upon her ; but to one who loved her with passionate devotion, earth could furnish no sight more sad than that delicate, worn countenance, crowned by its hair prematurely gray. That she had in her youth possessed a rare loveliness there was no room to doubt. Any one familiar with the pictures of the famous beauties of seventeenth and eighteenth century France must have been struck by her resemblance to their type. On a hundred canvases and squares of ivory we may see those fine patrician features, those delicate brows, that forehead of beautiful contour, those perfectly moulded outlines, and that slender neck which bore the head so loftily. Upon how many of those fair necks the axe of the guillotine fell ! But we do not read that one of them ever drooped in craven fear.

Looking at Madame Prévost, it was easily to be perceived that she, too, would have faced the mob howling for the blood of aristocrats, the tumbril and the scaffold, with the same proud composure, the same matchless dignity tempered with disdain of those noble ladies of the *ancien régime* whom she so strikingly resembled. She had indeed faced in her youth scenes hardly less terrible. She had lost father and brothers on the battle-field; she had wedded the lover of her choice in the midst of the roar of cannon, the red horror and tumult of war; and in the same hour sent him back to his post in the front, not to meet again until, when all was lost save honor, he returned to her, ruined in fortune and broken in health. She had faced then the last and perhaps worst enemy of all : the poverty which entails perpetual struggle—a struggle that, together with his old wounds, had after a few years killed her husband ; and which, when she had laid him away with the comrades he had tardily joined, she continued to face for her widowed, sonless mother and her four young daughters. The signs of this struggle were graven in deep lines upon a countenance still full of ineffaceable beauty and yet more ineffaceable distinction, on which was also to be read the impress of the courage, the fortitude, and the patience with which she had met the misfortunes that had fallen upon but never overwhelmed her.

Since a minute passed and she still continued to write without lifting her eyes, Yvonne crossed the floor and looked over her shoulder. She was not surprised to find that her mother was addressing the man whom she had just ushered into the house.

"Mamma," she said quickly, "there is no need to write that letter. Mr. Burnham is here."

Madame Prévost started so violently that a blot of ink

dropped from her pen upon the fair sheet of paper half covered with her small, regular writing. She turned and looked up at her daughter with an expression of amazement.

"What do you say, Yvonne?" she asked. "Mr. Burnham here!"

"Yes, mamma, he is here. I came to tell you. I was at the sugar-house when the steamer came by, and I saw that it dropped some one at the landing. Since we were expecting no one, I thought I had better see who had arrived; so I came over at once and met this man on the lawn. He is in the drawing-room now, waiting for you."

"Did you ask him why he had come?" inquired Madame Prévost, pushing aside her letter with hands which trembled excessively.

"No. I only asked him if you were expecting him, and he replied that you were not; that, business having called him to Bayou Tèche, he thought he would take advantage of the opportunity to call and see you—or something to that effect. Courage, dear! After all, it is no worse to see him than to write to him."

"Oh, yes, it is much worse!" said Madame Prévost, rising to her feet. "His coming is a bad sign—a very bad sign, Yvonne!"

"Let us hope not, mamma. Perhaps it is only, as he says, that he was in the neighborhood on other business, and so thought a personal interview with you would be better than an exchange of letters."

Madame Prévost shook her head.

"I doubt if he has any other business here than to see me—and the plantation," she said. "It looks badly, his coming. There would be no necessity for an interview if he were content to continue taking his interest; but if he demands his money, Yvonne, the end has come. We are ruined."

"Don't think that he will demand it until he tells you so," said Yvonne, putting her arm around the slender, trembling figure. "Mamma dearest, it is not like you to be so unnerved. Shall I see him for you and ask what is his business?"

"No, no!" answered Madame Prévost. "I must see him myself. It is foolish to be so unnerved; but I think my courage is not what it was, and I have been fearing this so long."

"Ah, God help us!" cried the girl, with a passionate intonation. "So long indeed! Oh, what would I not do to spare you all this horrible anxiety and suffering! But I can do nothing—nothing! And you must go and be tortured for no fault of your own by this low-born usurer——"

"Hush, hush, Yvonne!" Calm came back to Madame Prévost at the sight of her daughter's excitement. "Let us never forget justice. The man has a right to demand his money; and if he shows little consideration and no generosity in doing so, we must remember and allow for the fact that he *is* low born and low bred. Perhaps, as you say, I anticipate the worst without cause. We will soon know, for I must see him at once. Do I look composed? I should not like to show any signs of agitation." She held out her delicate hand and regarded it for an instant. "Yes, it is quite steady again. So now I will go. Do you stay here, dear; and I will return as soon as possible to let you know the object and result of his visit. Whatever it is, my child, we must meet it with courage, you and I, for the sake of the others."

She kissed tenderly the wistful young face, smiled reassuringly, as long habit had taught her how to smile, and left the room with a step as firm, a bearing as composed, as if she were going to meet a friend instead of a foe, an honor instead of a humiliation.

CHAPTER II.

IT was with the same bearing, the same composure of manner and expression, that Madame Prévost entered the fine old room, where the unwelcome guest still stood by one of the windows, looking out upon the verdant levels of the smiling country. She was half way across the polished floor before, hearing her light step, he turned and advanced to meet her.

"How do you do, Mr. Burnham?" she said with grave courtesy. "It was a surprise to me to hear from my daughter that you were here, since I was on the point of writing to you."

"So I supposed," replied Mr. Burnham, thinking better of an idea of shaking hands which had crossed his mind when he turned and advanced from the window. Now, as of old, he felt himself overawed and ill at ease in the presence of this woman, whom he knew to be his debtor, but whose graceful dignity was as unimpaired as if she had been still the beautiful heiress whom he, the son of her father's overseer, had once beheld across an impassable gulf. The thought of that past time, of the great change in their relative positions, was much more in his mind than in hers as they sat down opposite each other.

So many changes had come to Madame Prévost that she had ceased to be struck by surprise at any of the altered conditions which surrounded her. The man now facing her was only a creditor, who held for the moment her fate and that of her children in his hand. That she had known him once as an uncouth boy, who owed his first chance in life to her father's kindness, was a fact hardly present in her thoughts ; but it was overwhelmingly present in Burnham's. The success he had achieved meant more to him here than anywhere else. Vividly present in his recollection was the envious bitterness with which in his youth he had regarded this house and its inmates—the gallant boys who now filled soldiers' graves, and the radiant girl so far above him ; and that he should find himself now in a position to become the owner of the house and dictator of the destiny of those within it was as sweet to him as gift of fortune ever was to any man.

He had swelled with an almost rapturous sense of his power as he approached the dwelling which was to him what no other dwelling in Louisiana, nor in the world, could be ; and this had been intensified rather than lessened by the latent scorn he had read in Yvonne's eyes and manner. But now, confronted by Madame Prévost, her aspect still full of the distinction which impresses even the vulgar, and her manner unchanged in its gracious though formal courtesy, he felt himself sink again into the place and stature which had been his originally. It was the effort to overcome this feeling, to assert the rights of his changed position, which, after he had taken the chair that a motion of the lady's hand indicated, made him say with more abruptness of tone and manner than he had intended :

"I understand, of course, that you were about to write concerning the payment of your note to me."

"Concerning the note, yes," answered Madame Prévost. "I was about to write and inquire if you would not be satisfied for a little longer with the payment of the interest, since I have not yet been able to arrange to meet the debt."

"Hum!" said Mr. Burnham, looking down lest his eyes might betray that this was what he had desired as well as expected to hear. "I am afraid I have given as much time as I can, although I'm sorry to disoblige you. But I have need of my money; and business is business, you know."

"I know it very well," replied Madame Prévost quietly; "and ask nothing but what is business-like. I am paying an interest on the money which is surely as high as you could obtain from any other investment, and therefore I supposed that it would not inconvenience you to let the note run a little longer."

"How much longer?" asked Burnham, the roughness of his tone being an echo of the resentfulness with which he recognized that, in her definition of what was business-like, she made it clear that she had no intention of asking a favor.

"That I cannot exactly say," the lady answered. "I can only assure you that I am anxious to pay the money as soon as I possibly can. Meanwhile the interest——"

"You are mistaken about the interest," he interrupted. "It is by no means as high as I could obtain by many other investments, which are continually offering themselves to me. I could have placed the money twice as advantageously several times lately if I had been able to command it; but I disliked to press you. I—" he hesitated—"I don't forget my early connection with your family."

The lady bent her head slightly in acknowledgment of the remark. Nothing was farther from her gentle spirit or her noble manners than any touch of arrogance; but, in his uneasy consciousness of inferiority, Burnham thought that he read it in that gesture. His face flushed, his voice took a rougher tone, as he went on :

," I don't forget either what that connection was. I owe something to your father, who helped to educate me ; and I've paid it by keeping a roof over the heads of his daughter and his grandchildren. The overseer's son wasn't good enough to be your friend or associate in the old days ; but it's doubtful if any of those who were would have invested their money here to oblige you, as I have done."

His listener lifted her eyes and looked at him with a glance in which there was more wonder than disdain. In truth, there is to a lofty soul inexhaustible food for wonder in the brutalities of which a coarse nature is capable ; a wonder which sometimes merges into compassion for those who are separated by so wide a gulf—the gulf of absolute non-comprehension—from things noble, generous and refined. Something of this feeling made Madame Prévost's tone still courteous, although very cold, when she spoke :

" The old friends to whom you have alluded are not only now very few, but are not in a position to help others, as you must know well. Were it otherwise, I should not need to be your debtor, although I cannot acknowledge that by lending some money and receiving a very high rate of interest upon it, you have ' kept a roof over the heads ' of my children and myself."

" No," he responded, with increasing insolence of demeanor, " I don't suppose you would acknowledge it if I had given you the money without any interest. It would lower your pride to be under an obligation to *me*."

" There is, happily, no question of an obligation," observed Madame Prévost calmly. " You have lent me money on ample security, and I have paid you the highest interest you could possibly obtain. It is therefore a business transaction, out of which we will, if you please, leave all personal discussion."

"I suppose, then, you are ready to close this business transaction by paying my money?"

"On the contrary, I have already told you that I am not ready to do so, and shall be glad if you will be satisfied with the interest for—let us say, a year longer."

He smiled sardonically.

"And there's no obligation in that—oh, no! I'm to be out of my money so much longer, and see good investments lost to me for want of it; but I must be satisfied with my interest and the honor of lending money to Madame Prévost, and expect no gratitude from her for a favor."

"Mr. Burnham," said that lady, rising from her chair, "I see that it is useless to prolong this conversation. I am loath to think that you have come here—to a roof under which you never received anything save kindness—in order to insult me. I prefer to believe that you are not aware of the offensiveness of your manner and speech. But our business ends here. My note is due to you in a few days. To-morrow I will go to New Orleans to see my lawyer, and he will communicate with you regarding it. I now wish you good-day."

She stood waiting for him to leave; but, instead of accepting the dismissal he had brought upon himself, Burnham remained motionless, staring up at her. No sign of passion ruffled the dignity of her aspect, but there was a look on her face that recalled the father and brothers whose shades might almost have risen to cast him from her presence; and, with a sudden sense of shame, he felt that he had justified the scorn which his uneasy soul had always suspected, and which he now plainly read in her glance and on her lips. Consternation, too, seized him ; for this was not the end he had wished to bring about. Nothing was farther from his desire than to be forced to relax his hold on a property which he coveted with his whole soul. Madame Prévost was right in saying that, though he had indeed meant to be offensive, he was not aware of the extent of his offensiveness. He had been led away by the opportunity to utter thoughts which had long rankled within him ; and in giving himself this gratification he had counted, as an ignoble nature always counts, on the power he possessed, on the apparently absolute certainty that a woman who owed him money which she could not pay would not dare to resent whatever he chose to say. Confronted now with the consequences of his mistake, he murmured a few words of hurried apology.

. "Sorry to have offended you ! Hadn't the least intention of anything of the sort," he protested. "Pray sit down again, Madame. We haven't even begun to talk of the business that brought me here."

Madame Prévost did not sit down again, but she regarded him with a look of surprise in which a questioning was mingled.

"We have talked," she said, "of the only business which we possess in common. I am at a loss to imagine what else you can have to say to me."

"I have a good deal to say if you will sit down and listen to me," he continued. "In the first place, since it is not convenient for you to meet the note at present, I'm willing that the payment should be deferred a few months longer."

Madame Prévost sank back into her chair. Who can blame her ? The reprieve meant much to her ; and for the sake of those "others" of whom she had spoken to Yvonne, no sacrifice was too great—not even the sacrifice of accepting a favor from this obnoxious man. But in resuming her seat she did not change the cold reserve of her manner.

"I understood you to say——" she began.

"You understood me to say that I wanted the money for better investment," he interposed. "But if you cannot pay it, I must do without it a little longer, that's all. I'm a plain man and a little rough in my ways; but I meant no offence when I said that I did not forget what your father had done for me, and that perhaps I had been able to do for you what none of your fine friends of the days when I was only the overseer's son would have done. However, we'll let that pass; only I *am* glad it's fallen to me to help you when you needed help. And it's my desire to help you still further : to—to arrange matters so that this property may remain always in your family."

Madame Prévost looked at him with growing astonishment as he stumbled through these sentences. Was it possible that she had, after all, misjudged the man ; and that under his apparent brutality there was really some spark of generosity, of grateful remembrance of the past?

"I think," she said, after a moment's reflection, "that it will be necessary for you to explain yourself further."

"That is what I'm about to do," he answered. But it was evidently not an easy task. He hesitated again, cleared his throat, drew out a handkerchief with which he wiped his forehead, and then, clinching it tightly in his large hand, went on with what seemed an abrupt change of subject: "Has your second daughter—Miss Diane, I think you call her—ever mentioned to you that when she was in New Orleans last spring she met my son?"

"Never," replied Madame Prévost, with an unmoved countenance ; although an instinct of what was coming flashed upon her.

" Ah !" said Mr. Burnham, " that is the way with young people. They seldom mention these things to their parents. Well, Miss Diane *did* meet my son, and he was very much taken with her. What she thought of *him* I don't know ; but there's no reason why she shouldn't think well of him ; and the upshot of the matter is that I've come here to propose to you that we arrange a marriage between them—that's the way your old French families manage things, I know. And then I'll hand over your note and the mortgage, with the understanding that you are not to be disturbed as long as you live, and that the place is to go to Miss Diane at your death. In this way you'll be relieved of your debt and the estate will remain in your family, since one of your daughters will be the owner of it, together with my son."

There was a moment's silence after his voice ceased—a moment in which Madame Prévost felt as if she were suffocating. It is not too much to say that in all her long struggle with misfortune the hardships of fate had never seemed to her so cruel as at this instant, when she had been forced to listen to a proposal to barter her daughter for the discharge of a debt. A passionate sense of the indignity offered, the deep humiliation involved in such a proposal, overwhelmed her as she had never been overwhelmed before. Every drop of blood in her veins seemed on fire, and for once all gentleness left her. Those who knew her best would hardly have recognized her in the lady who rose with an air so haughty, and whose glance rebuked the presumption before her voice spoke.

" It would have been better," she said, clearly and proudly, " if you had ended this interview as I desired, a few minutes ago. I should have been spared an insult, and you would have been spared hearing that money difficulties have not driven me to entertain the thought of selling my daughter."

The color rushed in a dull, red flood over Burnham's face. Her tone cut like a whip, and again he felt himself at fault and despised. This time he too rose to his feet and stood facing her.

" If you think it an insult that I should speak of a marriage between your daughter and my son——" he began.

But she stopped him by a gesture.

" I think," she said, in the same cool, clear accents, " that you have made a mistake which need go no further. Let me repeat that you will hear from my lawyer, and that there is nothing to detain you longer."

" You are not afraid to turn me out of your house in such a way as this—the house which is as good as my own ?" he demanded. " You had better stop, I think, Madame Prévost. I know your pride—who should know it better ?—but pride will make a poor shelter for you when I foreclose my mortgage, as I surely will if I go out at your bidding now. Look here ! It is really I who have been insulted by the manner in which you have seen fit to take a very liberal offer. But I know the ideas in which you've been brought up—ideas that are out of date now, I can tell you ; and I'm willing to give you a little time to consider and consult with Miss Diane. She's a young lady who knows the world ; and, from what my son tells me, I think you'll find that she looks at the matter rather differently from yourself."

" Do you mean to imply that my daughter has given your son any encouragement to—offer himself in this manner ?" asked Madame Prévost haughtily.

" He believes that she has, at any rate, or he wouldn't do it ; for Jack thinks very well of himself," said Burnham, with a meaning nod. "Take my advice and consult with Miss Diane."

A horrible fear seized Madame Prévost. Could that which he implied possibly be true? Could Diane, her beautiful Diane, have given encouragement to the pretensions of the son of this atrocious creature? She had known of such things, of women who had so stooped, so degraded themselves; but that Diane was capable of it was incredible to her. And yet—

He saw her hesitation, and pressed his advantage.

"You had better take time to consider," he repeated. "It won't make much difference to *me* whether you agree or not, for the place is bound to be mine in any event; but I'd like to gratify my son, and I should think you'd like to know that your daughter will be mistress of it after you are gone. Besides, it would certainly kill the old lady to leave here. You ought to think of *her*. Old people can't stand changes."

Madame Prévost turned white. With an unconscious seeking for support, she put out her hand and grasped the back of the chair in which she had been sitting. Her mother! It was true what this man said: to be forced from her lifelong home would surely kill her. Was it not well, then, to take the time offered—to temporize, to treat this proposal with such form of respect as would at least not exasperate the father and son who made it, and in whose hands such power rested? Never had bitterer cup been held to her lips, but the painful schooling of adversity told. She recognized that she could not allow herself to resent this indignity as she longed to do, and after a short struggle answered:

"I will refer your son's proposal to my daughter. I am sure that his—hopes have misled him, and that she has never possibly given him any encouragement ; but it is best that she should speak for herself. I will let you hear from me on the subject.''

'' I think you'll find it all right ; my son's not likely to be mistaken,'' Burnham replied, with an air of offensive confidence. And then, feeling that he should make some concession on his side, as paving the way for a more cordial understanding, he added : '' Meanwhile, you can send the interest on the note for three months longer. By the end of that time I hope matters will be satisfactorily settled. And now I'll bid you good-day.''

CHAPTER III.

After Madame Prévost left the little sitting-room, Yvonne remained for a moment motionless, listening to the sound of her footsteps as they crossed the hall. When the closing of the drawing-room door told that she had entered upon the dreaded interview, the girl turned with a deep sigh, and seated herself in the chair which her mother had vacated before the open escritoire.

She had now laid aside the broad shade hat, and her countenance was fully revealed in the strong light pouring upon her from the open window, through which she absently gazed. It was a countenance in which were perceptible inherited traces of the mother's beauty, but much modified, less delicate, more forceful. In fact, there was in the face a touch of masculine vigor, which often caused people to say that Yvonne Prévost would have made a handsome boy, although she was not a remarkably pretty girl, judged at least by the standard of the rest of her family.   The hazel eyes, which were her greatest beauty, were like those of a boy in their frank, open, fearless expression ; and so were her resolute mouth and chin ; while the peculiarly refined loveliness for which her mother and grandmother had each in her generation been famous showed itself in the delicacy of the upper portion of her face. Her complexion was a clear brunette ; and her dark-brown hair, cut short around her brow, added, by its careless picturesqueness of tossed and tumbled locks, to her boyish look.

Indeed Mr. Burnham was not the only person who spoke jestingly of Yvonne as '' the man of the family,'' while to the girl herself it was a fact in which there was no jest. From her earliest youth it had in great measure fallen upon her to supply the masculine element—that is, the element upon which others depend—in a family altogether feminine. She had for years been her mother's sole confidante and counsellor in the difficulties which continually beset them, and with which they never troubled either the grandmother, who knew only the traditions of a luxurious past and the memories of her sorrows, or the three girls younger than Yvonne, to whom they were equally anxious to secure as far as possible a youth unclouded by the shadow of such stern cares as it was their part to meet and wrestle with.

And from being confidante and counsellor, Yvonne had advanced to the office of practical assistant, to taking the place which would have been hers had she been born a son instead of a daughter of the house. In an almost literal sense she put her hand to the plough, and spared her mother the expense of a manager by looking after the entire management of the plantation herself, with the assistance of an old servant of the family, intelligent and devoted to their interests. Friends stared, wondered, remonstrated ; for on all Bayou Tèche such a thing had never been known before as a girl who superintended the work of a plantation—going herself into the fields and the sugarhouse, and having as keen an eye for every detail as if she had been a man.   But no one could say that the result was not good, the work not well done, the plantation not better cultivated than it had been since the war.   Yvonne troubled herself with no theories of what was or what was not a woman's proper sphere ; she simply accepted the task laid before her, however unusual in its nature, as unnumbered women have done through all the ages, before ever the clamor arose for woman's rights ; and proved her right to assume the work by fitly discharging it.

And there is in work conscientiously undertaken and honestly performed such power to interest and satisfy that the girl would have been happy in her labor, in the modest consciousness of success, and the growing hope of making life brighter by her exertions for those so dear to her, but for seeing the burden of care which she could not lessen constantly weighing upon and visibly aging her mother. Always more or less the case, this was especially so at times of acute crisis like the present.   The heavy debt which her father had been compelled to lay upon the war-desolated plantation rested like an incubus upon them ; and as she looked out now over the green old garden, with its hedges of roses and groves of orange and fig, she was steadily facing the fact that there was scarcely more hope of paying it now than there had been ten years before.   The only hope, if Burnham demanded his money, was to find some one else willing to lend the same amount for the same security and interest.   But what respite was there in that ?   Sadly she shook her head.

" Oh, to be free from this intolerable slavery of debt !"

she thought. "I would walk barefoot around the world if I might, by so doing, find the means to set us free, and relieve poor mamma before this misery ends by killing her."

But those who have known much trouble learn, if they are wise, one thing—never to brood upon it. That way madness lies ; and not only madness, but all the lesser evils of embittered natures, ruined tempers, lessened energies, and the melancholy that destroys. Young as she was, Yvonne had learned this lesson. With an effort she threw off the thoughts that clamored about her like a pack of hounds ; and seeking, as long habit had taught her, some distraction for her mind, she turned to the open desk beside her.

"While I am waiting I may as well look for those papers mamma wants," she said to herself ; and from the pigeon-holes filled with letters and documents she began to take out one bundle after another (most of them yellow with age and tied together with bands of faded tape), and to read the endorsements written upon each in various old-fashioned handwritings. The papers of which she was in search were presently found and laid aside. But since Madame Prévost did not come, and it was necessary to continue to divert her mind as far as possible from the consideration of what was passing in the dreaded interview, Yvonne went on half-absently, taking out and examining documents, many of which had been untouched for years. It was indeed a very slight degree of attention which she bestowed upon them—listening the while for the sound of an opening door, of voices, steps—until suddenly, having pulled out a drawer which slightly resisted her touch, as if long unopened, she found a package of particularly time-yellowed papers, on which was written in the handwriting

of her great-grandfather, " Titles of estates in Santo Domingo.   H. de Marsillac."

She started then, with new interest ; for here were the
records of a page in the family history with regard to which
she had never been able to obtain the degree of information
she desired.   She knew that her great-great-grandfather
had been the sole representative of a family of refugees
from Santo Domingo, who, like most of the survivors of
the massacre which followed the uprising of the slaves in
1791, had fled to Louisiana ; but beyond that fact she had
been able to learn very little.   Everything available concerning the history of the colony, as well as of the great
wave of bloodshed and horror which had whelmed it in
ruin, she had read with avidity ; but this did not satisfy
her wish for more personal information.   So it was with a
sense of interest, which made her for the moment forget
her preoccupation, that she looked at the papers in her
hand, tangible links with that far-away past, that chapter
which, for her family as for others, had closed so tragically.

" I wonder nobody ever told me that these papers were
here," she thought.   " I suppose they were long since forgotten.   Probably no one has ever looked at or touched
them since my great-grandfather laid them away.   Well,
they will give a local habitation at least to the fancies I
have always woven about the place, the time, and the people.   As soon as I have time I shall look over them, and—
Ah, there is mamma at last !"

Her quick ear had caught the sound of Burnham's exit,
of Madame Prévost's last formal words in the hall, and
then of the step which came slowly towards the sitting-
room.   She thrust the package of papers back into their
drawer, and, rising, turned eagerly to greet her mother as
she entered.   " Well ?" she said quickly ; but even the

monosyllable died away half uttered on her lips as she saw the face with which, all need for self-control gone now, Madame Prévost met her.

"Mamma!" and the girl sprang forward. "What is it? What has that man said to you?"

Madame Prévost laid her hand on the young shoulder, as if on a welcome support, and so stood for an instant. Then she answered quietly :

"Only what we feared, Yvonne. He wants his money —at once, if possible ; if not, within three months."

"It is more than I should have expected of him to give even so much grace," said Yvonne. "Sit down, mamma, and do not look so heart-stricken. Within three months we can at least find another creditor, and so frustrate his intention of finally possessing the place."

"The amount is so large that I fear it will be almost impossible to find any one else to lend it to us," said Madame Prévost. "Mr. Clarke has never encouraged me to hope so. And—I am not sure even of the three months. He yielded that only because I, on my side, yielded something which I am ashamed to tell you."

"Ashamed !—*you*, mamma !" The girl knelt down beside the chair into which her mother had sunk, and softly stroked the hand which lay in her own. "As if it were possible that you could ever do anything of which you would have need to be ashamed !"

"Yvonne"—Madame Prévost suddenly sat upright and spoke with energy—"has Diane ever mentioned to you that when she was in New Orleans last spring she met this man's son?"

"Burnham's son?" asked the young girl, in surprise. "Certainly not. I never heard before that such a person existed."

"But he *does* exist," replied Madame Prévost ; "and he met Diane, and—how can I say it !—he proposes to marry her, and the father proposes that I shall pay my debt with my daughter."

"Mamma, you are not in earnest !"

"Yes, terribly in earnest, my child. It sounds like a melodrama, but it is exactly the proposal to which I have listened. And, being assured by Mr. Burnham that his son has reason to believe that his suit will be favorably received by Diane, I have agreed to consider the proposal far enough to consult her with regard to it."

Yvonne looked at her mother with eyes full of compassion.

"It was even worse for you than I feared," she said, in a low tone. "I could never have imagined anything like this. But while it is plain that we must face the worst as far as the debt is concerned, you do not think it possible that Diane——"

"No," said Madame Prévost as she paused, "I cannot believe it possible that Diane has given this man the warrant for his presumption which he asserts. But do you wonder that I feel degraded in my own eyes, as if I had sunk low indeed, in even considering such a proposal? Yet to refuse—that was to bring ruin upon us at once ; and I was not brave enough to face that, Yvonne."

"Mamma," cried the girl, "how can you blame yourself? What else could you do? As if he did not know well—the despicable creature !—that he had to deal only with a woman helplessly in his power ! Do you think he would have ventured to make such a proposal to a man? He would have known that he would have been flung out of the house—and, oh, that I had been a man to do it !"

"There are some things certainly for which men are useful," said Madame Prévost, in a faintly whimsical tone. "But let us not waste our energy in futile anger, *chérie.* Go and tell Diane that I wish to speak to her."

"Not at once, darling! Give yourself time to recover from what you have just passed through."

"On the contrary, Yvonne, I must know at once—I cannot have a moment's peace until I do know—what Diane will think of this. Go and bring her quickly."

"Shall I return with her?"

"Certainly. This is no secret. It concerns us all, and every one will soon know the result."

CHAPTER IV.

LEAVING the sitting-room to do her mother's bidding, Yvonne crossed the hall, and, running lightly up the wide, shallow, and dangerously polished steps of the great, curving staircase, reached the second floor, where, passing noiselessly by the door of the chamber in which her grandmother was taking her *siesta,* she entered another chamber containing two white-draped single beds, which indicated a double occupancy. It was the chamber shared by herself and Diane ; and, while large and lofty as all the apartments of the mansion were, was sparingly furnished with the same quaint, old-fashioned furniture which, with scarcely any modern additions, filled the rest of the house.

And seated at this moment before a Louis-Seize toilet-table was a girl who, from her appearance, might have been one of the gay group who played at blind-man's-buff with Louise de la Vallière on the *tapis-vert* of Versailles ; or one of those who shared the rural simplicity of the Petit

Trianon with Marie Antoinette.   For if the peculiar revival
or survival of a type which made Madame Prévost so " like
an old picture," as people always said, was only slightly to
be perceived in the personal appearance of Yvonne, it was
strikingly reproduced in Diane, the second daughter and
beauty of the family.   Like her mother, she resembled not
so much the Frenchwomen of to-day as those women of the
past, whose charms have been resolved into dust for nigh
upon two centuries.   Here in undimmed freshness were all
the traits which the countenance of Madame Prévost now
only suggested—the curling tresses of sunny hair straying
lightly across the fair forehead ; the brows delicately arched
over eyes sometimes tender, sometimes sparkling, but always full of possibilities of disdain ; the lips which well
deserved the old simile of Cupid's bow ; the exquisitely
rounded cheek and chin ; the complexion of lilies and
roses.

No wonder that Diane had made a sensation when she
entered society for the first time the winter before in New
Orleans ; or that the grandson of her grandfather's overseer, struck by her patrician loveliness, conceived the idea
of reaching at a single bound the social height towards
which he painfully toiled, by an alliance so desirable from
every point of view save that of the money which he had
no need to consider.   Yet so much wisdom had he learned
in the course of his struggles for social recognition that he
made no attempt to approach Diane in the character of a
suitor while she was shining in those elevated regions,
where he was barely tolerated ; but, patiently biding his
time and keeping in mind her beauty and distinction, he
waited until the moment was ripe for proposing to unite
his father's ambition and his own.

As Yvonne entered, her sister looked around with a

smile.   She had just finished arranging her hair, and was contemplating the result with satisfaction.

"How do you like this Psyche coiffure, Yvonne?" she asked.   "I think it is very becoming.   Look at the effect in profile."

She turned her graceful head—than which Psyche's own could not have been more charming—as she spoke.   At another time Yvonne would have appreciated the effect as much as herself, for she was the first and foremost of Diane's admirers ; but just now she gave only an indifferent glance at the coiffure as she replied :

"It is very pretty.   But I haven't time to admire it just now, Diane.   Mamma has sent me for you.   She wishes to speak to you."

"What about?" asked Diane, with some surprise ; for such a summons was unusual.

Yvonne hesitated an instant.   Then she answered the question by another :

"Diane, when you were in New Orleans last winter did you meet a man named Burnham—a son of the Burnham to whom, as you know, mamma is in debt?"

"Burnham!" repeated Diane, opening her pretty eyes a little wider in growing astonishment and the effort to remember.   "It is likely that I may have met him, but I don't recall him at all.   Why do you ask?"

Yvonne uttered a low, unmirthful laugh as she answered :

"Because you made so deep an impression upon him that he has sent his father to make a proposal for you."

"For me !   A proposal of——"

"Of marriage—yes."

"Yvonne, you are surely jesting !"

"Jesting !"   Yvonne's dark eyes gave a flash.   "Do

you think I would jest on the subject of a proposal from such a person ?"

" But it is so astonishing !" said Diane, leaning back in her chair and regarding her sister. " I am not sure that I ever saw the man—I certainly don't recall him ; and that he should have seen me, and been sufficiently impressed to make a proposal months after the meeting, is almost incredible, you will admit."

" It would not be incredible if he had never seen you," replied Yvonne ; " for although he must have admired you, as every one who sees you does, there is more in the proposal than admiration for *you :* there is a question of— But never mind that just now. Come to mamma, who wishes to speak to you before replying to this insult."

" I should not call it an insult," observed Diane dispassionately, as she rose. " It is a presumption, perhaps——"

" How great a presumption you don't understand," Yvonne interposed, impetuously. " This man, whom you cannot even recall as an acquaintance, asserts that he received encouragement from you which leads him to confidently expect a favorable answer to his proposal."

" That is most extraordinary," said Diane. " Let me think if I cannot recollect him." She paused in an attitude of consideration, her finger pressed to her lip. Then suddenly she looked up and laughed. " Why, certainly I do !" she exclaimed. " I met him at one of the Mardi Gras balls, and later once or twice at some large entertainment. He is one of the people who are not exactly in society, you know—only on the outskirts. I had forgotten all about him ; but I do remember now that, as far as could be observed on such a limited acquaintance, he seemed rather smitten by my charms. But that was not sufficient-

ly uncommon to be remarkable," added Diane, with frankness.

"Then that accounts for the matter," said Yvonne. "I
know how you treat people—how you smile in every man's
face, no matter how insignificant or even odious he may be,
as if he possesses your most favorable regard ; and how they
all believe that you mean something by it, not knowing that
you forget them as soon as they are out of your sight."

"But if I do," said Diane, "that is no reason why I
should not be pleasant to them while they are in my sight.
In fact, I don't know how to be anything else."

"That is true," replied Yvonne, recognizing the perfect
sincerity and simplicity of this assertion. "You really
don't know how to be anything else, so I suppose one
should not blame you. But come ; we must not keep
mamma waiting longer."

They left the chamber together, and ran down-stairs to
the sitting-room, where they found Madame Prévost pac-
ing up and down the floor. She paused at their entrance,
and looked first keenly at Diane, then interrogatively at
Yvonne.

"It is as we supposed, mamma," the latter said in reply
to the look. "Diane is barely able to recall having met
the man, and of course gave him no ground for the presumptuous confidence he has expressed."

Madame Prévost breathed a low sigh of relief, then an
swered :

"I did not think that Diane could possibly have encouraged him as his father represented, but I feared there
might be some ground for—misapprehension."

"I never dreamed of encouraging him," Diane said
quietly. "Such an idea is, of course, quite absurd. But
perhaps he was foolish enough to think that I did. As

Yvonne was saying a moment ago, it may be that my manner is sometimes misleading—though I'm sure I haven't the least intention of making it so—and an underbred man does not always understand these things."

"Of course he does not," said Madame Prévost; "and it is something you will do well to remember. You cannot treat an underbred man with ease and informality. He is certain to presume upon it, as this man has presumed."

"But there will at least be no difficulty in answering him, mamma," said Diane, with unruffled calmness. "You need only present your compliments to his father and decline the honor of the proposed alliance. It was hardly necessary to send for me for so simple a thing as that."

Madame Prévost looked again at her eldest daughter, as if inquiring whether she might not accept this decision as final, and not trouble Diane with any consideration of the consequences which would flow from the refusal thus unequivocally stated. There seemed no reason why she should be troubled, since the last thing either of them desired was that she should give any other answer. But, with her love of frankness, Yvonne answered the look by saying :

"I think Diane should know everything, mamma. I have no fear of her changing her mind."

"Neither have I," said Madame Prévost, "but is there need to pain her by a knowledge of difficulties which cannot be averted? However, it is perhaps better that she should understand the situation. Sit down, my dear" (this to Diane), "and I will explain to you the whole matter."

She sat down herself as she spoke ; and Diane, with a surprised expression, threw herself in a careless attitude

on a chintz-covered lounge, and drew Yvonne down beside
her.

"Come, counsellor," she said, smiling. "Nothing can
be decided without your help, although it does not seem
to me that there can be anything further to decide in this
case."

"Not to decide—of that I am sure—but to know," said
her mother. "Briefly, then, my dear : what Mr. Burnham came here to propose to me was this—that a marriage
should be arranged (in the fashion of our old French families, he was good enough to say) between you and his son,
for and in consideration of which he would cancel my debt
to him, and I should be left undisturbed in possession of
this place for the term of my life, with the condition that
it would pass to you and his son at my death. In other
words, he proposed that I should pay my debt—which he
had already satisfied himself that I could not meet—by
selling *you*. I answered, as you may imagine, by request-
ing him to leave the house. But then, Diane, he asserted
that his son had reason to be hopeful of a favorable reply
from you, and insisted that I should at least refer the offer
to you. It was a bitter humiliation to me to entertain it
even for the length of time necessary to observe such a
form ; but much depended on my making this concession,
and so—I agreed to do so, and leave the decision to you.
Thank God you are able to tell me that the man's presumptuous hopes had no foundation."

"Not the very least," replied Diane, with unmoved
quietness, "as far as they rested on anything that occurred
in our very slight acquaintance. But he probably reckoned
on something else, mamma—on the possibility that I might
be willing to do even this to help you."

"Diane !"

. It was a simultaneous cry from mother and sister—a cry of astonishment, of appeal, of something like fright. Diane in reply looked from one to the other.

" Why not ?" she asked, still quietly. " Since I can do nothing else, why should I not do this ?"

CHAPTER V.

THERE was a moment of silence, so much were Madame Prévost and Yvonne confounded by Diane's unexpected question. Then her mother answered, in grave tones :

" Because, my dear, there are some things which cannot even be taken into consideration. And this is one of them. Not to save Beaulieu—not to save our lives if it came to that—would I consent to such a sacrifice. Perhaps the man *did* count on this generous impulse on your part ; and thought, too, that I might play the *rôle* of the parent who makes such bargains. But he has only shown his incapacity to understand anything elevated in character or motive, and we need not consider him further. There only remains to decline his proposal, and forget it as soon as we can."

But Diane shook her Psyche-like head.

" I cannot consent to that, mamma," she said. " The proposal is made to me, and I have a right to accept it. It will be my act."

" Your act—but, Diane, you are mad ! I will not permit it."

Diane smiled. " Oh, yes, you will," she said, " when you consider that you should not stand in the way of my making so advantageous a settlement in life !"

"Diane !" It was Yvonne who now seized her arm and shook her angrily. "How can you jest on such a subject? It is shameful !"

Diane turned and looked at her sister, and certainly there was no jesting in her glance.

"I am in earnest," she said. "As far as I can perceive, it rests with me to relieve mamma of her debt and to secure her home to her. Do you think I would hesitate over that? Because I have never said much about our difficulties, you can't suppose that I have not been aware of them. There is no good in talking of disagreeable things when one can do nothing ; but when the opportunity comes to do something, then one should act. I have always thought that there would never be an opportunity for me, since I am such a useless creature ; and I confess that I have often envied you, Yvonne, your power of helping. But now my opportunity has come, and I shall take it. I will accept this man's offer."

Again there was a moment's silence ; for neither Yvonne nor her mother knew what to make of such an attitude as this on the part of Diane, of such totally unlooked-for resolution as her last words expressed. A gentle and charming docility had been so entirely heretofore one of her chief traits of character that they were wholly unprepared for any determination to act according to her own will and in opposition to their wishes. Obstinacy, self-assertion, in Hélène or Ninon they would have understood and reckoned upon as possible ; but in Diane—they looked at each other with a consternation which was speechless, until Madame Prévost presently spoke :

"My dear child, you mean this most generously ; but I must say again that it is absolutely out of the question for me to allow anything of the kind. Understand once for all that to see you sacrificed in such a manner would be far worse to me than anything else which could possibly happen. It is not even a subject to be discussed. Let me hear no more of it."

Generally, when Madame Prévost spoke in that tone her children yielded implicit obedience ; but on this occasion Diane broke the rule.

" I think, mamma, we must speak of it a little further," she said ; " for I am quite in earnest and quite resolved. I shall be sorry to do anything which you disapprove ; but when it is a question of gaining so much by a single sacrifice, I am bound to make the sacrifice—even against your wishes. You are thinking of *me*, but I am thinking of how I should feel when I saw you driven from your home after I had refused to help you."

" And do you think," asked Madame Prévost, " that I would not rather be homeless, and if need be penniless, than let you marry the son of that man ?"

" Perhaps you would," replied Diane ; " but it is for me, not for you, to make the choice. And let us look at it reasonably, mamma. I am a French girl, and we know that a French girl is expected to make *un mariage de convenance*."

" Because you are a French girl," said Madame Prévost, " you should know better than to confound *mariage de convenance* with what the gross English mind calls a ' marriage of convenience.' *Convenance*, my dear, as you are perfectly aware, is not convenience, mercenary or otherwise. It is propriety, suitability—all those things which wise parents endeavor to secure in arranging anything so important as a marriage for a child. But where is there any propriety or suitability in a marriage between you and the grandson of my father's overseer ?"

"It is possible that there might be more than you think," replied Diane. "Of course, it is very bad that his grandfather should have been what he was, and that his father should be what he is. One must shrink a little from these things"—despite herself a shudder crept over the girl's delicate frame—"but, until we know to the contrary, we may suppose that the son is an improvement on his father and grandfather, as we often find to be the case in the sons of self-made vulgar men. The sons have had advantages of wealth and education which their fathers did not have, you know. And don't you think we should give this Mr. Burnham the benefit of the doubt? It is a point in his favor that he made no impression of any kind on me. I did not even remember having seen him ; and, you know, if he had been *very* objectionable in appearance or manner I should have recollected him."

There was something humorous, had any one been in the mood to perceive it, in the seriousness with which the girl advanced this plea ; glancing appealingly from her mother to Yvonne, as if sure that they must acknowledge the force of it. But the aspect of neither was encouraging. Plainly, they were not prepared to accept the fact that he had not been able to impress himself upon her recollection as evidence in the suitor's favor.

"Diane," said her sister, "it is simply revolting to hear you talk in that manner. You know you don't think those things ; you know that there is no one who would shrink sooner than yourself from any connection with people of such atrocious antecedents and such shocking vulgarity and brutality. For this proposal proves a vulgarity so hopeless that it leaves nothing more to be said or done. The men —father and son—who are capable of *this* would be capable of anything. And the son is no better than the father.

How could he be ? And for you to endeavor to make us believe that you think he might be is really worse than nonsense—it is a false pretence of which I would not have believed you capable.''

'' Poor Yvonne !'' said Diane, patting her sister's arm, and quite unvexed. '' You are angry because, like mamma, you are thinking of me. But what I have said is quite reasonable, and it is best to look at matters reasonably ; for, even if all you say were true, it would not alter the necessity of the case. And, since I must marry the man, it is surely better that I should think well than ill of him.''

'' You shall *never* marry him !'' cried Yvonne fiercely. '' We will never allow you to do so !''

'' My dear,'' replied Diane, almost pityingly, '' you cannot prevent it. I see clearly that it is the thing appointed for me to do—a necessity of fate against which there is no good in struggling, and 1 shall not struggle. I shall simply make the best of it, if there be any best in it ; but, in any event, I shall do it.''

Again the note of clear, inflexible resolve in her voice struck on both the mother's and sister's ear, and again they looked at each other with that strange sense of helplessness which the unexpected, especially in manifestations of character, usually produces. Then, the imperative mood being proved clearly useless, they tried remonstrance and appeal. But Diane was unmoved. In her playful, gentle way—a way so associated in their minds with her customary docility that its effect was now bewildering—she answered the appeals, but yielded nothing. And when Madame Prévost finally and positively refused to communicate her answer to the Burnhams, she only said quietly :

"I am sure you will not force me to act for myself. That certainly would not be very *convenable.*"

"Diane," exclaimed her mother, "I do not know you!"

"No, mamma," she answered, "I do not think you do. I have been so purely ornamental hitherto that you have never thought of me as possibly useful, or as possessing any will or character of my own. But I really do possess a little, and I am quite determined to do this thing. So write to Mr. Burnham and tell him that we accept his proposal."

"I would rather die!" cried Madame Prévost passionately. "Diane, you think that you are self-sacrificing, but you are really cruel."

It was a thing so almost unexampled, at least in the knowledge of her younger daughters, for Madame Prévost to lose her self-control, that Diane stared for a moment at her mother, and then suddenly dropped upon her knees beside her.

"Mamma," she said earnestly, "*I* would rather die than cause you any pain which could be avoided ; but it seems to me that in this I am bound to disregard your present pain for your lasting good. And not yours only. Think of *grand'mère* and of the girls ! But I don't desire to be obstinate, and it is not necessary for me to say that I don't desire to marry Mr. Burnham. Tell me, therefore, mamma, is there the least—the *very* least—hope of your being able by any other means to pay your debt ?"

This was a crucial question indeed ; and, confronted with it, Madame Prévost could only gaze helplessly into the face uplifted to her.

"We can sell the plantation," she said desperately, at last.

Diane rose to her feet, smiling a little—a rather sad and hopeless smile.

"And if the plantation were sold, where would be your means of support?" she asked. "No, I see clearly that this which is offered is our only resource. Mamma, Yvonne"—she looked at them appealingly—"let us make up our minds to what must be and face it bravely. It seems absurd for me to offer such advice to you who have already faced so much which you spared the rest of us. But I knew of it all the time ; and, now that my turn has come to take my share of the burden, you should not refuse my help. This one thing has been reserved for me to do, and this one thing I alone can do. Therefore, if you love me, accept my resolution as final, and let us talk of it no more."

And then Yvonne, forgetting her anger, sprang forward and put her arms around the slender young figure standing so upright in its resolve.

"Diane, dear Diane," she cried, "it is *I* who never knew you ! Much as I have always loved you, I did not know that you have the soul of a hero. But you shall not be sacrificed—that I solemnly swear ! There must be *some* means to pay this debt, and I will find it. Only give me a little time. Don't insist on letting these people know your decision at once. The man has offered mamma three months' grace : let us accept it. Let her write to him and say, if you insist upon it, that his offer will be taken into consideration, and that three months hence he shall have his answer. Meanwhile I will move heaven and earth to save you ; and if I fail—well, then I promise to accept your decision and say nothing more against it."

Such a proposal as this from any other girl would have seemed the mere expression of a passionate protest, if not wildest folly ; but from Yvonne it had a more serious significance. Her thorough knowledge of the family resources, as well as her business-like qualities, were well known to every member of the family ; and she had already been able to do so much towards practically improving their fortunes that it was no wonder Diane looked at her now with a gleam of hope in her eyes.

"O Yvonne !" she said, "do you really think there is the least possibility of your succeeding ?"

"How can I tell until I try?" answered Yvonne. "Heaven helps those who help themselves. I can only say that I will leave *nothing* undone to gain success. Only give me three months."

There can be no doubt that Diane was glad of any excuse for delay, brave and resolute as she had appeared ; added to which her faith in Yvonne was so great that she agreed willingly to the compromise suggested. So it was settled that Mr. Burnham should be answered in the manner indicated.

"And for three months," Diane stipulated, "we will not speak again of the obnoxious subject. I shall try to forget it, and also try not to hope too much ; for not even you, Yvonne dear, can accomplish impossibilities."

"I feel," said Yvonne, "as if, for the end I have in view, there were no such things as impossibilities."

CHAPTER VI.

"YVONNE, Yvonne !" cried a gay young voice, "what *are* you doing, poring over those dreadful old papers, instead of coming out on the gallery with us ?"

It was Ninon—a tall slip of a girl, still in short frocks—who, standing in one of the open windows of the sitting-room, with a background of soft, purple night behind her, looked in on Yvonne, who, seated at the old escritoire, was examining, by the light of a student's lamp, the package of yellow papers which had roused her interest in the afternoon, and which she had then laid aside for future examination. The recollection of them had come to her some hours later as a welcome distraction from other thoughts ; and she had gone into the sitting-room to look over them at this un-usual time.

"Presently, Ninon," she replied, without looking up. "These papers are not at all dreadful ; they are very inter-esting, and I will come and tell you about them in a few minutes."

Ninon shrugged her shoulders.

"As if musty old things like those *could* be interesting !" she said.   But she knew Yvonne too well to persevere fur-ther ; and, turning, she went back to the two white-clad figures she had left seated on the gallery in the faint radi-ance of a young moon—a golden crescent hanging in the western sky.   "There is no use in trying to tempt her," she reported.   "She is absorbed in some old papers, which are so interesting that she promises to come presently and tell us about them."

"Poor, dear Yvonne !" said Hélène, the third sister, with a laugh.   "She thinks that because they interest her they will interest us.   It's a great mistake.   But we must pretend to be interested, because she is really so good in helping mamma look after our affairs."

"Yvonne ought to have been born a boy," said Ninon, in the tone of one who cannot but remark a mistake of Providence.   "It would have been so much better for her,

as she likes business and things of that sort ; and so much
better for *us*, since she could then look after our affairs to
more advantage, and perhaps *make* money instead of just
saving it. I hate saving money !" added this young person, in a quiet but very decided voice.

"Do you suppose anybody likes it—except, perhaps,
misers and people of that kind?" inquired Hélène. "It
would be a satisfaction, however, to know that we were
even saving money, because then there would be a chance
of some day spending what was saved ; but I fear we are
not even doing that. It goes to my heart to see how worried poor mamma looks sometimes ; and Yvonne is beginning to have a caréworn expression after the Committee of
Ways and Means has been in session."

There was a soft sigh from where Diane sat, leaning back
in a low wicker chair, and gazing at the golden crescent in
the violet sky.

"It is true," she observed ; "but they have both always
been so anxious to keep their worries from us that it seemed
a pity not to gratify them, especially since there was no
good in knowing unpleasant things if one could not help
them."

"One might prefer to know them, all the same," said
Hélène, who was afflicted with a full share of the failing
of Eve. "I don't think we ought to be treated quite so
much like children. There was a man here to-day to see
mamma," she added, after a moment's pause. "Do you
know what he came for?"

"I suppose you mean a man who came to see her on
business," Diane answered quietly. "His name is Burnham. He is from New Orleans."

"Oh, the son of grandpapa's overseer ! I have heard of
him. What business could *he* have with mamma ?"

"She owes him some money, Hélène, if you must know."

"And did she pay it?"

"Not yet," replied Diane, still calmly regarding the sky. "But she has made arrangements to pay it—in three months."

"It was a pity she could not pay it at once. It must be very disagreeable to owe that kind of person anything."

"Very disagreeable indeed ; but sometimes even owing is preferable to paying when the sacrifice to be made in order to pay is very great."

Hélène looked sharply at the speaker. "You are growing mysterious too," she said. "What sacrifice must be made?"

"There is always a sacrifice involved in every debt, which somebody must pay, you know," answered Diane vaguely.

"That may be," returned Hélène pertinaciously ; "but what I want to know is whether any particular sacrifice is to be made for this debt. Does mamma, perhaps, think of selling the place?"

"No," replied Diane, with sudden energy ; "she does not think of it ; and I beg you, Hélène, not to trouble her with any questions. It is, of course, annoying to owe anything which one cannot pay ; but she has arranged, as I have said, to meet this debt within three months ; and that is all there is about it. Since she is so anxious to keep such annoyances from us, the least we can do is to respect her wishes by not prying into them. *Knowing* is not *helping*, and if we all worried together it would not help matters in the least : it would only make them worse."

"Yvonne ought to be a boy !" reiterated Ninon. "Then there would be one of us to go and *do* something."

"You are quite right, Ninon," Yvonne said, unexpectedly drawing near. "I have always wished that I were a boy; but never, I think, so much as to-night."

"Why to-night especially?" inquired Ninon. "Has anything happened?"

"Yes, something has happened," answered Yvonne. "I have found an old paper which seems to me—don't laugh, all of you!—as if it may contain a faint, wild, distant hope of fortune for us."

"Fortune!" they all repeated, in different tones of surprise and incredulity. "For *us*, Yvonne?"

"A fortune as distant as if it were yonder," said Yvonne, pointing to the crescent moon hanging like a fairy boat in the sky before them; "yet perhaps—mind, I only say *perhaps*—existing for all that."

"But where, pray?—where?" cried Ninon eagerly.

Yvonne sat down in one of the chairs scattered about. Even in the moonlight they could see that her eyes were shining strangely.

"Those old papers which I was reading when you spoke to me, Ninon," she said, "interested me very much, because they are the records of things that seemed to belong to another world. They are title-deeds of the estates our great-great-grandfather lost at the time of the insurrection of the slaves in the island of Santo Domingo."

"But there can be no hope of a fortune in them, Yvonne," said Diane; "for you know we have always heard that the estates were totally lost."

"I am not so foolish as to think of the estates," replied Yvonne. "But I have found a paper which states that, being suddenly forced by the uprising of the slaves to fly for his life, Henri de Marsillac, our great-great-grandfather, buried at his home a large amount of gold and other valuables which he was unable to take with him."

There were quick ejaculations from three young voices.

"A buried fortune! How exciting!" cried Hélène.

"Yvonne, you are dreaming!" said Diane; while Ninon flung herself on her knees at her sister's feet, put her elbows in her lap, and looked up, with her eyes gleaming out of the mane of loose, dark locks she tossed aside.

"O Yvonne!" she exclaimed, "do you believe it?"

"I *must* believe that there was such a thing," answered Yvonne; "for the memorandum I have found is in the handwriting of Henri de Marsillac; and relates that, being taken by surprise in the uprising, and obliged to escape hurriedly, he buried, in a place which he describes, both gold and jewels. Now—be quiet, Ninon dear!—you know it is possible that this fortune was long since discovered—perhaps by his son, perhaps by others; but again there is a faint possibility that it may be there buried yet."

. "Gold and jewels!" repeated Hélène, in an awed tone. "And there all this time—buried, waiting for us! O Yvonne, what a romance if it should prove true!"

"I am afraid there is no hope that it is there yet waiting for us," said Diane. "If Yvonne found this memorandum, of course others have seen it; and no doubt the fortune was unearthed long ago."

"In that case," returned Yvonne, "would the paper be there at all? Or is it likely we should never have heard of such a thing? You know how often *grand'mère* has talked of the stories of Santo Domingo, which her father-in-law told her. Among them all would she have forgotten such a thing as the recovery of a buried fortune?"

"No," the girls agreed. "*Grand'mère* would know. Let us go at once and ask her about it."

There was a simultaneous movement; and the next moment four young figures, with Yvonne at their head, entered the drawing-room, where Madame Prévost and her mother, Madame de Marsillac, sat reading by the light of a shaded lamp. The corners of the large, foreign-looking room were shadowy ; but the centre of radiance about the table at which both ladies were sitting brought out with a picture-like distinctness their figures—especially that of the elder lady, herself a picture in every sense, and one which an artist would have delighted to paint. The delicacy of her regular features, the fine, clear pallor of her skin, were admirably contrasted by her silvery hair, arranged in a series of puffs on each side of her face—an arrangement eminently becoming ; and rendered more so by a coif of lace, which, just touching with its point the ivory-like forehead, left exposed the puffs of silvery hair, but fell in two lappets on each shoulder, thus framing the face in the softest drapery. It was a work of love and of artistic pleasure to Denise (the lifelong maid of Madame de Marsillac, who had laughed at the idea of freedom parting her from her mistress) to dress that beautiful hair, and arrange over it the fine lace which she guarded so carefully.

A queen all her life long had been this stately old lady, from the days of her beautiful, petted youth, when parents had idolized and suitors fought for her glances, to the present time, when her subjects had narrowed down to a few faithful hearts, all of whom, however, were absolutely loyal. *Grande dame* she was to the tips of her slender fingers, and so rigorous and punctilious in her ideas of the proprieties of life that her granddaughters mingled much awe with their love and admiration for her. This was evident in their manner whenever they approached her ; and at the present time even impetuous Ninon held back and allowed the eldest sister to explain their errand.

They were a pretty group—all so girlish, so simple, in

manner and dress, and all more or less preserving in the third generation the beauty of the mother and grand-mother. If this beauty lost in them something of its distinction of aspect—save in the case of Diane—it was at present replaced by the ineffable bloom of youth ; and they formed a band to gladden a mother's eyes and heart with their fair, sweet young looks.

" *Grand'mère*," said Yvonne, advancing into the circle of lamp-light, " we have come to ask you a question."

" I hope that it is one which I can answer, *mes enfants*," replied the old lady, lifting her eyes with a smile. " It is easy to ask questions, as you know ; but to answer them—that is sometimes very difficult."

" You can answer this, *grand'mère*," continued Yvonne. " It is only to tell us whether you ever heard of such a thing as a buried fortune on the De Marsillac estates in Santo Domingo."

" I have heard," replied Madame de Marsillac, without the least hesitation, " that my father-in-law's father, your great-great-grandfather, buried some amount of money—how much I do not know—on the eve of his flight from his estate. This is certain ; but"—the girls drew nearer in breathless eagerness—" the sum was never recovered, because he died at the Cape from his wounds ; and even if it had been safe to search for it, no one but himself knew where he had concealed it."

" Did he not leave some memorandum—some description of the place ?" asked the eldest sister, restraining the others by a gesture.

" Not that I ever heard of, and I should have heard of it if he had," answered Madame de Marsillac.

" But he did, *grand'mère*, he did !" cried Ninon, unable to restrain herself longer. " And Yvonne has found it."

"Yvonne has found it!" repeated Madame de Marsillac, looking at Yvonne with an expression of surprise. "When and where?"

"Half an hour ago, *grand'mère*, in a package of old papers which I was examining out of curiosity," Yvonne replied. "Here is what I found."

She made a step forward and placed in her grandmother's hand a yellow, stained sheet of paper—a single sheet, which, folded closely, might readily have lain concealed between other and bulkier papers for more than the century which had elapsed since it had last seen the light. There was a pause of intense silence as the old lady opened and placed it immediately beneath the lamp, then slowly read the lines of faded writing within. All eyes were bent upon her face, as if to judge by the manner in which she received this communication from the past how far they were to credit it. The silence was long—or seemed long to the excited fancy of the young people grouped around her—before she lifted her eyes and, looking across the table at her daughter, said, in the voice of one who is deeply impressed:

"This is very strange! How often I have heard my father-in-law say that his father had died leaving no clue to the place where he had concealed everything of value which he could lay his hands upon when forced to fly for his life! And yet here, in the writing of Henri de Marsillac himself, is a full description of the spot where he buried both money and jewels."

"How could it possibly have been overlooked so long?" asked Madame Prévost, in an awed tone, as she held out her hand for the paper.

"It was within another paper," said Yvonne—"an old deed, which was passed over, no doubt, as of no value, and might have been even partly opened without revealing its enclosure.   But I read it on account of its quaint phraseology, and when I turned the page I found this folded within."

" Read it, mamma !—read it aloud !" cried Hélène. " Let us hear what it is."

" Yvonne should read it, since she was its discoverer," said Madame Prévost, with a smile at her eldest daughter.

And so Yvonne, standing beside the table, and holding the paper within the radiance of the circle of lamp-light, read aloud the following words, which may be thus translated into English :

"Having learned, through the warning of my faithful servant, Jacques, that an insurrection of the slaves is hourly to be expected, I have determined to join my family at the Cape without delay.   And since it would be rash to attempt to carry valuables with me in the disordered condition of the country, I have concealed everything of the kind—to wit, the sum in gold which I have recently received from M. Brissot-Saget in payment for the estate of La Coupe, my wife's jewels, and all our plate—in the place which I now describe, for the benefit of my children, should I myself be prevented from returning to secure them :

" On the second terrace of the garden, at the east side of the sun-dial which stands in the circle containing the statue of the nymph, I have buried everything.   Should I not reach the Cape alive, Jacques will convey this, with my other papers, to my wife.

' HENRI DE MARSILLAC.

MILLEFLEURS, August 22, 1791."

Profound silence followed for a moment upon the reading of this document, now first seen by other eyes than those of the writer since the night it was penned in distant Santo Domingo. Every one was conscious of a thrill of something like awe in hearing this message of the dead, delivered at last to the fourth generation of his blood, after the lapse of a century. It was the voice of Madame de Marsillac which finally broke the silence.

"Jacques was faithful indeed," she said. "He accompanied his master on his flight to the Cape; and, when they were met by the insurgent slaves, died defending him. Thanks to the speed of his horse, M. de Marsillac escaped; but he was desperately wounded, and died a few days later. So it happened that, although he reached his family and saved his papers, he failed to tell them or to make them understand where they would find *this* paper. At least so we may conjecture, for we know very little. My father-in-law's mother never recovered from the horrors of that time. She died soon after they reached Louisiana, and two of her children followed her; so that he, a child of six years, was left sole survivor of the family."

"And he never thought of reading valueless title-deeds," remarked Yvonne; "so this one scrap of value among them escaped his knowledge. The question now is, has it yet any value?"

No one felt able to answer this question, and all eyes turned again toward the grandmother, whom, in French fashion, the children had been trained to regard as the head of the house, as if seeking an oracle there.

"Who can say?" replied Madame de Marsillac. "A century has passed; the land has been in the hands of the revolted slaves from that day to this; no one can tell whether the money M. de Marsillac concealed has not long ago been found and taken."

"But," said Yvonne—and what emphasis her clear young

voice lent that potent word !—" if by any chance it should still be undiscovered, that money is *ours*, and ours alone."

Her grandmother nodded. "There can be no question of that," she answered. "You who are gathered here—your mother alone in her generation, and you four girls in yours—are the only living descendants of Henri de Marsillac."

Yvonne's glance passed over the persons thus indicated—over her mother's noble, careworn face ; over the delicate, girlish aspect of her sisters, dwelling longest on Diane ; and, as if she drew inspiration from the sight, as if in that moment she saw all the struggles of the past and all the hopelessness of the future, she spoke as not one of those present had ever heard her speak before, with a passionate earnestness and decision that seemed for the moment to transform her.

"Then," she said, "with the help of God, I will find that money if it still remains where Henri de Marsillac placed it !"

———

CHAPTER VII.

It was two or three hours later, and the entire household was wrapped in silence and stillness, when Yvonne and her mother—the Committee of Ways and Means, as Hélène called them—were alone together in the chamber of the latter. Through the open windows a soft breeze from the river entered, wafting back the light curtains ; while Madame Prévost, reclining in a low, deep chair, looked and listened to Yvonne, who, seated before her, erect and eager, was talking earnestly ; the shaded lamplight from the table beside which they sat falling on her picturesque head, her animated face, and her girlish figure in its simple gown of white muslin.

"There is nothing else to be done," she was saying. "The money must be sought, and there is no one but myself to seek it."

"But, my dear," said her mother, "such a thing, when one comes to consider it practically, is madness. How is it possible for you to go to that island to look for money concealed a century ago? It would be a wild and hopeless expedition if you were a man, but for a young girl to undertake such a search is out of the question."

"Mamma," was the grave reply, "nothing is out of the question which *must be done*. And there is not anything more certain than that this must be done. It seems to me no less than a miracle that I should have found that old paper, which has lain hidden from all eyes so long, just when our need is most desperate. And because I have found it at the time when it means most to us, I believe firmly that the money buried by Henri de Marsillac is still to be found where he concealed it. At least, you must admit there is a strong probability that it is still there; and so would it not be madness indeed if we failed to look for it?"

"It might be worth while perhaps," Madame Prévost answered, "if there were a man to go——"

"But since there is no man, *I* must go."

"Yvonne," said her mother, "you have played the part of a man so long in our affairs that I believe you half forget that you are not one. There is nothing more impossible than that you should go on this wild quest. The mere thought of such a thing is absurd. You are dreaming, my dear—dreaming a fairy tale."

"Is there much that is suggestive of a fairy tale in the condition of our affairs?" asked Yvonne dryly. "Is there much encouragement to dream in the reality of our debts, or in the resolution of Diane to sacrifice herself? Do you understand that, gentle as she seems, Diane is immovable in her resolve? As certainly as she lives she will marry Burnham's son if we cannot pay the debt at the expiration of three months. And do you know any means by which we can obtain the money to pay the debt?"

Madame Prévost shook her head as she looked at her daughter's intensely earnest face.

"Did you hear me swear to her," Yvonne went on, "that I would move heaven and earth to find the means to save her? It must have been an inspiration which made me say this; for I knew there was no hope—that we had already tried every possible means of raising money to pay the debt, and failed. But when I looked at Diane and thought of what she was resolved to do, I felt that there was nothing impossible except to permit such a sacrifice; and so I pledged myself—wildly, desperately, hopelessly, one might say. I would 'leave nothing undone,' I said; although I felt that there was nothing to do. And then— then, mamma, there came into my hands, by a chance so strange, the old paper, written as if it were to meet this need, by that man standing on the verge of his death a hundred years ago. And what it says plainly is that if I will go to a certain spot in the island of Santo Domingo, I shall find the means to save Diane, to pay your debt, to give us all peace and independence. Do you think I can hesitate? Do you think *anything* could keep me back? No—not lions, not devils in my path, far less considerations of what is or is not proper for a young girl to do."

"Yvonne, you astonish, you almost frighten me!" said

her mother, startled by this passionate vehemence. " These
are new ideas indeed."

" Not more new than the needs which draw them forth,
mamma," said Yvonne. " If I wished to do this merely
as an adventure, or even merely for the money *as* money,
you would be right to have no sympathy with me and to
refuse your consent. But when you consider what it really
means—that I *must* go, however painful or difficult it may
be, since there is no one else to go, in order to find Diane's
ransom, your freedom, peace for dear old *grand'mère* in
her last days ; and security from indigence, the worst
trouble, the worst temptation of existence, for poor Hélène
and Ninon—you will see as I do, that it is one of the
supreme occasions of life, when mere proprieties must be
cast aside, and one must act without regard to what the
world may think or say."

" But the practical difficulties seem insurmountable,"
Madame Prévost yet protested. " Even if we could raise
the money——"

" The money *must* be raised—there is no question of
that."

" Still, how can you undertake, alone and unattended,
such a journey ? How can you secure yourself against robbery and violence on that horrible island ? You do not
know of what you are talking. If you were a boy now, it
might be possible——"

" Then," cried Yvonne, springing to her feet, " *I will
be a boy !* We will remedy the mistake of Nature. Don't
look at me as if you thought I had gone mad, mamma.
What I mean is that I will put on a boy's dress, and no
one will suspect that I am anything else."

" Yvonne, this is most wild, most insane of all !"

" No, mamma, no ! Instead of that, it is a happy inspiration. Why did I not think of it before? How it simplifies everything! It is not I, Yvonne Prévost, who will go, hampered by petticoats and proprieties; but a boy, a delightful boy, who need be troubled by neither. What shall we call him? Oh, Henri de Marsillac of course, after his great-great-grandfather!"

"But there is no De Marsillac living," said Madame Prévost, bewildered.

"And he will not be living except in a dream, a masquerade. Oh, I am perfectly enchanted with the idea! Mamma dear, don't you see how charming it is? It is not for nothing people have called me the man of the family, I will *be* the man of the family, and do all that a man can or dare do, so help me God!"

What a picture she made at this moment, standing so straight in her slim, young grace; her face flashing eager resolve from every eloquent feature; her voice dropping over the last passionate, earnest words! . Madame Prévost gazed at her as one fascinated. The contagion of such self-forgetfulness, such courage, such resolve, was irresistible. She felt herself carried away, so that all power of objection failed her. And it was not only that the need was desperate, the occasion supreme, and the hope almost miraculous in its opportuneness, but it was not an ordinary girl who proposed to do this wild and daring thing, but Yvonne—Yvonne, who had won the right to assume such duty and such risk; who had proved her capabilities, her judgment and her resource; so that the positions of mother and daughter were often reversed, inasmuch as the latter supported while the former depended. And the habit of dependence asserted itself now. · In her heart Madame Prévost felt that Yvonne was capable of anything, even of sustaining such a part as she proposed. Besides, since it was impossible that she could go properly protected and attended, the mother, bred in French traditions, and shrinking with horror from the new code of independence for girls, was much more ready to consent to her masquerading in male attire than to her going alone in her own character. And so after a moment she said, almost in a whisper :

" If I consent to this, Yvonne, it must be a profound secret. No one must know it but ourselves—you and me——"

" And one more—me, mamma !" cried a voice which made them both start. " You cannot leave me out of the secret, whatever it is."

It was Diane, who, having noiselessly entered in time to hear her mother's last words, now advanced across the dark, polished floor, a vision of ghostly fairness in her clinging white night-robe.

" You must excuse my interrupting you," she went on ; " but I have been waiting so long for Yvonne that at last I thought I would come and find out why the consultation was so prolonged ; although of course I know that you are talking about this romance of a buried fortune."

" It is no romance at all, but a reality," said Yvonne. " No one can doubt the evidence of that paper, together with *grand'mère's* testimony of what was always known. There is nothing of which we may feel more certainly assured than that our great-great-grandfather buried his valuables in the place he describes. The only doubt is whether they have been left undisturbed until now."

" And that doubt is equalled only by the greater difficulty of finding out anything about it," said Diane, curling down on a rug at her mother's feet. " In fact, as far as I can perceive, the fortune, even if undisturbed, might as well be buried in the heart of Africa, so far as we are concerned. It is all very well for Yvonne to declare that

she will find it, and for the rest of us to cheer her resolution ; but when it comes to considering the matter in cold
blood, as I have been considering it for an hour past, one
perceives that we are dreaming of impossibilities."

" On the contrary," said Yvonne, " it is settled that I
am going to seek it."

" Indeed ! When ?"

" Immediately. There is no time for delay, as you well
know. At the end of three months the Burnham debt
must be paid. Within that time, therefore, I must go to
Santo Domingo and find this money, if it is to be found."

Diane looked up at her sister in silence for a moment ;
then, in a voice altogether changed, she asked gravely :

" Yvonne, are you in earnest ?"

" Perfectly in earnest," said Yvonne. " How can you
imagine otherwise ?"

" But it is impossible. You cannot go alone."

" I *must* go alone. Do you think that considerations of
les convenances are for those whose situation is as desperate
as ours ?"

" I was not thinking of *les convenances*," said Diane.
" I was thinking of danger—real danger. You are as brave
as a lion, Yvonne ; but you are only a girl, all the same ;
and I don't see how it is possible for you to undertake
such an expedition as this alone. It would involve risks
for a man."

" And *I* shall be a man—for the time," said Yvonne.
" That was the secret which you overheard us discussing,
and which you must strictly keep. Since we have no man
even remotely belonging to us to do this thing—no brother,
uncle, or cousin—and since you are so far right that, setting *les convenances* aside, I fear a girl could hardly encounter all the difficulties and risks involved. we have de-

cided that I shall cease to be a girl for the time being ; that
I shall put on masculine dress, and become the boy I have
always desired to be."

" O Yvonne !"—Diane's tone was full of horror and consternation—" suppose you were discovered ?"

" I shall not be discovered, Diane. Don't frighten
mamma by such suggestions. I am confident of my ability
to support the part, and not less confident because it will
give me a sense of fearlessness such as a woman can never
know. It will be your brother, not a helpless sister, who
will go to find and bring back your ransom."

" Yvonne, Yvonne !"

Even as Yvonne had done in the other scene between
these three, Diane now sprang to her feet and threw her
arms about her sister.

" I would rather have *you* than a hundred brothers !"
she cried. " It is for me that you are going to do this
reckless thing—I know it. But you must not. Mamma,
tell her that she must not. There is no saying what may
befall her, and it is better that I should be sacrificed than
that we should lose Yvonne."

" Diane, be silent !" exclaimed Yvonne, fearing that her
mother's hardly extorted consent might be recalled. " You
have no right to interfere. Mamma, don't listen to her."

Poor Madame Prévost sat motionless and silent, torn by
a struggle such as only a mother could know. Diane's
words seemed to make more real to her the dangers surrounding the wild enterprise to which Yvonne had pledged
herself ; but, then, Diane's presence also intensified her
consciousness of the other danger—more real, more menacing, more pressing—which threatened the girl herself.
Was it not well to dare any risk which might result in res-
cuing this self-devoted victim from a fate against which

every fibre of the mother's heart revolted? Yes, it was hard to make the choice ; but since it must be made—

"Diane," she said suddenly, in a low, clear tone, "Yvonne is right. As there must be one sacrifice or the other, hers is the better. She will undertake a difficult, even perhaps a perilous, task ; but she can hope for the help of God, because her motive is absolutely unselfish. She is also right in thinking that, since she must go alone, the attire of a man will be a protection, and enable her to do many things which she might not otherwise be able to accomplish. Extraordinary emergencies require sometimes extraordinary exertions to meet them, and we cannot always look at things in a conventional light. It will almost break my heart to see her go away on such a wild and hopeless quest——"

"Not hopeless at all, mamma dearest !" cried Yvonne, as her mother's voice broke down in tears. "Call me fanciful if you will, but I do not believe I found that paper at such a time for nothing. I shall come back to you with Henri de Marsillac's buried fortune. I am sure of it."

"But, O Yvonne, are you not frightened to think of all you must go through to reach it?" Diane asked, looking at her with wide eyes.

"Frightened ! No," Yvonne answered. "I had no feeling of the kind when I thought of going as a girl ; but as a boy—how *could* one be frightened as a boy ?"

"I think I have heard of boys and even men who were sometimes frightened," said Diane. "But if no one is to know of your transformation—and indeed I am sure *grand'-mère* would die before she would give her consent to such a thing—how are you going to accomplish it ? Where will you cease to be a girl and become a boy ?"

This was a practical difficulty, in the face of which Yvonne remained silent a moment or two. Then, her young mind being accustomed to rapid reflection and decision, she said :

" I shall have to go to New York to find a steamer for Hayti ; so it is there the transformation shall take place. Cousin Alix lives there, and she will help me. We must take her into our confidence, but no one else. *Grand'mère* and the girls must know, of course, that I have gone to the island ; but not *how* I have gone ; while our friends and acquaintances had better not know even that. They would only laugh at the idea of my going to seek a buried fortune. So *they* must only be told that I have gone to New York to visit Cousin Alix. It is really nobody's business where I have gone, but we don't want to create an unnecessary mystery."

" By no means," said Madame Prévost. " It is very necessary to account for your absence, and 1 am glad I can truthfully say that you have gone to visit Alix."

" It seems really providential that Cousin Alix should have gone to New York to live," remarked Diane. " Without her assistance, you would find it hard to meet the practical difficulty of changing from a girl into a boy and back again."

Yvonne smiled. " I wish there were no worse difficulty in my path than that," she said. " But there is yet one more person to be taken into our confidence, as far as the mere fact of the journey to the island and the object with which I go is concerned. That is Mr. Clarke. We must go to New Orleans to-morrow, mamma, to see him. It will be necessary to borrow more money on our sugar crop, for I must have enough to enable me to meet any extraordinary demands that may arise."

"And if you fail?" observed Madame Prévost, whose heart sank at this.

"If I fail we shall be ruined," replied Yvonne calmly. "But we shall be that if I do not go. And I shall not fail."

PART II.

CHAPTER I.

" The end of the matter is, Bertie, that the doctors give no hope of your overcoming this constitutional weakness unless you live for two years at least in a warm climate."

Herbert Atherton rose from his seat opposite his father —the two men had been lingering over their after-dinner coffee and cigars together, as was their custom ; for each was partial to the society of the other—and stood for a few minutes meditatively on the hearth-rug, with his back to the fire. He was a tall, slender man, handsome, and possessing an air of distinction which does not always accompany good looks ; but a certain narrowness and hollowness of chest, together with his blond fairness—that peculiar fairness which invariably denotes a certain lack of vigor— would have told a physician at a glance in what direction lay the constitutional weakness of which his father spoke. It was indeed an inherited weakness ; for his mother, whom he strikingly resembled, had died early of consumption.

" In short," he said at length, in a quiet tone, " I have to choose between sentence of death and sentence of banishment. But who is to tell that the last will avert the first ? After I have given up all my interests in life, professional and social, and idled away two years in some invalid resort, who is to guarantee me against dying at last, as so many other poor devils have died who were persuaded to do the same ? But if the dying must be done within a limited space of time, I should much prefer to make shorter work of it and die in harness, with the satisfaction of *living*, rather than merely *existing*, to the last."

" You mistake the case, my dear boy," said his father earnestly. " The doctors have spoken very frankly, and they assure me that your lungs are not seriously affected at present ; but there is a weakness, a predisposition to—the disease we fear, which makes it necessary for you to live for two years at least in a climate that is warm, equable, and healthful. At the end of that time—if you give up all work and live as much as possible in the open air—they say that the weakness will be overcome, and your prospects for a long life as good as any one's."

" Very kind of them to offer such assurances," said the young man sarcastically. " It is the old story, I fear ; and if I consulted my own inclination, I should take my chances for life or death here, rather than consent to this banishment with all that it involves."

" But you will not consult your own inclinations, Herbert ?" said his father, yet more earnestly. " You will think of me and of your future. What are two years at your age ?"

" Very much," replied the other : " more than they would be either earlier or later ; for just now, as you well know, I am on the road to success ; but if I drop out of the race, others will step in and gain all for which I am striving. Life does not halt an instant for any man."

" It is hard, my boy—I know it is hard !" the elder Atherton said, looking up at him with deep sympathy. " It grieves me as much as it grieves you to see you drop out of the race, as you express it, even for a limited time——"

" It is *not* for a limited time," interrupted the other,

turning his face away. " Don't you see ?—this is final. It means that if I am to live at all hereafter, it will be as one of the great army of invalids and valetudinarians idling away existence in ' health resorts,' with no aspiration in life beyond that of avoiding cold and nursing a vital flame that will continue to grow feebler year by year. Father, I would rather die sharply, quickly. If you would only not press the point of this going away——"

" But I must, Bertie, I must !" said the father, rising and laying his hand upon his shoulder. " I must beg you to do it for my sake, if not for your own. You know what you are to me. Is it necessary to tell you that since your mother died I have not had a thought except for you and your future ? Every hope I have in the world is bound up in you ; and for my sake, therefore—that this inherited curse may be averted, and I may not be left desolate in my age—I implore you, my son, to follow the advice of the doctors and go away."

Only a selfish and callous nature could have withstood such an appeal, uttered by a father who, although usually reserved in the expression of affection, had proved his devotion by every act of his life. Indeed, so well did the two understand each other that Herbert Atherton had never for an instant doubted his father's love any more than the comprehension and sympathy which were always to be felt under his quiet reticence. What he was to him he knew without need of speech ; but the speech itself— the very unaccustomedness of which lent it additional force —touched him deeply. The quiver of the older man's voice, even more than the words he uttered, gave him a poignant sense of what he owed to this love which had always encompassed him, but had never before demanded anything. What it now demanded was that he should live, even if in order to do so he must sacrifice all that made life of value to his young ambition ; even if he must fall into the routine of that semi-invalid existence which he had watched in others with a sense of dread and repulsion produced by the lurking fear that it might be his own fate. ˙ He had always vowed in his heart that he would not submit to it ; that when the time came to choose he would take a quick death in preference to a lingering death-in-life ; but now that the time *had* come, he saw that such choice would be but selfishness. For his father's sake he must accept life on any terms that might be granted him, however bitter they might be. And so it was that after a short pause he replied quietly :

" My dear father, the expression of your wish is enough. Of course I will go since you desire it, and since such is the medical sentence. Have the doctors indicated any particular place of banishment, or am I to be allowed to choose within the rather vague limits of ' a warm climate ' ?"

" They have not recommended any particular place," answered Mr. Atherton, relieved by an acquiescence more prompt than he had expected. " It is left for you to decide where you will go. But since, in connection with the warm climate, Dr. Talford mentioned a sea-voyage as desirable, I have myself thought of the West Indies."

" The West Indies !" repeated Herbert. He shrugged his shoulders with a gesture of indifference. " Why not? They offer a wide field in which to do nothing, and are at least not overrun with invalids, like Florida and Southern California. If a man must drop as a wreck out of the stream of life, I fancy that a West Indian island is as good a place as another to be stranded upon."

" You distress me by speaking in that manner," said his

father. " There is no question of your dropping as a wreck out of the stream of life. You are only asked to take certain precautions against a possible danger ; and I see no reason to doubt the assurance of the doctors that, these precautions taken, such a danger may never arise. So let us face the necessity cheerfully"—he sat down again in his chair—" and decide what is best for you to do."

To face the prospect cheerfully was a little beyond Herbert Atherton's powers ; but to face it philosophically was at least within his reach. So he, too, sat down again and lighted a fresh cigar as he inquired :

" Have you any plan to propose ?"

" Yes," replied his father ; " I have a plan which I hope you will approve. I sympathize so deeply with your objection to being ordered away to vegetate in idleness, that I have been considering what can be done to make the banishment less irksome to you, and I have decided that the only possible thing is to provide you with some occupation and interest."

" Rather difficult to do if I am condemned to a valetudinarian existence for two years," answered the young man despondently. " But I am open to any suggestions. Only don't ask me to become a fisherman or a botanist. Those are the only things the West Indies seem to suggest."

" I shall certainly not propose either of those pursuits to you," returned Mr. Atherton, smiling. " My idea is very different. Have I ever mentioned to you that I possess an interest in a sugar estate in the island of Santo Domingo ?"

" I don't think you ever have. Isn't it rather a singular investment ?"

" On the contrary, it has proved very profitable—until lately. Together with some of my friends, I was induced to enter into the speculation by a man on whose judgment and integrity we had implicit reliance ; and the result was all we anticipated so long as he was alive to manage the property. But, unfortunately, he died rather more than a year ago, and since then affairs have been by no means so satisfactory. The person who has the management of the estate now is a man whom he trained and in whom he had the greatest confidence. This confidence induced us to leave matters in his hands when poor Burton died ; but we are not at all satisfied with his management. It is necessary, therefore, that we should send some one to look into affairs ; and it has occurred to me that this may serve as an occupation for you. You can go out, examine into matters, take as much or as little of the responsibility of management as you care to assume, and meanwhile discover how the climate of the island—said to be the best in the West Indies—suits you.''

'' It sounds quite promising,'' replied Atherton ; '' and leads one to think that in making your investment you foresaw the possibility of some day needing to find an occupation in the tropics for an invalid son. At least the existence of the estate provides me with a spot a little more definite than the equator towards which to turn my face. For of course I'll go, overhaul the agent, and perhaps— who knows ?—turn sugar-planter and lotus-eater, and never come back again. What, by the way, do I know of Santo Domingo ? Very little, I fear, except that it was the Hispañola of Columbus and the scene of many romantic and tragic histories.''

'' It is the richest, the most beautiful, the most undeveloped and the most unfortunate of the West Indian islands,'' said his father. '' You will find some books about it in the library, which I collected at the time we bought the sugar estate. Since then I have met many business men and planters from the island, and they all agree in describing the climate as one of rare perfection. It was that made me think of sending you there."

"You don't know how grateful I am to you for giving me an object to lessen the weariness of enforced exile and idleness," said the young man earnestly. "It seems to put a different face upon the necessity of going. And this reminds me—did Talford say anything about how soon I should go?"

"The sooner the better," answered Mr. Atherton reluctantly. "He wishes you to be in the tropics before the severe weather sets in. And if a thing is to be done——"

"'Then 'twere well it were done quickly,'" quoted Herbert, as he rose to his feet again. "I shall find out to-morrow when the next steamer for Santo Domingo sails. Meanwhile there are one or two places I have promised to look in on to-night. Even a condemned man may be permitted to make his *adieux* to his friends."

CHAPTER II.

TEN days later, and in the brightness of a December afternoon which had still a touch of Indian summer mildness, the two Athertons stood together on the deck of the Clyde steamship bound from New York to Santo Domingo. With hatchways closed and ready for departure, she lay at her pier, taking her last consignment in the form of passengers before sailing. Father and son each wore an air of cheerfulness, assumed for the benefit of the other ; and in the intervals of exchanging those last words which always seem so inadequate, they watched with some surprise the number of passengers arriving, accompanied by the usual *impedimenta* of steamer trunks and deck-chairs.

" It begins to look as if Santo Domingo really formed a part of the civilized world," observed Herbert presently. " The steward tells me that every state-room is taken, and these people are in appearance quite like the average of the ordinary ocean-travelling public. I have felt as if I would be setting sail for a place as distant, vague, and far removed from the conditions of modern life as the Fortunate Isles ; but the illusion begins to be shattered by these dapper men of business, and these fashionable-looking women, with their bouquets and attendant friends. One might fancy one's self on the *Majestic* or the *Umbria.* Where are the West Indian creoles one would naturally expect to see, with their picturesque languor and grace ?"

" There are some of them here, I think," said Mr. Atherton. " I have seen several typical West Indian faces. On the whole, I find the appearance of the passengers more satisfactory than I expected, and I hope you may find some companionable people among them."

" Doubtful," replied the young man, in a disparaging tone, which was the result of his deep though concealed depression of spirit. " But I am fortunately very independent of companionship on an ocean voyage or elsewhere, Ah, there is the signal for departure ! Good-by, my dear father, good-by !"

" Good-by, my boy !" said the father huskily. ' God bless you ! And, whatever you do, take care of yourself."

" I shall have nothing else to do, so don't be afraid of my failing in that duty," answered the son, with an attempt at cheerfulness. " God bless *you*, sir ; and again good-by !"

It was as their hands unclasped and the father hurried

away down the gang-plank that an echo of his last words struck on Atherton's ear.

"Good-by, my dear, good-by! Take care of yourself, and may God take care of you!"

These words, spoken close beside him, with a fervor of accent uncommon even in such farewells, made him half unconsciously look around to see who had uttered them. His glance fell on a lady who was in the act of embracing a slender, handsome boy of eighteen or nineteen years. She seemed to restrain with great difficulty an inclination to tears as she kissed him repeatedly. Then, saying earnestly, "May you have the success your heroism deserves!" she turned to follow the rest of the shore-going contingent down the gang-plank.

A few minutes later, as the ship moved slowly out of her dock, a group composed of the friends of those on board gathered at the end of the pier and waved their farewells with many fluttering handkerchiefs. Apart from them, however, stood two persons: one a gray-haired man, who only watched, with a sadness he no longer made any attempt to disguise, the tall, well-known form which carried away with it his heart and hopes; and the other a delicate, dark-eyed lady, who on her part no longer restrained the tears which dimmed her power of seeing the slender figure waving her so bravely a last farewell from the deck of the receding vessel.

When the wharf with these figures upon it finally disappeared from view, as the *New York* steamed down the bay, Atherton turned from the rail against which he had been leaning, in contemplation sad as that of his father; and, telling himself that the depression which weighed upon him must be cast aside, began to pace the deck, to inhale the sea-breeze which came from the vast ocean expanse towards which they were hastening, and to make some attempt to interest himself in observing the fellow-travellers whom fate had granted him.

It was then that his glance fell again on the boy whom he had before observed ; and he was struck by the dejection which his attitude expressed, as, standing at the extreme end of the after-deck, with one arm passed around a stanchion, he kept his face steadily turned towards the land they were leaving. The pose of the young figure seemed to Atherton to express a despondency almost akin to despair ; and the droop of the head was suggestive of tears, which might have dropped into the green brine below. " Poor boy !" he thought, as he recalled the fervor of the farewell he had overheard ; and then he remembered the last words of the lady, which even in that moment had faintly excited his surprise—" May you have the success which your heroism deserves !"

Heroism ! That was something uncommon ; and, glad of anything to divert his thoughts, Atherton, as he paced back and forth, cast curious glances now and again at the slight, motionless figure, while idly wondering what form the heroism in question took. Whatever it was, it certainly did not just now sustain a manifestly sinking heart. But there is a wide difference between a sinking heart and a sinking courage ; and Atherton, knowing this, felt his sympathy so touched by the sadness of the lonely boy that at last, pausing, he proved his interest by speaking.

" We are likely to have a fine night," he observed ; for the sun was now sinking over the land in a clear bed of gold.

The boy started at the sound of his voice, and turned towards him a face on which there was an almost offended look. The expression surprised Atherton ; yet in the midst of his surprise he was struck by the character of the countenance thus revealed—its mingled delicacy and strength, the virile resolution of the clear-cut mouth, the feminine sweetness of the brow and eyes, the spirited intelligence which breathed in every feature, and the striking picturesqueness of the whole. As he gazed at it, saying to himself, "What an attractive face!" its owner evidently remembered that he had no cause for offence in the fact that this gentleman had addressed him, and answered coldly, yet courteously, as he looked away again :

"So it appears."

It was now Atherton's turn to start ; for the voice which replied would have been singularly sweet and refined even for a woman, with an accent that could not be described as foreign, yet which was clearly produced by the habitual use of some speech more musical than English. Every one knows that there is no more unmistakable indication of character and breeding than the voice ; but there are some persons peculiarly susceptible to the effect of these inflections and intonations which express so much, and Atherton was one of those persons. His interest in his young fellow-traveller was sensibly quickened by the discovery that he possessed a voice altogether exquisite. But for this he would probably have turned away from one so plainly indisposed to meet his advances ; as it was, he rather surprised himself by making a second effort at conversation.

"That doesn't mean, however, that we may not find it a little rough when we get outside. Are you a good sailor?"

"I think I am rather a good sailor," the other replied, still keeping his face turned away, and speaking with marked reserve. "But this is my first long voyage, so I am not sure."

' Short voyages are worse than long ones for testing certain sailing qualities," Atherton said. "Then you are not a West Indian?"

"No," was the quick reply, and the face turned towards him again with a flashing look of interrogation. "Why should you think so?"

"I can hardly say that I thought so. Only—this is a West Indian ship, and your appearance and voice are suggestive of something foreign."

There was a moment's pause, and then the boy replied with an effort, as if disliking and resenting the necessity to speak of himself: "I am from Louisiana."

"Ah, a French creole!" said Atherton involuntarily. "That accounts for the suggestion. Pray excuse me!" he added. "I had no intention of making personal remarks, but I am always interested in the study of national types; and am never brought into contact with a stranger that I do not find myself at once mentally determining from what branch of the human family he springs. There is usually very little difficulty in deciding."

"I should think," said the boy, with the manner of one who is drawn into talking against his will, "that to decide at once would be quite difficult, unless you possessed a very wide knowledge of the different types of humanity."

"On the contrary, a very moderate amount of the knowledge derived from travel renders one quite familiar with the marked types," Atherton answered; "and their various interminglings are readily traced. A glance is generally sufficient to enable me to ticket satisfactorily all those whom I encounter. But, you see, there was more than a glance required to ticket *you*," he added, smiling.

The other did not smile in reply. He hesitated a moment before answering, looking out again over the wide expanse of tossing waters to the vanishing city and the pale winter sunset beyond ; and then saying abruptly, " You will do me a favor if you will not attempt to ticket me at all," he turned and walked quickly away.

It says much for Atherton's amiability that he was more amused than indignant as he watched the slender young figure hastening across the deck. In fact, he was conscious of a sense of pity for the boy's folly and the mistake he had made. For not to gauge accurately the quality of those with whom the chances of life bring us into contact is to be guilty sometimes of very great mistakes. Without entertaining any undue sense of his own importance, Atherton was thoroughly aware of the enviable position which he occupied in the eyes of the world ; and was as well assured that his advances would have been rebuffed by no other passenger on board as that he would not have thought of making them to any other. It was his custom to hold aloof from all casual acquaintance, not so much from superciliousness as from a fastidiousness, which made him slow in choosing friends and associates. Indeed, according to the invariable rule of such a temperament, his friends were few and his associates generally characterized him as " difficult to know." He was himself surprised at the impulse which had prompted him to address this young stranger, and he could not but smile at the unexpected repulse he had received.

Naturally, however, he decided that he would hereafter ignore one so ungracious ; therefore it was with surprise, unmixed with pleasure, that on taking his place at the dinner-table he found the seat on his right occupied by the young Louisianian. The surprise was as great, the pleasure evidently as little, on the side of the latter as on his own. He glanced up quickly as the chair was swung around ; and when he saw who dropped into it, a deep flush mounted to his face and he looked away. It is probable that he felt conscious and ashamed of his rudeness on thus seeing the object of it beside him again ; but Atherton read his manner otherwise, and his own face took an expression familiar to those who had at times made advances which *he* did not care to receive, as he turned slightly in his chair, so as to present his shoulder to the offender, and began to examine the *menu*.

His order given, he glanced up and down the table, and, with the practised eye of a man accustomed to much travel, had no difficulty in determining the different types which composed the thirty or forty human beings whose numbers sea-sickness had not yet diminished. Half a dozen he at once perceived belonged to the class of the omnipresent German commercial traveller, who is overspreading all the countries of the world and the islands of the sea. Another group were distinctively West Indian—quiet, olive-skinned men, with great, slumberous, black eyes, who spoke Spanish among themselves. Only one showed in his chocolate-colored complexion the trace of negro blood. Then came a pair of alert young Americans, civil engineers, going down to assist in the construction of a Dominican railway ; a number of nondescript individuals, who might be either tourists or possible investors, or both ; and finally several ladies, who, as was to be learned by the conversation briskly carried on between them, were the wives and daughters of planters residing on the island.

By the time dinner was nearly over the swell of the Atlantic surge could be distinctly felt, and the steamer began to swing to it in a manner which shortened the ceremony of dining for several passengers. Atherton, quietly proceeding with his dessert, saw his right-hand neighbor turning pale, and was not surprised when he suddenly rose and

left the table as abruptly as he had quitted him on deck.
He smiled with a slight sense of sardonic amusement.
" Not such a very good sailor, after all, my young friend !"
he thought.

A few minutes later, having finished his coffee, he went
on deck for a last glimpse of the lights of Sandy Hook.
The night was clear and sharply cold, but the briny breath
of the sea came to him with a sense of refreshment.   As he
stood filling his lungs with it, the starlight of a radiant sky
revealed the wide expanse of tossing waves, which the
lights of the ship, gleaming across them, showed to be
foam-crested.   There was a promise of boisterousness in
these racing, yeasty surges, which now and again leaped up
as if in wild sport, and smote the sides of the vessel, sending aloft a shower of spray ; but as yet the sea was not
very rough, and Atherton paced the limited deck-space
with a sense of keen enjoyment.

Already he felt a reaction from the depression consequent
upon departure, and a conviction that the voyage alone
would do much for him.   Although he had struggled
against it, he knew that this enforced rest was really what
he needed.   Ever since his return from university life
abroad, he had been working too hard—ambition with him
proving even a keener spur than the need of making money
with other men.   And this intense application, this burning the candle of life at both ends, had developed the constitutional weakness which else might never have appeared.
Now he must perforce rest ; and the keen, salt breath of
the sea seemed to scatter his dark forebodings of a life
doomed in its prime to invalid inaction, and to tell him
that there was nothing wrong which Nature, the great
healer, could not restore without the help of other agencies.

He was not tempted to enter the smoking-room, where a

sound of tongues—most of them speaking English with a German accent—testified to the love of talking, which is a distinguishing characteristic of a large portion of the human race. So he paced back and forth in the starlight, with a renewal of that sense of pleasure in mere existence which had been lost to him for some time.

It was in one of his turns around the deck that he presently observed the dark outlines of a figure sitting in a chair placed under the shelter of the after-cabin. At first he paid no attention to it; but when he returned again and yet again from a tramp which extended as far as the bow of the ship, and had even taken in the hurricane deck, to find the same figure still motionless in its place, he began to wonder a little who was as fond of solitude as himself. In order to satisfy this faint curiosity, he dropped into a vacant chair beside the other, that he might take advantage of its shelter to strike a light for his cigar; and, as he struck it, glanced at the quiet figure.

A pair of large, startled eyes—which seemed to him even in this brief instant beautiful as those of a fawn—met his own, and he saw that the lover of solitude was the boy whom he had addressed before dinner. A certain sense of vexation crossed his mind as he recognized him, mingled with regret that he had taken the seat; but to leave it now with any abruptness would be to give to the incident of the afternoon an importance which it did not deserve, and to let an ill-mannered boy suppose that the rudeness had power to affect him. He therefore remained quite still, smoking placidly; and had so far abstracted his thoughts that he had almost forgotten the presence of his silent companion, when the latter suddenly spoke.

"I think, Monsieur, that I owe you an apology," said the sweet voice with the slight French accent which had charmed his ear when he heard it before. "I fear that I was very rude when you spoke to me this afternoon. I did not intend to be so. I only wanted just then to be alone with my thoughts, and so—I hardly knew what I said."

"It was of no importance," answered Atherton, whose sense of vexation melted away as if by magic under the influence of those exquisite tones. Just to keep that voice sounding in his ear he would have forgiven a much greater offence. "It was really my fault for disturbing you," he continued. "I can only plead a good intention. I perceived that you were feeling despondent, and I fancied a little distraction might be good for you."

"I have thought since that perhaps what you meant was a kindness, and that I was very ungracious," added the boy. "But, you see, I did not take it in that way. I only thought of you as—presuming."

"By Jove!" said Atherton to himself, too much astonished for indignation. "What kind of a youngster can this be?" Aloud he said, in a tone of good-natured irony : "Your royal highness must accept *my* apologies. It is certainly not my habit to be ' presuming.' "

There was a moment's pause, and then the boy said, catching his breath a little :

"I am afraid I have been rude again. I should not have used that word. Of course it strikes you as absurd."

"Rather, I confess," Atherton replied, a little dryly. "Naturally, I don't know how exalted your rank may be ; but unless it is very exalted—and I have never heard that there are princes in Louisiana—you are undoubtedly guilty of absurdity in thinking that a man presumes because he addresses you without an introduction."

"You are right—I see that now," said the boy hastily, with a humility in his tones which was strikingly at variance with the suggestion of arrogance in the objectionable word. "You must excuse me. I forget many things which I should remember. I will endeavor not to forget again that I am only an insignificant boy, whose loneliness you pitied, and who should have been grateful for your kindness instead of repulsing it."

Again Atherton felt any possible anger disarmed by those accents, which seemed breathed like music out of the darkness.

"I think," he said, "that if you will take the advice of a man a good deal older than yourself, you will be slow to repulse any one until quite sure that such repulse is deserved. Otherwise you will make many enemies, and perhaps lose some friends. And one just entering upon life can hardly afford to begin by either making the one or losing the other."

"'Hast thou a thousand friends, it is not enough; hast thou one enemy, it is too much,'" murmured the boy, as if to himself. "Yes, your advice is good; and I really have sense enough to know it of myself. But when you addressed me I was feeling so miserable that I resented any intrusion upon my wretchedness."

Now, this was not at all the confession to be expected of a potential hero. But so strongly did the witchery of the voice continue to assert itself, that Atherton felt more than ever attracted to the speaker.

"I fancied that was how you felt," he said after a brief pause, "and since I was feeling low-spirited myself, I was more inclined to sympathize with you. Are you alone?"

"Entirely alone. I have not even an acquaintance on board, and a little while ago I should have said that I did not desire one."

"I may suppose, then, that you would not say so now?"

"No. I am not sorry to know *you*, who, I think, are kind ; but I shrink from the thought of indiscriminate acquaintance, and I hope I may be left alone."

"There is not much difficulty generally in being left alone," observed Atherton, smiling under cover of the darkness at the thought of what an opinion of his own importance the boy must have. "Unless one has something very remarkable to distinguish one, the world is, as a rule, only too ready to leave one alone."

"That again is true," the other replied ; "and I should not have needed to be reminded of it. You must think me very foolish, but I—I need a little time to adjust myself to a new situation. I have never been alone before, and I am going into a strange country with a responsibility upon me which is rather trying."

"You are very young to have responsibility thrown upon you," said Atherton, recalling the words which had first attracted his attention to the speaker.

"Young or old, we must not shirk our burdens ; especially if there is no one else to take them up," the other answered with a sigh. "And so, having many things to think of, I hoped that no one on board would notice me, and that I should have the time of the voyage to consider my plans. This is why I was so startled and, I confess, annoyed when you addressed me."

"Well," said Atherton, "I am glad you have been so frank. Hereafter I promise that I will not address you unless you take the initiative ; and I do not think you have much annoyance of the kind to fear from the other passengers. My impression is that you will be left as much alone as you can possibly desire."

There was a few minutes' pause. The motion of the vessel had now very much increased, and she was swinging to the fast roughening sea in a manner calculated to prove very trying to a landsman. The boy presently observed, in a low voice :

" I seem to say nothing but ungracious things, and yet I don't mean them. Perhaps when I feel better I shall be able to express myself better. Just now I—I think I shall go to my state room. Good-night, and pray believe that I am not ungrateful for your kindness."

He rose as he spoke, but a sudden lurch of the ship sent him reeling back into his seat.

" Take care !" said Atherton. " If you don't want to sustain an injury, it is necessary to be careful on shipboard until you get your sea-legs. Where is your room ? I'll help you to it."

" Oh, thanks !" said the other, hastily ; " but I think I can manage to reach it alone. I will be more careful."

He rose again ; and, this time keeping his feet and balancing himself with the roll of the vessel, he passed around the cabin and out of sight. Atherton rose also ; and walking slowly forward, thought :

" What a remarkable boy !"

———

CHAPTER III.

ROUGH and boisterous were the seas which the *New York* encountered as she passed Hatteras, of stormy fame ; and few were the passengers who did not more or less succumb to the dreaded malady which lies in wait for those who go down upon the deep in ships. Atherton was not surprised that for two days he had no further glimpse of the boy who so much interested him ; nor that when he met him on the third day he was looking very pale, as he lay back in a deck-chair gazing at the sea, which, now comparatively smooth and brilliantly blue, spread its tossing waves to the far horizon. His appearance, at once so delicate and so lonely, revived the sympathy which Atherton had first felt, and brought his steps involuntarily to a pause in front of him.

"Good-morning !" he said ; "I believe it was agreed when we parted that the initiative in any further intercourse should come from you, but I may be permitted to inquire how you are feeling. You have evidently suffered from the rough weather of the last two days ?"

"Very much," the boy replied, looking up with a smile at the tall figure standing over him. "I was very sea-sick, and I am still feeling the effects of it. I find that I am not a good sailor at all. And you—have you been well ?"

"Oh, yes ! I am an old yachtsman, used to the roughest tumbling Neptune can give. You needn't fancy yourself a bad sailor, however, because you have felt the weather of the past two days. It has been uncommonly nasty."

"Yes ; but to-day makes amends. Is it not glorious ? This is, indeed, Byron's ' deep and dark-blue ocean.' "

"So you know ' Childe Harold ' !" said Atherton, drawing forward another chair and dropping into it. "That is a little uncommon with the youth of the present day. Which is a pity. For the morbidness of that interesting exile was healthfulness itself compared to the morbidness of *fin de siècle* verse-makers ; and the poetry is magnificent."

"It seems so to me," said the boy. "As I have sat here watching the waves in their long, ceaseless rolling, those lines ran constantly in my mind :

> " ' Roll on, thou deep and dark-blue ocean—roll !
> Ten thousand fleets sweep over thee in vain ;
> Man marks the earth with ruin—his control
> Stops with the shore : upon the watery plain
> The wrecks are all thy deed ; nor doth remain
> A shadow of man's ravage, save his own,
> When for a moment, like a drop of rain,
> He sinks into thy depths with bubbling groan,
> Without a grave, unknell'd, uncoffin'd, and unknown.' "

Familiar as the stanza was to Atherton, it seemed to him that he had never heard it before, so much did the noble measure gain from the music of the tones which uttered it. Gazing out over that majestic expanse of waters, which since the birth of time has never been wholly stilled, the speaker, as if he forgot his listener and only gratified himself by uttering aloud the lines which haunted him, recited them with a melody of intonation, a depth and perfection of expression, which justified Atherton's exclamation :

" What a voice you have ! Where did you learn to recite like that ?"

The boy turned his face towards him with a surprised look.

" Was it at all extraordinary ?" he asked. " I only spoke as I felt. The music of the verses seemed the only fit expression for the feeling which the sea excites."

" I should have said that only a poet or an actor could have spoken them as you did," Atherton replied ; " while few poets and not a great many actors possess such a voice. You are really a very astonishing boy. If I might hazard a guess, you have been brought up by a woman, and a woman of singular intelligence and refinement."

" Yes," was the quiet reply ; " my mother is all that."

" And you are perhaps the only boy in a family of girls ?"

"Right again"—and now for the first time Atherton heard him utter a low, musical laugh. "I have three sisters, but I am the only man of the family."

"That accounts for your feminine ways, and also for the fact that you seem to look at things in general in a manner rather unlike what one would expect in a boy."

"I hope you don't think that I am a—milksop?" asked the boy anxiously.

It was Atherton's turn to laugh.

"Oh, no!" he answered. "If I had thought that I should not have mentioned the feminine ways. It is the bravest men who sometimes have most of the woman in them ; and refined natures often dare more than coarse ones, because they can feel the incentive of a higher motive. Indeed, I should not be surprised"—he spoke deliberately—"if you proved a hero."

As he had anticipated, the last word made his companion start. He turned around in his chair, and his face was quite pale as he asked :

"What do you mean ? Why do you say that ?"

"To be frank with you," Atherton answered, " because I have already heard heroism attributed to you. Don't look so startled. It was only by the lady who bade you good-by on board the day we left. I was standing close beside you, and I could not avoid hearing her say that she wished you ' the success your heroism deserved.' That first drew my attention to you. One does not sail with a hero every day, you know."

There was a short interval of silence, and then :

"My cousin—for the lady you mention was my cousin—spoke extravagantly," said the boy. "It seemed to her heroic that I should undertake this voyage, and—and also some matters at the end of it. But there is really nothing heroic in it at all. There was nobody but me to go. As I have said, I am the only man of the family."

If Atherton thought the family not very well provided which had only this man to depend upon, he was far from uttering the thought to one for whom he felt a deepening attraction.

".I should like," he said after a pause, " to know your name."

" My name"—the other hesitated for a moment—" is Henri de Marsillac."

" Quite a fitting name for a hero," said Atherton. " It sounds romantic enough to suggest all manner of heroic adventures."

" It was the name of my great-great-grandfather," was the quiet reply ; " but I never heard that he had any specially romantic or heroic adventures, although he died tragically enough. He was a planter in the French colony of Santo Domingo, and was killed in the insurrection of the slaves."

" Then you have a connection, and a very close one, with the island you are about to visit."

" Yes," answered the other, and then paused. He was evidently not to be drawn into any personal details ; and Atherton, whose interest in him was different from the curiosity which desires to know such details simply for the sake of knowing them, saw this, and changed the subject.

" What a history that island has had !" he said musingly. " The cradle of the New World ; the Hispaniola of Columbus ; the disputed battle-ground for centuries of Spaniards, French, and English ; ravaged by buccaneers, baptized in blood ; swept a hundred times by fire and sword ; the theatre of constant warfare, culminating at last in massacre without a parallel, and in its fairest portion being abandoned into the hands of African savages. Yet it still remains as fair, as productive, and as undeveloped as when the keels of the caravels first cut its shining waters, and the eyes of the immortal discoverer first rested upon the beauty of its heights."

"You are familiar with it?" asked the boy, looking at him a little curiously as he lay back in his chair gazing out over the blue, flashing surges ; as if in fancy he saw the caravels before him, and the figure of the heroic admiral standing in the prow of his flag-ship, searching with eager eyes for the desired land.

"No," he answered, "I have never seen it ; but I have lately been reading much about it, and what I have read has fired my fancy exceedingly. I really think I shall enjoy a sojourn which at first wore only the aspect of a disagreeable exile."

"Is it to the Spanish part of the island you are going ?" the boy asked, after some hesitation.

"My immediate destination is Santo Domingo city, the capital of the Spanish part of the island," Atherton replied. "My further destination is a certain sugar estate, into the affairs and management of which I have a commission to inquire. I should like to take you along with me," he added, with a smile. "Since you come from Louisiana, you ought to know something about sugar, while I know absolutely nothing."

"I know a great deal about sugar," the other answered simply. "At home I manage a sugar estate."

"You !"

"I. Why not ?"

"Well, really there is no reason why not, except that you look rather young for such responsibility," Atherton replied. "Suppose, then, that you continue your journey with me to the sugar estate and give me the benefit of your knowledge ?"

" I leave the ship at the Cape," was the serious reply. " My business is in Hayti."

" I hope it is not business which will take you into the interior of the country ; for by all accounts it is not safe there."

The other shrugged his shoulders. Plainly he had no intention of being expansive on the subject of his business.

" One cannot stop to think of risks," he said ; then added : " If you know nothing of the raising or making of sugar, why do you undertake to examine the affairs of a sugar estate ?"

" I am," said Atherton, " one of those unfortunates who, being under sentence of death, have a partial reprieve given them by the judges whom we call doctors, in the form of an order to go and live in a warm climate. Hence I am going to the West Indies ; and my choice of Santo Domingo is determined by the fact of the existence of the sugar estate, which, ignorant as I am of sugar affairs, affords me at least the shadow of an interest and an occupation—of both of which I am greatly in need."

The boy looked at him with an expression of quick compassion in his face.

" Are you in earnest ?" he asked. " Do you mean that you are under sentence of death in—in any immediate sense ?"

" Sometimes I think that it is in a very immediate sense. Then again I listen to the voice of Hope speaking through the doctors, and telling me that if I live for two years in a warm climate I shall be cured, or at least reprieved for an indefinite length of time. Left to myself, I should not have listened to them ; I should have positively refused the *rôle* of an invalid health-seeker and preferred to make shorter work of dying. But I have a father, who is not only devoted to me, but of whom I am the only child. It is for his sake that I have followed the advice of the medical gentlemen and that I am here."

"You were right," said the boy, with an air of decision that sat strangely upon his youthfulness. "Even if you had believed there was no possible good in it, you should have consented for the sake of your father. But there must be good in it. You have no look of an invalid."

"I sincerely hope not," replied Atherton. "But this enforced exile is hard on my father too. He will miss me very much."

"He would miss you still more if you obstinately stayed at home and died," rejoined the other. "Does he live in New York?"

"My father? He may be said to live everywhere. His business extends from San Francisco to New York, and he has headquarters in both cities. If you read newspapers much you have probably seen his name now and then. It is George Atherton."

"I think I have seen it. He is what is called a railroad and bonanza king, isn't he?"

"Some such foolish term is sometimes applied to him. He is simply a man who has large interests in railroads and mines, and has made a great deal of money out of both. I am rather proud of my father. He is of sturdy English stock, and was hardly more than a boy when he came out from the old country and went to California, in what are known as 'the flush times.' Without any advantages of capital or friends, by sheer pluck and intelligence, and perhaps some luck—one must give fortune its due—he succeeded from the first. He was rather advanced in life when he married my mother—who, now, that I think of it, was a countrywoman of yours : at least her people came from New Orleans—and after her early death he never married again. From that time he has lived for only two things—business and me. Determined to equip me for the race of life with every advantage, he sent me abroad to an English, then to a German, university ; and when I came back no one could have been more delighted than he that I had no will, because he is so rich a man, to be an idler. And indeed I am too much his son for idling to be to my taste. I threw all my energy, all my ambition into my work ; and all that I desired was opening before me—when the blow fell. 'Drop everything ; go away for two years !' The doctors said it glibly, but it was worse than a death-sentence to me. It was a sentence to a death-in-life, which I had always dreaded more than death itself."

The speaker paused, his voice dropping at the last words, as he gazed from under the rim of his cap straight out over the boundless leagues of shimmering water. He had for a moment forgotten the companion to whom he had been speaking, in the sudden wave of bitterness roused by the thought of his enforced exile, of his thwarted ambition ; and it was a sigh breathed by that companion which made him glance around. He never forgot the look of exquisite pity and sympathy which was shining upon him from the beautiful hazel eyes.

"How sorry I am for you !" the boy exclaimed. "Do you mind my saying that ? I know that there are people who do not like to be pitied. But it seems so hard—to have everything that life can give, and to be obliged to drop it all and go away, with such a fear in your thoughts. Oh, how many different kinds of trouble there are in the world !"

"Very many, indeed," said Atherton. "But although I am not one of the people who object to being pitied, I must not take your pity under false pretences—at least not too much of it. When I am despondent I think of falling into lifelong invalidism, if I live at all. But at other times I believe that I shall get well, and that the two years I shall lose will be all. I have determined to live for that time the life of Nature—to exist as much as possible like an animal in the open air—and I think Nature will cure me. I have solemnly thrown physic to the dogs."

"Which is good," said the boy, smiling. "I believe that Nature *will* cure you, as this delicious sea-air has cured my sea-sickness. For there is the luncheon bell, and I really feel as if I can once more face the table."

CHAPTER IV.

WITHIN the next few days the friendly intimacy of the two travellers advanced apace. They were almost constant companions, to the exclusion of all other companionship on the part of either. Sitting for hours on deck, their chairs drawn together, each with a book which neither read very much, they sometimes talked, their talk wandering over many wide and various fields ; or lay back dreamily, drinking in the beauty of the marvellous, restless plain of flashing waters, which deepened in tint with every onward league toward the tropics, until at last it became an unimaginable expanse of lapis-lazuli, dazzling, sparkling, impossible to describe, filling the wide sea-circle with the long liftings of its gentle swell, fanned by the warm breath of the trade winds.

Most of the passengers fancied that they were relatives, or at least travelling companions—the tall, fair, languid man and the dark, delicate, picturesque boy ; but there was no opportunity to put these conjectures to the proof by questioning. The genial, talkative Germans ; the young engineers, who bloomed out in white duck suits as soon as the weather gave the least encouragement ; and the inquisitive tourists or possible investors, with strong nasal voices which had a penetrating quality that carried their sound from one end of the deck to the other—all passed them by as hopelessly "unsociable ;" while the feminine contingent, remarking among themselves that they looked "interesting," had no chance to determine whether this interest existed in more than appearance.

"The captain says that we shall be at Turk's Island to-morrow morning," said Atherton, as he dropped into his chair beside De Marsillac on the sixth day of the voyage—a day like a flawless jewel in its splendor. The voyage had now become a kind of lotus-eating. The long lift of the waves, the warm caress of the wind, the soft whispering of the sea, all lulled to repose : a quietude made for dreams. And such dreams were in the eyes of the boy who looked now with a start from the entrancing azure of sea and sky to the face of the speaker.

"Shall we ?" he asked, adding involuntarily : "I am sorry."

"Are you ? Why ?"

"Because the ocean grows more beautiful every day, and the voyage more pleasant. Also because, if we are to be at Turk's Island to-morrow, we shall reach the Cape the day after."

"And you regret that ? Most persons are glad to reach their destination."

The other did not answer immediately. He looked back at the flashing blue plain, which spread its billowy leagues to the farthest verge of the horizon ; and Atherton observed that a shadow seemed to fall over the sensitive face.

"I am afraid I am not so brave as I have fancied," he said presently, in a low tone. "I find myself shrinking from the unknown and the difficult, now that they are close at hand."

It was then Atherton's turn to be silent for a moment— a moment in which he reflected again, as he had reflected before, how strangely reserved as well as how strangely attractive was this remarkable boy. Close as had been their association for several days—that association of shipboard which with most people has the effect of immediately unloosening the tongue upon all their private affairs—he had let drop no word to indicate the nature of the business which was taking him to a place so remote as Hayti. On the contrary, he had carefully avoided anything which might lead to the subject, and his present expression of shrinking reluctance was the first indication either of the nature of his mysterious errand or the feelings with which he regarded it. Slight as it was, however, it was quite enough to excite Atherton's concern, already vaguely stirred.

"Would you object," he said suddenly, "to telling me the nature of the business upon which you are bound? I think you must be aware that I do not ask the question from idle curiosity or any desire to pry into your affairs. But I really fear that you may have in view something rash, if not dangerous ; and, being so much older than you are, I feel that I might give you the benefit of my experience of the world in the form of advice."

Somewhat to his surprise, De Marsillac looked at him

with a grateful expression in the frank, clear eyes he had come to know so well.

"It is kind of you to speak in this manner," he answered. "I have thought of asking your advice on some practical points before we part ; for I am sure you are to be trusted."

"I think that I am," said Atherton, smiling. "At least I cannot imagine the temptation which would induce me to betray your trust. I am right, then : you are going upon some rash enterprise?"

"I suppose you will think it so. I am going"—he sent a quick glance around to be sure that no one was within earshot—"to seek some money which my great-great-grandfather—he of whom I told you, who was killed by the insurgent slaves—buried before he left his home."

"Good Heavens !" exclaimed Atherton, startled. "Do you really mean it ? This is worse than 1 feared—a more rash and dangerous enterprise. My dear boy, the thing is impossible ! How could you have dreamed of attempting it—you, alone?"

"Because, as I have already told you, there was no one else to attempt it," the boy answered quietly. "It was for me to go, or for that money to remain hopelessly lost where Henri de Marsillac placed it a century ago."

"Men will risk a great deal for money," said Atherton, gravely ; "but I confess I am surprised that one so young as you should be willing to undertake so much for it ; unless, indeed, it is the romance of the thing that has attracted you. A boy's imagination is easily fired by a suggestion of hidden treasure."

The face of the particular boy in question suddenly grew cold, as if he withdrew within himself ; and his voice had a plainly offended accent when he spoke :

"I have not thought of this money as a treasure, but simply as a sum deposited by its owner—does it matter whether in a bank or in the earth?—for the benefit of his rightful heirs. There is no romance in the search for it which I have undertaken; and if you think me mercenary because I am willing to run all risks to obtain it, I can only say that it is easy to despise money when one possesses it."

With the last words he rose and walked away.

Atherton was so much astonished by this abrupt departure, and by the equally abrupt end of his confidence which it intimated, that he sat quite still and silent, staring after the young figure which walked down the deck and disappeared into the cabin. Then a pang of self-reproach seized him. He had repelled the boy's confidence—that confidence so tardily, yet at last so readily given—and had wounded his feelings besides. What a mistake to speak as he had done, if he indeed desired to influence the lad! Nothing, he now perceived, could have been better calculated to offend than the imputation of a mercenary motive in the first instance, and of a romantic imagination in the second.

"One is very much of a fool sometimes," he remarked meditatively to himself. "I should have remembered the susceptibility of a youthful spirit. And, apart from the unwisdom of uttering them, my remarks were foolish in themselves. For whether it is merely a desire for money—which, as he observed, it is no doubt easier to despise when one possesses than when one lacks it—or whether in reality his imagination *has* been fired by romantic dreams of buried treasure, one thing is at least certain : he has the courage of a paladin in that delicate frame of his, and he will risk his life in this wild search unless some one interferes. Now, I am the only person who can interfere ; for

I am the only person he is at all likely to admit into his confidence. So it behooves me to apologize at once, and endeavor to retrieve the mistake I have committed."

But, like many a man before, Atherton was to discover that it is easier to commit a mistake than to retrieve it. For one thing, repentance is not always accepted ; and for another, opportunity for apology may not be given. When he went into luncheon he found the chair on his right vacant, and vacant it remained throughout the meal. Its emptiness increased his regret ; and on his return to the deck he paused beside a closed window which he knew to be that of De Marsillac's state-room, and lightly knocked.

" Who is there ?" asked a quick, startled voice within.

" It is I—Atherton," he replied. " Come out on deck. The day is too divine to lose an hour of it, and I have much to say to you."

" I cannot come," the voice responded. " I—I have a headache. I am lying down."

" Shall I come in and talk to you a little ?"

" Oh, no, no—thanks ! When I have a headache I must be quiet—and alone."

" Well," in a disappointed tone, " in that case I will not trouble you ; but I hope you'll feel better after awhile and come out."

An inarticulate murmur answered him, but a murmur which evidently contained no promise of coming out ; and, after waiting a few moments longer, he quietly walked away.

" Odd," he thought, as he settled himself in his chair with a cigar, " how much that boy's voice is like a woman's. Any one who did not know the contrary would have sworn that there was a woman behind that blind. And there was a suggestion of tears in the voice too. I wonder if he could have taken my words to heart to that extent? It seems incredible, and yet—he is a queer boy! I must manage to make matters up with him at all costs before we reach the Cape."

De Marsillac's headache allowed him to appear at dinner, but he was very silent; and when afterwards Atherton and himself went on deck, where day had given place to night with tropical rapidity, an air of reserve still hung about him, which made it a little difficult to return to the subject of the morning. When they were again established in their respective chairs on the after-deck, however, Atherton determined that the interrupted confidence should be resumed, and at once led the conversation in that direction.

"I am afraid," he began, "that you thought me unsympathetic this morning when you told me the nature of your business in Hayti. But you were a little hasty in that conclusion. I was in reality deeply concerned—I may say shocked—to find that you had such a project in view, and it was the expression of this feeling which you misunderstood."

"It does not matter," the boy replied somewhat coldly. "There was no reason why I should have expected sympathy from you. One should not talk of one's private affairs to strangers. The mistake was mine."

"The mistake is yours now," said Atherton, with some energy. "If I seemed unsympathetic to your confidence this morning, you are now repulsing a very sincere interest —or attempting to do so. But I have no intention of allowing it to be repulsed. I apologize for anything which I may have said inadvertently to offend you, and acknowledge that I was foolish to attempt to criticise motives of which I knew nothing."

There was a silence. De Marsillac did not answer at once, but kept his face turned from his companion towards the vast beauty of the night, throbbing with the deep pulsations of the ocean, and the radiant glory of myriad stars shining out of the great arch of purple heaven above. Caressing winds breathed about the ship as she sped onward ; while the low murmur of the seas through which she cut her way was like the whispering of soft voices—an infinitely lulling sound. The spell of the night seemed to lie over the wide world of waters, hushing them to a deeper repose than that which they had known by day, and perhaps penetrating also into the spirit of the boy. At least, when he spoke at last it was in an altered and gentler voice.

" If I was a little wounded by your criticism, it was because you seemed to believe that I was either actuated by a love of money or by a foolish romance in undertaking to recover what my great-great-grandfather endeavored to secure from robbery for his descendants. But I fail to perceive what there is in my enterprise which should make either of these motives appear to you a matter of course. Even if I had no special need of this money, would I not be very foolish if I made no effort to recover it ? You are, it seems, a very wealthy man, Mr. Atherton ; but if *you* heard of such a deposit, to which you had an undoubted and lawful right, would you not make an effort to obtain it ?"

" That would depend, I think, upon the probabilities of the case," Atherton answered. " I should need to be very certain in the first place that the deposit in question existed——"

" *I* am certain. Presently, if you care to hear, I will tell you why."

" Then I should desire to be assured of at least a fair probability of success in my efforts to recover it. Now, my dear boy, what probability is there of your success ? Have you thought of all the practical difficulties surrounding your task?"

The other uttered a low, rather sad laugh, as he repeated :

"Have I thought of them ! I have thought of little else since I first learned of this thing. They are great, I admit ; but have you ever heard of any other way of overcoming difficulties than by meeting them ?"

"There is no other way," Atherton agreed. "But they must be met with prudence as well as with courage in order to overcome them. Yet here you are alone, going to seek money which your ancestor buried a hundred years ago in an island which has been ever since in the hands of the negroes whose revolt made the concealment necessary. Do you suppose they would allow you to carry away any treasure found in the country, however clear your right to it might be ?"

"No, I do not suppose so, and therefore I know it is necessary that the search should be made secretly."

"And how do you propose to do this ? Have you friends on the island ?"

"Certainly not. I have only myself to rely upon ; yet, nevertheless, I believe that I shall succeed. If my motive were either the mercenary or the romantic one with which you credit me——"

"Do not say that ! I have retracted my hasty opinion —for judgment it was not—and I am sure that your motive is worthy of the courage which supports it."

"I do not think that any one could have a better," said the boy in a low tone. "But what I was about to say is this—that, were my motive no higher than those of which you spoke, I might, in the face of the great difficulties which confront me, believe success impossible and my efforts foredoomed to failure ; but since it is a motive which makes me feel, like Sir Galahad, that

" ' My strength is as the strength of ten,'

I firmly believe that I shall succeed.   I believe that as I found at a moment of supreme necessity the paper, hidden for a hundred years, which told of this treasure, if you care to call it so, I shall also find at my need the means to carry out my undertaking.   It sounds fanciful, superstitious perhaps ; and yet it is surely neither fanciful nor superstitious to believe that God helps those who have faith in Him, and who earnestly ask His aid."

Again what haunting music in the tones which uttered these words, as the speaker looked out over the cradling, whispering waters of the mysterious, encompassing sea ! The strange magic of the voice touched and stirred Atherton in a manner he could not understand.   There seemed in it a suggestion of all things noble, generous and tender. He thought of the mother and sisters of this lad who had set forth, like a knight-errant indeed, with resolve so high and hope so dauntless, upon a quest so difficult.   The cousin had been right who had prayed he might have the success his heroism deserved.   It *was,* heroism, no less ; and if it was also folly—well, heroism is often but a touch removed from that which the cold and prudent of the world call by the other name.   This Atherton knew well ; but, even while he recognized the possible folly, his heart thrilled to the heroic spirit.   He suddenly extended his hand, and laid a light, firm touch on the other's arm.

" I think it neither fanciful nor superstitious to believe that you will find the means to carry out your undertaking," he said.   " We must give the matter careful consideration in the time remaining before you reach the Cape, and form the outline of some plan which on landing you can endeavor to carry into effect with what modification circumstances demand."

CHAPTER V.

WAKING next morning to find themselves anchored off a low, white, palm-dotted coast, around which the waves were flashing over hidden reefs ; with a brilliant clearness in the atmosphere, an ardent warmth in the sunshine, and a deeper blue, if possible, upon the wide expanse of ocean, the passengers of the *New York* were assured of being at last well within the tropics.. It was the island of Grand Turk which lay before them—a line of foliage-embowered houses fringing its beach, and in the interior a ridge of barren-looking hills. The accommodation-ladder was let down the side of the ship ; boats from the shore lay around the foot of it waiting for passengers, and various parties for going ashore were formed as soon as breakfast was over.

"Shall we go, Henri ?" asked Atherton, turning to the boy whom he had begun to address familiarly in this fashion. "Turk's Island does not probably offer anything of a very interesting nature to sightseers, but we can at least stretch our legs on land and vary a little the monotony of a day which I believe is to be spent lying here."

"Oh, yes, I think we should certainly go !" the other replied, with an inflection of young eagerness in his voice.

"Come, then," said Atherton, casting a critical eye over the boats, and motioning to the oarsmen of one which looked particularly smart and clean in a coat of white and blue paint, to draw near for them.   A little later they were rapidly rowed over the mile of sparkling water that lay between the ship and the line of dazzling shore ; the boat was steered in to the steps of the wooden pier, they landed, and were presently walking along the glaring white sands of Turk's Island, taking in comprehensively the line of small wooden buildings on one side, and the wide ocean prospect on the other.   "And now," said Atherton, "if we are to play the part of sightseers, we must find the salt works which are the chief industry of the island ; after having seen which we can with a clear conscience devote ourselves to idling."

They were not long in finding signs of the principal industry of Turk's Island.   Just behind the single line of houses which fringe the curving shore are the salt ponds, where sea-water is let in to evaporate and deposit the crystallized salt which has made the name of this barren little Bahama isle known to the entire world.   Great mounds of salt, white and glistening as snow, were piled along their margins ; and having tasted a few grains, Atherton declared their duty accomplished.

"And now," he said, hearing the echo of voices, "I fear that the party from the ship who came ashore just before us, having taken in all the rest of the island, are turning their steps and their cameras towards the salt ponds. Lest we should point a moral against sightseeing by appearing in their photographs, let us at once retreat."

He moved as he spoke into a lane which led back in the direction they had come ; and, the village being more remarkable for length than depth, they were a moment later again facing the sea.

"Are we now to indulge in idling?" asked De Marsillac.   "But Turk's Island appears deficient in places suitable for that amusement. Returning to the ship seems the only alternative to walking indefinitely over glaring sand in the hot sunshine."

"I don't think we shall need to walk very far in this direction," said Atherton, turning to the left, "before we have the shore and ocean to ourselves. Then we will find a bit of shade, where we can rest and talk."

Beyond the village limits, which were indeed soon reached, they found a long stretch of beach, upon which the surf curled creamily and the sun beat hotly, so they were glad to seek the first shade which offered—that of a large tree, with spreading roots and foliage, which grew by the wayside. Throwing themselves down here, they bared their heads to the fresh breeze sweeping in from the flash-ing plain of waters stretching to the verge of the horizon, and were silent for several minutes, drinking in the wide beauty of the scene.

"Nothing that has been said of the charm of the sea is exaggerated," murmured the boy at length, with a soft, deep sigh. "I think I should like to live on an island, in order to be surrounded by it on all sides."

"You might take your choice among a thousand or so of these Bahama cays," said Atherton. "Or it might be better to go down into the Caribbean Sea, among the Vir-gins. Or, better yet, the isle of Tortuga, that old home of the buccaneers—from whence they descended upon what is now Hayti, and upon Jamaica—is, I believe, again unin-habited and open to settlement."

"I should not care to make a home in a place so asso-ciated with pirates and their deeds of blood," said De Mar-sillac. "Don't think that I am descended from any of those freebooters. Our family records are quite clear of such stain. After the eastern end of Santo Domingo had been declared a French colony, our ancestor, Raoul de Marsillac, a 'cadet' of a noble Breton family, came over in some official capacity, purchased large estates and remained in the island. It was his great-grandson who was killed at the time of the insurrection."

"Which removes you six—or is it seven?—generations from the Breton cadet," observed Atherton. "Yet I fancy he looked something like you; for you are singularly like the French type of a century and a half ago, as one sees it in the portraits of that time. Powder your hair, dress you in the fashion of that period, put a sword at your side, and you might be the original Raoul de Marsillac going beyond seas to seek his fortune. And I think that you would like to be going to reconquer those rich lands which your forefathers made the wonder of the world for their productiveness."

"You are right," was the reply. "It seems a shameful thing that this island, so marvellous in its beauty and fertility, be lost to civilization. I should of all things like to reconquer and reclaim it. But since that cannot be, I am determined at least to recover that small part of all my people lost there of which I know."

"You have infected me with your hope that you may be able to do so," said Atherton. "I have been giving the matter much consideration since we talked of it yesterday; and the more I think of it, the more probable it appears to me that such a deposit may have remained undisturbed during the century which has elapsed since it was buried. Do you know exactly where the estate of your ancestor is situated?"

"Yes, exactly. It is on the Plaine du Nord—a famous plain of the northern province, where the insurrection began—four leagues from Cape Français, now Cape Haytien."

"Good ! Have you by chance a map with you ?"

De Marsillac replied by producing from the inner pocket of his coat a folded piece of thin paper, which proved to be a map of Santo Domingo. Spreading it out between them, the two bent their heads over it ; and Atherton, having located the Plaine du Nord, said :

" A plan has occurred to me which I judge from this map to be entirely feasible. Here at the head of the Plaine du Nord is, you perceive, Sans Souci, the palace of the black king and tyrant Christophe ; and beyond that again, higher in the mountains, is the citadel which he built, and which all who have seen it describe as the most wonderful thing of its kind, not only in the West Indies, but in the world. As intelligent travellers, we must see this citadel ; and since the estate of your family lies immediately on our route, what is easier than that we should pause on the way and make our search without any one being the wiser ?"

" *We !*" repeated the other, lifting startled eyes from the map to the face of his companion. " But *you* are not going to Hayti ?"

" Am I not ? There you are mistaken. Nothing so important calls me to Santo Domingo that I should pass a country so unique without examining its political and social conditions. And, then, there is the citadel of Christophe, of which I have just spoken. One should on no account leave that unseen."

The boy sat up, pushing back with a quick gesture the clustering locks from his forehead, so that they formed a tumbled, curling mass around his face, to which the sun and the sea had given a Murillo-like color that added to its picturesqueness.

" It is impossible !" the young voice said hurriedly. " You are only thinking of doing this on my account—and

I cannot allow it. Mr. Atherton, you must not think of such a thing !"

" And when, Monsieur de Marsillac, did you recover seignioral rights in the island of Hayti ?" asked Atherton good-humoredly. " I really do not think you have the power to forbid my landing at the Cape ; and for the rest, I was foolish enough to imagine that you would be rather glad of my assistance in your undertaking."

" And so I would," the other replied eagerly, " if—if things were different. But as it is, what you propose is impossible. It cannot be thought of."

" But why not?" asked Atherton, surprised by this vehemence, and perhaps a little disappointed as well ; for he had anticipated a very different response to the announcement of his intention.

The boy looked at him for a moment without reply, and in that moment many things rushed through his mind. He suddenly colored, and the clear hazel eyes fell as if in shame.

" I am afraid you think me very ungrateful for your kindness," he said, in a low voice. " But it is not so. I feel it deeply. Only I also feel that it would be very selfish to accept such a sacrifice of time and comfort as would be involved in your breaking off your voyage, and running the risk of many inconveniences if not dangers, in order to serve the interest of a stranger. It is very kind—it is *more* than kind—of you to think of it. But, all the same, you must not do it."

" All the same I intend to do it," Atherton replied. " If you did not wish me to take a part in your adventure, you should never have told me anything about it. Somewhere within me there is yet the spirit of a boy, and what boy would not be fascinated by the prospect of a search for hidden treasure?—although I believe you don't like your ancestor's hidden wealth to be called by that name."

" Only because it makes my search seem wild and absurd, like a dime romance. You know what you thought when I told you of it first."

" Ah ! but since then I am quite converted to your views —so much so that I mean to have a share in finding this treasure. You see, as I have told you, I am a man very much in want of an interest—a want which I do not feel that a sugar estate in Santo Domingo is at all likely to fill. In all seriousness, my boy, I have determined to see you through this affair, which you are too young ever to have undertaken alone ; and which will require all our united fund of wisdom, cunning, and contrivance to carry to success. So let us say no more about it."

" I must say how grateful I am—how much I feel your kindness——"

" It is really unnecessary, since it is I who am obliged to you for furnishing me with an adventure such as I could never have hoped for ; and incidentally for an excuse to visit a country which must be interesting, if only from its unlikeness to all others, and the novel conditions on which it rests. Now, there are many practical details to be arranged when we reach the Cape, but meanwhile the chief point is settled : we undertake this search together ; and if the first Henri de Marsillac's treasure remains undisturbed where he buried it, the second Henri de Marsillac shall obtain it ; and here is my hand upon that."

Half-laughing, he held out his hand as he spoke, and the Henri de Marsillac to whom he pledged his assistance could not fail to place his own within it. As it chanced, their hands had never met before, nor had Atherton noticed that of the boy farther than to observe that it was very slender and delicate. But as it lay now in his grasp he became conscious of the fact that it was even more slender than he had imagined ; and, although firm and vigorous, clothed in a skin fine as satin.

" By Jove !" he said involuntarily, looking down at it. " What a hand—small and soft as a woman's ! You can never have played ball very much, or rowed, or——"

" No ; I never cared for athletic sports," said the other, coloring, as he quickly drew back his hand. " There are other things that seem to me better worth a man's doing ; as horsemanship, fencing——"

" So Raoul de Marsillac would have said. You are, I see, a survival of another race in more than appearance. But I fear, Sieur de Marsillac, that it will require other hands than yours to dig for your inheritance."

The Sieur de Marsillac glanced rather ruefully at his hands.

" I am afraid they are not good for much in that way," he said. " But we must get those whose business it is to dig ; and if you give me a pistol or a sword, I will show you that I can at least defend my inheritance."

" You would have surely had to defend it, and the end of the matter would probably have been that the spot out of which the inheritance was taken would have served as the grave of the inheritor, had you proceeded to the search with only such hands as the country could have furnished. My dear boy, what a good thing it was—if you will allow me to say so—that we sailed on the same ship !"

The boy looked up with a light of almost passionate gratitude on his face.

" It is for me to say that," he exclaimed ; " and I do say it with all my heart. It was such great good fortune— for me—that I wish I could send a message across these leagues of ocean to tell those who are suffering anxiety on my account what a helper I have found."

CHAPTER VI.

A MORNING of wide, tropical splendor—fresh, delicious, filled with the very breath of Eden ; the sleeping ocean a flashing expanse of blue and silver ; the sky a great vault of lucent turquoise, and a pale, misty, magical coast ; a vision of azure mountains, melting and blending in the most exquisite lines, while about their lordly heads were gathered cloud-wreaths of softest beauty and shining radiance—this was the picture to be seen from the deck of the *New York* as she steamed towards the famous bay of Cape Haytien, once the Cape Français of the French, and earlier yet the Guarico of the Spaniards.

Atherton, who was the first of the passengers on deck, tapped on the closed window of De Marsillac's room.

"Come out !" he cried. "This is no time for sluggardly repose. We are in the most historic waters of the New World, and in sight of its loveliest coast. Come out !"

"In a moment," an eager voice replied. And it was hardly more than that when the slight figure emerged from the cabin door and joined Atherton, where he stood watching the entrancing picture which every minute more clearly revealed.

"I am endeavoring to fancy the feelings of Columbus, when this coast first appeared to him," he said. "With what a thrill he must have descried those dream-like heights, which were to be in beauty as in richness the culmination and crown of his discoveries. Had ever explorer

before such a reward !   Could even his wildest dreams have
fancied *such* a New World !   And yet it seemed an earnest
of the misfortunes which were to befall him on this Isle of
Hispaniola, that in the bay we are entering, on Christmas
Eve of 1492, the *Santa Maria* was wrecked.''

"Was it here?" the boy asked. "Strange that so
heavenly a spot could have been the scene of such a misfortune !"

"Not strange at all to a sailor's eye.   Ask our captain,
who has been lying off for several hours waiting for daylight to enter the harbor, what *he* thinks of it."

But nothing could be considered now—not even the
memory of the great admiral viewing from his doomed
flag-ship the wondrous coasts opening before him—save the
picturesque beauty unfolding as they drew nearer the land.
The magical, cloud-draped mountains receded into the
background ; while close at hand bold, verdure-clad heights
rose abruptly out of the flashing tides that broke in white
surf against the cliffs and detached masses of rock that
formed their base.   Light, lovely mists were curling about
them, crowning their summits and lying in their green
gorges.   All was fresh, radiant, enchanting, as if Nature
had just left the hand of God.   Slowly steaming in, they
rounded that rocky headland, crowned with plumy palms,
which the Cape thrusts into the sea, and to which clings
the old fortification of Fort Picolet, its guns commanding
the narrow, winding channel ; and saw opening before them
the superb bay, with space on its broad bosom for a navy to
ride, and with such noble sweep of shore, such divine frame
of distant sapphire heights, as not even these "summer
isles of Eden" can elsewhere show.

"Magnificent !" exclaimed Atherton, as his glance took
in the wide, land-locked expanse.   "No wonder the buc-

caneers seized such a harbor.   And yonder is the town they founded—the historic ' Cape.' "

Yes, there it lay—the old town which later became the Paris of the West Indies, and later yet the scene of the most horrible atrocities of the negro revolt.   Viewed across the emerald waters of the harbor, its mass of gayly tinted buildings presented a strikingly picturesque appearance, as they occupy a narrow plain which lies between the shore and two noble mountains which rise abruptly in wooded steeps behind.

De Marsillac watched with fascinated gaze the gradual revealing of this spot as they drew nearer.   His thoughts were with the past, with those of his own blood who had lived here their gay, luxurious, careless lives, lapped in ease and pleasure until the storm in which they perished burst upon them.   He thought of his great-great-grand-father dying there, after that wild midnight ride for his life ; and of the wife he left, with her infant children tak-ing refuge on a foreign vessel, and sailing away, broken-hearted and penniless, out of this beautiful bay—a paradise transformed into a hell.   He was still silent when, the ship having dropped her anchor in front of the town, there came borne across the water the sweetest, clearest, most musical chime of church-bells that ever delighted the ear. As the silvery sound reached them, he looked up with a quick glance towards his companion.

" What an exquisite welcome !" he said.   " Does it not seem a good omen that *that* is the first sound to greet me from the island ?"

" We will hope so," Atherton answered.   " Certainly the appearance of things is calculated to raise one's spirits. Whatever the town may prove on nearer view, it is delight-fully picturesque seen from here ; while the natural setting of the bay is the most beautiful I have ever beheld. Somewhere in our view along these shores is the place where, out of the material of the wrecked caravel, Columbus erected the fort of Navidad—the first European settlement in the New World, though one with a most tragic fate."

"Everything about this island seems to lead to tragedy," said the boy. "There is a blood-stain everywhere—and yet how divinely beautiful it is !"

"Where is the site of the fort of Navidad?" repeated the purser, who came up at the moment, and to whom Atherton put the question. "Over yonder, I believe, near the village of Petite Anse. And there"—he pointed to the westward side of the bay, where, dim, misty, inexpressibly fair in their azure robes, rose the mighty forms of the mountains that divide Hayti from Santo Domingo— "stands the great citadel of Christophe. It is on one of those highest mountains. With a good glass the walls can be clearly perceived from here."

"I must see that citadel," observed Atherton. "From the descriptions given, it is well worth a visit."

"If you are going on with us, you can't manage it at present," the purser said. "We sail to-morrow morning."

"I have decided to stop here," was the reply. "When does your next steamer come along?"

"Probably in about two weeks. But you'll not have a very lively time spending two weeks at the Cape with nothing to do."

"'Nothing to do' is a condition I seldom suffer from," answered Atherton. "I shall have much to do ; for in that time I intend to see, if not all, at least a good part of Hayti. I shall go ashore after breakfast to look up quarters—and there is the breakfast bell."

"What is this I hear, Mr. Atherton?" asked the captain, as they took their seats at table. " Are you thinking of leaving us here ?"

" I have decided upon doing so," replied Atherton. " I want to see something of Hayti, and I am afraid that if I don't take the present opportunity I may not have another. I may leave Santo Domingo by another route, or interest may be lacking, or—or any one of several things. Moreover, I shall have my young friend Mr. de Marsillac as a companion at the present time, which would not be the case later."

The captain glanced a little curiously at the " young friend" indicated. Like others, he had been perhaps slightly repelled by the remarkable reticence of this particular passenger for the Cape. The business of every one else on board—whether it were logwood, sugar, tropical fruits or railroads—was well known ; but this boy had kept his own counsel so resolutely that no one knew what object or interest was taking him to the island. Secretiveness, which is not a very agreeable trait in any one, sits with a peculiarly ill grace on the young ; and the frank sailor was not to blame if he felt otherwise than attracted towards this exceedingly secretive youth.

" I hope you'll be repaid," he said ; " but I very much fear that you'll find accommodations so bad that you'll wish yourself back on the *New York* before we have been gone very long."

" Mr. Schlagenbach," said Atherton, bowing to a friendly German across the table, " has promised to see if he cannot get me quarters with some friends of his. In that case I can make the Cape my headquarters, and carry a camping equipment with me when I take excursions into the country."

" That will be best," several voices said approvingly ;

and then a shower of advice descended upon Atherton from the surrounding travellers, most of whom knew the different ports of Hayti well.

"For my sins," said one, "as well as for logwood, I must stop here and go to Port de Paix in one of these small sailing vessels that they call in Santo Domingo a *goleta*. I only wish I had your chance of continuing on the *New York*. Hayti wouldn't tempt me much."

"It will not tempt Mr. Atherton a second time," said another, with a laugh. "But it's worth while to see it once, since there's nothing in the world like it."

It was not until breakfast was over that De Marsillac, drawing Atherton aside, asked if his intention to land at the Cape could not even yet be changed. "I thought of the matter all night," he added wistfully; "and it seems too great a sacrifice on your part for me to allow——"

"You said something of that kind yesterday," interposed Atherton with good-humored impatience; "and I believe I told you I had no intention of asking your permission to land on the soil of the Republic of Hayti. Consider that I have made the same statement again, and that the discussion is at an end. Can my man do anything for you? I have told him to put up my traps and be ready to land this afternoon. Meanwhile we'll go ashore and see what my German friend can do for us in the way of finding quarters; then come back for lunch, and afterwards bid Captain Rockwell and his good ship adieu. Nonsense!"—as the other attempted to speak. "Let us have no more of this. *Allons!*"

It was with a strange thrill that De Marsillac found himself treading the soil of Hayti. A row of about a mile over the sparkling water of the bay had brought them to a dilapidated pier, where they landed, and whence a few steps led them to the principal street of the city of ruins.

For such they found it to be. The appearance of the town, viewed from the deck of the ship, had not at all prepared them for its reality, nor had even the description of those who knew it well. It is indeed impossible to conceive anything like this city, on which fire, sword, and earthquake—the hand of man and that of God—have alike done their worst. In amazement the two newcomers walked along the uneven, dusty streets, filled with refuse of every possible description, where great piles of stones lay as they had fallen in the great earthquake of 1842, and regarded with constantly increasing wonder the immense extent of the ruins which testified what the town had once been, with its stately houses built entirely of stone, its well-paved streets, its open squares decorated with fountains ; its churches and public buildings worthy of the opulent, luxurious city which existed here in the colonial days. The walls of those once splendid dwellings stand now great piles of shattered masonry, overgrown with the luxuriant vegetation of the tropics. On every side the gaze fell upon carved arches, pillars, and balconies, over which creepers ran riot ; superb flights of stone steps ; courtyards and roof-less salons, in which were growing full-sized palms, bananas, and other trees ; while amid these wrecks of past splendor the present inhabitants have erected low, insignificant dwellings of wood—many of them mere cabins—and all the scenes and conditions of an African village are to be beheld in the midst of these melancholy ruins of an overthrown civilization.

"It is something for which no description can prepare one," said Atherton, as they threaded their way amid the piles of *débris*. "These ruins attest a past magnificence far exceeding one's conception—and in their midst, without attempting even to lift a fallen stone, burrow a race of savages !"

"You have never read the accounts of St. Méry, who visited the colony before the insurrection, and who particularly describes the magnificence of the Cape, else you would not be surprised," said De Marsillac. "For myself, I have the strangest sensations as I walk these streets, as if I were the ghost of one of the old dwellers here. I have read, heard, dreamed so much of the colonial life—for the subject always possessed a peculiar fascination to me—that I seem to have made a part of it. I feel as if I had seen all this before ; as if I had been one of those who feasted and revelled within these walls ; as if I had once passed up and down those steps"—he pointed to a stately flight of stone steps leading from the street to a great carved doorway, behind which were roofless, partially fallen walls and a wilderness of tropical growth—"to and from a waiting carriage, into which I was handed by a gentleman with powdered hair and a sword at his side——"

"You must, then, have been a woman in those days," said Atherton, glancing at him with a smile.

He was surprised by the flame of color that mounted into the young face, only a moment before so absorbed in imaginations of the past.

"What an absurd dreamer you must think me !" said the boy, looking away. "But, dreams apart, I wish I knew which one of these masses of ruins belonged to my great-great-grandfather and was the house in which he died."

"If you lived here in a former state of existence, you ought to know. But, seriously, have you no clue—do you not know the name of the street on which it was situated ?"

"It was, I think, in the Rue St. Louis ; but how can one tell whether the streets still bear their old names? The people look so forbidding that I feel a hesitation in addressing any of them."

" I will inquire," said Atherton ; and, pausing, he addressed a barefooted policeman in fluent French. The man stared, shrugged his shoulders, muttered something unintelligible, and walked away.

" Probably he does not understand you," said De Marsillac. " I believe the educated class alone speak French. The others speak a *patois* called Creole, which must be a good deal like the *patois* our Louisiana negroes speak."

" You understand that, I suppose ?"

" Oh, yes ! One catches it from the negroes in one's childhood."

" It may enable you, then, to talk with these people, which will be a distinct gain in enabling us to dispense with an interpreter. But tell me now, if you were here alone, what could you possibly do to effect your object ?"

De Marsillac gazed around at the heap of overgrown ruins, the neglected streets, the throng of strange, black faces filled with hereditary suspicion and dislike of the white man, and his heart sank within him. What, indeed, could he do? How different from his Louisiana, and the negroes who were there his faithful friends and assistants ! What foolish daring, what presumption of ignorance, had brought him here with so vague an idea of the difficulties that would confront him ! He turned his gaze to Atherton's face.

" I fear that I could do nothing—alone," he said. " But I still believe that God will give me success ; and I believe it more than ever since He has sent you to help me. For it seems to me almost a miracle—men being so selfish as they are—that you should do this for me, of whom you know so little."

"Men are, certainly, as a rule, very selfish," Atherton replied ; "and I have no reason to suppose that I am in any striking degree an exception to the rule. Yet I am resolved to do this ; although, as you justly remark, I know little of you. But yonder, if I mistake not, comes my good friend, Mr. Schlagenbach ; and I judge from his beaming expression that he has succeeded in obtaining for us the lodgings desired. If not, I think we had better seek shelter in the ruins of your ancestral house than attempt to find our comfort in such an inn as the Cape is likely to furnish."

But Mr. Schlagenbach's news justified his beaming expression. The tall, friendly German was overflowing with satisfaction.

"I am happy to say that my friend will have pleasure in receiving you," he said to Atherton when they met. "And you are very fortunate, because he has a comfortable house on the outskirts of the town ; and, since his wife is just now in Germany, there is no one but himself to occupy it. Therefore he can put several rooms at your disposal."

"1 am delighted to hear it," said Atherton ; "and more obliged to you than I can express. Will you add to your kindness by introducing us to your friend, so that we can make our arrangements ?"

"Oh, with great pleasure ! We will go at once to his counting-house. It is on this street, a little farther along."

The street they were now following, which ran parallel with the shore and was more closely built than any other, was chiefly lined with business houses, structures of wood gayly painted, in the second stories of which the families of the merchants lived, as was evident from the glimpses of furnished rooms obtained through the open windows, and the household scenes on the balconies. These shops were well filled with goods, and trade seemed brisk. But the condition of this principal thoroughfare was hardly better than any of the others, while it was filled with a motley throng of black people ; very few colored (that is, mulatto) faces being seen, and fewer still white, with the exception of a group or two from the *New York*. Negresses passed along, trailing freshly starched dresses over the filthy sidewalks, and wearing brightly striped handkerchiefs tied in picturesque turban fashion around their heads. Others, in short blue cotton gowns and bare black legs and feet, carried bundles of one kind or another on their heads, holding themselves surprisingly erect, and walking with an inimitable ease and savage grace. The men were less remarkable, and seemed to De Marsillac much like any average throng to be found on a Southern plantation, or the docks and negro quarters of a Southern city. Here and there faces of intelligence, indicating education, were to be seen ; but the majority were of a very low intellectual and strongly animal type, with now and again a countenance of revolting characteristics.

"If you want to fancy yourself on the Congo, you ought to go and take a glimpse of the market yonder," said Mr. Schlagenbach, as he nodded in the direction of a cross-street. "It is on the next square. And it is not mere report but verified fact that human flesh has been offered for sale there."

"Impossible !" cried Atherton, with an expression of disgust and incredulity.

"Ah ! you say 'impossible' because you know not Hayti," replied the other. "Get those who live here to tell you what *they* know. But here we are at my friend's place."

He turned as he spoke into a large warehouse filled with merchandise of various descriptions, the odor of green coffee strongly predominating ; and made his way to where a short, rotund German of middle age—dressed, like most men in the tropics, in white clothing—was seated at a desk. He stepped from his high stool as the trio approached ; and Mr. Schlagenbach, benignly smiling, introduced his companions to Mr. Hoffman.

" We are very glad to hear," said Atherton, after shaking hands, " that, owing to Mr. Schlagenbach's kind recommendation, you will afford us quarters during the short stay which we expect to make at the Cape."

" It is something which we who live here expect to do for our friends," the German replied. He was a stolid man, with none of Schlagenbach's beaming friendliness, but a certain air which seemed to say that what he promised he would perform. " If we did not," he added, " they would fare very badly. Ever been in Hayti before, Mr. Atherton ?"

" Never."

" And you don't come on business ?"

" Merely to see the country."

" Ah ! Then I fancy you will not require any quarters longer than a good opportunity offers for getting away. Meanwhile, since my family are absent, I can put my house at your disposition. Have you come ashore at present prepared to remain ?"

" No ; we only came ashore to look at things and make the arrangement now happily concluded. We will return to the ship, and come ashore with our luggage this afternoon."

" If you will name an hour, I will meet you at the wharf with my carriage."

"You are exceedingly kind.   Under those circumstances it would be better for you to name the hour yourself."

"Shall we say five o'clock, then ?   That will give you time to settle comfortably before dinner.   By the bye, how many rooms do you require ?"

"Three.   I have with me an English servant."

"Very well.   They will be prepared—oh, no more thanks !   We expect, as I have said, to do this kind of thing here on the island, and I am glad to have the pleasure of meeting you.   I need hardly say that your father's name is well known to me."

"And therein," said De Marsillac, in a low voice, as they left the warehouse, "lies the secret of Mr. Hoffman's obliging readiness to take us under his roof.   You asked me a little while ago what I should do without you, Mr. Atherton.   I begin to perceive clearly that I should do very badly indeed."

CHAPTER VII.

At five o'clock in the afternoon, their luggage having already been sent ashore under care of Atherton's capable English servant, the two friends shook hands with the genial captain and such of the passengers as had formed their acquaintance, went down the ladder at the ship's side to the boat awaiting them, sprang lightly into it as it tossed up and down on the green waves, and were rowed across the bay to the city lying under the shadow of its superb heights, where their adventure was to be carried out to the final issue of success or failure.

According to his promise, Mr. Hoffman met them at the

wharf with a light carriage, such as those foreigners who do business in the Cape but live outside generally use.

"I have sent your man on with your things," he said to Atherton, who glanced around. "Jump in, both of you, and we'll be at my place in fifteen minutes."

Complying with this request, they rattled away in an opposite direction from that which they had taken in the morning, crossed a stone bridge over a dry watercourse, and, driving along a road which followed the shore, with masses of overgrown ruins on its landward side, presently descried before them a red roof showing with picturesque effect above a great mass of greenery, which Mr. Hoffman pointed out as his residence.

It proved to be a very attractive place. The large house, although single-storied and rather slightly built of wood, was an ideal dwelling for tropical purposes, with wide doors opening in every direction to take advantage of every sea or land breeze, and broad verandas completely encircling it, as it stood in the midst of a garden filled with luxuriant trees, shrubs, and flowers. The rooms in readiness for the newcomers were all that could be desired in cleanliness and neatness; and when they sat down to dinner there was something very suggestive of home to the young Louisianian in the black faces of the servants who waited upon them. Mr. Hoffman apologized for shortcomings on the ground of his wife's absence, but to the two who had feared faring so differently there seemed no need for apology at all.

Dinner over, the host proposed that they should adjourn to the veranda to smoke; and while he and Atherton lighted their cigars, their companion walked away from them to another side of the building, where he paused to contemplate the picture spread before him, with the strangest possible mingling of thoughts and feelings.

It was a picture to rouse many thoughts, apart from its personal significance to himself. The air was perfectly still, hardly the whisper of a breeze stirred the heavy tropical foliage drooping around the veranda ; and the waters of the wide bay seemed sleeping like an inland lake, while the masts and spars of the ships lying at anchor upon it showed like marine etchings in the delicate mingling of starshine and moonshine, an exquisite radiance in which the hushed waters, the far outlines of shore and mountains, the town gleaming with lights, and the dark, majestic heights above it, were all touched with a mysterious beauty and charm. What memories of the past rushed upon the mind of the gazer as he stood looking out over the tranquil scene !— memories of the great Genoese, for whom no doubt these waters slept as softly and plashed as caressingly, as if they had not betrayed him to shipwreck, and whose eyes first gazed upon the enchanting beauty of these shores ; memories of the doomed defenders of Navidad, with the unwritten tragedy of their fate ; memories of the buccaneers sailing into this noble harbor with their booty from plundered Spanish galleons, and founding, in piracy and bloodshed, the town which was to be a hundred times washed in blood ; memories of colonial wealth and splendor, and of the constantly arriving ships laden with their dark freight of slaves from Africa—the black cloud which was to whelm in ruin the prosperity it helped for a time to build ; memories of the terrible scenes of the insurrection, the continuation beyond seas of the not less terrible scenes of the French Revolution, and of the wave of savagery which had submerged forever this fairest and most fertile spot of all God's earth !

"That seems a nice boy, Mr. Atherton," Mr. Hoffman had meanwhile remarked, as the slim young figure passed out of sight around a corner of the building.

"He is a very nice boy," Atherton agreed ; "a descendant, by the bye, of one of the old proprietors of the colonial days. His people owned large estates near here, and he is anxious to visit them—in fact, that is his chief reason for coming ashore at this place. I suppose there will be no difficulty in paying such a visit ?"

"That depends upon how far he wishes to go," the other replied. "There are parts of the country that are neither agreeable nor safe for foreigners ; but if the estates are in the immediate neighborhood of the Cape, he might venture to visit them, although I should not advise him to mention the fact of his being the descendant of their former owner. The hatred and suspicion of the negroes towards white men are inextinguishable, and would naturally be greater towards the representative of one of their old masters."

"I should have fancied that a century of independence might have eradicated such feelings," Atherton observed.

"A century of independence has eradicated nothing and improved nothing in the character of this people," was the reply. "In point of fact, the whole truth has never been told to the world in regard to Hayti, else civilized nations would grow ashamed of protecting in a farce of self-government a race of savages as steeped in barbarism as their fellow-countrymen on the west coast of Africa."

"Everything which I have heard and read has led me to the same conclusion," said Atherton ; "but, from certain dark hints which are let fall by those who know the country, I fancy the worst is *not* known outside. For instance, what do all these stories about cannibalism amount to ? I confess that I have heard them with incredulity."

"Very likely," said the German dryly. He smoked for a moment in silence. "Most strangers hear them with incredulity," he added ; "but there is nothing more certain than that they are true, and that the constant effort of the government is to ignore and hide this crime rather than expose and suppress it."

"But do you, a resident of the country for years, of your own knowledge declare this thing ?" Atherton persisted.

"Of my own knowledge !" repeated the other with emphasis. "I have not seen the cannibals at their feasts—if that is what you mean—but, short of that, I know it as thoroughly as I can know anything, as thoroughly as every one else on the island knows it. Why, it is a fact that the police are bound to examine the basket of every peasant who comes in to market, to prevent the smuggling in for sale of human flesh, and that time and again it has been seized. Don't you know that the mysterious disappearance of children, carried off to be sacrificed at their Vaudoux rites, keeps every mother on the island in terror ? Look yonder !"—he pointed to the immense mountain overshadowing them, where, midway up its dark side, a light gleamed like a star. "That light indicates the dwelling of a Vaudoux *papaloi*, or priest. There, it is well known, the negroes go to celebrate their infernal mysteries, of which the worship of the serpent is chief ; but they would tell you that they do not offer human sacrifice. Yet it is only a few years since two white men—one an American, the other a Dominican—witnessed the murder of human victims in that very spot."

"*There !*" said Atherton, gazing in horror-struck fascination at the light which seemed to shine with so baleful a glow out of the deep obscurity surrounding it. "In sight of a seaport where contact with the outer world might be supposed to produce some glimmer of civilization —what horrible audacity !"

"No particular audacity was required," replied his host

quietly. "But these facts will give you some idea of how shallow the civilization of Hayti is, and will indicate what I meant when I said that I would not advise your young friend to venture too far into the country in the attempt to visit the former estates of his family. If he disappeared—well, do you know what was said in open court to the jury by the advocate of a negro who had murdered a Frenchman in Port au Prince! '*Après tout, ce n'est qu'un blanc de moins.*'"

"He will not disappear," said Atherton grimly. "I think I can promise so much. But in going into the country for a few days I shall want a guide. Do you know any one trustworthy whom you could recommend?"

Mr. Hoffman smoked meditatively for a moment before he replied:

"I will speak to one of my servants to-morrow, who may be able to obtain for you what you want. He is an American negro, with a very low opinion of the Haytians, and he may find some Jamaica or Turk's Island negro, of whom there are a few here, for your service. How soon do you want to start on your expedition?"

"As soon as we can get ready."

"And is your destination only the old estate of which you have spoken?"

"By no means. We wish to see as much of the country as possible—taking in, of course, the famous palace and citadel of Christophe. There is no difficulty in visiting those places?"

"None at all in visiting the palace, but you will need a permit from the general commanding this department to enable you to enter the citadel."

"I thought it was in ruins?"

"So it is—partially, at least. But, all the same, no foreigner is allowed to enter it without a permit. If you wish to go there, and it is decidedly worth your while to do so, we will apply for a permit to-morrow."

"By all means, if necessary. How many days are required for the excursion ?"

"Not more than two. That is the time usually occupied in going and returning, and seeing the palace and fort."

"I shall take more time. There is no need for haste, and we will visit my friend's family estate *en route*."

"Is it situated near here ?"

"It is in the Plaine du Nord. That is near here, is it not ?"

"Very near. Passing around that great mountain yonder, you soon enter upon it. It is a magnificant plain, covered with the ruins of old estates ; and, if it were in the hands of any other people than these, would be again the wonder of the world for its fertility. Does Mr. de Marsillac know the exact situation of his family place ?"

"Exactly enough for all practical purposes. I think we shall be able to locate it without difficulty. I shall also take a camera with me ; for I wish to obtain a number of photographs, and I have an idea of doing a little prospecting in the hills. This country should abound in minerals ; and yet, I believe, there has never been any attempt to prospect it."

"It has never been in a condition—at least, for a century past—to make prospecting possible, or its results (if any were found) very valuable," said Mr. Hoffman dryly. "But I don't think that even the Spaniards ever looked here for gold. The mines they worked were all in the Dominican mountains."

"Gold is not the only valuable mineral," said Atherton. "But what I chiefly wish to gratify is a scientific curiosity by finding what the hills contain. Therefore I shall take with me a geological equipment—hammer, pick, and shovel. I presume there will be no objection to my exploring a little in this manner?''

" There is no telling to what these people will object," was the discouraging reply. " I think that if I were going to attempt anything of the kind, I should carefully avoid opposition, by prospecting only in a quiet place and to a limited extent."

" I think I can promise that my prospecting will be to a very limited extent, and in a very quiet place," said Atherton, smiling. " I can obtain the necessary tools here, I suppose?"

" I will obtain them for you. It will excite no attention for me to do so, but a stranger is always an object of attention and suspicion. I must warn you, however, that you will not find any accommodation in the country. You can get a night's lodging at Milot—the village of the palace of Sans Souci—but I doubt if it will be of a nature to tempt you to remain there longer than one night."

" I shall not even ask for that. I intend taking with me a camping outfit. In expectation of such excursions—for I have come to the West Indies to spend some time—I have a light tent and several hammocks. My servant is also experienced in camping. He spent last summer with me on a hunting tour in the Rocky Mountains. We will take provisions with us, and ask no accommodation from the people of the country."

" A very good plan," said Mr. Hoffman approvingly. " Well, I will do what I can for you ; and I hope"—with a rather doubtful accent—" that you may not get into any difficulties. It is necessary to bear in mind that it is very easy to get into difficulties in Hayti."

"I shall bear it in mind," answered Atherton, amused at the evident solicitude of the speaker lest he himself might be involved in the difficulties which he feared for these rash strangers.

The more rash of the two strangers—that one the extent of whose rashness was indeed only gauged by some anxious hearts far away—was still gazing out over the shadow-haunted bay and shores, when a little later Atherton came up and laid a hand on his shoulder.

Now, as more than once before, he was struck by the manner in which the boy shrank from anything like personal contact. He drew the shoulder abruptly away as he turned, with a slight contraction of the brows, to see who had approached him.

"Did I startle you?" Atherton asked. "You must have been very much absorbed in your thoughts."

"So I was," the other answered. "For the moment I was at home, thinking of my people and of all that has brought me here, upon what seems to you so wild a venture."

"It is beginning to lose its wild character as one comes down to practical details," said Atherton, drawing forward a large bamboo chair and settling himself comfortably. "I have just been discussing these details with our host, and we have pretty well arranged them. I came for you to talk matters over a little further ; but just now he is engaged with a visitor, so we'll lounge here and wait his leisure. Meanwhile I'll light another cigar—you don't smoke, sensible boy !—and you shall tell me something about your people. I fancy that your sisters must be very attractive."

"Why do you think so ?" asked the other, with surprise.

"Don't be too much flattered when I say because I

judge of them by yourself. It is impossible not to fancy that the qualities which render you an uncommonly attractive boy must exist in an accentuated degree in them."

"And you are quite right in fancying so," was the quick reply. "Any attractive qualities that I may possess certainly do exist in a very accentuated degree in my sisters—at least, in one of them. No one could be more attractive than my sister Diane."

"Diane !" repeated Atherton. "What a charming name—Diane de Marsillac ! It suggests some court beauty of old France."

"And that is what Diane looks like !" cried the boy. "Everybody says so ; and, in fact, one can see for one's self how much she is like the pictures of the famous beauties of the time of Louis Quatorze and Louis Quinze. You might think her one of them restored to life—and there is not one more beautiful than herself."

"You are more enthusiastic than brothers usually are over the charms of a sister," observed Atherton, amused and interested. "She must be very fascinating, this fair Diane."

"She is that above all," was the serious answer. "She fascinates every one—not a special class, like some women, but *everybody*. Young and old, rich and poor, black and white, there is not any one who knows her and who does not love Diane. And that," the speaker added, half unconsciously and in a changed tone, "is her misfortune."

"Why ?" inquired Atherton, surprised and yet more interested by the thrill of emotion which had suddenly come into the expressive voice.

"Because there is a love, if one can call it love, which is more cruel than hate," was the unexpectedly passionate reply, "a love more to be dreaded than death ; for it is more ruthless, more unsparing. This love it has been the fate of my poor Diane to inspire ; and she will be sacrificed to it unless I—I alone—can save her."

" Pray tell me what you mean," said Atherton, suddenly sitting upright and speaking in a tone of such interest as demanded response.

And the voice, with its thrilling inflections of passion and pathos, told him. Loneliness and the deep human need of sympathy overpowered with the speaker all considerations of prudence ; and so, here in distant Hayti, Atherton heard the story of the home on the Bayou Tèche, and of all that had brought the descendant of Henri de Marsillac to seek the wealth which the latter had striven to save.

Whatever was most sympathetic, most generous, and, it may be added, most chivalrous in the nature of the listener stirred at the recital as he listened ; and he said to himself that the whim which had led him to break off his voyage to accompany this lad on his adventure had been well followed.

" I am very glad that you have told me this," he said presently. " If I was anxious to help you before, I am much more anxious now. With such a motive I do not wonder you have crossed the sea and are ready to encounter any risks to seek what is yours—and theirs. And we will find it, never fear for that ! Your Diane has gained another champion. Time, labor, money—we will spend them like water, but she shall have her ransom. I pledge myself to that."

Even in the dim light he could see that De Marsillac looked at him with glowing eyes, and that for the first time, of his own motion, he extended his hand.

" If we succeed or if we fail," he said, in a tone of exceeding sweetness, " I can never thank you more than I thank you now for the aid without which, as I clearly perceive, I could do nothing."

" But, as it is, we will together do everything," answered Atherton confidently. "And when we have succeeded you shall reward me for whatever I have accomplished by introducing me to this fair Diane, whose sworn knight I hereby constitute myself."

CHAPTER VIII.

THANKS to the efforts of Mr. Hoffman—who showed himself extremely anxious to fulfil the injunction to speed the parting guest—and thanks yet more to a lavish use of that talisman which proves an " open sesame" in all countries, the third day after their arrival at the Cape found the travellers equipped and ready to set forth upon their journey.

It was a morning of such radiant freshness and brilliance as only these enchanted tropical regions know. The warmth of the sun was tempered by the breeze already blowing from the limitless expanse of silver sea ; and the wide, flashing bay, the distant sapphire heights, and the great, green masses of the Mornes rising above the picturesque town, were all bathed in an atmosphere of the most exquisite beauty.

It was a scene upon which the eyes of the strangers had not ceased to dwell with delight since their arrival ; but to-day they were for the first time heedless of its loveliness in the excitement attending their departure. Before the veranda stood five horses—two passably good, three very sorry—on one of the last of which several servants were packing the camping outfit : tent, hammocks, etc. Gilbert, Atherton's well-trained English servant, was directing and assisting ; while the guide—a chocolate-colored Jamaica negro with an intelligent face—stood by, offering now and then a word of advice. On the veranda Mr. Hoffman was also bestowing some last words of advice upon his departing guests, who assured him of their intention to be as prudent and cautious as possible. Presently Gilbert, approaching his master, announced that all was in readiness.

"You are sure nothing is forgotten ?" Atherton asked.

"Nothing, sir, I think."

"Then we are off ! A thousand thanks for all your kindness, Mr. Hoffman ; and I trust we shall be able to report on our return a successful expedition."

"I sincerely hope that you may," was the cordial reply. "I'll expect you here, of course, on your return."

Hands were shaken ; Atherton and his companion mounted ; Gilbert, with the guide leading the pack-horse, followed ; and they rode out of the gates of the merchant's pretty residence.

Their way lay directly through the town, so that they had another comprehensive view of its squalor and filth ; its immense masses of overgrown ruins, with their picturesque aspect and unspeakably tragic suggestions ; its flimsy houses, and its throng of black faces. Followed by curious glances, they rode through the unevenly paved, crowded streets, by the grass-grown, ruin-encircled *place* where stands the church with its musical bells, and so reached the northeastern gate of the city, where, passing a barefooted sentry, with whom their guide exchanged a few words, they found themselves in the open country, upon a broad, hard road which led across saline flats and around the base of the great mountain known as the Western Morne.

" Here we are at last, fairly on our way to the place we have come to seek," said Atherton when the town was left behind them. " Of what are you thinking, Henri, that you are so silent ?"

The boy whom he addressed started, and turned towards him a pair of eyes shining with that excitement of the mind which is like a strong stimulant in its effect upon the body.

" There are so many things of which to think !" he replied. " But just then I was thinking of my great-great-grandfather riding for his life along this road, carrying his death wound with him, on that awful night of the first outbreak. I am the first of his blood to ride here since then."

" A second Henri de Marsillac retracing his steps, with the gulf of a century between !" said Atherton. " It is certainly a thought to stir many memories, especially when one recollects why you are here. I fancy, by the bye, that the first Henri rode that race with death as much to save the secret which he carried as to warn the Cape—which by that time must have needed little warning—and to see once more his wife and children."

" Who can tell ?" the other answered. " There were reasons enough, God knows ! But I hardly think he thought of *that* after it was done. Events followed too fast. He and his faithful Jacques at once set out to save themselves, and carry the news of the insurrection to the Cape ; but they met a party of the insurgent slaves and were forced to fight. They had firearms and fast horses, which the others had not ; so, although poor Jacques was killed, my great-great-grandfather escaped—but with a mortal wound. His horse was a splendid animal, and carried him away from the fiends through whom he had fought his way. Can you not fancy horse and rider as they dashed madly along this road—the man staunching the blood from his wound as best he could, and praying, no doubt, just to keep his senses and his seat until he should reach the lights of the Cape that shone ahead, while hell itself seemed behind in the burning glare which lighted the Plaine du Nord from the plantations where the slaves were making a carnival of murder ?"

"One would think you had been with him," said Atherton, "you seem so well acquainted with every detail."

"Oh, that is not remarkable ! I have heard the story so often, and pictured it to myself in connection with all I read of that time. In fact, I fancied it so clearly that the only strange thing now is to find myself here, where it happened. I can hardly believe that that is not a dream."

"We will prove it a most solid reality. And if we find untouched what Henri de Marsillac buried on that night, I hope his spirit may have the satisfaction of knowing it."

"I am glad you don't hope that it may be ' by to see,' " said the other, with a slight laugh. "Great as my regard for and interest in him have always been, I confess I could not hope that. But let us speak of practical things. Shall we seek the estate to-day, or go to the palace and citadel first ?"

"My plan is to locate the estate to-day—that is, find exactly where it is—and then go to Milot for the night. To-morrow we will see the palace and citadel, and return ; and to-morrow night we will spend in the home of your ancestors. How long we will remain there depends on—circumstances."

"Yes," in a low voice. Then abruptly : "When do you suppose we shall reach the Plaine du Nord ?"

"Very soon, I think," replied Atherton. "You see,

we are turning quite away from the shore and rising to higher ground."

In fact, they had already entered upon that famous plain. The barren saline flats were left behind, and on each side spread an expanse of rich but almost wholly uncultivated land. On the side of the road—the ancient French highway, still, after the neglect of a century, in a state of good preservation—grew, tall and thick, trees which had originally been planted for hedges ; while here and there a plantation patch was the only sign of cultivation, although large tracts were covered with what seemed at first sight a species of scrub timber, but which proved to be coffee-trees left to grow wild. Soon also there appeared ruins of gateways and houses, all built so durably of stone—the gateposts and *façades* of the dwellings handsomely carved—that they had, in a measure at least, resisted every agent of destruction employed against them. In what remained of these mansions no one dwelt ; but near the gates were frequently seen the palm-thatched cabin of some negro descendant of the slaves who once tilled these broad and fertile lands, now again abandoned to Nature.

"I am afraid the search will be a little difficult," said Atherton. " Who could have imagined that the country-seats of the old proprietors would be so numerous ! What a paradise this plain must have been before the insurrection !"

It required indeed no great stretch of imagination to picture its beauty and fertility when covered with superb plantations and stately homes, its broad fields of cane and sugar divided by citron hedges, and the whole crossed in all directions by roads so admirably constructed that their stone bridges, culverts, and ditches still remain after the lapse of a century.

" A paradise indeed !" echoed the other, glancing over

its wide expanse, bounded by glorious masses of azure mountains, cloud-crested against the deeper azure of the sky. "And now given up to utter ruin and desolation. *Eh bien!*" turning quickly to the guide, "do you know where is the village of Grande Rivière?"

The man nodded assent. "Oh, yes!" he replied. "Grande Rivière over yonder," pointing eastward.

"Very well. Take us towards Grande Rivière. The estate we seek is in that neighborhood, about a league distant from the village."

"But if we go to Grande Rivière, we mus' leave this road to Milot—and road from Grande Rivière to Milot pretty bad."

"That does not matter. We have all day before us, and we desire to visit that place first."

It was after they had, in accordance with this direction, taken the road leading from Petite Anse to Grande Rivière that the guide pointed out the ruins of great estates on every side. Riding slowly, they paused now and then to ask information of the persons they met—all negroes of the class of agricultural laborers, if the term can with any propriety be applied to those whose labors are so small. But none of these were able or willing to give the information sought. Some merely stared when questioned, muttered a word or two in *patois*, and went on ; others knew of such a place, but were very indefinite in their description of the locality where it might be found.

"All big fools, dese Haytian niggas !" said the Jamaican, with scorn, after one of these encounters. "Bes' not talk to 'em any mo', sah—look for ourselves."

"We must be near the place, I think," observed De Marsillac, whose excitement, though restrained, was now intense. "Let us ride on."

On they rode, the country around them growing constantly more beautiful, with wooded hills making a background for the rich plain ; and ever beyond, the blue majesty of the great mountains enthralling the vision.

Presently, attracted by a magnificent avenue of royal palms —the finest they had yet seen—which led from massive gate pillars of stone towards the ruins of a large house beautifully situated on the crest of a gentle hill, beyond which rose bolder heights, they paused again, and Atherton said :

"This may be the place we seek—at least I think we should examine it. We may find some one to tell us what estate it is, and if——"

He was stopped by an exclamation from his companion, who pointed to one of the stone pillars on which was deeply carved the name :

" Millefleurs."

Doubt was now at an end. The situation, the name, both indicated that the De Marsillac estate was found. Turning into the gateway, the party rode along the avenue of palms which, fully a mile in length, crossed what had once been fertile fields, but was now a scrub-covered waste. The stately stems of the royal trees, exquisitely tapering, rose on each side to a height of fifty or sixty feet, where the great fronds of plumy foliage then sprang out and mingled high overhead, forming a vista which framed at its termination the house towards which it led. Viewed from a distance, it was difficult to believe this house a ruin, so nobly did its walls still crown the eminence on which they stood, and so little of decay was visible. But when the end of the avenue had been reached, and, dismounting before a handsome flight of stone steps, where the attendants were left with the horses, the two explorers (for such they felt themselves) ascended to a broad terrace, they saw that what stood before them was indeed but a shell. Like the ruins of the Cape, it was roofless, while great trees grew within its walls, and vines of many kinds rioted through the empty doorways and windows.

For a moment both remained motionless, regarding in silence this melancholy wreck of a once stately and beautiful home. With Atherton it was but another proof of the complete destruction which had overwhelmed the civilization of the island and doomed it to barbarism ; but to the descendant of those who had for long years made this the seat of their gay, luxurious life and boundless hospitality, it had a more personal and tragic significance. Yet it was not so much upon those days of prosperity that his thoughts dwelt, as upon the insistent recollection of that night of terror when the last possessor of this house had fled from it —to meet his death and leave a fortune lost behind him. Again the thought, " Since then, I am the first of the race to stand here !" brought with it a sense of something akin to awe ; and, seeing how he was wrapped in memories of the past, Atherton laid an imperative hand on his arm.

" Come !" he said. " There will be time enough for dreams when we return. At present we must satisfy ourselves without delay that this is the place we seek."

" The place we seek !" repeated the other, quickly rousing himself. " How can there be any doubt ? The name —the situation——"

" Then let us lose no time in finding the spot of which we are in search. Where shall we look for it ?"

" In the gardens. They must be in the rear of the house."

" Come, then, and leave the ghosts behind, at least until we find what we seek."

"Poor ghosts!" said the boy, with a sigh, as they moved away.

"And why ' poor ghosts ' ? They had their day—which is more than many ghosts can say—and enjoyed it royally."

Passing around the ruins of the house, they found a wilderness which had once plainly been a place of delights. A series of terraces cut out of the hillside were covered by a tangled, luxuriant growth of such vegetation as only the tropics can produce. Evidently every tree, plant and shrub which could lend adornment had been brought thither ; and, all restraining care long since removed, had, as if exulting in recovered freedom, converted the beautiful pleasure-ground into a very jungle—an unimaginable mass of broad green leaves and glowing blossoms ; of twining, climbing parasites, and trees of magnificent growth spreading thick crowns of foliage. Great bushes of heliotrope filled the air with fragrance ; roses grown into trees were covered with cascades of blossom ; immense clusters of pink and yellow lilies flaunted in the sunshine ; the scarlet hibiscus burned like a flame ; bamboos clashed their tall, feathery spears together ; ferns and palms of countless varieties grew everywhere ; and over all myriads of vines, among which the passion-flower and many-hued convolvuli were conspicuous, rioted in wild grace.

To penetrate this overgrown, enchanting wilderness appeared at first glance almost impossible ; but closer inspection revealed the fact that what had formerly been broad walks and rose-lined avenues were not even yet wholly impassable ; and the two companions, making their way wherever it was possible to do so, found everywhere evidences of the beauty and luxury with which the old possessors had surrounded themselves. Balustrades and vases wrought in stone still held their places ; while here and there were the empty basins of fountains once filled with crystal water brought from the neighboring hills ; water that also fed a great swimming-bath in a spot so picturesquely secluded that Diana and her nymphs might have sported in it. But, look where they would amid all this wild luxuriance of loveliness, they failed to find a sun-dial within a circle, so completely had the rampant vegetation obliterated all but a few demarcations of the grounds.

"One thing only is certain," said De Marsillac, when, disappointed, they finally returned to the first terrace, from whence they overlooked all that lay below : " the spot we seek is on the second terrace. '*On the second terrace of the garden, at the east side of the sun-dial which stands in the circle containing the statue of the nymph* '—that is what Henri de Marsillac wrote."

" It is explicit," replied Atherton. " A circle—a sun-dial—a statue. We should be able to find those things, for the place seems only ruined and abandoned : nothing apparently has been taken away. I should judge that it has never been occupied since Henri de Marsillac left it ; which makes me sanguine that, when we discover the indicated place, we shall find what he buried untouched."

Evidently his companion was also sanguine. Hope had again taken possession of him like a flame, had lighted a scarlet flush on his cheek and wakened a shining glow in the brown eyes.   He did not answer immediately, but stood, studying with eager intentness every feature of the scene below. Suddenly he pointed to where a large group of citron-trees rose out of a mass of lower verdure on the second terrace.

" Does it not seem to you that those trees form a circle?" he asked. " It looks to me as if they have grown up from what was originally a hedge. If so, that may be the place. Let us go to it.''

Without waiting reply, he ran down the stone steps which, still in a state of perfect preservation, led from one terrace to another, and began breaking a way through the dense growth that intervened between himself and the citron-trees. Atherton followed ; and, after a few minutes of difficult work which made the latter wish for a hatchet, they reached the group, and found that, as the boy had divined, they had indeed grown up out of what was once a hedge, much of which still remained in the form of tall bushes. Forcing a passage through these, they entered a circle so completely enclosed by its wall of tall, green foliage, so secluded, and so wrapped in the deep stillness that comes from the absence of all signs of human life, that it was like a spot enchanted. The same thought struck both, as they looked around. Within this charmed and, as it were, sentinelled space any operations might be conducted with impunity from observation. A better place for such work as they had to do could not be imagined. But was it the place they sought ?

Impossible at first to say. The whole interior of the circle was overgrown with the same luxuriant vegetation which existed elsewhere, covering the space so entirely that what else it contained was purely a matter of conjecture. Only one fact was plain—no statue stood there. If the other silent witness for which they looked, if the sun-dial was also missing, then one of two things was certain : either this was not the circle sought, not the place where Henri de Marsillac and his servant had buried the money and jewels, or else the objects which marked it had been removed. They looked at each other with the same apprehension.

"We have a circle, but everything else seems lacking," said Atherton. "I fear this is not the place."

"We cannot decide yet," answered the other. "I believe that it *is* the place."

"Then where are the sun-dial and the statue?"

"We do not care where the statue may be, if we can find the sun-dial. That alone is necessary. The other might be overthrown, broken, carried away; but no one is likely to carry away a sun-dial. Where would it be situated? Ah, how stupid I am! In the centre of the circle, of course. There we must look for it."

Again waiting for no reply, he plunged into the tangled mass of plants and vines and made his way towards the centre. Reaching it after some difficulty, he paused and glanced up at Atherton, who had followed closely.

"Are we exactly in the centre now?" he asked.

"Exactly enough," Atherton replied, beating down the riotous growth around them with a stick which he carried. "And I see no sign of a sun-dial."

"How can you tell?" cried the boy, in a sharp, nervous tone. "It—it *must* be here!"

He moved a few paces as he spoke—and suddenly his foot struck against something buried in the luxuriant verdure; and, stumbling, he almost fell. Atherton caught his arm; but he drew it quickly away, and with a cry fell upon his knees.

"It is here!—it is here!" he exclaimed, with a sob of passionate excitement and relief. "I have my hands upon it—oh, thank God!"

Other hands were upon it also the next moment—hands which paid no heed to thorns and briars as they tore away the closely matted vegetation covering that which, once cleared, revealed itself as indeed the old sun-dial beside which Henri de Marsillac had buried his treasures.

CHAPTER IX.

"No," said Atherton half an hour later, "it will not do to alter our plans. We must go on to Sans Souci and the citadel, in order to support our character of sight-see-ing travellers."

There was a mutinous light in the brown eyes that looked up at him. The pedestal on which the statue of the nymph erstwhile stood had been found on one side of the circle ; but its present occupant, instead of the nymph, was the slender figure of the boy. His attitude as he sat care-lessly on the block of stone had, in these sylvan surround-ings, a suggestion of faun-like grace ; while his face, from which the hat was pushed back, with its flush of excite-ment, its shining eyes, and damp, clustering curls, was brilliantly handsome as he lifted it towards Atherton, who stood beside him.

"Why should we support a character in which nobody is interested ?" he asked, with some impatience. "Who has noticed us ? Who will care whether we are sight-seeing travellers or—or anything else ?"

"Let us once give reason for the suspicion that we are anything else, especially seekers of buried valuables, and I fear we should excite an interest far too lively for our com-fort or perhaps our safety," Atherton answered. "We must conduct this affair with every precaution that pru-dence can suggest. And although I grant that it is hard, having found the place of the treasure, not to assure ourselves at once that it is there, still it is but a short time that we have to wait for the assurance ; and our safety depends on our exercising due discretion."

"How can you tell," demanded the boy, "that while we are gone it may not be discovered——"

"After having remained undiscovered for a century? Ask your common sense if that is possible."

"Or we might be killed by some accident, and never re-turn ; *that* is possible, you must admit."

"Possible, but not very probable, I hope. I am sorry to thwart your wishes, but my judgment tells me that it is necessary for the success of our plans that the original pro-gramme should be carried out. We must go on."

"But if I insist upon staying?" said the boy passion-ately. "After all, it is *I* who have come here to seek what is buried in this spot, and it is on my success that every-thing depends."

Atherton felt himself growing angry. He did not take into consideration the intense excitement which possessed the speaker ; nor how hard it was, in the face of long ex-pectation wrought to battling hope and fear, to turn away still in suspense, knowing as little as he had known in dis-tant Louisiana whether or not Henri de Marsillac's hidden treasures did or did not lie untouched beside the old sun-dial. He only perceived an unreasonable obstinacy and folly, as well as forgetfulness of all his efforts to make success possible.

"Very true," he replied coldly. "It is your interests alone which are at stake in this matter ; and if you choose to risk them, I have no right to prevent you from doing so. Stay if you like. I fancied you something more than a foolish child ready to throw away everything rather than restrain impatience ; but that, it seems, is what you are."

He turned and walked away, leaving behind him on the pedestal of the nymph a very crestfallen person. To have full liberty accorded to do that which is unwise or wrong is with some natures the surest means of rousing reflection, awakening conscience, and preventing such action. So it was now with De Marsillac. Thus suddenly granted what he asked, shame overtook him. He had no thought of resenting Atherton's last words ; he was only struck with a deep sense of his own ungrateful perversity displayed towards one who had done and was doing so much for him ; and, springing from his seat, he followed the tall figure still striding away. In his eagerness to make amends for the folly which had wounded his friend, it hardly cost him a pang to turn his back upon the sundial.

"Mr. Atherton !" he cried. And then, as Atherton paused and turned, he went on quickly : " Forgive me for being so obstinate and foolish. I will certainly go on, if you think it best."

"I am *sure* it is best," Atherton replied. His anger melted at once at sight of the contrition and appeal in the beautiful eyes uplifted to his own. What strange power did this lad possess to disarm him at a word? He asked himself the question with something of wonder, as he laid his hand on the young shoulder. " My dear boy," he added, in his kindest tones, " do you think I would ask you to go if I did not know what success means to you, and how necessary it is to take every precaution against failure ? Suspense is hard to bear—do you suppose I am not feeling it in sympathy with you ?—but you who have borne it from Louisiana to Hayti can surely bear it from Millefleurs to La Ferrière and back."

" There is no comparison," was the reply. " The first

had to be borne, but this—to have stood on the spot and yet not know——"

"You may know ; for, after all, there is no reason for suspense. We may be sure that had the spot ever been disturbed, the sun-dial would not be standing where it is : it would have been overthrown, cast aside. Those who secured the treasure would never have left it untouched, nor paused to put it back in its place."

"That is true" (reflectively). "The fact that the sun-dial stands there is proof that what lies beside it is undisturbed. Thank you for the suggestion. And yet—and yet it makes me desire still more to secure at once what has waited for me so long."

"It can wait a little longer. What are twenty-four hours after a century ?"

"Nothing, of course," the boy answered. "But we—that is my family—have had so many misfortunes that—you will think me very superstitious—I feel as if it were hardly possible for good fortune to come to us. One grows to feel that way, you know. And so I can never believe in the reality of what we hope is buried there until I see it. And, if it exists, I have a fear that if I turn away from it now I shall never be so near it again."

"Come," said Atherton once more, taking forcible hold of his arm and leading him on. "This is superstition indeed ; and if I listen to you longer, I shall be foolish enough to be moved by it. Let us get away at once !"

The sun was setting when the travellers, descending the rocky hill above Milot, down which their road wound, saw before them, in the exquisite evening light, the beautiful valley like a dream of Paradise, covered with verdure and dotted with cocoa palms, its village embowered in groves of luxuriant fruit-trees ; while crowning the brow of a hill at its farther end shone majestically, against a background of verdure-clad mountains, the yellow walls of the palace of Sans Souci.

" What a picture !" cried Atherton, reining in his horse. " I doubt if the world can match it for mingled softness and grandeur. African savage though he was, Christophe knew well how to choose the site of his palace. Nothing more beautiful could be conceived."

" Nothing," assented the boy beside him. " It looks like an ideal abode of peace ; yet one shudders to think what atrocities it has witnessed."

" Do not think of them. Nature forgets, and why should not we ? Heaven ! what a fate it was that consigned this island into such hands ! If it were any other land one would be tempted to make one's home forever in such a spot as this."

" Beg pardon, sah !" said the guide ; " but it'll be dark in a few minutes, and we better go on to Milot and find lodgin' 'fore night."

" Do you mean to say that we could find any lodging in that village fit for our occupation ?" asked Atherton.

" Schoolmaster, sah, got pretty good house. He take you in."

" We will not trouble him. We have brought a tent and hammocks, and intend to camp in some pleasant place outside the village."

The man glanced at the great, furrowed mountains, above which rested dark masses of cloud that the sunset was gilding with glorious, coppery gold.

" 'Tent bery good when we got nuffin else, sah," he remonstrated ; " but house better to-night. See big clouds yonder ? Sure rain 'fore mornin'."

So into the village of palm-thatched houses, sheltered

under great, spreading banana, guava, and mango trees, they rode ; black faces looking at them on every side, though with less curiosity than would have been displayed in any other country village ; for of the few travellers who come to Hayti all go to Sans Souci and the citadel, so that the people of Milot are more acquainted with the appearance of strangers than any others outside the seaport towns.

The schoolmaster proved to be a perfectly black man, but speaking pure French. He put his house at the disposal of the visitors with a courtesy which left nothing to be desired—in that respect at least, though much might have been desired in others. Although the best in the village, it was little more than a hut ; and it was necessary, in order to secure a night's rest, to hang the hammocks they had wisely brought.

They were repaid, however, for any discomfort, not only by the fact that the rain came down in pouring torrents, from which their tent would have proved but an ineffectual shelter, but also by the discovery that their host was an educated and intelligent man, from whom it was possible to obtain much information. He spoke with reserve upon the present condition and government of Hayti, nor did they press him to expand upon that point ; but of the past, of the recollections and traditions still existing in this spot of the reign of the black King Christophe, he talked freely and interestingly. It was Atherton who presently made a diversion of topic.

"These mountains ought to contain mineral wealth," he remarked, "since the mountains of Santo Domingo near by are known to abound in it. Has nothing of the kind ever been discovered ?"

The man shook his head. "I think not, Monsieur," he replied. "Had there been any mines, Christophe would have had them worked, though it had been necessary to place an overseer over every miner. You know how he forced the people to cultivate the sugar estates. *Ma foi!* they had never to work so hard in the days of the old proprietors."

"But Christophe probably possessed no knowledge of mines," Atherton answered. "I agree with you that he would certainly have had them worked, had he known of their existence. I am aware that this is not supposed to be a gold country; but there are other minerals besides gold, some of which it is more than likely these mountains contain."

"It may be so, Monsieur. I do not know. No one, to my knowledge, has ever looked for them."

"I have thought of looking as we go up into the mountains to visit the citadel. It is not likely that any one would object?"

"I do not see why any one should object, Monsieur," was the guarded reply. "But our people are inclined to be suspicious of strangers ; and you know that even if you found a mine it would not be possible for you to own it."

"I am aware of that, and should not expect to profit by any discovery I made. My curiosity is purely scientific, and, of course, I shall not allow it to lead me very far. But these mountains offer a most interesting field for exploration——"

"Why do you talk in this manner?" interrupted De Marsillac, speaking in English. "Do you really think of wasting time on this pretence?"

"Be more guarded," replied Atherton quietly. "One never knows how much of a language presumably unknown might be understood. I thought I explained to you the object I have in this—prospecting."

"But I thought it was to be done after—after——"

"We had accomplished our purpose? You are right. But it may be well to pick up a few stones in these mountains, if we can do so without too much delay."

"Ah, pray let there be no delay! The pre—the prospecting is not worth delay."

"I promise you that the delay, if any, shall be so little that even your impatience will be able to bear it for the sake of the end in view ; and that end I will explain to you more fully to-morrow."

After the rain of the night, the morning was of the most exquisite freshness and beauty, when the two friends—having presented their permit to visit the citadel to the general commanding the station, who graciously intimated that they might proceed—went to view the ruined palace of Sans Souci.

Imposing as it appeared from afar, they were not prepared for the magnificence to which it testified in the grandeur and extent of the buildings, though shattered by earthquake and destroyed by time. Climbing the long flight of steps leading to the esplanade, they paused in amazement before the palace, still majestic in its architecture and its strength, notwithstanding that trees are growing amid its roofless chambers and fringing its broken archways ; still forming, as it stands in its superbly commanding situation, with the lovely valley at its feet and the noble heights of the great mountain range behind, a lasting monument of the wonderful and terrible man who erected it. Within, the different apartments connected with his story were pointed out to them : the throne-room where he held his court, while his trembling subjects knelt before him with averted faces ; the salons, once furnished with all the luxury of Europe and hung with costly tapestries ;

the chapel where—can it be possible he ever prayed?—and the room (now inaccessible from a falling stair) where he ended his life by his own hand when the downfall of his power had come. On the terrace stands the great *caimito*, or star-apple-tree, under which he was accustomed to hold audiences with his officers ; while all around are the ruins of buildings—stables, storehouses, arsenals, barracks, and other offices—indicative of the busy throng of life once called into existence here by a despotic will, and now pervaded by the silence of death.

"No description prepares one for it," said Atherton, as, forgetting the need for haste impressed upon them by their guides, they wandered over the wonderful place. "One must see it in order to believe that anything so amazing ever existed here."

"What superhuman energy he must have possessed, that terrible Christophe," said De Marsillac, "to have accomplished this and the erection of the fortress, of which one is told such marvels, in the space of fourteen years—for that, I believe, was the length of his reign !"

"And what a thirst for luxury and beauty, as well as power," added Atherton. "Here, in his ruined palace, let us at least say this for him : that he alone of the rulers of Hayti has done anything save destroy. Among them all Christophe alone strove to create—strove indeed with the ignorance and boundless cruelty of a savage, but with a fierce genius, an indomitable will, and a blind groping towards civilization, from which one cannot withhold a certain tribute of admiration. He seems to me something of a black Peter the Great—at least, the strong desire of each was the same : to raise a barbarous people at once to a state of civilization."

"The comparison is most unflattering to Peter the

Great," replied De Marsillac, " and I think most unde-
served by Christophe—but here comes George to remon-
strate again on our delay."

The guide was this time so pressing in his representa-
tions of the necessity for reaching the citadel before the
heat of the day that he succeeded in his object of drawing
them away from this place of beautiful desolation and
tragic memories, and starting without further delay upon
the ride to the fortress of La Ferrière.

Leaving Milot, their road, which soon became a mere
trail, led them into the heart of the giant hills, passing at
first through groves of wild coffee and banana trees ; then
into the marvellous forests which cover these great heights ;
along the bases and skirting the brinks of immense precipices ; growing steeper with every mile, but opening at
every turn such enchanting views of land and distant sea
that its difficulties and roughness were almost forgotten.
Wonderful tropical growths of tree and plant and vine
lined their way, and filled the deep green chasms far below
them, where waters—often unseen, then again flashing like
silver into sight—filled the solitude with their music ;
while over the broken masses of verdure-clad heights the
gaze passed to rest on fairy valleys, and then on the blue
plain stretching to the glittering azure of the bluer sea.

At the end of two hours they were thousands of feet
above that sea, far in the bosom of the mountains, remote
from all signs of human life, in a region full only of the
wildest grandeur and most infinite loveliness of Nature.
And as they went onward yet onward, upward yet upward,
their wonder grew at the thought that into these apparently inaccessible wilds, along this steep and difficult way, the
material for and ordnance of a fortress had been conveyed
by wretched, toiling men.

"If one could forget that, it would be possible to enjoy the beauty much more," De Marsillac said. "But I cannot banish from my mind the recollection of the unspeakable sufferings endured by the unhappy slaves of your black Peter the Great, as they dragged up these tremendous hills the stones and mighty guns of his citadel above."

"Poor devils!" said Atherton. "Dead as they are, one must pity them. But why think of these things since they affect you so much? You have the heart of a woman, my dear boy!"

"Do women alone compassionate suffering?" asked the other, turning away his face. But he said no more of the victims of the cruel king.

There was indeed scant opportunity for conversation, as they climbed the last and steepest ascent to the summit of the mountain—five thousand feet above the sea—which the famous fortress crowns, and saw its mighty walls at last towering above them.

Nearly a hundred feet in height, and from fifteen to twenty feet in thickness, these walls seem in their stupendous massiveness to form part of the rock on which they stand. Though rent in places by earthquake shocks, even the earthquake could not cast them down; and they still cover the entire peak of the mountain, rising abruptly from the very edge of its precipitous sides. Words fail to describe adequately this marvellous proof of what human effort can accomplish under the compulsion of a tyrant's will.

The custodian—an old and ragged negro—having been summoned, the visitors were admitted through a ponderous door into the grim darkness of the tower, whence a covered way led to the deep fosse, over which they crossed on a narrow plank (the drawbridge having disappeared) into the interior of the immense edifice. Once within, amazement became, if possible, even greater. Through gallery after gallery, filled with long rows of cannon, they threaded their way ; and as they looked at the great guns— heavy fifty-six and thirty-six pounders—which frowned through every porthole and guarded every approach, they were hardly able to believe the undoubted fact that these stupendous engines of destruction were conveyed to the spot by the unaided and almost incredible labor of man alone. Certainly no one seeing them, and regarding with awe the mighty walls built to receive them, can doubt the statement that at least thirty thousand human beings perished in the construction of this wonderful fortification.

As it was his intention to make this citadel a last and impregnable retreat in case of attack—especially from the French, whose return he always feared—Christophe accumulated within it vast stores of ammunition and also of treasure. In the magazines built for the first are still to be seen thousands of flints and balls ; while the accounts given of the immense quantity of gold, silver and precious articles found here after his death would seem fabulous were not the names on record of those who became rich from the plunder of the treasure-vaults of La Ferrière.

Into these vaults the two visitors were led ; and it was with the strange sensation of realizing a fairy tale that they saw the great old chests, clamped and bound with iron, which had contained the tyrant's treasures ; their locks broken and their lids wrenched off, just as they were left by the plunderers who sacked the castle.

"It was a splendid looting," said Atherton, looking at his companion, as they stood—a strange group enough, in the fitful light of a torch which their guide carried—in the dark vault beside the empty chests. "Thirty millions of dollars are said to have been found here. What a com-

mentary on the wealth of the island, when one considers
the regal luxury in which Christophe lived and the vast ex-
penses he was constantly incurring !"

"How do you think he accumulated it ?" asked De
Marsillac.

" Primarily, no doubt, by appropriating the wealth of
the old proprietors, of which, in the form of money, there
must have been an immense amount ; and, secondarily,
from the labors of the people whom he forced to cultivate
the sugar estates by the most cruel methods.   But whether
by the one means or the other, these chests, with their
story of hidden riches, have a suggestion for us.   Do you
know what it is ?"

" Not a suggestion of robbery, I hope ?"

" No.   And not a suggestion, either, so much as an assurance that there is nothing improbable in the belief that
one of the rich proprietors of this rich island might readily
have had a very considerable amount of solid cash in hand
to secrete when surprised by the insurrection.   Now we
will see the empty tomb of the great savage who built this
marvellous monument for himself ; and then go up on the
walls for the view, which must be glorious."

<hr>

CHAPTER X.

It is doubtful if the earth can show anything more beautiful than the view from the walls of the fortress of La
Ferrière.   Magnificent in extent—for the lofty mountain
dominates all the northern portion of the island—it is also
of surpassing loveliness, from the blending of land and sea
in the vast picture, and the exquisite tints with which Na-

ture robes herself in these enchanted regions. Immediately around, and far as the gaze can sweep eastward, are mountains and yet again mountains, broken, tossed, confused ; green near by, since covered to their summits with dense tropical verdure, but melting afar into the most ethereal azure. Among them lie valleys so completely enclosed that it seems as if no outlet were possible from them ; and deep gorges where the foot of man has rarely, if ever, penetrated through the luxuriance of vegetation which fills them. Clouds abound, enveloping the highest peaks in soft white masses, sun-kissed to dazzling splendor ; piled rampart-like behind others, and yet again moving majestically across the sky, and turning some great mountainside to darkest purple with their shadows. But, noble as are the forms and masses of the immense furrowed heights, and heavenly as are the tints in which they drape themselves as they recede, they cannot detain the gaze from the wide scene northward—the long sweep of the magical blue plain to the city and bay of the Cape, and the boundless expanse of shining ocean beyond, flashing to the horizon. On the left the isle of Tortuga, that old home of the buccaneers, rises picturesquely out of the waters which surround it ; while to the right the lovely Bay of Manzanilla lies ; and farther still the dream-like heights of Monte-Christo stand between a yet more dream-like sea and sky.

And of the air which comes to these high battlements, fresh with the salt freshness of the sea, fraught with the thousand perfumes of the odorous land, and pure as the heaven into which it blows, what words can speak ! It is delightful and invigorating as an elixir of life ; and Atherton, while expanding his lungs with it, said to himself that there was healing in it for any ill that mortal frame could know ; and that, whether by accident or design, he had been red to the land of all lands which suited him best. Again and yet again, gazing over its outspread beauty and thinking of its untold fertility, he marvelled at the fate which had befallen this enchanting island, so rich in all that Nature can give in her most prodigal mood.

"One would like to turn buccaneer and reconquer it," he said ; and De Marsillac smiled.

"I have been thinking that," he answered ; "and wishing that we were in the robust days when it would have been done without a moment's hesitation."

"As far as that goes, these days are quite sufficiently robust," said Atherton. "We have not developed any very high conscience with regard to the rights of savages to occupy a land they cannot develop—as witness the march of Europeans into Africa. Yet here is a land more beautiful, more fruitful than any part of the Dark Continent, left in the hands of absolute savages, because, forsooth ! the nations are like watch-dogs :

" ' . . . snarling at each other's heels.' "

"Absolute savages indeed !" said the other. "I wonder, by the bye, if this terrible precipice down which we are gazing is what was called ' the Grand Boucan ' because of the vast number of wretched creatures whom Christophe had hurled over it ? That was one of his favorite modes of execution, you know."

"What an awful pleasantry—the Grand Boucan !" observed Atherton. "Yes, I fancy this must be the place ; for, sheer and steep as the mountain sides are all around, this is the most sheer descent of all. A man flung from this wall would fall at least a thousand feet—probably more."

"Perhaps the bones of his innumerable victims are

whitening down there yet," said the boy, gazing as if fascinated into the abyss. Then suddenly he looked away, very pale. " Does it not make you dizzy and faint to gaze from such a height ?" he asked his companion.

The latter smiled. " No," he replied. " I have tested my head too often in mountain-climbing. Two years ago I ascended the Matterhorn. That settles once for all what kind of a head one has ; for if it fails *there* one does not return to tell the tale."

" But why risk your life on the steadiness of your head —merely to climb a mountain ?"

" Ah ! that is a question which cannot be answered to the satisfaction of anybody who does not know the fascination of such climbing and such danger. As for me, 1 am fond of exploring in all forms ; and if I am doomed to be an idler, I shall become a wanderer and endeavor to leave no spot of the globe unseen. Will you wander with me ? It is thanks to you that I am here to-day ; and I think— in fact, I am sure—that we should make good comrades."

The boy laughed. " You forget," he said, " that I am the man of the family at home. They could not do without me."

" I did forget that important fact," replied Atherton ; " although you have told me of it before. But when you have arranged the affair of Mademoiselle Diane, there will be nothing to detain you longer."

" On the contrary, there will be everything. I attend to the plantation ; I see to all matters of business ; I—in short, I am *necessary* to them."

" Happy boy ! To be necessary to anybody is a great privilege ; but when it is to an entire family of charming women, the privilege becomes immense."

" You are laughing at me," said the other simply.

"You think I exaggerate my own importance ; and it is not strange you should think so, since I look—since I am so young. But they would all tell you the same thing at home. And now isn't it time we were starting back ? We have seen all the castle ; and if we are to reach Millefleurs before night——"

Atherton glanced around. The group of their attendants were at some distance, evidently listening while the old custodian dilated, as his gestures showed, upon the Grand Boucan ; and the Jamaica guide translated his words for the benefit of the Englishman, whose countenance was a study of disgust and horror. The two were thus left quite alone together on the high wall of this strange citadel, amid the solitary hills.

"We will start soon," Atherton then answered. "But first let me explain to you more fully than it seems I have yet explained why I think the pretence of looking for minerals necessary. Stones, even if they possess no real value, are heavy. If I fill a couple of sacks, which I have taken the precaution to bring, with specimens picked up in these hills, do you not understand that it is in order to empty them out at Millefleurs—should we find what we hope for —and substitute for them the gold which we could not otherwise carry without rousing suspicion ?"

"You have thought of everything," said the boy ; "and I am most ungrateful to find any fault. Of course you are right, and I understand now why you talked of minerals to the schoolmaster at Milot last night."

"Believe me, we cannot take too many precautions to avoid any risk of suspicion. If it were once known that we were engaged in raising hidden treasure, do you think you would be allowed to retain even the least part of it ? And now, taking all these things into consideration, can you support with philosophy the thought of spending another night in Milot should we reach there late, and not returning to Millefleurs until to-morrow?"

"If I must, why"—with a sigh—"I can. But is it really necessary? Can you not merely pause on our way down long enough to pick up some stones? I suppose any stones will do."

" I should prefer some containing mineral in observable quantity, if possible ; for I have Mr. Hoffman to consider as well as the guide. These hills are certain to contain deposits of one kind or another."

" Well"—with another sigh—" you must do what you think best, and I will try to be patient. But it will be rather a joke upon us if we carry the stones to Millefleurs and do not find the gold."

"I have no doubt of finding the gold ; but whether I had doubt or not, I should carry the stones," Atherton answered. "A wise general does not wait to load his guns until he is in the presence of the enemy. Now, one last look over this scene of Paradise, and then *allons!*"

*　　*　　*　　*　　*

It was an hour later, as they were descending the steep road along which they had ascended not more laboriously, that Atherton, who was riding in front of the cavalcade, suddenly called a halt by stopping his own horse.

" George," he said, turning to address the guide, " I see another trail here leading off from ours. Do you know anything about it?"

" No, sah, nuffin," George answered decidedly. " Neber been anywheres here 'cept to de citadel."

" Where do you suppose this probably leads?"

" Ober de mountain to some valley, sah, where dere's a

village. Can't lead nowheres else. Mus' be pretty far off, too," he added.

"Well, I am not interested in its ultimate destination, but I am going to follow it for a short distance; for I think it goes deeper into the hills than ours."

"Lord, sah!" remonstrated the startled George. "Ain't we deep 'nough in de hills now? Better stick to de road; might git los' in all dis wildness."

"How can we possibly get lost if we keep the trail? All we shall need to do when we want to return is to retrace our steps. Gilbert, have you the prospecting tools ready?"

"Yes, sir, all ready," replied Gilbert.

"Then follow me, all of you. Henri, you have no fear of being lost, I suppose? I merely want to take a look at those hills over yonder."

"Not the least fear," De Marsillac said readily and truthfully enough; for Atherton's last words to him as they mounted beneath the castle walls had been : "It will not do to find my mineral deposit immediately *on the road*. That, you know, would be too easily verified. So don't be surprised if I lead you into some less accessible spot."

The less accessible spot was to be sought now; and, with an earnest hope that this trying but indispensable pretence might soon be over, the boy turned his horse into the scarcely perceptible trail which Atherton's keen glance had perceived. Branching abruptly from their road, it wound off around the shoulder of the mountain in a southeast-wardly direction, and speedily plunged into an even wilder region than any they had yet seen. Giant heights, forest clad to their crests, enclosed them; deep green gorges opened below; and, save for the path they were following, there was not a token of man's presence in all the solitude of Nature.

Continuing to wind around the hills rather than descend abruptly like the road they had left, the trail led them on until it finally dipped to cross the mouth of a deep, narrow ravine, through which a hidden stream flowed with much sweet music of falling, tumbling, rushing water. And here Atherton halted again.

"I can find no better place than this," he said to De Marsillac, who was near him. "In such cañons one looks for minerals, because the erosions of the water have through long ages laid bare the secrets of the rocks. Then dismounting, "Gilbert, give me my hammer."

"Shall I come with you, Mr. Atherton?" asked the man, as, dismounting in turn, he brought the implement desired.

"Yes. Bring a pick and the sacks. George, you will stay here with the horses. Henri, what are you about?"

"Coming with you, of course," the person addressed answered, as he swung himself out of the saddle. "Do you think I have no spirit of an explorer?"

Atherton laughed.

"You can't be of the least service," he said; "and you'll find it very hard work to break through this undergrowth. But come along if you like. We shall follow up the stream."

Following the stream proved to be difficult work, so dense was the growth along its banks; while overhead branches and foliage intertwined so closely that sunlight was entirely excluded, and a dim, green twilight reigned. The soil was covered with a thick tangle of ferns, moss, and an immense variety of plants for which the strangers knew no name; interlacing vines leaped from tree to tree, and luxuriant parasites filled every open space; while through this exquisite world of greenery the flashing water came in crystal pools, which mirrored the feathery tendrils and gorgeous blossoms drooping above them.

Although taking little interest in the search for minerals, save that of wishing it well over, De Marsillac was struck by the manner in which Atherton seemed bent upon thoroughly carrying out the form of seeking. Wherever along the banks of the stream the least outcropping of rock appeared through the luxuriant vegetation, he paused to examine it; and after one or two of these pauses seemed to become as interested as if the search had been a reality instead of a pretence. At least so the observer said to himself, until at last, becoming weary of the struggle through the dense undergrowth, and of a tramp which seemed leading them farther and farther into the wildest recesses of the hills whose steeply towering sides rose above them, he ventured on a remonstrance.

"Don't you think," he said, as they paused for the fifth or sixth time where aqueous erosion had laid bare a ledge of rock on the side of the stream, "that this would serve your purpose without going farther?"

Atherton, who was bending over the spot, breaking off fragments of rock with the pick, looked up, somewhat flushed and breathless.

"Without going farther!" he repeated, and then he laughed. "A curious thing has happened. Sham has turned into earnest. I have found gold!"

"What! really?"

"Yes, really. Do you know it when you see it? Here is a piece of ore showing free gold." He drew from the outside pocket of his coat a small fragment of quartz, and pointed to one or two tiny spots upon it. "This," he said, "is what miners call 'float'—brought down the stream from a vein above. As certainly as we stand here, my dear boy, there is a mine—a genuine mine—of gold in these hills."

"It is very strange that you should have chanced upon the signs of it," said De Marsillac, looking with wonder at the bit of ore which told so much. "But you are not going to search for the mine itself, are you?" he added presently. "*It* does not concern us."

"It concerns us to have something genuine to show for our prospecting, and something astonishing too. Gold has never, I think, been found before in these Haytian mountains. Consequently, this is an immensely interesting find; and you must bear with me while I follow it up."

"Will it be of value—to you?"

"To me—no, nor probably to any one else. But you don't consider scientific curiosity. I must find where this float has come from."

Further remonstrance would have been both useless and ungracious. The boy sighed—partly from weariness, partly from longing to turn his face towards Millefleurs—but made no remark; and followed the toilsome ascent of the gorge, when the speaker, returning the pick to Gilbert, went on.

It was perhaps unfortunate, at least De Marsillac thought so, that Atherton's interest was stimulated by finding other bits of float, as they followed the stream, which led them with every step higher as well as deeper among the hills; for the spirit of a prospector was now thoroughly aroused in him, and none the less because cupidity lent no zest to it. The find could be, as he had already remarked, of no value to him; nevertheless, his interest was intensely excited in tracing out this secret of Nature, which, hidden from the eyes of other men for centuries, was now revealed to his.

So on, still on they went, Atherton growing more absorbed as the scent, in hunting phrase, grew warmer ; and De Marsillac more fatigued from the double labor of forcing a way through the undergrowth and of climbing, for they were now ascending the mountain which headed the gorge.

And here—as Atherton knew must be the case—he found at last that which he sought. Cut by the action of the stream in its downward course, the vein from which the float had come was revealed on either bank—a distinctly marked strata of unmistakable gold-bearing quartz.

Atherton uttered an exclamation as exultant as if he had been a Colorado miner seeking his fortune, when he saw the ledge of stream-washed and decomposed rock.

"Eureka !" he cried. "I knew it must be here. Henri, we have found the mine !"

CHAPTER XI.

De Marsillac was not in a condition to join in Atherton's exultation. He was, in fact, completely exhausted. The determination not to acknowledge weariness had made him follow resolutely on the long, fatiguing tramp and climb ; but it afforded him no voice now with which to reply to his companion's words. He could only lean against a tree breathless, with his heart beating painfully.

"Better sit down, sir," said Gilbert, who, not so absorbed as his master, saw and pitied the boy's plight. "You look quite done up. It's been tough work getting here."

"I forgot you were not an old mountaineer like myself," said Atherton, glancing round ; "or I shouldn't have pressed on so fast. Gilbert, haven't you anything to give him?"

"I don't need anything," the boy said, with pale lips. "I'm only—a little out of breath. I'll be all right in a few minutes."

"This'll put you right quicker, sir," said Gilbert, producing a pocket-flask. "I always carries something of the kind on such hexpeditions. One never knows what'll 'appen, 'specially in a country as wild as this—for wilder *I've* never seen."

De Marsillac did not refuse the draught offered him, and soon felt the benefit of it, so that he was able to move forward and examine the find.

"And this is a gold mine!" he said, looking at the seam of quartz from which Atherton was knocking fragments.

"This is a gold mine!" the other replied, with the note of triumph still in his voice. "Isn't it a remarkable thing that I should have found that piece of float, which turned pretence into reality? Now, if this were only in any other country, you might take from here a fortune greater than the one your ancestor lost."

"But, since no white man can own property in Hayti, it can really be of no benefit to us."

"Except to serve our special purpose ; and to give me the opportunity to indulge in a little vanity, since I have had eyes where every one else has been blind."

"But, after all, what could ignorant negroes know——"

"Bah! who talks of ignorant negroes? Where were the eyes of the buccaneers, who were keen enough for gold when they found it in other forms? Where were the eyes of the French colonists—of your own Breton ancestor, Monsieur Henri? As for the Spaniards, they were sent by the natives into the mountains eastward of this, so they were not to blame. But I know now what I have always suspected—that the gold crown which the cacique wore who received Columbus so kindly when he was shipwrecked at the Cape, came from a spot nearer home than that shrewd gentleman cared to admit."

" Do you think it came from this spot ?"

" From this identical vein ? Possibly not. But where there is one gold vein there are others. Gilbert, bring the pick and knock off as much of this ore as possible. I wish now that I had brought George along, but it was necessary to leave some one with the horses."

" You might have left me," said the boy. " I am not of much use here."

" We'll make you of use in a moment. You shall fill the sacks."

But before filling the sacks it was necessary to have the wherewithal to fill them ; and, since this was lacking until the pick—now sending through the forest the sharp and unaccustomed click of metal ringing upon rock—had done its work, the boy sat down and watched with a strange sense of unreality the scene before him.

Was it a dream from which he should presently wake, or was he really here, on this high mountain-side of Hispaniola, the vast tropical forest stretching below like a green sea, and all around the silent majesty of untrodden heights ; while two men, whom three weeks before he had never seen, were digging at his feet for the gold which had remained undiscovered by Spaniard, Frenchman, or African, though known, beyond doubt, to the original possessors of the island ? If a dream, it was certainly a fantastic one, and what would be its end ? He looked at Atherton. What strange chance or fate was it which had brought across his path this man, who seemed so quiet, yet was in fact so dominating, as his whole conduct of this matter proved? The situation seemed too unreal to be anything but a dream ; and yet——

"Now, Henri"—it was Atherton's voice breaking on his reverie—"here is your work.   Come and fill the sacks with this ore."

"Beg pardon, Mr. Atherton !"—Gilbert stood up, exhausted from his prolonged and unaccustomed labor—"but how much of this rock do you want knocked off ?"

Atherton measured with his eye the pile collected.   "Almost as much again, I suppose," he said.   "Why do you ask ?   Are you done up ?"

"Pretty much, sir—not being used to this sort of work."

"It is rather hard to be turned from a valet into a miner at a moment's notice," said Atherton good-humoredly. "But your recommendation to me has always been that you were not an ordinary valet.   You've roughed it with me before this."

"Very true, sir ; but not quite in the line of the present work.   As soon as I've rested a bit, though, I'll be ready to go on."

"I don't think," continued Atherton reflectively, looking from the man to the considerable pile of ore—accumulated so soon because the surface rock was decomposed and therefore easily broken—"that you'll be able to carry much more than that amount down the gorge.   You had, therefore, better fill one sack and take it down ; remain with the horses, and send the guide up to fill and take down the other."

The prospect of being relieved from miner's duty was plainly very agreeable to Gilbert.   He obeyed with alacrity, filled the sack, threw it over his shoulder, and, staggering somewhat under its weight, disappeared in the thick undergrowth as he made his way down the hillside. They heard for some time the sound of his descent, marked by the sharp crack of breaking boughs ; then silence settled again over the wide, wild solitude of gorge and mountains.

" It will be some time before he gets down to the trail and the other fellow gets up here," said Atherton, as if struck with a sudden thought. " I'll employ the time in following this vein along the mountain, for it must have outcroppings. It would be very interesting if I should discover some trace of ancient work. Are you sufficiently rested to come with me ?" he asked his companion.

" Certainly," was the quick reply. " Do you think I am so lacking in strength that a mere climb could knock me out, except for a few minutes ?"

" Well, I have seen more apparent Samsons," remarked Atherton with a smile ; " although no doubt you make up in pluck and endurance what you lack in muscular strength. Come along, then. But put that flask lying there on the bank in your pocket : you may need it again."

" That is not at all likely," ignoring with a somewhat lofty air the flask, which Gilbert had neglected to replace in his own pocket.

" Then *I* shall take it ; for I am not at all ashamed to say that it is within the limit of possibility that I might need it myself. Anybody is likely to be knocked out by a steep and difficult climb."

De Marsillac made no rejoinder, but followed the speaker as he struck off from the stream in a slanting direction up the mountain ; explaining as he did so that this would likely be the course of the vein.

The result justified his anticipation ; for now again he discovered outcroppings which would have been hidden from eyes less keen than his own. The climb was very steep, the growth not quite so dense as along the stream, but quite sufficiently so to make passage through it exceedingly fatiguing. Very little interested in tracing the course of a vein, however rich in precious metal, which could be of no possible advantage to any human creature in whom he felt the least concern, the boy beguiled the ascent by admiration of the marvellous wealth of verdure around them. Beautiful tree-ferns—loveliest of all tropical products, except the royal palm—met the eye on all sides ; together with such effects of leaf and vine and flower, and such variety of orchids, as might have driven a botanist wild. But presently he observed a new and singular effect —delicate, fairy-like wreaths of mist creeping among the trees and enhancing the beauty of the scene. So exquisite were these trailing, lace-like veils that it was not until they suddenly thickened that he awakened to a sense of what they were, and called to Atherton, who, some distance in advance, had eyes only for his mineral search :

"A cloud is settling over us. Had we not better return ?"

"A cloud !" repeated Atherton, starting up from his examination and glancing around. "By Jove, yes !—one of those you admired so much from the citadel, perhaps. It seems very light—a mere vapor ; but we must retrace our steps at once, lest it should grow more dense and make return difficult."

They turned ; but nobody who has ever watched the rapidity with which a cloud gathers about a mountain-top, or who has ever had the misfortune to be caught in one, will be surprised to learn that in five minutes they were standing still, wrapped in thick white mist, and unable to tell in what direction their path lay.

"Here is a nuisance !" said Atherton. "But no doubt

the cloud will lift shortly, so that we can get our bearings.
It is better to wait, although I am pretty certain our way
is in this direction."

" I am certain of nothing," answered the boy, " except
that it is down-hill."

They waited for what seemed to them an interminable
time, but was in reality not more than ten or fifteen minutes, when, the increasing density of the cloud proving
that it had settled to remain, Atherton decided to proceed.

" Get lost ?" he observed, in reply to a suggestion of his
companion. " There is no danger of that. Even if we
don't keep exactly the right direction for the place we left,
a down-hill course will take us out of the cloud, and then
we can get our bearings. Waiting here is mere waste of
time."

He started off with energy. But a tropical forest and
an enwrapping cloud are likely to exercise a restraining influence upon the greatest energy. To break through dense
undergrowth when able to perceive surroundings, and know
in some degree at least what direction is being followed, is
a rather confusing process ; but when a white mist shrouds
every object at more than a yard's distance from sight, it
becomes more bewildering than can be expressed. Atherton very soon relinquished all idea of anything except preserving such a downward course as would soonest take
them out of the cloud ; but, mindful of the dangers of unseen precipices and hidden pitfalls, he found it necessary to
proceed with caution—which meant with a slowness really
exasperating, in view of the fact that the day was far advanced towards sunset. That the quick night of the tropics
should descend upon them before they reached the spot
from which they had wandered was, he knew, their only
danger ; and, blaming himself silently but severely for hav-

ing been led away by the interest of his find, he crashed on through the thick vegetation, obliged constantly to pause and turn aside from some more than usually impenetrable mass of giant parasites, until—all sense of even general direction altogether lost—they at last emerged from the enshrouding mist, to find themselves on the mountain-side, with a vast world of verdure spreading around them, and not a sign or token to tell in what direction lay the gorge which they had ascended.

De Marsillac looked at Atherton. "Have you any idea where we are?" he asked.

"Oh, yes!" was the reply with well-assumed confidence. "I have a very clear idea that we are on the side of the mountain where we have been all the time, and that our course to reach the stream which will guide us out of this wilderness is northwest."

"And which direction is northwest?"

A simple question—a question most easily answered by the aid of a compass or of the sun—but terribly hard to answer when lacking both in a strange country. Atherton looked around, and, experienced woodsman as he was, his heart sank. Shut in as they were by forest, with the sun sunk out of sight behind the mountains, and twilight— such short-lived twilight!—already falling, what hope had he of telling what was north, south, east, or west?

"I am afraid," he replied after a moment, "that I have somewhat lost my orientation, as the French say. But we may be very near our place—it is hard to tell in such thick woods—so I'll try what a shout or two will do. If the guide has come up and is anywhere within sound of my voice, he'll answer."

He shouted; and it is safe to say that if the doctors who were accountable for his presence here had heard him, they would not have thought there was much the matter with his lungs. Shout after shout he uttered, making the forest ring, waking echoes from the hillsides, and rousing many strange birds to answer with shrill cries. But no human voice replied. Pausing, he and De Marsillac strained their ears to listen ; but after the mocking echoes ceased, silence fell as before. Then the two looked again at each other and Atherton smiled.

"Plainly, that rascal has not come up yet," he said. "Well, it is impossible that we can remain here until night falls, waiting for him to arrive and answer us. Failing anything else, I must follow my own judgment of what our course should be. We will go this way."

And, followed by the boy, he started off.

CHAPTER XII.

AN hour later, with night fallen upon them, in the deep heart of a forest so dense that they were in almost absolute darkness, worn out with stumbling over invisible vines and laboriously breaking a way through obstructing undergrowth, the two wanderers paused, to look their situation, if they could not look each other, in the face.

"We are lost !" said Atherton. It was the first time he had acknowledged the fact, which had been abundantly clear for some time. "I am ashamed of myself as a woodsman ; but when we came out of that infernal cloud, I must have turned in exactly the wrong direction, so that there is no means of telling where we are now."

"What can we do ?" asked De Marsillac. He had kept up bravely, following the guidance of Atherton in their laborious tramp through the wilderness in which they were plunged ; but it was now evident from his voice that he was quite overcome with weariness.

"I am afraid there is nothing we can do except spend the night in the woods," Atherton answered. "And if we can find an open space, we had better remain quiet. As soon as the sun rises I shall know in what direction to strike out. But now we know nothing of our whereabouts, and are surrounded by hidden perils which make movement very unsafe."

"Then," suggested the boy, "had we not better stay where we are than wander farther, looking for an open space which is difficult to find ?"

"No ; because later in the night there is a moon, and when it rises I should like to be able to see something of our surroundings. Here we can see nothing. If we could manage to climb a little higher—but I can tell from your voice that you are used up."

"Oh, no !" was the prompt reply, while into the voice rushed the rallied energy of will. "If you think it best, I am ready to go on."

"Be sure, then, to follow me closely and cautiously ; for a fall over some precipice would form a tragical termination to our adventure."

Onward then again, and this time also upward, increasing thereby the strain on heart and lungs. Atherton, accustomed to mountaineering and always a hardy climber, had very little idea how painfully his companion, with lips parted to breathe but never to complain, was laboring behind him. Now and again they paused ; but, finding the thick growth still all round them, Atherton again pushed on, sure only of one thing—that he was mounting upward. "And if I can only reach the crest of the ridge," he thought, "I *must* find clearer space."

So on, still on, breaking through boughs which swept their faces ; plunging waist-deep into beds of fern or broad-leaved plants ; slipping across wet moss ; falling over entangling vines ; and all the time unable to tell into what hidden pitfall the darkness might betray them.

Happily, in their wandering they had left behind the cloud which was the source of their trouble, and were now upon a different and somewhat lower portion of the ridge. At least Atherton judged that it must be lower—a gap between loftier heights—when, to his great relief, they presently emerged into a comparatively open space, which was evidently the summit ; for he at once perceived that he overlooked another world of dim, mountain forms towering against the sky, and deep valleys and gorges.

" We are on the top of the divide," he said ; " and can use our eyes again—which is something to be thankful for. This starlight seems quite brilliant after the darkness we have been groping our way through ; does it not ?"

But his companion was once more without power to reply. He sat down and made no effort to do more than recover his breath, of which a last bit of very steep climbing had almost entirely deprived him.

" My poor boy, you are completely exhausted !" exclaimed Atherton " Here ! take a good pull at this flask. It has been very trying work, especially the last climb. Now we will take things easy for a while. After all"—throwing himself upon the ground—" it is a good thing to be so tired that one is indifferent to everything except the mere privilege of resting."

" Resting is a good thing," said the other, who was sitting with his back and head reclined against the trunk of a palm ; " but I can't agree that it is good to be tired—so unspeakably tired ! If we had had another hundred yards to climb, I fear I should have dropped in my tracks."

"Why didn't you say so and call a halt? There is no wisdom in trying to force one's self to exertion beyond a certain point, and no disgrace in acknowledging fatigue."

"If one has not very much strength, one must make up for it with pluck," said the boy. "Did you not say so yourself? And there are few things one cannot force one's self to do if one tries. I have always believed that. Weakness is often only another name for giving way."

"I am prepared to testify that it is not an infirmity of yours," observed Atherton. "There are not many men of double your physical strength who would have followed me without protest or complaint as you have during the last two or three hours."

There was a moment's silence. Praise—honest praise—is sweet to every child of man ; and possibly those few words, simply and sincerely spoken, repaid the listener for all he had endured. But he did not answer them · only after a moment said :

"I think my predominant thought as I toiled up the hill was what a fool I had been ever to wish for adventures and fancy I should enjoy them. If this is a specimen adventure, I shall be satisfied hereafter to walk in commonplace paths."

"You think so now ; but if you have the real love of adventure, you will feel differently when you are once housed and fed. Adventures are often more enjoyed in retrospect than at the time of their occurrence. I grant, however, that one must have a strong physique to enjoy them thoroughly."

"And yet you——"

"Have not a strong physique, you would say ? I believe that is a mistake. Did I climb this mountain like a man who has anything the matter with him ?"

" You certainly did not. But are you not afraid of the exposure, if we must spend the night here ?"

" I am afraid of nothing—for myself. For you, however, I am exceedingly concerned. Such exposure is new to you, though not to me ; and if there were any possible means of finding or making a shelter——"

" But you know there is none. And why should I suffer more than you ? I am young, I am healthy ; and if the air on this summit is a little chilly, how fresh it is, and what delightful odors come to us from the forests and gorges below !"

It is indeed impossible to conceive anything more delicious than the sylvan fragrance which night draws forth from these tropical forests, the wild, sweet freshness of growing things, which is carried by the land-breeze far out to sea, to suggest to the voyagers on some passing ship— strangely mingled with the musical wash of waves against the vessel's side—pictures of great, serrated, forest-clad, cloud-swept heights ; and of deep green gorges, through which clear streams flow between banks where vegetation runs riot in unspeakable luxuriance, and the air is heavy with countless aromatic odors of blossom and leaf.

" They are delightful," Atherton agreed ; " but I should appreciate an odor of food much more just now. Heavens, how hungry I am, now that I have time to think of it !"

The boy sighed : nature with him, too, clamored for support. " It is best not to think of what we can't possibly get," he remarked practically. " We will have to tighten our belts like Indians. And you can smoke. That is said to deaden the pangs of hunger."

" And what will you do ?"

"Oh, I will inhale some of your smoke ; or, better yet, I will sleep ! I am very tired ; and, you know, ' *qui dort dine.*' "

" I wish I did know it ; for, in that case, I should soon be sleeping myself. But as it is, I will light a cigar and wait for the moon. She ought to appear very soon now."

" I fear it is not so late as you think ; for the hour of her rising is quite late. And when she comes, what can she show us more than we see now—mountains and trackless forests ?"

" Well, that remains to be seen. At all events, she is our only hope, until the sun appears."

Then for a time there was little more conversation. The boy, with his head leaning against the trunk of a royal palm, fell asleep, completely worn out by the exertions of the day. Atherton sat, silently smoking, and anathematizing the folly which had placed them in this exceedingly uncomfortable if not dangerous situation, while an hour or two wore away. It must have been at least ten o'clock before the moon, with a considerable slice taken from her waning disk, rose over the eastern mountains and flooded the whole wide scene with silver radiance. Nothing more wildly beautiful could be imagined. But Atherton was hardly in a mood to appreciate the magnificence of the picture, as his glance swept in every direction, eagerly seeking some clue to guide them out of the wilderness which surrounded them, and sought in vain. On every side towered great mountains, their mighty flanks clothed with impenetrable forests ; the moonlight falling upon their furrowed sides, but failing to pierce the deep cañons at their base ; and all wrapped as with a mantle in the majestic calm, the inexpressible solitude only to be seen and felt in remote, untrodden wilds.

Over the prospect, on the side of the ridge from which he had ascended, Atherton gazed in despair, and then turned his observation to the country on the other side. This in its general features was much the same, only he perceived that immediately below them instead of a ravine there was a valley—one of those spaces, fruitful and well-watered, which abound even in the recesses of the great heights. Hope suggested to him that there might be a village, or at least a hamlet, here ; for he remembered the trail branching off from the road to La Ferrière, which they had followed, and which the guide had said led, no doubt, to some village among the hills. Might not the village be here below them ? And if so, what would be easier than to obtain a guide there ; or, even without one, to follow the trail until it led them back to where they had left their horses ? The moon had not yet risen high enough to illumine the valley, which, being on the western side of the ridge, was in deep shadow ; but Atherton strained his vision in the attempt to pierce the obscurity sufficiently to tell if there were any signs of human habitation within its borders.

The cabins of these villages are, however, so insignificant and nestle so closely under the spreading shade of mango, banana, and palm trees, by which they are always surrounded, that to distinguish them at any distance even in daytime is difficult. It was not strange, therefore, that he failed to discern any such sign as he sought ; and he had resigned himself to waiting for the advent of day, when suddenly he perceived the most unmistakable of all the tokens by which man indicates his presence—a light.

There could be no doubt of it. A mere point in the distance, it still shone with a steady glow out of the obscurity which clothed the valley ; such a light as streams from the habitation of man alone, and spoke eloquently to the weary wanderers of the possibility of obtaining the food, shelter, and guidance they needed.

Atherton did not hesitate a moment after the friendly gleam had met his eye ; but walked over to where his companion still slumbered, and, laying a hand on the lad's shoulder, shook him.

" What is it ?" asked the latter, opening his eyes quickly, for the slumber cannot be very profound that is taken in a sitting posture, with no softer pillow than the trunk of a palm.

" A light !" replied Atherton. " A beacon to guide us out of this wretched situation. Evidently there is some inhabitant, or perhaps a village, in the valley below us, and we are going there at once."

" Are we ?" said the boy, rising to his feet. " It seems to me we would do better to remain here until morning. I dread plunging into the deep woods again."

" Nonsense !" answered Atherton vigorously. " Think of obtaining something to eat, not to speak of a better place to rest than this mountain-top !"

" But the woods ! Think how dark they are and how tangled ; and how certain we shall be to lose our direction as soon as we are in them again."

" We shall not lose our direction. I have the points of the compass clearly in my mind now."

" *Eh bien,*" said the boy, shrugging his shoulders in his French fashion ; "lead on. But I am certain you will wish yourself back before you have gone very far."

" And I am certain I shall not, whatever you may do," Atherton answered, as he again took the lead, and set off at a brisk pace down the mountain-side.

Facilis descensus held good here as elsewhere. They had less fatigue than in ascending, and went down at a more rapid rate ; but hardly with less difficulty, as far as breaking their way through the undergrowth was concerned. Into these dense shades sunlight can scarcely penetrate ; and the moon's pale rays, even had they not been on the shaded side of the mountain, would have had little power to pierce the thick canopy of foliage under which they plunged. Guiding himself, therefore, more by touch than by sight, Atherton crashed along, sending back now and then a brief warning or direction to the boy following him ; trusting that he was keeping his general direction, but certain of nothing in these bewildering shades. It was breathless work ; but after an hour they found themselves on level ground, and emerged into a valley encircled by giant heights, and looking an ideal abode of peace and Arcadian happiness, as its cluster of palm-thatched huts lay under the broad shadow of fruit groves by the side of a clear, babbling stream.

CHAPTER XIII.

" Now," observed Atherton, as they paused in momentary admiration of this smiling spot, " are we not more than repaid for the labor that it has cost us to reach here ?"

" Before answering that," said his companion, " we will see what kind of reception we meet. You know what Mr. Hoffman told us of the dislike and suspicion with which white people are regarded in these places."

" Oh, a fig for dislike and suspicion, if they give us food and shelter !" Atherton returned. " We will select the principal house for our application, and I have no fear of the result. Come !—only a few steps farther, and our labors for the night are over."

Following a path along the margin of the stream, they approached the shade-embowered hamlet, which still seemed wrapped in deep repose until they were within a very short distance of it.   Then suddenly on the still night air there rose the sound of singing—a weird, monotonous chanting of many voices, that evidently issued from a building which they were immediately approaching : a long, low, palm-thatched edifice of wood.

Atherton paused.   Something in the character of the sound recalled to his memory all that he had heard of Vaudoux meetings—how they are held at dead of night, generally in remote spots where no eye of the uninitiated can behold them, and where any stranger who should present himself would run the utmost risk.   What could this strange singing indicate but some such gathering?   And if so, it behooved them to be cautious.   He looked at his companion, who had paused also.

" I think," he said, " that it will be well to ascertain what this means before we allow our presence to be known."

" If we were at home," replied the boy, " I should know very well what it means.   I should say that it was a negro religious meeting, and that they would soon begin to shout."

" But since we are in Hayti," said Atherton, " there is danger that it may be a religious meeting of another kind. It may be one of the Vaudoux gatherings, of which we heard such terrible stories at the Cape."

" I don't believe those stories," answered the other. " A form of Vaudoux exists among the negroes in Louisiana, and therefore I know it is absurd to talk of it as a regular worship with priests and sacrifices.   It is simply a survival of African sorcery, practised by some negroes on others more ignorant than themselves, and connected more or less with a horrible African dance.''

'' You forget that Louisiana is as different from Hayti as from the interior of Africa,'' said Atherton. '' But, whether matters have been exaggerated or not, we must know what this is before going farther ; for should it prove to be what I suspect, our danger would be extreme. Let us get into the shade.''

As he spoke he stepped out of the bright moonlight which lay upon the path ·into the deep shade of a thicket of mimosas, which, with other luxuriant growths, extended up to the building from which the singing proceeded. Safe from observation here, and moving with extreme quietness, they approached the house in the rear ; and found it so rudely and carelessly built that they were able to see clearly all that was taking place within by looking through the chinks of the wall, while keeping carefully in the shelter of some large, broad-leaved plants which grew immediately against it.

What they beheld was a scene so weird and so entirely a verification of all they had heard and read that they could not doubt they were indeed looking upon a meeting of Vaudoux worshippers ; and even their pressing bodily wants were for a time forgotten in the interest it awakened. For wild and terrible are the stories told in Hayti of this fearful idolatry, which, introduced in the days of the French Colony by slaves from the west coast of Africa, and practised secretly then, is now so widely diffused that it is impossible to say what order of Haytian life is free from its degrading superstition. It is at least certain that, although nominally forbidden by law, the sect is so powerful in numbers and influence that few officials are brave enough to incur its enmity ; and that especially in country districts it flourishes almost unchecked, even when it takes its most awful form of human sacrifices and cannibalism. It was owing no doubt to the remoteness of this spot, upon which the two wanderers had stumbled, that the temple into which they looked stood within the borders of a hamlet instead of being as usual buried in the forest ; and that there seemed no pretence of secrecy in the celebration of the dark rites now going on within.

At the end of the long apartment, which was all that the building contained, there stood a kind of altar, beside which, on chairs draped with red cloth and elevated on a throne-like platform, sat a man and woman—evidently the priest and priestess. Both were pure negroes, of the ordinary Haytian type ; and both were dressed in long gowns girded by red sashes. The man wore also a red handkerchief bound around his forehead, above which stood erect the peculiarly knotted hair that marks the Papaloi, or Vaudoux priest. A throng of men and women filled the room, all of whom were singing the monotonous, barbaric chant which had first attracted the attention of the lookers-on ; and all were moving their bodies in slow, swaying motion ; while every eye was fastened on the altar, upon which stood a box containing the serpent which was the object of their idolatry.

De Marsillac shuddered. "This is horrible !" he whispered. "All that we have heard must be true. Let us go away."

"Not yet," Atherton replied. "Think what an unlooked-for chance to witness one of these meetings ! Men have risked their lives by going in disguise to see what we see now without any risk at all. Of course we must presently go back to the forest ; for we cannot show ourselves until daylight after this. But we will not go until we have seen whatever——"

He paused abruptly in his speech ; for the chant suddenly ceased and silence fel'—a profound, complete silence, which lasted for several minutes. Then, rising to his feet, the Papaloi began to speak—at first in low, rapid tones ; then louder, with increasing excitement, until at last he fairly shrieked his utterances. To Atherton these were mostly unintelligible, from the *patois* in which they were spoken ; but the young Louisianian comprehended enough to be aware that the speaker was extolling the worship of the serpent in which they were all engaged ; that he urged his followers to be faithful to this adoration, and to obey implicitly the commands of Vaudoux ; promising them freely temporal and also spiritual rewards. The degree to which he had wrought upon the emotions of his listeners was soon apparent from the cries that broke from them, and in the increased motion of their bodies—a nervous shaking, apparently beyond control, that passed like a wave over them. Some prostrated themselves before the altar, others with lifted hands uttered petitions ; when, perceiving that he had raised their excitement to the proper pitch, the speaker suddenly broke again into the chant, now wilder, higher in key, more barbaric in its strange rhythm than before ; while added to it was an accompaniment that seemed to transport the assemblage to frenzy— the peculiar sound of the Congo drum.

The scene which followed soon became indescribable. Still singing, the people began to dance, shaking violently with the nervous trembling already mentioned ; some of them hissing and wriggling like snakes, and all filled with what seemed a veritable diabolic possession. Louder grew the chanting, more frenzied the movements of the dancers —some in their fury tearing off portions of their clothing— while above all sounded the note of the drum : a strange, wild echo from the deep African forests whence this infernal worship came. As the red light of the smoking torches, which alone illuminated the room, fell over the scene, it was hard to believe that these savage creatures, dancing their horrible dance with demoniacal energy, had ever left those dark forests, or been brought into the faintest contact with any form of civilization.

" It is too dreadful to witness," said De Marsillac, averting his face with a gasp of horror. " Oh, let us go away !"

But Atherton's hand fell on his arm with a detaining grasp.

" Wait !" he answered. " We will go after a moment, but I must see the end of this. What can be to come next ?"

He was soon answered. The drum ceased, and, as if under the influence of a spell, instantly the whole frantic assemblage became quiet and silent again. But now the silence had in it a sinister, menacing quality of expectation —such expectation as that of the tiger when, crouching motionless but quivering in the jungle, he waits the coming of his victim. Like so many human tigers these men and women now waited, their glistening eyes fastened on the altar. Plainly, something terrible was about to take place. Atherton felt himself growing cold with undefinable horror.

Presently the Papaloi arose, made an obeisance to the serpent, and, passing behind the altar, drew forth from beneath something which he brought forward and laid before it.

" My God !" said Atherton in a sharp whisper to his companion. " They have brought out a child !"

" A child ! Impossible !" exclaimed the other, turning to look once more through the aperture from which he had averted his face.

It was a child undoubtedly—a female child of six or seven years, bound hand and foot—that lay before the altar. A stir of horrible eagerness passed over the assemblage, but the silence still remained unbroken while a stalwart young negro detached himself from the throng, and, approaching the throne, knelt before the priestess, or Mamamloi. What he said was not audible to the concealed and now horror-stricken observers (it was, in fact, a request that they might offer the sacrifice of the " goat without horns") ; but her gracious assent was evident, and immediately two other negroes came forward and lifted the child to her feet.

" They are going to murder her !" cried De Marsillac, seizing Atherton's arm. " Oh, for God's sake, let us do something before it is too late !"

" What can we do ?" asked the other. " We ourselves would be murdered if our presence was discovered ; for"— he swore a great oath, which was surely not recorded against him—" the infernal devils are indeed about to offer a human sacrifice !"

At this moment the Papaloi, knife in hand, again advanced to the child, who until now had seemed half-stupefied, but who, catching the deadly gleam of the blade, began to scream.

That scream was echoed by another cry as the Papaloi drew his knife across the victim's throat—a cry which made the whole assemblage start and look around, seeking the person from whom it had proceeded. A breathless minute passed in this scrutiny, then some one shouted, " Outside ! —search outside !" and a dozen men rushed from the building.

Meanwhile when De Marsillac, with that involuntary cry of overmastering horror, dropped fainting at his feet,

Atherton had known that there was not a second to lose if their lives were to be saved. One quick motion of his hand to his pocket gave him the assurance that his revolver was there ; then, picking up the insensible boy, he retreated as rapidly as his burdened condition would allow through the bushes which had sheltered them, and spent the minute which meant their salvation in putting all the distance possible between himself and the temple ; so that by the time the searchers had rushed out and were beating the bushes where he and his companion had been standing, he was a hundred yards away. He was aware, however, that their fate was sealed unless he could find some place of immediate concealment. To gain the forest, burdened as he was, before he could be overtaken was impossible ; so, with senses quickened by the awful nearness of the danger, he looked around, seeking some refuge, as men only seek that on which life and death depend.

But where was refuge to be found in this haunt of murderers ? His eager gaze swept the scene around him, while the voices of the searchers seemed to his excited fancy to be drawing every instant nearer ; but he perceived no shelter which could serve any purpose of concealment. Filled with a sense of despair, he was about to place the boy upon the ground, and, standing over him, kill as many of the wretches seeking them as possible before the inevitable end —an end which gained new horror from the thought of what would follow death—should come, when suddenly he thought of the stream. As they approached the hamlet he had observed that its banks, especially in one place, were washed out, forming cavities on each side. Here was a hiding-place which might pass unnoticed save in case of a prolonged and careful search—such search as would not be likely to be made, since the wretches would hardly suppose that strangers could have wandered into this remote spot. It was an instant's work to gain the bank of the stream, break through the bushes fringing it, and let himself and his still insensible companion down over the crumbling edge.

Underneath he found, as he thought would be the case, a perfect place of concealment. During past flood-times, when swollen to a raging torrent, the stream had chiselled out these hollow spaces, from the projecting surfaces of which a green curtain of bushes and vines now drooped. Atherton pushed these aside, and into the cavity behind thrust the body of the boy ; then, crouching beside him, waited, pistol in hand, for what should come.

What came were many trampling feet upon the path above him, and much talk in a language of which he only now and then caught a word he understood. But the tones of the speakers told him they were of differing opinions—some for searching farther, some for returning ; and it was also evident that the latter were in the majority. As a matter of fact, these last were of the opinion that the cry had been uttered within rather than without the house, by some novice not yet hardened to the offering of human victims, who was ashamed or afraid to confess it. "For how," they argued, "could a stranger possibly have been present ? Or when had such a thing ever been known as that any one from the outside penetrated here ?"

Perhaps the others were ready to be convinced, feeling secure of their impunity in crime, and anxious to return to the horrible feast awaiting them. At all events, after a pause and discussion just above the spot where Atherton crouched grimly waiting, they retraced their steps ; their voices gradually died away, and silence reigned again over the wide, beautiful scene, which had so suddenly been transformed into a very gate of hell.

CHAPTER XIV.

WITH the aid of the water near by, it was not difficult to revive the insensible boy. Atherton dashed it liberally over his face ; and, when he stirred with a reviving gasp, raised the flask to his lips. "Drink !" he said, in a tone of such imperative command that the other obeyed without protest or hesitation ; and after a moment was able to withdraw himself from support and sit up alone, though trembling excessively.

"Did they murder her?" he asked then, in a horror-stricken whisper. "My God, I can still hear her cry !"

"It seemed unnecessary on your part to echo it, however," replied Atherton. "In consequence, we have had as narrow an escape from death as we are likely ever to have."

"Did I cry out so as to be heard?" asked the other. "I did not know it. And I fainted too ? That is strange. I never fainted before in my life."

"You never before had such occasion. I don't blame you for fainting ; but it was your cry that brought the whole pack of devils at our heels."

"What shameful weakness on my part !" said the boy in an accent of intense contrition. "How did we escape?"

"I picked you up and ran for it. There was nothing else to do. If you were not a light-weight I could never have done it."

"You *carried* me ! Oh, I can never forgive myself ! What a position to place you in ! You would have been justified in leaving me to my fate. But"—with a violent shudder—"thank God and thank you that you did not !"

"I should have made a fight if the worst had come,"

said Atherton. "I had seven shots, and I knew I could answer for that many of the miserable wretches. But of course we should have been killed at last—and *eaten!* That was the most appalling thought."

The boy drew nearer to him with an involuntary movement.

"Where are we now?" he whispered. "Are we safe?"

"Not yet, but we soon shall be. I am only waiting to give those who pursued us time to return to their devilish worship before we make our way back to the forest."

Ten minutes passed, which seemed an hour; and then, bidding his companion remain quiet, Atherton rose.

"I am going to reconnoitre a little," he said. "On no account stir until I return."

Leaving the cavity where they crouched, and standing on the edge of the shallow stream, he cautiously parted the bushes growing along the bank and looked over the valley. There was no sign of human presence; and, after listening intently for some seconds, he sprang to the surface of the bank and disappeared, leaving De Marsillac a prey to the keenest anxiety and fear.

At another time the boy would have followed, despite the injunction to the contrary which he had received; but now, acutely conscious of his late ignominious failure in self-control and the consequent peril in which it had placed them, he felt that he owed Atherton, who had saved his life at the risk of his own, the return of implicit obedience as long as this situation of danger lasted. He waited, therefore, for what appeared an interminable length of time, until at last he heard a slight sound above, and the next moment Atherton dropped over the bank again.

"All clear!" he reported briefly. "I have been as far as the village, and found no one watching. They are all

at their infernal orgies, and now is our time to escape.
We must go at once."

"I am ready," replied the boy, rising as he spoke.

The bank once mounted, he was conscious of an access
of vigor from the sight of the hamlet and the thought of
the danger lurking there. It was true that a sense of
deadly sickness came over him at the recollection of what
he had witnessed, and of what was no doubt now going on.
But it was a sickness which did not incapacitate, but on
the contrary lent such wings to his feet that he was in advance of Atherton when they gained the forest and once
more breathed freely, knowing themselves at last safe from
pursuit.

Pausing on the edge of the deep woods into which they
were about to plunge, Atherton glanced back over the
scene that so short a time before had looked to them an
idyllic Arcadia in its peaceful serenity and beauty.

"At this moment," he said, "there is nothing I would
not give to be able to level a field-piece upon that abode of
devils and wipe it out of existence. Yet I must turn my
back and go away ; knowing that what we have seen to-
night will be repeated again and yet again."

"Is there *no* possibility of punishing them in any way ?"
asked De Marsillac. "If these atrocities are against the
law, can we not inform the authorities of what we have
seen ?"

"And do you think the authorities would act upon any
information given by foreigners and white men ? You
have not grasped the idea yet of what Hayti is."

"But it seems appalling to do nothing. Think of the
unutterable horror of it ! Can you ever forget the cry of
that child ?"

"Not soon, I fear. But the scene when I went back—

don't ask me to speak of that. Ah, how the recollection sickens me !''

" I would not hear of it for anything !'' cried the other hastily. "For God's sake, let us get away—far away ! I never before knew how a coward feels ; but now I am afraid —horribly afraid.''

" There is now nothing to fear,'' said Atherton, as they went on. "Not one of those cannibals would leave his awful feast ; and besides they are drinking, and will soon be helplessly intoxicated. What a glorious opportunity to go in and kill the whole of them—devil-worshippers and murderers as they are !''

" I would rather have killed them at the moment of the murder. If I had had a pistol 1 should have shot that Papaloi as he turned with the knife. Nothing could have held my hand—I am sure of it.''

" It would have been a well-merited punishment, and possibly not more dangerous in its results than what you did. But, after all, we have not come to Hayti to constitute ourselves avengers of blood. Remember what lies yet untouched in the garden of Millefleurs.''

As if struck by a shot, the boy paused, and, turning, faced his companion. They were not yet in a forest so dense but that some stray beams of moonlight filtered through the foliage and showed to each the pale face of the other.

" What did I say to you yesterday ?'' he asked in a quick, tense tone. " Did I not say that we might die instead of returning there ? You laughed at me then. But how near death we have been to-night ! And how do we know that even yet we are out of danger ?''

" I think that we are,'' replied Atherton. " It is rather curious that you should have said that yesterday ; but it was only one of those chance shots which events afterwards turn into a prophecy. You certainly can't pretend that you had any premonition that we were to run into such danger as we have been exposed to."

"No," answered the other, "I had no premonition further than what I told you, and you called superstition—the belief that if I did not then take what I came to seek I would not have another chance to do so. And now"—he spoke in a tone of despair—"I am sure that I never shall."

"This is ridiculous folly!" exclaimed Atherton impatiently. "I would not have believed that a boy of so much pluck could be guilty of it. What is to prevent your returning? Here we are safe; and we have only to wait a few hours for daylight to find our way back to our men and horses."

"You don't know how exhausted I am," said the other, confessing it for the first time. "I shall never be able to get back to the place we left. And we cannot seek help, and you certainly cannot carry me again; and so——"

"And so we are to perish like the babes in the wood! A very pretty programme, truly. If the worst came to the worst, I would show you whether or not I could carry you again; but it isn't coming to that. We are going to find a place to rest, and sleep if we can; and to-morrow you will laugh at this nonsense. Come!"

He took the boy's arm and drew him on. They were still following the stream, and a few minutes later they found themselves in a leafy glade among the hills—a spot fit for a fairies' meeting-place, where the ground was free from undergrowth, and the moonbeams fell through the exquisite fronds of tree-ferns, while all the solitude was made musical by the sound of water.

"Here is a good resting-place," said Atherton. "Sit

down on that bed of ferns, put your back against that tree, and now we will address ourselves to a light collation of bananas."

He began emptying his pockets as he spoke, until a large pile of this nutritious fruit lay before them.

"There is one great advantage in being lost in the tropics," he said, as he turned down the skin of one : "nobody need starve here. There is no better food than this."

"When did you get these ?" asked his companion with surprise.

"When I returned to the village. It was only to lift one's hand and help one's self, and fortunately my pockets are deep. Half a dozen or so of these and a little brandy and water, and you will be ready to go to sleep, and wake to-morrow quite fresh and ready for our tramp over the hills."

"You must think me contemptibly weak," said the boy after a few minutes' silence, "and, I am afraid, as weak in mind as in body."

"I think nothing of the kind. But you are completely used up ; besides which, your nerves were terribly shaken by the awful scene we witnessed ; so it is no wonder our situation looks to you much darker than it is."

"You say my nerves are shaken," said the other, after another brief pause. "I suppose they are. The gleam of that knife is before my eyes all the time, and the cry of that child rings unceasingly in my ears."

He put his hands before his face, as if to shut out the scene his fancy so vividly painted, at the same time shuddering convulsively.

"What you want is rest," said Atherton kindly ; for he saw that it was a case of shock to the nerves that would not soon pass away. "Try to think of something else. And get to sleep as soon as possible. There is nothing like sleep to bring the nerves back to their proper condition."

"And you?"

"I shall not sleep. I have no inclination to do so; and I think it, on the whole, safer to keep watch. I haven't the least apprehension of any danger, but it is well to be on the alert."

"Then we must keep watch and watch," said the boy earnestly. "What time is it now?"

A ray of moonlight enabled Atherton to answer: "Ten minutes past one."

"Then I will sleep two hours, and you must wake me, so that I can watch while *you* sleep. Promise me to do so, or I will not consent to sleep at all."

"Very well, I promise. Now let us have no more talk. In fact, I am going to stroll about a little while I smoke."

"You will not go far?"

"Certainly not. I shall not lose sight of you. Have no fear."

The last words, instead of offending the listener as they might have done a little earlier in their adventure, fell upon his ear with a soothing sound. He was for the first time in his life—as he had truly said—in the strong grasp of fear : that passion, or emotion, of which those who are physically brave know so little, but which is one of the worst sufferings the human soul can be called upon to endure. Every fibre of his body, as well as his whole spirit, was sick with the horror of the appalling scene he had witnessed. He could not divest himself of the fancy that the forest around was filled with the dark faces of cannibal murderers; and all the stories he had heard in the Cape from Mr. Hoffman and his friends rose in memory—terrible stories of human ghouls robbing graves in order to feed upon the dead ; or, worse yet, of those who had been thrown into what was only a simulation of death in order that they might be resuscitated, killed, and devoured ; of the fearful *loup-garou*—the monster whose business is to steal children for these feasts ; of a slain youth found with a cane driven into his heart, through which the blood had been sucked ; of an unhappy woman taken ill on the road, whose husband left her in a wayside house while he rode to the nearest town for medical aid, and who, returning, found that she had been murdered—cut into pieces and *salted down.*

These blood-curdling tales—all resting, though he had not known it at the time, on absolute evidence—might rouse only a passing shudder when told on a pleasant veranda with lamplit rooms behind, the security of companionship and the near neighborhood of power ; but *here,* in these deep mountains, so wild, so remote, with the celebration of a cannibal feast near at hand, and with the consciousness of an escape so narrow from a fate the most awful, it was no wonder that their recollection filled the boy with a thrill of terror altogether new to his experience. So he had asked, like a child, not to be left alone ; and there was comfort in the sight of Atherton's tall form passing and repassing to and fro ; in thinking of the weapon he carried ; in reliance upon his courage and resource already so abundantly tested ; and even in a whiff from his cigar which came now and then, strangely mingled with the aromatic odors of unnumbered plants and flowers. After a while even the gleam of the murderous knife was forgotten, and the heart-piercing cry of helpless childhood ; the young head drooped, and Atherton, when he approached, saw with satisfaction that his companion was sleeping the deep sleep of weariness and exhaustion.

When next De Marsillac opened his eyes, daylight was all around him ; and the pale man standing over him was saying :

"Sorry to disturb you, but it is time we were moving."

"You did not wake me, after all !" cried the boy, springing up. "You broke your promise—you let me sleep all night !"

"Yes," was the cool reply ; "because it was better you should sleep at night than that you should break down by day. How do you feel?"

"Quite rested. But you have had no sleep at all. How could you act so ?"

"For the very good reason that you needed sleep and I did not—or, at least, I could do without it. I am glad you are feeling better. Here are three or four bananas. When you have breakfasted we will start."

The other smiled as he took the bananas.

"One would think we were on a desert island," he said. And then the smile faded, as he looked up with a recollection of horror dawning in his eyes. "Was it a dream ?" he asked. "Did we really see——"

"The Vaudoux worship and the human sacrifice ? Yes. I am sorry to say there was no dreaming about it. But don't think of it now. What we have to do is to get away from here as soon as possible."

"I am ready : let us go at once. I shall not breathe freely until we have put the mountain between ourselves and that place of abominations."

"We are not going *over* the mountain," replied Atherton calmly. "We are going *around* it, by the trail we partly followed yesterday, and which must lead to the village we have seen."

The boy started. "Do you mean to go *there ?*" he asked.

" Not to the village immediately. I hope to be able, by
skirting around it, to escape observation. But we must
find that trail. I cannot risk the danger of further wan-
derings in these mountains, when there must be a path
leading out of this valley, to find which will mean safety."

" But if we should be seen ?—they will know that we
were the spectators of their meeting last night."

" Let them know it. Last night we had to fear the rush
of a multitude, with their passions already inflamed to the
utmost—human tigers thirsting for blood. To-day they are
scattered, many no doubt yet helplessly drunk ; those who
may be sober capable of understanding the argument of
this," and he touched significantly the pistol in his pocket.

De Marsillac turned a shade paler than he had been before, and did not speak for a moment. Then he said
slowly :

" Don't you think it would be better to take the fatigues
and dangers of the mountains rather than run the risk of
having to use that ? If you killed any of those wretches
and even escaped with your life, what would follow in a
country where white men are hated and justice unknown !"

" I shall not kill any one except in self-defence," answered Atherton. " Wretches as they are, I have no desire to be their executioner ; and it would certainly be unpleasant to figure in a Haytian court either as murdered or
murderer. ' *Après tout, ce n'est qu'un blanc de moins,*' "
he added with a laugh, recalling the story Mr. Hoffman
had told. " But find that road we must. So *allons !*"

Retracing their steps of the previous night, they soon
reached the margin of the forest ; and saw before them
again the Eden-like valley, with its picturesque hamlet
clustering amid groves of fruit-trees. In the clear, delicate light of early morning—for the sun had not yet ap-

peared over the high crests of the encircling mountains—
it seemed steeped in an even deeper repose than when beheld by moonlight. No sign of human presence could be
perceived about it, and Atherton repeated his opinion that
all the inhabitants were sleeping off the effects of their
orgy of the night before.

"And now," he said, looking around with the eye of a
veteran mountaineer, "I begin to think that it will not be
necessary for us to enter the valley at all, nor even to skirt
it for any considerable distance. There is but one natural
outlet from it, and that is the gap in the hills on our left.
We will make for that, and I am sure we shall there find
a trail."

The gap of which he spoke was on the eastern side of
the valley, while they stood on the northeastern ; so that
the distance between the two points was not very great, and
there was no necessity for leaving the shelter of the woods ;
while, to the great relief of De Marsillac, they increased
their distance from the village with every step. These
steps were also less difficult than if taken higher on the
mountain side, where the forest growth was so dense and
the riotous parasites so many that progress was a constant
struggle. On this lower level walking was easier ; and,
since they made all possible haste, they reached the gap
within an hour ; and found, as Atherton had anticipated,
a well-defined trail leading through it.

"Thank Heaven for so much !" said Atherton when
they had turned their backs on the valley and village.
"Now we must pray that we may meet no wayfarers to report our presence here. This would make a perfect place
of ambush."

It was not a cheerful suggestion, but of the fact there
was no doubt. This narrow pass through the mountains,

with its trail running along the side of a steep height, densely wooded above, and with a green chasm below, in which could be heard but not seen the tumbling fall of waters, offered every facility for assassination. No better covert could a murderer desire than the thickets overhanging the path ; and no better hiding-place, were hiding-place desired, for the body of his victim than the verdure-filled *arroyo* below.

But the two who now followed the trail had stout hearts. Although they knew not what moment might bring them face to face with some one bound for the village, who would carry there the news of the presence of strange white men, they walked on with cheerfulness and energy ; inspirited by finding themselves on a path instead of wandering through the trackless forest ; and yet more inspirited by leaving behind the scene of all the horrors of the night. Now and then Atherton glanced at his companion with mingled wonder and admiration. How slight he looked !—how frail a frame for such work as this—for long hours of weary tramping, of exposure, fasting and danger ! Yet what a brave spirit animated that slender body and looked out of those clear, brown eyes ! After they had been walking for about two hours, he uttered a thought which had been in his mind for some time :

" Since we have come so far in safety, we might rest for a short while. We are neither of us in very good condition for athletic exercise this morning."

The boy glanced at him suspiciously.

" I think," he said, " that you suggest that on my account. But I am not such a weakling as you imagine. Remember, *I* slept last night."

" But *I* did not. So I hope you will allow me to be a little tired. We will take fifteen minutes for rest ; and, that our minds may be at ease, we will conceal ourselves while doing so."

He led the way as he spoke up the hillside which rose above them, and where they found themselves in the midst of the same riotous tangle of every variety of plants and creepers with which they were already so unhappily familiar. A few steps were sufficient to put them in perfect seclusion ; for entering within the shelter of one of those strange fig parasites—which, having seized and strangled in their embrace some stately tree, drop their long tendrils to the ground from its branches, thus forming a green tent —they were absolutely secure from observation.

Still, the boy was not at ease in mind.

"You are doing this on my account," he repeated. "I am certain that, on your own, you would not halt when haste is so necessary. And I assure you that I am perfectly capable of going on."

"You will be yet more capable when our rest is over," replied Atherton. "You must remember that we have already taken a great deal out of ourselves, and have had nothing to sustain our strength but a few bananas."

"All the same, you would not do it if you were alone," persisted the boy. "You think that I will break down again as I did last night, and I don't blame you for thinking so. I behaved like a fool, and a very weak one at that. In consequence, I am suffering all the pangs of self-contempt this morning. But I am not going to repeat my folly and weakness."

"That is exactly as I thought," said Atherton. "You would prefer to drop in your tracks, as you admitted last night that you came near doing. But I object to so ill-judged a display of the triumph of spirit over matter. My dear boy, you remind me forcibly of some valorous young recruit whose bravery outruns his physical powers, and who has not yet learned discretion, or patience with those limitations of strength which exist, in more or less degree, for all of us."

"Ah, you are kind to try to restore my self-respect! But I can never forget how I failed last night," answered the other. "Nor can I ever forget that you saved my life, in return for my endangering yours."

"Well, are we not told to return good for evil?" laughed Atherton. "Bah! you make too much of all this. By the time we have gone round the world together, and been in a dozen or more adventures, you will take such trifles as a matter of course. Now let us talk of Millefleurs, where I hope we shall be to-night."

"To-night!" (in a tone of incredulity). "Where do you think we are now?"

"Unless I am very much mistaken, very near the place where we left our horses."

"Why do you think so?"

"I think so from the general direction we are following, and from the fact that this trail is evidently on the other side of the mountain, upon the flank of which we lost our way. It will, I believe, finally lead us safely around to the mouth of the cañon where I found the drift from the gold vein."

"Oh, then, pray let us get on! There is surely no reason why we should waste time here."

"The time is not wasted that recruits one's strength. However, since you are so anxious, we will be moving. I wish I had some definite idea how much farther we shall have to go, and whether we shall find our people where we left them."

"What would have become of them if they are not there? They surely would not go away without us."

"There is no telling what folly those who are accustomed only to act under orders may commit when left to themselves. But I have some reliance on Gilbert. He has a strong habit of unquestioning obedience, which may keep him quietly waiting until I appear."

. He proved to be right—in degree, at least. Waiting for them Gilbert was ; but not very quietly, as they discovered by the time they had advanced a mile or two farther. For suddenly as they walked on through the wild, beautiful solitude, they were startled by a sound of distant firing.

"What on earth can that be !" cried Atherton, pausing to listen. "Pistol shots ! Can our men have been attacked, or are they fighting a duel ?"

"Perhaps they are firing as a signal to us," suggested De Marsillac.

"That is exactly what they are doing," said Atherton, as, after a short interval, another shot or two were heard. "Gilbert thinks we may be guided by the sound. That settles the question of our being in the right way, and of their being where we left them. Now let us see if they can hear a shout."

About ten minutes later the men and horses were in sight ; and the long, weary tramp of the wanderers ended where it had begun.

CHAPTER XV.

IT was late in the evening of the same day when a very tired party arrived again at the gate of Millefleurs. Many hours had passed since the two wanderers found themselves back in the place whence they started, and every one of those hours had been filled with employment of one kind or another. Atherton's energy was astonishing. No one familiar with the aspect of the languid passenger who had lounged on the deck of the *New York* would have recognized him in the man who so indefatigably exerted himself and compelled exertion on the part of others. For finding that, owing to his absence and the consequent alarm it had excited, no more ore had been brought down than the single sack he had sent by Gilbert, his first act, after the pressing bodily needs of himself and his companion had been attended to, was to dispatch the men for a further supply. Then, after a very short rest, and despite the remonstrances of De Marsillac, he returned himself to the head of the gorge, in order to select the best specimens from the vein. All of this occupied time ; following came the loading of the ore upon the horses, the slow return to Milot, the bargaining there for another pack-animal to divide the load—secured with much difficulty through the good offices and on the security of the schoolmaster—and finally the journey to Millefleurs.

One point, however, was successfully achieved as a direct result of their misadventure—the guide was dismissed. To get rid of him before the important search should be made had been a difficulty which confronted them all along, and which chance now happily removed. For in consequence of a night-long vigil, together with much unaccustomed labor with the pick, this gentleman of leisure found himself more completely used up than were the two young men who had tramped all night over the hills. When he learned, on reaching Milot, that they did not intend to take the direct road to the Cape, but to diverge again to the old sugar estate, he evinced so much reluctance and carried his protests so far that Atherton summarily dismissed him, with permission to take his way to the Cape by any road that pleased him.   Then, greatly relieved, they turned their own faces in the direction of Mille-fleurs.

As a result of these many delays, it was dusk when they reached the old, carved pillars at the entrance to the avenue of palms. Riding up this avenue, the fading light veiled all signs of decay in the house they were approaching until it almost seemed as if lights might gleam from its windows and hospitable figures come hastening forward to greet them as they neared the broad terrace before it. So strong was this impression that there was something of a shock in the aspect of the dark and silent ruin which confronted them, with its roofless walls and empty chambers, when they ascended the terrace steps ; for, striking as had been its sadness by day, it was far more striking now in this waning twilight, that in itself was full of infinitely melancholy suggestions.

But there was no time to indulge in the thoughts and memories it roused, since they had the practical work before them of making all their preparations for the night before darkness fell.

" What do you say, Henri—do you care to spend one night of your life within your ancestral walls, if not exactly under your ancestral roof ?" Atherton asked of his companion, and smiled at the emphatic negative he received.

" I shall see ghosts enough outside," the boy answered. " I have no desire to meet the company which would marshal within."

" Then we will not intrude upon them," said Atherton. " But I hardly imagine they will object to our camping here on the terrace. I think, however, that we need not pitch the tent.   We are not likely to sleep very much to-night."

"I should think not !" returned the other, whose pulses were beating so excitedly that he marvelled to hear the thought suggested.   What he would have liked would have been to go directly, without delay even for refreshment, and settle, once for all, the question of what was to be found in Henri de Marsillac's hiding-place beside the old sun-dial.

He was forced to repress his impatience while supper was prepared and taken—his own performance, or lack of performance, with regard to it calling forth strong rebuke from Atherton—and then to witness preparations for repose instead of for the labors which awaited them.

"We will sleep until midnight," Atherton announced. "The moon will by that time be risen, and we can go to work."

"I—hoped we should go to work at once," said De Marsillac in a disappointed tone. "We would sleep better after we had satisfied ourselves."

"*You* might," Atherton replied ; "but I can answer for Gilbert and myself that we shall sleep very well before undertaking any more work, and shall then work better for having slept."

"I am a selfish wretch to forget how tired you must be, and that you did not sleep at all last night," said the boy remorsefully. "Of course you must rest. But I shall not sleep, so I will be able to wake you at whatever hour you desire."

"There is no necessity for that. You must take some rest also. I shall wake easily enough, never doubt."

"There is nothing I could not sooner do than sleep *here* —to-night," was the reply, in a tone of such earnestness that his companion perceived the futility of further remonstrance.

Indeed Atherton's heart smote him a little for condemning the speaker to several hours longer of suspense ; but, apart from the fact that he was by this time physically worn out, and knew his servant to be very nearly the same, he also knew that it was necessary to wait until the moon had risen before they commenced the work that lay before them. Saying, therefore, " I hope you'll think better of it and go to sleep ; but if you should be awake, call me at twelve," he threw himself into his hammock and was soon sleeping soundly.

But De Marsillac had been right in affirming that nothing was less possible to himself than to sleep in this spot, haunted by so many associations ; on this night which was to decide whether his long journey, with all the risks it involved, had been taken in vain or was to be fully rewarded. While Atherton slept, he paced like a sentinel up and down the terrace in the wonderful tropical starlight, which makes the term darkness, as applied to night in these regions, a mere form of expression. The obscurity was no more than a softening veil thrown over the wide landscape, every feature of which stood clearly revealed in the exquisite radiance of the shining worlds, thick-sown on a field of deepest blue.

It was a memorable vigil—one never to be forgotten by the young spirit, which was thrilling with imaginations. What a company indeed of ghosts were about him as he paced to and fro before the ruined home of his race ! From the shattered walls and empty doorways came the shades of the gay, luxurious men and women of the past, bowing over jewelled snuff-boxes, rustling silken petticoats fresh from Paris, telling the last scandal from the court of Versailles. And behind them followed dark, savage forms with knife and torch—children beyond seas of that hydra-headed monster, the Revolution of France. The gay figures were swept away in a hurricane of tears and blood ; the sky grew red with the flames of burning homes ; and a lurid cloud of carnage and barbarism, never again to be lifted, settled upon the land. For how dark that cloud remained, who could know better than one who had witnessed only last night the scene he shuddered to recall, the terrible scene of devil worship and cannibal murder ? Despite his efforts to keep his mind from the awful memory, it returned again and yet again to that picture, which seemed the supreme expression of all that this fated island—made by God so fair, rendered by man so horrible—had shown him. From the dark ruins of the Cape, with their sinister and tragic memories, to the great fortress built by infernal cruelty and cemented by blood, the desolated plains and deep forests had but one story to tell, and that story was epitomized in the gleam of a deadly knife and a child's helpless cry. " *Haiti, Haiti, pays de barbares !*" What could the descendant of men who had once made it the wonder of the world for fruitfulness and wealth add to these true and bitter words from imperial lips ?

In thoughts and fancies like these the long hours passed, until at last the moon came up the eastern heaven—a strange, mournful presence, as the waning moon ever is, but still able to flood the world with silver light. Her rays, shining in his face, presently awoke Atherton ; and, starting up, he looked around. A slender, dark figure was standing at the edge of the terrace, silhouetted against the wide radiance which had paled the stars.

" Henri !" he cried—and then as the boy turned, " Why have you not called me ? Is it not time ?"

"It is half-past eleven," was the reply. "I was waiting for twelve o'clock."

"And you have not rested at all! Foolish boy! Well, since her lunar majesty is fairly risen, eleven will answer for us as well as twelve. Here, Gilbert!—wake up, man! It is time to go to work."

Gilbert rather slowly arose; and if he had given utterance to the thoughts in his mind, he would probably have declared that a master less given to the pursuit of adventure was to be desired by a servant who, on engaging to perform the duties of a valet, had not anticipated being called upon to supplement them with the tasks of a miner and treasure-seeker. Nevertheless, when he had shaken off the sluggishness of sleep, even his phlegmatic soul felt a faint thrill of the expectation and suspense which filled the others, as, shouldering the picks, they took their way towards the second terrace of the garden, as Henri de Marsillac and his faithful Jacques had taken their way on that August night a hundred years gone by.

Reaching the circle with less difficulty than on their former visit—for Gilbert wielded a cutlass with good effect in clearing a path—they found it sufficiently illuminated by the moon's rays to dispense with any other light. Very few words were spoken as they set themselves to the task in hand. First thoroughly clearing the ground around the dial, which had so well and so long stood guard over its trust, they fell to work digging—Gilbert and his master alternately using the pick; for De Marsillac proved quite as incapable of effective labor as Atherton had foretold when he observed his hands the day they sat together on the beach of Turk's Island.

"Your will is good enough," he said, after the boy had made an ineffectual effort to do his part of the labor required; "but your strength amounts to nothing. Give me the pick."

There was no alternative but to obey—the most gallant will in the world being unable to create muscular strength. And so the person chiefly concerned in that which was sought was forced to stand by inactive while the search was conducted.

But the work required was, after all, not very great. Evidently time pressed when Henri de Marsillac and his servant had likewise worked here; and their shallow hiding-place would soon have yielded its treasure had suspicion ever been directed to the spot. For the excavation of the searchers had not reached a depth of more than two feet when there was a sudden, sharp sound, as the pick—at that moment in Gilbert's hand—struck on metal. De Marsillac, who was leaning against the sun-dial, uttered an exclamation as sharp; while Atherton, quietly looking on with his hands in his pockets, called out to Gilbert:

"You have struck it! Go on at that spot."

Ten minutes later the top of an iron-bound chest was laid bare; twenty minutes later two men were eagerly digging around it; and thirty minutes later they had made their excavation sufficiently large to attempt to lift it out. But the attempt resulted in a complete failure; the weight which it contained was beyond their joint strength to stir.

"By Jove!" said Atherton, looking up at the pale boy who stood on the margin of the excavation, "you have found your fortune indeed! This chest must weigh at least a thousand pounds. It is useless to think of lifting it without further assistance, and that cannot be had. So we must open it where it stands."

"How do you suppose that two men brought it here in the first place?" asked De Marsillac.

"They did not bring it here filled. They must have deposited the chest and then filled it—as we must empty it. Do you observe how much it resembles those treasure-chests of Christophe that we saw at the citadel? Evidently every planter possessed such a receptacle for the safe-keeping of money and valuables. And since the key of this was taken away in the pocket of its owner, we must imitate the soldiery of Christophe and break the lock. Give it a few blows with the pick, Gilbert."

A few blows well directed, and the work was done. Then, stepping aside, Atherton motioned the boy, still standing above, to descend.

"Come," he said, "and lift the lid. You alone have the right to do so."

It was a moment of such intense excitement and suspense that the speaker did not wonder to see how the slender hand trembled as it lifted the lid.

What they beheld was a sight which again carried them back to that long past night of terror, and made them feel as if its very breath was upon them. For they could perceive with what frantic haste articles of all kinds had been flung headlong into the chest before it was closed and locked. That which first met the eye was a piece of amber satin, some rich drapery apparently, that had been torn down to form a covering under the lid. This removed, they saw beneath a quantity of silver plate—massive, richly chased and much tarnished—with which were mingled indiscriminately jewel-cases, and boxes evidently containing trinkets and articles of value.

"Take out that plate, Gilbert," said Atherton, as the owner stood silent and motionless, looking down on the disordered mass, as if struck afresh with the infinite pity of the old tragedy. "We must see what is beneath."

He stooped as he spoke, and himself lifted one of the jewel-cases, touched the spring and threw back its top. There was an immediate flash of diamonds, as brilliant as if they had not lain buried in darkness for a century. Indeed, there seemed an accumulated brilliance in the flood of light they emitted as the soft moonbeams fell upon them for the first time in a hundred years.

"Jewels for a princess!" Atherton exclaimed. "You have reason to thank your ancestor for saving these, Henri."

"A necklace!" said De Marsillac, taking the case containing the sparkling ornament in his hand. "It shall be for Diane. It seems made for her neck."

Atherton smiled as he looked at the speaker. He liked the boy's devotion to his sister ; and a pleasant vision rose before his own imagination of a fair, slender throat around which those dazzling gems might fitly clasp.

"The woman does not live who would not be enchanted with such a gift," he said. "It may be that you will find your fortune rests chiefly in these jewels. They are of great value as well as beauty."

"No," the other answered. "My great-great-grandfather speaks expressly, in the paper of which I have told you, of jewels and plate as well as of gold. We have found the jewels and the plate : the gold must be here."

"Beg pardon, sir !" said Gilbert, who had now lifted out the heavy silver, consisting of massive dishes and richly ornamented vessels of many kinds ; "but I think the gold is 'ere."

Atherton and the boy looked eagerly into the chest, and saw a number of bags of soft leather, tied tightly and packed closely together—so closely indeed that it required considerable effort to dislodge and draw forth one. Once drawn forth, the string confining its mouth dropped away at a touch ; and, opening it, the boy took forth a handful of yellow, shining pieces—*louis-d'ors*, as a glance showed. The gold was found.

There was a moment's silence as he held out his hand for the other to see. And meanwhile before his mental gaze stood two pictures, clear as if beheld with bodily eyes. Not the haunting shades of Henri de Marsillac and his faithful servant burying this gold with feverish haste—for the moment they were forgotten—but a group of youthful figures on the gallery of an old house ; and a girl who, pointing to the crescent of the moon now shining above them in the tropic heaven, said, " A fortune as distant as if it were yonder ; but perhaps existing, for all that." And again : the shaded lamplight falling on the faces of two women grown old in sorrow and bereavement, and on fair young faces unfitted for the harsh struggle of life ; while, as one who utters a vow, the same girl cried, " With the help of God I will find that money, if it still remains where Henri de Marsillac placed it !"

And now it was found. And had not God helped the brave, unselfish heart ? Had He not raised up a friend but for whom success would have been impossible ? Even as Atherton was saying, " My dear boy, I congratulate you with all my heart," the gold dropped in a shower at his feet, and he found his hand imprisoned in the clasp of two other hands, while a voice broken with a hint of tears cried :

" But for you I should never have found it !"

*   *   *   *   *

" Now," said Atherton, a little later, " a very important part of our work is yet to come. We have to provide for safely smuggling this gold into the Cape and out of the country. And in this you will see the useful part which my sacks of ore—those sacks which you were so impatient with me for spending time in filling—will play. Gilbert, go and bring one of them here."

As Gilbert departed, Atherton went on :

"I fear we must leave the plate. It is too bulky to take away in addition to the gold. I am sorry for the necessity, since not only is it exceedingly handsome, but would be of untold value to you from its age and family association. But there is no help for it : the sacrifice must be made."

"It is so slight a sacrifice, comparatively, that I shall not grieve over it," said the boy. "I know that you are right : it is impossible for us to take away anything so bulky."

"It would be to risk—nay, almost certainly to incur—detection, and the loss of what is far more important. So, when we have taken out all the gold, we will put the silver back in the chest and cover it up again. Perhaps a hundred years hence *your* great-great-grandson may come to find it."

"One thing is certain," answered the other : "I shall never come myself. Let me once leave this horrible island, and not ten times the value of what lies before us here would bring me back again."

"The same inducement which brought you now would if necessary bring you back again," said Atherton, "or I am greatly mistaken in you."

"Yes" (reflectively), "for the same purpose I would do as much again. But, thank God, it can never *need* to be done again ! Diane's ransom is here."

"How much is required for the ransom ?"

"The debt is twenty thousand dollars."

"You have it and to spare, many times over. In that chest there is gold to the value of at least a hundred and fifty thousand dollars."

"How can you tell?"

"By a very simple calculation of the number and weight of the bags. And that sum was a small price for anything so valuable as a sugar estate in this island in the old days."

"Perhaps it was a small estate, or perhaps the uncertainty of the times was taken into consideration in the price. At all events, I am grateful that it was sold for any price; and grateful beyond measure to Henri de Marsillac who placed that price in safety here."

"Don't forget to be grateful for the jewels, of which there seems to be many besides the diamonds. Here are some beautiful emeralds. You will be immortalized in the family annals when you go home laden with these spoils."

"They will all be pleased," said the boy, thinking of the eager young faces that would bend delighted over such fascinating heirlooms of the past.

Atherton, pursuing his researches, then lifted the lid of a box of sandal-wood. Within was a great confusion of trinkets: lockets, rings, chains, miniatures. One of the last, set in a frame of pearls, he held up to the light, which was sufficiently bright to show that it was a picture of a lovely young woman, dressed and coiffed in a fashion of two hundred years ago.

"Here is a treasure," he exclaimed. "An ancestress who carries her patent of nobility in her face. Ah! why do not women look like this now?"

"Diane looks like it," said the boy, taking the miniature from his hand. "It might almost be a likeness of her." He turned it over, and engraved on the golden back read the name, "Yvonne d'Aulnay." "Ah, I know who it is now!" he said. "She was the wife of Raoul de Marsillac, of whom I have told you—the first of the family who came over here. In some way she impressed herself deeply on the memory of her descendants; for I don't think there has been a generation since which has not had an Yvonne."

"Yvonne!—a quaint but charming name. Breton, I think."

"Oh, yes! Breton without doubt."

"It suggests the noble châtelaine of some old château in wave-washed Brittany, as much as Diane suggests a beauty of the court. Have you an Yvonne as well as a Diane in your own generation?"

"Certainly. It is my——"

In Heaven's name, what was he about to say? An instant more and the heedless tongue would have told all. Absolutely cold with horror at the narrowness of the escape, he paused abruptly in a manner which could not have failed to arouse Atherton's surprise if Gilbert had not created a diversion at the moment by staggering into the circle with the sack of ore. -

The beautiful miniature and the unfinished speech were at once forgotten, and Atherton eagerly went to work to assist in the carrying out of his plan with regard to the gold. The greater part of the ore was emptied out of the sack, which held about a hundred and fifty pounds; the bags of gold, weighing each ten pounds or thereabouts, were then placed in it—care being taken to make them as much of a solid mass as possible in the centre, and to line the sides with pieces of ore, of which a number were also placed on top before the sack was closed. This done, Atherton felt it carefully over; lifted it from the ground and set it down again, to be sure that no jingling sound was heard to betray the presence of coin ; and then declared that no one could possibly suppose it to be other than what it purported to be—a sack of ore.

It was then conveyed away ; another brought, and the same operation repeated ; a process which was continued until the sacks which they had filled with ore were all filled with gold, and the chest was empty. Into this was then replaced the silver plate, and upon it the discarded ore. The lid was closed again, the excavation filled up, all signs of disturbance as much as possible effaced, and three weary but intensely well-satisfied persons turned away from the old sun-dial as the faintly flushing east showed that the sun himself was about to rise on a new day.

CHAPTER XVI.

" There is one thing I must do before we leave here," said Atherton ; "and that is, take some views of the place."

It was several hours since they had turned away in the flushing dawn from the sun-dial. They had slept—De Marsillac heavily after the vigil and excitement of the night—had breakfasted, and were now taking their ease on the terrace, beneath the shade of a great mimosa, which spread its branches over them like a green umbrella. Atherton had decided to delay their return to the Cape until the afternoon, so as to avoid notice as much as possible by passing through the city after dark ; and they had therefore some hours still before them to while away as best they could.

Neither found this difficult ; for both had endured so

much fatigue and been so constantly on a strain for two days that rest was a thing to be welcomed and enjoyed, even if it had not been sweetened by the consciousness of success in their undertaking. The last fact, however, was so agreeable that they had been discussing it at length, and bringing its reality fully before them by contemplating the jewels, which lost none of their beauty when seen by day ; until Atherton made a sudden diversion by the speech recorded above.

"I had forgotten that you brought a camera," said his companion. "You have not used it."

"The opportunities for doing so have not been very great, if you remember. The camera was not always at hand when it would have been of use. I should have liked exceedingly to take a view of that Vaudoux meeting, if such a thing had been possible——"

"Don't!" said the other, lifting his hand quickly. "Don't recall that awful scene ! I am trying—oh, so hard !—to forget it."

"You will not succeed. Neither of us will ever forget it. I am sure that years hence a word or an allusion will recall it so vividly that we shall feel the same thrill of horror which we feel to-day."

"Is it decided that we say nothing about it—that we do not report it at all ?"

"I shall inform Mr. Hoffman and abide by his decision. He knows the people, and can tell whether or not it is worth while to make any report. From what I have heard, I do not believe that the testimony of a white man would have any weight. If it possesses any, I would willingly submit to the inconvenience of acting as a witness to punish those murderers. But you—would you be willing to be detained here indefinitely for the purpose ?"

The boy looked at him with startled eyes ; evidently this thought had not occurred to him.

" No," he answered after an instant : " I should not be willing. Now that my work is done, my object attained, I can allow nothing to delay my return. I must leave by the first ship."

" Then nothing must be said of the matter until after you are gone. We don't want to attract attention to our movements and doings until that money is safely out of the country."

" Do you anticipate any difficulty in getting it out safely ?"

" Not if my plan is successful—as I think it will be. And here comes in the great benefit of having found a genuine vein of gold. I shall make a present of my discovery to Mr. Hoffman, and he will probably know some Haytian to whom he can impart the secret on his own terms. If the Haytian (in whose name alone anything can be done) and himself decide to open the mine, they will want an assay of the ore. To obtain this they must send specimens to New York, and I shall advise that a sufficient quantity be sent to make what is called ' a working test.' You, fortunately, are going, and will take charge of the sacks to oblige me. What follows ? The sacks, without difficulty or remark, are conveyed on shipboard as containing ore. They do contain enough for the purpose desired, and therefore neither you nor I am guilty of falsehood."

" You think of everything," said the boy gratefully. " What should I have done without you ! But will you derive no benefit whatever from your discovery of the gold ?"

" I shall derive the benefit I desire—that of enabling you to take your coin safely out of the country. For the rest, I am quite willing that Mr. Hoffman shall make all

that he can out of it, in return for the services he has rendered us."

"And what" (with sudden energy) "is to be your return for the inestimable services you have rendered me?"

"My return," said Atherton lightly, "is in the pleasure
it has given me. What did I tell you when we first talked
of this matter on Turk's Island? Did I not say that I was
an idle man, to whom such an interest was a welcome
boon? In fact, if you come to the question of indebtedness, it is I who am indebted to you for one of the most
exciting adventures of my life. It is not every day one has
a chance to seek for treasure—and, better yet, to find it."

"What can I say to you!" answered the other, looking
at him with eyes that had seemed to him from the first
time he met them the most beautiful he had ever seen.
"You speak in this way to lessen my sense of obligation;
but you know that I owe you *everything*. You have given
me your time, your thought, your interest; am I to give
you nothing?"

"What can you give me, dear boy," replied Atherton,
touched by the intense feeling of the words, "except your
friendship—let us be sentimental enough to say, your affection? That I shall be glad to have."

"It is yours, and will be yours as long as my heart
beats," said De Marsillac earnestly. "Promise me that
you will believe it."

"Why should I not believe it? One is generally willing
enough to believe what one desires. I hope you will put
out of your mind any idea that you owe me gratitude for
the aid I have given you. I tell you again, in that matter
I pleased myself. I might not have entered on the adventure if I had not liked you; but it would have tempted
me, I think, had I liked you less than I did. Put all

thoughts of indebtedness aside, therefore ; and like me, if you like me at all, for such qualities as I have shown you, and such sympathy as I truly believe exists between us."

" I could not fail to like as well as to admire you for those things. I could not fail to feel how sympathetic, how unselfish, how altogether kind you have been," answered the boy, with the same deep earnestness he had already displayed. " But why forbid me to be grateful ?— because, whether you forbid it or not, I must be so."

" If you must" (shrugging his shoulders), " why, then, you *must,* and there is no more to be said. But 1 do not like it, because it seems to me in some degree a sordid sentiment, based as it is on a sense of benefits received. Now, I do not wish you to feel that you have received any benefits from me, but only such aid as friends may freely give and take."

" But, unfortunately, my part seems to be to take all and give nothing. What can *I* do for *you ?*"

" I thought I had made that clear. If you insist, however, on balancing obligation with obligation—which is to me a most objectionable spirit—why, I have already told you what you may do : you may introduce me to your sister, Mademoiselle Diane."

Dead silence for a moment—a moment filled with such embarrassment on the part of one, such absolute lack of any possible response, that it was amazing the other did not observe it. In that instant De Marsillac anathematized his own garrulous folly, which by want of reticence had brought this upon him, with a vehemence which, in the way of self-reproach, left nothing to be desired, but which was quite unavailing to provide a remedy. What could he say ? What frightful failure in the gratitude he had just expressed in even hesitating over his answer to such a request! At length he stammered lamely, awkwardly:

"You are jesting when you talk of balancing my obligations to you by such a request as that. After I have told Diane what you have done, you will need no introduction, should you ever meet her, but your name—that name which we will all 'set in our prayers.'"

How sweetly—as if to make amends for something lacking—the musical voice uttered those last words! Atherton could not but look at the speaker with a smile.

"That is a form of gratitude to which I cannot object," he said. "As for your sister, let me tell you that I shall not leave the matter of our meeting to chance. I intend to meet her. I have an idea, based on what I have seen of you, that she is wholly unlike the *fin de siècle* women whom one knows so well, and from whom I confess that I turn with a deep distaste. How often I have wished that I could summon back from the past some type that charmed my fancy! Now, I think that your sister must be the survival of such a type; only I wish that she were named Yvonne instead of Diane."

"Why?"—in a very startled tone.

"Because that quaint, Old-World name has captivated my imagination. I fancy the chátelaine whom it suggests as one of those heroic figures of women who now and then through the ages have done things so nobly brave that they shame the achievements of men. Gentle as a s int, proud as a queen, faithful to every trust, and capable of fighting like the Countess Matilda, or holding a fortress like many another gallant woman of the past—is that the type of your sister?"

"No" (reluctantly), "that is not Diane. There is nothing warlike in her. And, after all" (hesitatingly), "do you think you would really fancy a woman who possessed the masculine qualities of which you speak? I thought men liked women to be as feminine as possible.''

'' Bravery is not unfeminine. It is a quality as admirable in a woman as in a man ; and in the type of which I speak the woman lost no feminine grace by being brave. How is it with yourself? Would you not like a woman who had in her, under the softness of her sex, the spark of fire which might kindle into some heroic deed?''

''I—don't know.'' The brown eyes looked away from him over the plain towards the mountains, lovely in their blue-robed distance as ideals, hard and rugged in their reality as facts. ''A great deal of daring which the world would disapprove is sometimes necessary for a deed that might perhaps be called, by a stretch of terms, heroic.''

'' The world disapproved of the Maid of Domremy,'' said Atherton. '' One may imagine that her neighbors and friends thought it very objectionable when she donned armor and went forth to fight. You know we measure the value of such a deed—the right which the doer has to set the opinion of the world aside—by the object in view and by the end attained.''

The brown eyes, turning back again, looked at him gratefully.

'' I think you are right,'' was the somewhat wistful reply. '' If the object in view was very important, one might pardon a woman for setting aside the opinion of the world ; one might think she was right in considering the essentials rather than the appearances of conduct. But'' (hastily) '' we have wandered far from the subject of which we were speaking—the subject of my deep indebtedness to you. Will you add another favor to all that you have already bestowed upon me, and select a souvenir—a remembrance of our adventure—from among these jewels which but for you would never have been recovered ?''

He made a gesture of his hand towards the trinkets which lay before them in a glittering heap ; and Atherton could not but feel that his manner in preferring the request was the manner of one who does in truth, earnestly yet gracefully, beg a favor. The soft eyes looked at him so appealingly that refusal seemed impossible, unless he were prepared to wound deeply one whom he had so deeply obliged.

"My dear boy," he said lightly, "this is unnecessary ; for I can never possibly forget our adventure. But if my complying with your request will give you pleasure——"

"It will give me the greatest pleasure," interposed the other eagerly. "Nothing could give me more. It will be a great satisfaction to me in the future to think that you have in your possession something which will make you recall Henri de Marsillac and his gratitude whenever you look at it."

"You speak as if Henri de Marsillac himself was not to play any further part in my life," said Atherton. "On the contrary, I am determined that we shall see a great deal of each other in the future."

"But life is uncertain" (confusedly). "And, in any event, you must take the souvenir. I could not endure to look at these jewels if you refused to have any of them. Now, what will you choose ?"

"Not the diamond necklace," said Atherton, laughing. "Your hand seems to be moving in that direction, I perceive. Nor anything else of great value ; for, apart from the fact that these are family jewels, what should I do with bracelets or necklaces? If I followed my inclination I should say, give me the miniature of your beautiful ancestress——"

"Of course it is yours!" cried the boy with reckless generosity, putting out his hand to take up the pearl-set medallion.

But Atherton laid his own upon it with a restraining gesture.

"Stop, stop! Did you fancy me in earnest?" he said. "That miniature should be in the future, as it evidently has been in the past, a family treasure, not under any circumstances to be given to a stranger."

"You are not a stranger. You are the person but for whom it would still be buried in the earth, to be found, if ever found at all, by some ignorant negro——"

"No matter; I have no claim to possess the picture of Madame Raoul de Marsillac, and I was only jesting when I alluded to such a possibility. I was going to add, since that cannot be, you may give me a ring, if you can find an unobtrusive one."

"There are not very many rings," said the boy. "But, such as there are, will you select one?"

Atherton turned them over, and finally selected one which he slipped upon his finger. It held a single ruby, not very large but of rare beauty, with the true pigeon's-blood tint and of exceeding brilliance.

"I would not willingly deprive you of anything so lovely as this," he said; "but if you insist on my taking something——"

"I do insist," answered the other; "but I am disappointed in your choice. I wish you would choose something of more value."

"It is not a question of value, but only of remembrance," returned Atherton. "This is a particularly fine ruby, however, let me tell you ; and the ruby has always been my favorite gem. I like the rich color of its deep heart—symbol and emblem of passion. I shall keep this in memory of our association and our friendship. Are you satisfied now ?"

" Partially—if I must be. And now you must not forbid me to reward Gilbert for his services."

" But I do forbid it. To reward Gilbert's services is *my* affair."

" Oh, no, Mr. Atherton—no ! Your reward to him will not be mine. Don't prevent me. I would not willingly do anything against your wishes ; but I must give him at least five hundred dollars, or its equivalent, of the gold he helped to find."

" Obstinate boy, I much prefer that you should not. I will reward him fully, amply ; he knows that."

" Again, let me say, your reward is not mine. Help me, then, to decide how much of this French money is equivalent to the sum I mentioned."

" If you persist—and I see that you do—I suppose I must let you have your way in this also. We will attend to the matter presently. But now I want to take those views of which I spoke some time back. I am sure you will like to have one or two pictures of the place where your people lived and where you have found a fortune. Let me see ! I will take the house, the avenue, and the circle of the sun-dial, of course. Gilbert, bring my camera. Come, Henri ; I shall put you in the last picture."

" No, no !" (with evident consternation.) " That is not to be thought of. I—I mean the picture will be much better without me. Figures posing in photographs of famous scenes, or scenes of any kind, always strike me as impertinences. One wants to brush them away."

"I shall not want to brush your figure from that scene, where I consider that it will be most appropriate. And I am certain that your family will agree with me ; and will value the picture more if you are seen in it, standing on the spot where you found the treasure for them."

"It would be much more appropriate if *you* were standing on it," said the boy. "At all events, I cannot possibly consent to be taken."

"But this is nonsense. Why not?"

"Because I—I have an abhorrence of being photographed. And I think the picture should be of the circle and the sun-dial in their loneliness, not of me."

"I totally disagree with you. But it is easy to take two photographs : one of the empty circle, and one with you leaning against she sun-dial. I insist on this for myself ; and you are not going to refuse to gratify me in a matter so trivial."

No, he could not refuse, in a matter apparently so trivial, to gratify one to whom he stood so deeply indebted. The risk was, after all, slight ; faces in these photographs of outdoor, as he remembered with relief, being generally quite indistinguishable. And so, with deep inward reluctance but an outward show of yielding gracefully, he said :

"Of course if you put it in that way I cannot refuse. But I still think the scene would be better without me."

"What significance would the scene have to me unless your figure were in it?" Atherton asked. "No ; Henri de Marsillac the second must be standing where Henri de Marsillac the first buried his fortune. Come !"

Night had fallen when the travellers, having timed their arrival carefully, passed through the Cape without challenge of any kind, and rode up to Mr. Hoffman's door.

That gentleman greeted them warmly, and would have hurried them at once into the house, but Atherton paused and pointed to a large steamer which lay at anchor in the starlit bay.

" What ship is that ?" he asked.

" That is the Clyde steamer, from the other side of the island, on her return voyage," was the reply. " She sails for New York to-morrow."

LETTER FROM HENRI DE MARSILLAC TO HERBERT ATHERTON.

NEW YORK, December 31, 1894.

MY DEAR MR. ATHERTON : I have complied with all your directions concerning the ore : have placed it without delay in the hands of the assayer you designated, who will send direct to you a statement of the result.

Thanks to your kindness, which anticipated everything, I had no trouble in landing. As we were both anxious that no news of what was found in Hayti should return there, I told no one what the sacks really contained ; and they passed through the custom-house without examination, as ore. My heart was in my throat during this ordeal, you may be sure ; for I knew that if the gold were discovered I should have some difficulty in accounting for its presence ; and that other things might have to be accounted for, too. But the risk seemed to me better than the certain attention that would be excited by a story so sensational. I felt that I could risk almost anything rather than that—for which I had more reasons than I can tell you.

For now comes the hardest part of what I have to write. And, being so hard, I will make it brief. It is that I must now go out of your life entirely ; that you will never after this hear of me again ; and that I beg you to add one more kindness to the great kindnesses you have already done me, by putting me out of your memory altogether and making no inquiry about me.

And, indeed, why should you not put out of your memory one who will seem to you so ungrateful ? I can explain nothing ; I cannot even ask for your kind remembrance of what I was in the time we were together. I only assure you—and you will not believe this, nor can I blame you for disbelieving it—that as long as life lasts I shall hold your memory in my heart ; and that I shall pray unceasingly that you may be rewarded in fullest measure for all you have done to help one who needed your help most sorely, and thanks you for it now more than any poor words can say.

And so God bless you, and farewell !

HENRI.

PART III.

CHAPTER I.

"AH, Varigny! You are the very man I am looking for."

So said one young man to another, by whose side he dropped into a chair in the window of a New Orleans clubhouse. The person addressed glanced up with some surprise.

"Looking for me, Langdon?" he said. "What do you want?"

"Nothing very much," the other replied. "I only want to introduce to you a man who seems consumed with curiosity about the old French families, old French customs, and old French history of New Orleans. Now, I'm not at all informed on these subjects; but *you* must be, since you belong to a representative French family. He'll bore you, no doubt; but you've no objection to knowing him, I suppose?"

"If he is a friend of yours, certainly not," said Varigny.

"He's a little more than a friend: he's a distant relative, whom I wish was a good deal nearer. Some thirty or forty years ago a cousin of my father went to California, and his daughter married Atherton the millionaire. I believe he wasn't a millionaire when she married him, but he became one afterwards; and this is her son."

"It is not to his discredit that his father is a millionaire," remarked Varigny temperately. "What is he like himself?"

"A good deal like an Englishman—the genuine article, not the American imitation, you understand. He doesn't make a point of talking London slang ; and doesn't even let you know, unless it comes up naturally, that he is an Oxford man. He's quiet, well-bred, and without an ounce of pretension on the score of his millions."

"Why should a man have pretensions on the score of possessing millions which somebody else accumulated ?" asked the young Creole, with a quiet shrug of his shoulders.

"Why, indeed ? But one knows, all the same, that the pretensions of such men are often unbearably offensive—at least to that large proportion of the world which does not possess millions. But Atherton, you see, has good blood on his mother's side, and therefore knows better."

"That" (with gravity) "is no doubt to be considered. And is he here for any special purpose ?"

"No : merely as an idler. It seems that he is threatened with consumption, and the doctors ordered him to the West Indies. He found life dull there, and has come over from Cuba here. For lack of other interest, I presume, he is, as I have said, immensely interested in the Creole families ; so I am sure he will like to meet you."

"I shall be delighted to meet him. Where is he to be found ?"

"In the smoking-room at present—at least I left him there when I started in search of you, somebody having ·mentioned that you had come in. If you like, we'll look him up."

Varigny, assenting, rose—a slender man with a quiet manner and somewhat languid grace of movement, which did not conceal the latent nerve and fire that would be quick to answer to any demand made upon them. His face was strikingly handsome, with clear, olive tints, finely cut features, and brilliant dark eyes ; while his lithe, graceful figure, tapering to delicately small extremities, betrayed only to a practised eye the muscles of steel it possessed.

Langdon belonged in all respects to a different type. As commonplace as the other was picturesque in appearance, he was large-limbed, loosely built, and inclining to stoutness. But his good-humored face was not without attraction ; and his aspect was that of one sure of himself and his surroundings, with a comfortable conviction that he had little to desire in life which was not within his reach.

They speedily found the man, described as manifesting a consuming curiosity about old Creole families, where he had been left—sunk in the depths of an easy-chair, smoking, and listening with perfunctory attention to two club gossips talking such social scandal as flourishes for the benefit and by the aid of persons like themselves. "I know for a fact that the matter will end in a separation," one of them was saying as Langdon and Varigny came up.

"Are you fellows on that topic still ?" remarked the former. " 'At every breath a reputation dies,' might be truly said of you ! Atherton, here is a man who has the history of every French family in Louisiana at his fingers' ends, for the best of all reasons—that he is connected with every one of them—and who is himself a sample of their best. Let me introduce Mr. Varigny."

"Our friend Langdon gives me credit for more claims on your consideration than I really possess," said Varigny, as Atherton and himself shook hands. "I am by no means connected with every French family in Louisiana ; nor am I——"

"Don't say you are not a sample of their best," interposed Langdon. "For you must know that you are ; or if *you* don't, the rest of us know it so well as to make your knowledge non-essential."

" We'll waive that point if you insist upon it," Varigny responded, smiling. " I was about to say that I am not possessed of the exhaustive knowledge regarding them with which you credit me. But, for all that, I can possibly either answer myself or find some one who can answer any reasonable question Mr. Atherton may desire to ask about any particular French family. Or is your interest merely general in its nature?" he added, addressing that gentleman.

" It is both general and particular," answered Atherton, thinking, as he looked at the speaker, that between him and a certain boyish face which dwelt in his memory there was a striking resemblance of type, which in no respect amounted to personal likeness, but distinctly marked them as belonging to the same race. And perhaps he saw this the more clearly because his perceptions were quickened in all that related to that face by deep and stern resentment towards it—towards the frank lips that had deceived, and the beautiful eyes that had cheated him out of the interest and affection he had all his life so sparingly bestowed.

" Your history is so rich in romantic interest," he went on, as Varigny, having sat down, regarded him expectantly, " that one would need to be devoid of all imagination who did not find it fascinating. But it is likely that you are tired of hearing this ; and tired, too, of imparting information about its details to curious strangers."

" Not at all," replied the other courteously ; " provided that strangers do not talk to us of the extremely imaginative creations of certain novelists, and expect us to recognize them as types of Creole character and life. Of what has real existence, either in history or in the present, we arc quite ready to speak ; being ourselves perhaps a little proud of our past, and much attached to its traditions."

" Who would not be proud of such a past !" said Atherton. " It is not the fault of those from whom you are descended that this whole continent is not French instead of English to-day ; for the world has never known a more gallant, adventurous and hardy race than the early French settlers of America. Marquette, La Salle, Frontenac, De Bienville—the mere sound of their names recalls achievements of daring, marvels of iron endurance, such as no other race can show on the soil of the New World."

The young Creole smiled, and his dark eyes had a light of pleasure in their brilliant depths.

" *Je vous remercie, monsieur,*" he said ; and added, in the same language : " We think so, who have sprung from the race of which you speak ; but it does not naturally become us to dwell very much upon these things. There is one who would like to talk to you of them, however ; and that is my father. He is of the old order ; he has no taste, no love for the new. His mind is stored with memories, traditions, stories of the past ; and it is possible that you would be interested in meeting him."

" It is not only possible but certain," Atherton replied. " I should be extremely interested in meeting him."

" Then you must come over into our old French city ; for my father seldom goes beyond its boundaries, now that he has grown old. He never liked the new American city, but now he tries to forget its existence. It is still not very difficult to achieve that in the ' *Vieux Carré.*' "

" Which comprises within its limits all that is worth seeing or remembering in New Orleans," said Atherton. " I assure you that it will give me the greatest pleasure to make a pilgrimage to any part of it in order to form the acquaintance of your father."

"It is settled, then. Are you engaged for this evening?"

"I have no engagement which I cannot put aside."

"In that case I shall have the pleasure of calling for you at—shall we say eight o'clock? You are to be found——"

"At the Hotel Royal, quite in the heart of your old city. For the matter of that, how could one possibly think of being found anywhere else!"

"You do us and our old city too much honor. May I ask if your interest in these things has been awakened since your arrival here?"

"My interest in New Orleans, yes. In old French families—or, to speak more correctly, in *one* old French family—no. And this" (glancing around to satisfy himself that the gossips had withdrawn) "suggests a question which I have been anxious to ask of some one able to answer it authoritatively, as you no doubt can. Is it true, as I have been informed, that the family called De Marsillac is extinct?"

The young Creole looked surprised.

"The name is extinct," he replied; "for all the men who bore it were killed in the war. But the family still survives in the persons of Madame Prévost, born De Marsillac, and her daughters."

"She has no son?"

"None."

"There is positively no *male* alive who has a right to call himself De Marsillac?"

"I will not go so far as that," said the other, with a smile; "but I am certain there is none in Louisiana. Have you met some one calling himself De Marsillac?"

"Not only calling himself so, but taking all the rights which should accompany the name."

"And those rights," asked the young man with astonishment, "were—what?"

Atherton hesitated before replying. Deep as was his indignation against the boy who, he said to himself, had befooled and deceived him, some instinct—whether of past trust or past affection—held him back from denouncing him as an impostor and appropriator of that to which he had no claim. And while he hesitated Varigny went on :

"I ask the question because I do not know what rights a self-styled De Marsillac could claim. All that remains of the family wealth is a plantation on Bayou Tèche, which belongs to Madame Prévost ; on which, in fact, she lives. And, although that has been heavily mortgaged, she has lately been able to pay off the mortgage, and therefore no one could possibly claim it."

The mortgage ! How clearly at that word there rose before Atherton the picture of a wide, sleeping bay overhung by a tropical heaven ; of dim, mysterious, encircling mountains ; of the gleaming lights of a city from which the dark shadow of blood might never pass away ; of heavy tropical foliage softly rustling in the breath of a fragrant land-breeze ; while a voice full of music, and, he would have sworn, of truth, told him of a threatened home, and of a mortgage which might be paid only by sacrifice or by daring ! He looked quickly at Varigny.

"Do you know," he inquired, "where the money which paid that mortgage came from ?"

He did not think until after the words had left his lips how singular would be their sound in the ear of the man to whom they were addressed. In fact, the latter was for a moment confounded. Then, recovering himself, but with a stiffness of manner which told with sufficient clearness what he thought of such an inquiry, he answered :

"That is surely Madame Prévost's private affair. If I did know I should not feel myself at liberty to say."

"I beg your pardon," said Atherton. "The question escaped me unawares. Of course you could not be expected to answer it. I asked only because—well, because I am greatly puzzled."

"About the payment of the mortgage on Madame Prévost's plantation ?" asked the other, with growing astonishment. "Do you, then, know any of the family ?"

"None."

"And yet——"

"And yet I am curious about their private affairs, you would say. But it is not that I am interested, in so far as those affairs relate to *them* ; but—perhaps—to the De Marsillac who, you assure me, does not exist."

"You talk in riddles, Mr. Atherton. Do I understand that this De Marsillac claimed to belong to the same family as the Prévosts ?"

"I cannot say that, because the name of Prévost is new to me. I have heard it for the first time since my arrival in New Orleans. But he claimed to represent the De Marsillac who came to Louisiana as a refugee from the island of Santo Domingo."

"It is the same family ; there is no other of the name in Louisiana. Therefore the man who told you he represented it could only have been an impostor."

"That is what I am constrained to believe. And if so, these people of whom you speak—these Prévosts—should be put in possession of some facts relating to him."

"Facts affecting their interest ?"

"Very much affecting their interest."

Varigny was silent for a moment, as if reflecting.   Then he said :

"Do you know that you rouse my curiosity exceedingly?"

"There is no reason why I should not gratify it," Atherton replied, "except for the fact that in what so nearly concerns them I should perhaps first address the Prévosts.   Yet, if you are a friend of theirs, I may, by placing the matter in your hands, relieve myself of any responsibility——"

"No.   On consideration, I should much prefer that you communicated with them directly, since the matter seems to you important," said the young Creole.   "It is for them to take me into their confidence if they care to do so."

"But where shall I find them?"

"Their home is on Bayou Tèche.   But my sister is expecting a visit from one of the daughters of Madame Prévost next week.   You may, if you think it well, communicate your information to her."

"I shall be glad if you will afford me an opportunity to do so.   It may be too late for any practical result ; but, since her family are very much concerned in certain acts of the person calling himself De Marsillac, I do not feel justified in withholding from them my knowledge of what has been done."

"And I," said Varigny, "shall have pleasure in arranging for you to meet Miss Prévost as soon as possible after her arrival."

CHAPTER II.

It was with a more serious expression of countenance than he might have been supposed to wear as a result of learning that some one without right to do so had been masquerading as a De Marsillac of Louisiana, that Varigny, having parted with Atherton at the club, found himself a little later walking homeward along Royal Street.

A son of the old French city, his feet were naturally at home on the *banquette* of this its most famous thoroughfare ; and the preoccupied expression did not leave his face as he walked past the flashy saloons and concert halls, the cheap restaurants and oyster houses, which, as signs of invading Americanism, have spoiled the street in the neighborhood of Canal ; nor yet when, unmarred by such innovations, it stretched before him, a vista of wonderful picturesqueness, with the lines of its irregular roofs, gables, eaves and dormers cutting fantastically against the sky, and its long balconies of wrought iron projecting from the fronts of its variedly tinted houses. It was all familiar, as sights seen from infancy can alone be familiar ; but to-day he looked at it with a more than usually absent gaze.

Past the small, quaint shops, where French was the only language spoken by the French-looking men and women within ; past more green-shuttered, iron-balconied, quaintly tile-roofed houses ; past the Hotel Royal—no ordinary hostelry, but a landmark of history ; past the foliage-filled cathedral garden, beyond which the rear of the great church shows ancient and strong ; and so, still absent, preoccupied, unheeding, on to where the French Quarter ends with aristocratic Esplanade Street, lined with the homes of wealthy Creoles. A few more steps, then, entering and

passing through a garden, Mr. Varigny let himself into a
stately, wide-balconied house and was at home.

" Is that you, Adrien ?" cried a musical voice as he entered the hall ; and through a curtained doorway a girl's
bright young face glanced out. " Come ! I have news for
you."

" What news ?" asked Adrien, pushing aside the *portière*
and entering a room full of soft, delicate colors, and the
peculiar brightness of aspect which characterizes Parisian
rooms—as was not remarkable, since almost every object in
it had come direct from Paris, where the Varignys rarely
failed to spend a portion of every year. French of the
French, too, was the figure it enshrined. Octave Varigny
was not so handsome for a woman as her brother for a
man ; but she possessed the true Creole fascination of appearance and manner—a fascination difficult to define, but
still more difficult to resist, as one sees it in these delicately fashioned, dark-eyed girls who have grown up among
the roses and magnolias of the old French city. Such a
girl was Octave, polished to her finger-tips, yet with a gay,
childlike simplicity of character and manner which suited
her face, with its soft ivory tints, its mischievous dark eyes,
and the smiling lips, which answered her brother now.

" What news should it be except of Diane ? I have had
a letter from her. She comes to-morrow."

" To-morrow !" Pleasure flashed into his face. " That
is sooner than you expected. I have just said that she will
be here next week."

" To whom did you say so ?"

" To a man I met at the club, who has a particular reason for wishing to meet her."

" For wishing to meet Diane ! Who is he ?"

" You don't know him. His name is Atherton ; he is

a cousin of George Langdon and son of a California millionaire.''

'' Does he know Diane ?''

'' Not at all.''

'' Then why has he a particular reason for wishing to meet her ? Don't be so mysteriously reticent, Adrien. One has to *drag* out of you whatever one wants to know.''

'' You can't drag out of me what I don't know, Octave. The man of whom I speak is more mysterious than I am. I don't at all know why he wishes to meet Diane, except that it is to tell her of a certain De Marsillac whom he has lately met, who claims to represent the family of which, as we know, the Prévosts are the only representatives.''

'' But is that remarkable ? Do not people often assume names to which they have no right ?''

'' Very often ; but it seems that there has been something more than the assuming of a name in the case. Mr. Atherton says that this De Marsillac also claimed certain rights of the family.''

'' What rights ?''

'' He did not tell me. That is to be the subject of his communication to Diane. But he was deeply struck by hearing that Madame Prévost had lately paid the mortgage on her plantation, and asked if I knew where the money to pay it had come from.''

'' What a very impertinent question ! And you told him——''

'' That even if I knew, I should not think of speaking of Madame Prévost's private affairs.''

'' And then ?''

'' Oh, then he apologized. I really think the question slipped from him unawares ; but his manner left an impression upon me which I cannot shake off—a very disagreeable impression. Octave, *where did that money come from ?*"

Octave shook her head. " I don't know," she answered. " Somebody from Bayou Tèche told me that Madame Prévost had unexpectedly recovered a part of the family fortune which was supposed to have been lost. But I heard no details, and I am sure it does not matter. We are no more concerned to know how she obtained it than the man who asked the question."

" There you are mistaken. I am much more concerned ; for I am the friend of—Madame Prévost, and there is some mystery which connects this money with the person calling himself De Marsillac whom Mr. Atherton met."

" Did Mr. Atherton say so ?"

" No, but his manner implied it."

" If his manner implied it, why didn't you ask him distinctly what was the connection ?"

" Because I have no right to know more of the private affairs of the Prévosts than they choose to tell me. When he spoke of desiring to communicate his knowledge to some member of the family, I told him that one of Madame Prévost's daughters would be here next week, and that he could see her ; on which he said that he would certainly do so, since their interest was very deeply affected by the acts, whatever they may have been, of the false De Marsillac."

" But I cannot understand," cried Octave impatiently, " how their interest could be injuriously affected ; or how they could be in ignorance of his acts, if—as you say this Mr. Atherton implied—he had some connection with paying off the mortgage on the plantation."

Varigny spread out his hands with a significant gesture.

" I do not pretend either to understand or to explain,"

he said. "The man talked in riddles, and I did not choose to press him for an explanation."

" But Diane can have nothing to do with it."

To this positive assertion Varigny made no reply; so, after waiting for a moment, Octave repeated it with slight variation.

" You know that Diane can have nothing to do with it," she said.

" How can I know?" he inquired. " There is something mysterious about the paying of that debt. And we know this—that before it was paid, pressure was brought to bear upon Diane to induce her to save the property by marrying Burnham, the son of the old usurer who held the mortgage. The insolent cub boasted that she had agreed to do so."

" And if she had," said Octave boldly, " it was as one who would agree to go to the stake if no alternative offered. I knew that."

" You knew it ! And never told me !"

The girl shrugged her shoulders.

" Why should I have told you?" she asked. " You would have been furious ; you would have rushed to Bayou Tèche, and—and made Diane more miserable. For what could you have done? Had *you* twenty thousand dollars to pay the mortgage and save her mother's home ?"

" I would have obtained it. I would have pledged my credit to the utmost—to help Diane. You know it, and she should have known it."

" Perhaps you would ; and so have started in life with a debt for which you would have reproached her later, in your thoughts if not with your lips," said Octave, with a shrewdness beyond her years. " Diane would never have consented to that. I knew it, and so I said nothing. Besides, I hoped that the necessity might be averted—as it has been."

"But how? That brings us back to the first point. Where did the money come from?"

"That, as you told the inquisitive stranger who started the inquiry, is surely Madame Prévost's private affair."

"It is also *my* affair, if Diane is pledged for it again—as she may be. For who is this man calling himself De Marsillac?"

"An impostor it appears, since he has no right to the name; and you cannot think that Diane would have any connection with such a person."

"I am at a loss to know what to think," replied Varigny.

"Then I will tell you," said Octave. "Think that Diane is incapable of doing anything unworthy; and that whatever mystery there may be about Madame Prévost's affairs, or about this person called De Marsillac, it will prove to be a mystery which throws no shadow on her. Bah!"—with supreme scorn—"how little faith men have!"

"I have all possible faith in Diane," replied her brother. "You misunderstand me entirely. What I fear is that the person whom Mr. Atherton met did not take the name of De Marsillac without the knowledge of the Prévosts; and that if he paid the debt of Madame Prévost, Diane may be bound to sacrifice herself to him, as she would have sacrificed herself to Burnham."

"Such a fear is absurd," said Octave with decision. "But I will know all about the matter—if there is anything to be known—as soon as Diane comes. In the mean while I wish that I could meet this Mr. Atherton."

"You can be gratified. I have promised to introduce him to my father this evening. If you stay at home you will meet him."

" Then I shall certainly stay at home.   And if I cannot learn more from him than you have been able to do, I will give you leave to call me as stupid as—a man !"

*   *   *   *   *

It was a charming scene upon which Atherton entered that evening in the Varigny house. The apartment into which he was ushered, with its Parisian aspect, made a harmonious background for the group of persons assembled —a group consisting of the family and two or three friends —than whom no more distinctively French people could be found in Paris itself. Atherton felt that he had not appreciated before how purely the Gallic type had been preserved by these transplanted children of France until he saw this group, composed entirely of Creoles, with their faces, voices, gestures, all full of French vivacity and grace. But the most striking as well as the central figure of the group was the stately old gentleman whom Adrien presented as his father. He had a military bearing which rendered his military title of colonel less inappropriate than such titles usually are ; while his slender, erect form possessed the same look of steel-like strength which distinguished that of his son ; and his snow-white hair and mustache, both carefully cut and trimmed, contrasted admirably with his clear olive skin, his brilliant dark eyes, and fine, aristocratic features.

He received Atherton with great courtesy, and presented him to his wife, to his daughter Mademoiselle Octave, and to his old friends Judge and Madame Guichard and Dr. Latour ; after which he invited him to a seat beside himself.

" My son tells me," he then began, " that you are a stranger in New Orleans, and that you are much interested in our old city."

"I am a stranger in New Orleans—yes," Atherton answered. "But, since my mother was born here, my interest is perhaps more than a stranger would ordinarily feel."

"Your mother was born here ! May I ask her name?"

"Langdon—Mary Langdon."

"Ah !"—a very significant interjection. "I know the name. It belongs to the later time of New Orleans ; or, rather, to what we used to call the 'American Quarter,' as people now speak of the 'French Quarter.' "

"I regret," observed Atherton, smiling, "that this is the utmost I can do towards claiming connection with the true New Orleans. But, although my blood belongs to the other side of Canal Street, my interest, I assure you, is all on this side, in your fascinating old city."

"You find it fascinating ? Ah, it was once the only city in America worth living in ; but it is now a shadow, a ghost of what it was. As for the new city—bah ! it is a commonplace American town, with no distinction save what is lent by its connection with *us*."

"It is impossible to question that," answered Atherton very sincerely. "No city in America—I mean, of course, in the States—has a history so picturesque and romantic as that of New Orleans. And what is recorded of its past must be but a small part of what existed."

Colonel Varigny's lifted hands and shoulders signified that it was a smaller part than words could express.

"No one—not even my old friend Judge Gayarré—has ever been able to put on record all the brilliant and picturesque life of Creole Louisiana," he said. "Do you remember what Talleyrand said of French society before the Revolution ?—' *Qui n'a pas vécu avant* 1789, *ne connait pas la douceur de vivre.*' So it is of our Louisiana. Who did not know it before war and the American element changed it, does not know it at all."

"I told you how it was with my father," said the younger Varigny, approaching. "He is a conservative of conservatives, and has no love for the new order of things. But have you asked the question you desire to have answered? No? Mr. Atherton," turning to his father, "wishes a little information about the De Marsillac family. Am I not right in telling him that the family, as a family, is extinct, although the blood survives in the Prévosts?"

"You are quite right," replied his father. "Poor Achille de Marsillac and his two sons all perished in the war. I know of no family that suffered more severely. Gabrielle, the daughter—ah, there was a beauty for you!— who married Louis Prévost, alone represents the family now."

"Was there no other branch?" asked Atherton.

"Certainly not," was the decided reply. "The family had no branches—at least in Louisiana. You see, they had not been very long planted here. They were '*San Dominguais*'—that is, refugees from the island of Santo Domingo at the time of the insurrection of the slaves."

"Yes," assented Atherton, who had heard this fact before. "And you are sure there was no offshoot of the stem?"

"Perfectly sure. I have often heard Achille de Marsillac say that his father was the sole survivor of his family, while he himself was an only son. So you see there is no possible place for an offshoot."

"And yet," said Atherton, "I have lately met a young man, almost a boy, who not only called himself De Marsillac, but who seemed to have the family history at his fingers' ends."

"That proves nothing. He probably belongs to some obscure Creole family; and, borrowing the name of De Marsillac, thought it well to support his claim by allusions to the history of the family, which is sufficiently well known."

"Since Mr. Atherton is so much interested in the De Marsillacs," said Octave, approaching so unexpectedly that Atherton started a little as he turned towards her, "he may like to have an opportunity to meet a member of the family. You know, papa, we are expecting a visit from Diane Prévost."

"Certainly," assented her father. "A charming girl, but hardly so beautiful as her mother. A daughter of Madame Prévost," he added, addressing Atherton, "who, as I have said, now alone represents the De Marsillac family."

But Atherton was for a moment struck dumb. Diane! It was a name with which his ears were most familiar; but *Diane de Marsillac*, not Diane Prévost! Were they the same? And if so, who was the youth who, masquerading as Henri de Marsillac, claimed to be the brother of a girl who had no brother? He felt bewildered by these recurring clues to the mystery that seemed to grow deeper rather than clearer as he pursued his inquiries.

Octave, watching him closely, saw that he was visibly startled by the name of Diane. "What can it mean?" she thought; and her own curiosity waked as strongly as her desire to satisfy her brother.

"Papa is right," she said, addressing Atherton. "Miss Prévost is one of the most beautiful girls in Louisiana; and well worth meeting for her own sake, whether or not she can throw any light upon your mysterious De Marsillac."

"What possible light can Diane throw upon him?"

asked her father. "She can only repeat what I tell you—that she has no relation of the name."

"It will at least interest her to hear of this person who claims to be one," said Octave. "He seems to have taken a good deal of unnecessary trouble to deceive Mr. Atherton, who had never heard of the De Marsillacs. It was not in Louisiana that you met him?" she asked, turning to that gentleman.

"No," he answered. "It was in—the West Indies."

"The West Indies! But in that case he may have been a genuine De Marsillac. They were West Indians, you know."

"Octave," said her father irritably, "did you not hear me state that the only survivor of the West Indian family was the father of Achille de Marsillac?"

"Yes, papa; but there might have been some mistake about all the rest of the family perishing in the insurrection. Such mistakes are made sometimes."

"It was not a mistake in this instance," answered Atherton. "The person whom I met distinctly asserted that he was a Louisianian."

"And you know him well?"

"Quite well."

"And he was—that is, seemed to be—a gentleman?"

"I should have said at the time when I was associated with him, thoroughly so; in fact, of an unusual refinement. He struck me as one who had been brought up under altogether feminine influences, and he said——"

"Yes, he said——"

But Atherton, who had paused abruptly, did not continue at this question. He was silent a moment longer—a moment in which he decided that he would not be drawn on to speak further until he had a little more light upon the mystery which was puzzling him. Looking into Octave's eyes bright with interest and curiosity, he replied quietly :

"Pardon me, but I prefer to add nothing more. It is possible that I might be doing an injustice, for which I should be sorry. It is also barely possible that Miss Prévost may be able to throw some light on this person ; and if so, we will leave the matter of identifying him to her."

And, as if this was not sufficiently provoking, Adrien must needs murmur, as rising he strolled past his sister :

"You see, you have learned no more than I."

CHAPTER III.

"DIANE," said Octave, "I really think that you grow prettier as you grow older."

Diane, accustomed to admiration as to breath, smiled serenely in reply to this remark ; and, leaning back in a nest of silken cushions on a broad, low couch, regarded her friend appreciatively.

"You are very pretty yourself, Octave," she observed, with an air of candor.

"I—bah !" returned Octave. "I am ordinary, commonplace : you cannot walk down Royal Street without meeting a dozen girls who look like me. But you are remarkable—a beauty such as men rave over and artists paint. *Ma chère*, you should not bury yourself on Bayou Tèche."

"It has been very necessary, burying myself on Bayou Tèche up to the present time," said Diane simply. "But, now that mamma's debt is paid and her affairs easier, it is possible that we may go into the world a little more."

"You should go to Paris, and Carolus Duran should paint your portrait."

"Oh!" laughing a little, "that is more than we count upon doing. But it is settled that mamma will take a house in New Orleans next winter, and gather her friends about her again."

"That is charming news. May I say how glad we all were to hear that she had been able to pay her debt? O Diane! how could you have run the risk you did in promising to marry that dreadful man if she had not been able to pay it?"

"It was not a risk but a certainty," said Diane quietly. "I should undoubtedly have married him, had no means of payment been found; for it was the only way to save the home for mamma, *grand'mère*, the girls. But it is a mistake to say that I promised. Mamma would not allow me to promise; she only said that the offer would be taken into consideration. She did not want to say as much as that, but I made her do so."

Octave clasped her hands and looked up towards the ceiling.

"You are a heroine!" she exclaimed.

"No," replied Diane, with the same absolute simplicity. "It was a thing that in my mind did not admit of a question. People say now that it is not a girl's duty to sacrifice herself and her own inclinations for others; that she should say to her parents, 'Go, starve, suffer, do what you will: I shall not give up my chance of happiness and love for your sake.' But it seems to me that is only another name for selfishness. When one can do something—and has the opportunity to do it but once in a lifetime—for those one loves, those who have done all in their power for one's self, I think a girl is bound to remember that there is one thing better and higher than love and happiness in the world, and that is doing one's duty."

" But the need must be great, Diane, to justify such a sacrifice."

" Ah, *cela va sans dire !* Only extreme need will justify it—not merely wishes based on cupidity or ambition. But our need was very great. If you could know the long agony of the struggle I have witnessed—if you could know how I have prayed for the opportunity to help poor mamma—you would not think I could hesitate when the chance came. Yet, after all, it was Yvonne who saved her and me—not I."

" Yvonne !" Octave stared. " Why, what had Yvonne to do with it ? I thought—I heard—that your mother recovered some money which had been supposed lost——"

" That" (hastily) " is true. I only meant that Yvonne happened to find the papers and managed the affair. She is so clever and so brave, you know."

" Yes," assented Octave, but this time absently ; for she suddenly remembered Atherton and the mysterious De Marsillac. Now was her opportunity to question Diane and find out whatever was to be learned regarding this person. " I must not forget to tell you," she said quickly, " that there is some one here who desires very much to see you—a gentleman, a stranger in New Orleans."

" To see me ! Why ?"

" In order that he may inform you that he has lately met—in the West Indies, I believe—a person calling himself De Marsillac, and claiming to represent—— Diane, what is the matter ?"

Diane had sprung from her cushions and sat upright, with the color suddenly gone from her rose-leaf cheeks and her eyes opened widely in consternation.

"Who is this man?" she asked, or rather gasped. "What is his name?"

"His name is Atherton. He is rather an agreeable person, considering that he is said to be a millionaire; and—— Diane, what *is* the matter? Do you know him?"

"No, I never saw him," replied Diane hastily; "but I know—something of him. And I don't wish to meet him. In fact, rather than meet him, I would go home at once."

"Going home would not help you," said Octave, who was greatly astonished and intensely curious. "For he is so anxious to solve the mystery of the De Marsillac whom he met, and also to communicate to a member of your family some important intelligence affecting your interest which he possesses, that I think he would have gone to Bayou Tèche to see your mother, if he had not learned that you were coming here."

Then was seen the almost unprecedented spectacle of Diane in a passion. Color flamed into her cheeks and light flashed from her eyes as she stamped her foot upon the floor.

"How dare he be so intrusive, so interfering!" she cried. "What concern is it of his *who* the De Marsillac was, or how our interest is affected? Oh, how I detest meddlers and—and busy-bodies!"

"Then you know this De Marsillac?" asked the young girl, forgetting that questions so direct are not permitted by the code of good manners.

Diane looked at her for a moment in silence—a moment in which she seemed to hesitate how much to say or leave unsaid. Then:

"Yes, I know—him," she replied. "But I will not answer any questions of a presumptuous stranger about him."

"But *I* am not a presumptuous stranger ; and you will tell me who he is, will you not—for papa says that there is no De Marsillac living ?"

"Your father is mistaken," said Diane proudly. " *We* are De Marsillacs. We have a right to bear the name if we choose. I like the Spanish fashion of bearing the names of both parents. If we were Spanish, we should call ourselves Prévost y De Marsillac."

"True, but this man whom Mr. Atherton met is not one of you, so how has he the right ?"

"In the same manner that we have."

"But papa says——"

Again the girl stamped her foot in uncontrollable impatience.

"Your father does not know everything that possibly is to be known about our family," she said. "I do not choose to enter into our genealogical history for the benefit of Mr. Atherton. It is enough to say that I know the person of whom he speaks, and that I decline to gratify his curiosity respecting him."

Octave was silent for a moment, so much was she astonished by this strange heat and vehemence in one usually so gentle and placid as Diane. What could it mean? Who could the person be concerning whom she showed such interest and excitement? The recollection of her brother's fears and suspicions recurred to Octave. Was the man indeed some mysterious lover ?

"Diane," she said gravely, "tell me only one thing : are you bound in any way to this—person ?"

"Bound ! What do you mean ?"

"Oh" (impatiently), "you know what I mean ! Is he your lover ? Have you perhaps pledged yourself to marry him as you were ready to pledge yourself to marry Burnham ?'

Diane stared for a moment, as if the idea thus suggested was so amazing as to require a little time for taking it in; and then she astonished Octave still further by falling back on her cushions in a paroxysm of almost hysterical laughter. Now, to see any one laugh convulsively, uncontrollably, without possessing the faintest conception of the cause of the merriment, is somewhat trying to most people; and Octave was no exception to the general rule. She regarded Diane in silence for a minute or two, and then spoke stiffly:

"I have been fortunate in amusing you. But I really fail to see what there is so exceedingly ridiculous in the question I asked. You *have* had lovers—many of them, I believe; and you *were* ready to pledge yourself to marry Burnham."

"You know why," said Diane, sitting up again and wiping the tears of laughter from her eyes. "But there is nothing of the kind in this case. The—person of whom Mr. Atherton talks has indeed done us a great service, but he asks no reward for it."

"That is not saying that he does not hope for one," returned Octave suspiciously. "Diane, I believe—I really believe that you are in love with him."

"I have a great affection for him," said Diane; "but it is absurd to talk of being in love in the sense you mean."

"Why is it absurd? Mr. Atherton says that he is young, agreeable, a gentleman—Diane, how can you laugh in that manner when you know that I am so concerned? Because if you are bound to any one else it would break Adrien's heart."

"Oh, no!" said Diane—but she ceased to laugh, and her blush was beautiful to see—"it would not break his heart. Men's hearts are very—elastic, shall we say? But there need be no question of the kind ; for I am certainly not bound to any one."

"And you will not tell me who is this De Marsillac, whom papa and Adrien and Mr. Atherton have decided must be an impostor ?"

"An impostor !" If Diane's blush had been beautiful, her wrath was now splendid to see. "How dare they make such a charge against one of whom they know nothing—on the word of a prying, meddling stranger !" she cried. "I said that I would not see Mr. Atherton ; but I *will* see him, in order to tell him, once for all, that we know the De Marsillac whom he met, that we acknowledge his claim upon us and his right to do all that he did, and that to utter the word ' impostor ' in connection with him is—is an offence and an insult to all of us."

"Diane !" Octave simply collapsed into the depths of her chair. "I don't know you," she murmured. "I never saw you so excited before. There is no good in denying it—you *must* be in love with the man."

It was a little after this that Adrien Varigny found an opportunity to ask his sister if she had mentioned to Diane that Atherton wished to give her some information which might be of importance to her family.

"Yes," Octave replied, "I have told her ; and I think Mr. Atherton will find himself snubbed as it has perhaps never been his fortune to be snubbed before, when he begins to talk to her of the mysterious De Marsillac."

"Why ?" asked her brother, startled. "Does she know the fellow ?"

"Very well, apparently ; and deeply resents his having been called an impostor. She declares that he is no impostor, but has as much right to bear the name of De Marsillac as the Prévosts would have, did they choose to do so."

"Then we have all been mistaken, and there is another branch of the family ?"

"So it would appear ; but she is so far like Mr. Atherton that she talks in riddles. This De Marsillac must certainly be very mysterious since he inspires so much mystery in others."

"He *is* a mystery," said Varigny. "I do not understand at all who he can be, or how he is connected with them ; and still less how his doings have been able to affect their interest. Has Diane given you no information on these points ?"

"Absolutely none at all. She only denies that she is bound to him in any way ; in fact, she went into paroxysms of laughter when I asked the question."

"Paroxysms of laughter ! That does not sound like Diane."

"Nothing that she said or did was like Diane. You didn't suppose she could fall into a passion, did you ? But she was simply furious over what she called Mr. Atherton's meddling interference."

"In that case," answered De Varigny gravely, "I had better tell Mr. Atherton that it is unnecessary for him to volunteer information which is so entirely undesired. The matter is no concern of his ; and I think he is enough of a gentleman to drop it when he learns that Miss Prévost does not wish to hear anything that he has to say."

"Yes," observed Octave meditatively, "that will be best. Tell him that the family know De Marsillac, acknowledge him as a connection, and endorse all that he has done—whatever that may be. This is what Diane said that she would tell him, and I think it covers the case."

"Very completely," replied Varigny. He rose and took up his hat as he spoke. "So completely," he went on,

" that it will silence me as well as Atherton. I do not like mysteries—especially mysteries connected with men whom no one knows, and with money. The conjunction looks badly. Until Miss Prévost chooses to honor her friends with her confidence, her friends can do nothing but imitate her reticence in all respects."

" Papa will be certain to question her on the subject," said Octave hopefully ; for her curiosity was so much excited that the policy of reticence by no means commended itself to her.

" I will request him not to do so," said her brother. " The subject shall not be mentioned again unless Diane chooses to open it voluntarily."

" And if she never does ?"

" Then for me it is closed forever."

And with these words he left the room

CHAPTER IV.

So it came to pass that Diane heard no more of the information Mr. Atherton desired to afford her ; and that gentleman found himself unexpectedly checked, as if by a dead-wall, when Adrien Varigny ceremoniously told him that Miss Prévost was perfectly cognizant both of the existence and the doings of the De Marsillac whom he had met, and therefore any communication which he had thought of making to her was unnecessary.

" I am sure you will pardon me for also suggesting," added the young Creole, " that, since this is the case, it will be best to drop the subject, as far as any inquiries for this person in New Orleans are concerned."

"In other words, to respect the mystery of the family," said Atherton, smiling slightly. "You need have no fear. I will make no further inquiries. It is very evident now that it is not, as I was inclined to suspect, a case of imposture and robbery ; but that it is a family secret, with which no stranger has a right to interfere."

"It is at least a subject upon which they have a right to be reticent if they please."

"Undoubtedly ; and which has, therefore, lost interest for me. Why they should make a mystery of what they had a perfect right to do is their own affair, and I shall give it no further thought."

In saying this the speaker not only promised, as many of us often do, more than he was able to perform, but he also supplied much food for thought to Varigny. "*Make a mystery of what they had a perfect right to do.*" These words rang in the young man's mind ; and, though he would have disdained to ask an explanation—in fact, it is doubtful whether he would have listened to an explanation had Atherton volunteered one—it was impossible not to ask himself what was meant. What had they a perfect right to do ? What was it that had been done for them by this mysterious De Marsillac, in whose behalf even Diane the gentle was roused to passion ?

There is nothing which has such power to change and absorb a man as a question like this, which he is continually asking himself and which he has no power to answer. Diane was not long in perceiving a great difference in Varigny. He was all that courtesy demanded he should be in his father's house, and to his sister's guest, but he was no more. The pervading attention, the absorption in herself, the constant homage of look and manner even more than of word to which she had been accustomed from him

—these things were absent. At home he was silent and apparently preoccupied ; in society he drew back and allowed other men to surround her. There was no lack of other men ; but, first with wonder and then with a growing pang, Diane recognized that the only man for whose attention she cared no longer cared to bestow that attention upon her.

It was singular, perhaps, that she did not connect this change with the mystery which in her conversation with Octave she had left unsolved. But Diane possessed no great power of imagination. She had attached no importance to her own refusal to satisfy the curiosity of her friend or to answer Atherton's inquiries. She had been greatly relieved that the latter had not appeared to press his inquiries in person, and that the Varignys had abstained from questions which it would have been difficult to answer ; but she never for a moment thought of connecting the marked change in Adrien with her own silence on a subject which she would have said did not concern him at all.

How much the change in him concerned her, however, she felt daily more and more. With what a light heart she had come to New Orleans, relieved from the strain of financial trouble, and from the terrible possibility of having to sacrifice herself to the obnoxious Burnham ; free to take up her—what shall one call it ? Flirtation is too vulgar, love affair too serious a term to characterize what had existed between Adrien Varigny and herself. It had been impalpable as a perfume, but as exquisite, tender, delicate ; the first dawn of an attraction that needed only opportunity to broaden into the full glow of love. Diane had whispered no articulate hopes to her heart as she sped on her way towards New Orleans ; but she had been filled with a sense of delightful expectation—of something indefinite, yet certain as the coming of spring, the opening of flowers, the advance of roseate morning. And now suddenly a strange frost came into the air—a strange bar to all advance. What was it? Were men indeed so fickle? Had Adrien forgotten all that he seemed to feel when they last met? Poor Diane, waking to a knowledge of how little *she* had forgotten, asked herself these questions, but found no answer to them.

And then, even in her sweet nature, something like resentment roused. Was it necessary for him to indicate so plainly that he had changed? Need he be so distant? Need he, who last winter had claimed every moment of her society which he possibly could, now draw aside and leave her to others in a manner so marked? She lifted her graceful head with pride, even if her lip quivered, as she said these things to herself; and, while it was not possible for any one to be less of a coquette, there is not perhaps a woman living who would not, for the pang of wounded feeling and wounded pride at her heart, have smiled a little more sweetly on those who thronged around her to take the place of the one who had withdrawn.

Matters were in this state during the crowded, gayety-filled days of the Carnival, in which New Orleans excels all other cities of the world. Indeed, the true Carnival spirit survives here alone, whatever fictitious attempts may be made to revive it elsewhere. Mardi Gras in New Orleans means not only gorgeous processions, magnificent scenic displays, but the abounding mirth of all classes of the population—a casting aside of the cares of life; a return, as it were, to the Golden Age of childlike enjoyment for this brief period. And during these scenes, on Mardi Gras itself, when Canal Street is thronged from wall to wall with masks and revellers, the playful fooling never becomes disorder ; the whole city gives itself up to mirth, but the mirth does not degenerate into license. It was this which struck Atherton most as he sat, on that famous day, in the window of the club where his cousin had introduced him, and looked over the gay and motley throng which filled the street before him.

"This is the genuine thing," he said to Langdon, who sat beside him ; "this is the Carnival. In other places its attempted celebration is either a dismal failure—for more and more are the people of the world forgetting what mirth is—or it becomes a mere spectacle : a parade at which the populace stare, but in which they take no part. Here, however, it is the Carnival of the people. This scene carries one back to Carnivals in the Rome and Naples of the past. There is nothing perfunctory or make-believe in the gayety of these maskers ; and their pranks are to me better worth seeing than even the gorgeous procession of Rex."

"Rex's procession wasn't bad," observed Langdon, with the moderation of one who had witnessed many Carnivals. "In fact, it was expected to be better than usual this year, because Harvey—who is Rex, you know—is not only a very rich man, but a man of great taste. By the bye, I suppose you have heard who is to be his queen ?"

"Not I. Names are merely names to me here, you know. My acquaintance is very limited."

"That" (in an injured tone) "is your own fault, I am sure. You. might know everybody, if you would, and be *fêted* to your heart's content. We are not more fond of millionaires than our neighbors—perhaps not quite so fond —but we appreciate them, nevertheless ; and are quite ready to kill our fatted calves for them. But you will not eat the fatted calf after it has been killed."

"Perhaps I have been surfeited with fatted calves, and would prefer to be distinguished in some other manner than by the ticket 'millionaire.' Not that I go in for cheap cynicism on the subject of the world's worship of wealth. But I am not fond of profiting by it. Besides, I did not come here to enter society."

"I wonder what you did come for!" thought Langdon ; but he only said aloud : "Of course it's a matter of taste ; but there are a good many people here who would like to meet you, and whom I think you would enjoy knowing. You must certainly look in on the balls to-night, however. Rex's ball will be a magnificent affair. As I began to tell you, he has the most beautiful girl in Louisiana for his queen."

"Who is she ?" (indifferently).

"Miss Prévost—Diane Prévost. She—but what is the matter ? Do you know her ?"

"No," answered Atherton, who had given a start and glance of awakened interest at the name. "I do not know her at all, but I have—heard of her."

"From the Varignys, I suppose ? She is visiting them. Her family have not been living in New Orleans for some time, but she was here last winter and made a great sensation by her beauty. Adrien Varigny was considered to be first favorite then, but this season he has rather lost his place ; and Harvey, who is desperately in love with her, is making the best running. I'd like you to see her. She is not of the ordinary Creole type."

"I chance to admire that type very much."

"You can't fail to admire Diane Prévost, and she will be a sight worth seeing in royal robes to-night. I wonder" (with a laugh) "what Burnham will think of her ?"

"And who is Burnham ?"

"A young cad whose father has made a great deal of money, and who has therefore crept into the outskirts of good society. The story runs that, seeing Miss Prévost last winter, he was deeply smitten; and, being unable to approach her in any other manner, induced his father—who held a mortgage on Madame Prévost's estate—to offer him as a suitor, threatening to close the mortgage at once if he was refused. Details of the result are not clearly known. However, it is said that Miss Prévost took into consideration sacrificing herself, but that somebody or something came to her rescue. At all events, the debt was paid in money, not in flesh and blood; and Miss Prévost is here in more brilliant beauty than ever, to be the Queen of the Carnival."

"I have heard a story something like that before—in a dream perhaps," said Atherton quietly. "In my story the girl's brother obtained her ransom by a rather wild adventure."

"It was not *this* story" (very positively); "for there is no brother in the case. Miss Prévost has none."

"Then, of course, she is not the heroine of my story. There is a sufficient similarity, however, to induce me to take the trouble of seeing her; so you may count on me for Rex's ball to-night."

━━━━━

CHAPTER V.

REX'S ball was indeed a very magnificent affair; and Rex himself, an extremely good-looking young man, was a very imposing figure, in his royal attire. But he and his brilliant court were alike thrown into the shade by the dazzling beauty of the stately presence which stood beside him as queen. Dress, which is becoming to every one, was becoming to Diane in superlative degree ; and it is doubtful if a lovelier sovereign ever smiled upon the mimic pomp of a Carnival or the real splendor of a court. The costume which she wore was carefully copied from the period which her appearance strikingly suggested, and she seemed to have stepped direct from Versailles in the days of the Grande Monarque, or from the frame of some ancient portrait hanging upon its ·walls. Her robe of shining white-and-gold brocade, trimmed with priceless lace—the chief treasure which adverse fortune had spared to Madame de Marsillac—was fashioned in the mode of that by-gone court. About the rounded whiteness of her fair neck was clasped a *rivière* of diamonds splendid enough for a queen ; while above the luxuriant masses of her sunny hair—coifed high, but unpowdered—rested a crown of diamond stars, which flashed with every motion of the graceful head.

"Isn't she superb ?" said Langdon in a tone of intense admiration, as Atherton and himself came in view of this radiant figure. "There's not a woman to compare to her here to-night, and indeed one would have to go far to find one. Did you ever see a more striking resemblance to many of the famous court beauties of the past ?"

"I never did," Atherton answered very sincerely. "The type is wonderfully preserved. Some of those beauties must have been among her immediate ancestors." And as he spoke he recalled the miniature of Yvonne d'Aulnay, at which he had looked in the brilliant tropical moonlight, and of which a well-remembered voice had cried, "Diane looks like it !"

And Diane did look like it—marvellously, wonderfully like it. In her present attire she might have been thought its original ; and the last doubt which Atherton had entertained of her being the identical Diane of whom he had heard so much was finally and altogether dissipated.

" Well," Langdon remarked, " I must go and offer her my homage.   You will come and be introduced ?"

Atherton assenting, they made their way to the daïs where the mimic court was assembled.   Before the splendid young figure which was its centre, Langdon made his obeisance ; and then, drawing aside, said :

" Your Majesty will graciously allow me to present to you my cousin, Mr. Atherton."

Ah ! Diane, Diane, was it not in your power to restrain that start, which had in it something of terror, and that glance of dismay as the tall figure of the stranger bowed before you ?   Happily no one noticed either except the stranger himself.   But he must have had eyes in the top of the blond head which he bent so low ; for even before he raised it he knew what he should see : he knew that he should encounter just that look in the lovely, startled eyes which met his own—a look at once apprehensive and unconsciously appealing.

The appeal touched him ; for he perceived now what a very charming as well as beautiful face it was into which he looked—a face so sweet that to see it was to be fascinated by it.   And he remembered that this, too, had been said to him : " Everybody loves Diane.   Young and old, rich and poor, white and black—she fascinates every one." He remembered how he had listened with a smile, and now he felt and saw that it was true.   No one could resist the charm of this lovely countenance, on which was plainly to be read the stamp of a nature gentle and guileless as that of a child.   In the deception which had been practised upon him he could not believe that she had any part, or at least any blame. But she evidently knew enough of it to fear some revelation from him ; and, anxious to relieve her apprehension, he spoke at once :

"Your Majesty is kind enough, I am told, to welcome strangers to the court of your Carnival. You will allow me, then, as a stranger, to express my delight at all that I have witnessed ; and to hope that I may have the honor to —shall I be mediæval enough to say—'tread a measure' with your Majesty in the course of the evening, so that I may the more happily enshrine the occasion in my memory."

He purposely made his speech long, in order to give her time to recover herself ; and fanciful, in order to reassure her. Meanwhile his eyes were fastened on her, so that he saw the quick rise and fall of the diamonds on her bosom—those diamonds, in their antique setting, which he had held in his hand in the garden of Millefleurs, and had fancied clasped around just such a white young throat as that which they now encircled. In answer to his last words, she murmured something inaudible and held out her ball-card. He glanced over the list ; and seeing only one number vacant, placed his initials against it. Then, returning the bit of pasteboard with a bow of thanks, he was forced to draw aside to make room for others.

"I am sorry I came," he said to himself as he walked away. "I fear I have spoiled this girl's pleasure in the evening. She is no actress—that's certain ; for what a look of recognition and apprehension there was in her eyes when she saw me ! I would like to have an opportunity to reassure her—to let her know she has nothing to dread from me. But that is impossible, surrounded as she is at present. I must wait until our dance is due, and I only hope she may be able to put me out of her mind until she sees me again. Why did I ever come here and mix myself up with these people ? What possible concern was it of mine who Henri de Marsillac might be, or what right he had to the treasure he carried off ? I am rightly served for my quixotry, both on the island and here, by the dismay and fear with which that girl regarded me."

Pricking himself with the memory of her look, he found little interest in the scene around him, however well meriting the epithets with which the reporters of the press would characterize it in the morning papers. A floor of glass, perfect music, lavish decoration, beautiful faces and beautiful toilettes—each and all had long since ceased to have any intoxicating effect upon him, even if his mind had not been occupied with other thoughts. Hence the young ladies to whom he was introduced found him disappointing ; and, notwithstanding the aroma of millions which surrounded him, were not sorry when his perfunctory dances with them were over and they could turn to more agreeable, if less heavily gilded, partners. And, ungallant as the admission writes him down, there is no doubt the relief was mutual ; since the only event of the evening to which he looked forward with the least interest was his promised dance with Diane.

The time for this seemed to him very long in arriving ; and it is possible that his interest might have waned before it did arrive had it not been stimulated now and then by a vision of Diane, like some princess out of a fairy tale presiding over the revels of the gay throng. The very gleam of her diamonds had a fascination for him, linked as they were with the memory of the distant, blood-stained island where they had been found, and the mystery of the boy who had vanished out of his life. At length, as all things come to him who has patience to wait for them, he found himself again bowing before her, saying deferentially, "This, I believe, is our dance, if your Majesty is good enough to remember it," and walking away with the radiant figure on his arm.

It need scarcely be said that there was no thought of dancing in the mind of either, although the most seductive strains of the orchestra were ringing through the ball-room. A quick glance showed Atherton that a corridor without was almost entirely deserted ; and that a small apartment at the end thereof—a luxurious retreat, all foliage and soft-toned lamps and pleasantly placed seats, carefully arranged for purposes of repose and flirtation—might be counted on to be empty.   He turned and looked at his companion.

"Do you care to dance ?" he asked, speaking with deference, but dropping the tone of fanciful homage he had before employed.   "It strikes me that you may be tired and would perhaps prefer to sit out this waltz.   If so, do not hesitate on my account.   I am by no means fond of dancing, and I shall be glad of an opportunity to improve our acquaintance."

"I *am* a little tired," replied Diane tremulously.   "It is not easy to dance in a court train.   I—think I would prefer to sit out this dance, if we can find a quiet place."

"That is easily found," he said, and led her down the plant-decorated corridor to the room at its farther end.

This they found so far empty that only one pair of persons, engaged manifestly in a deep flirtation, occupied a palm-shaded corner.   These gazed disapprovingly at the intruders, until, finding that the latter had no intention of retiring, but, on the contrary, calmly established themselves in another corner, they presently rose and sauntered slowly away towards the ball-room.   It was when this event occurred that Diane, breaking in on some rather absent-minded remarks which Atherton was making, turned abruptly towards him.

"Mr. Atherton," she said quickly, "I cannot endure for you to believe—as you must at present believe—that we are unmindful of all that we owe you. Don't think us ignorant of it ; don't think us ungrateful for it ! We know and feel it more than we can say. It is with all of us written here"—she laid her hand on her heart—"and will never be forgotten."

This was so different from anything that Atherton had anticipated—the eager impulsiveness of the speech and the spontaneous acknowledgment of indebtedness took him so much by surprise—that for an instant he did not reply. He looked steadily at the beautiful face, all alive with feeling, as if admiring its charm or sounding its sincerity ; and then said calmly :

"May I ask, Miss Prévost, to whom you allude as ' we ' ?"

She flushed deeply ; but her eyes still met his own, frank and innocent as those of a child.

"I allude," she said, "to my family—my mother—all of us. We know that but for your assistance the—venture which saved us from ruin could never have been successfully accomplished."

He bowed. "You do me too much honor," he answered. "I speak with sincerity when I say that I am glad to have served you—glad that so much was true of the story which moved me : that there *was* ruin to be averted from one like yourself, and that I was able to assist in averting it."

"Do you mean," she cried, as if stung by his words, "that you doubt any of the story which was told you ? You do injustice—great injustice—to one who does not deserve it.   Believe me, the—person who told it you would never utter an untruth."

"Indeed !   How, then, am I to reconcile the statement of this person that his name was De Marsillac and that he was your brother, with the equally positive statement of your friends that there is no De Marsillac living and that you have no brother?"

She looked at him for an instant without speaking, the lovely color dying out of her cheeks, and her eyes seeming to plead against the sternness of his words ; and then she said in a low voice :

"It must seem very strange to you, and I cannot explain ; but both statements are true."

"Both, Miss Prévost ?   That is a bold assertion."

"It *is* a bold assertion—I know that ; but it is true. The person whom you know has a perfect right to call himself De Marsillac, and he has been a brother in every sense to me."

"I think," he said coldly, "that you are playing with words.   But it does not matter.   It is no concern of mine who has or has not a right to call himself De Marsillac, and far less whom you consider ' a brother in every sense.' I am glad, however, that you have opened the subject of a mystery upon which I had no intention of touching, because it allows me to explain how I have chanced to interfere with it at all.   Briefly, then : I was not only foolish enough to be both wounded and indignant when a boy for whom I had conceived a liking which amounted to attachment, and which I fancied was returned on his part——"

"It was, it was !" Diane interrupted earnestly.

"Threw me aside and vanished with a melodramatic farewell into mystery ; but I began to ask myself if I had not been lending my aid to imposture and possibly robbery."

" O Mr. Atherton !"

" Do the words shock you ? What else could I think? I have seen much of the world, but I have never yet found an honest man who veiled in mystery transactions in which there was no disgrace. The whole thing looked to me very suspicious ; and, besides being the dupe of a clever impostor, I had no mind to be his unconscious accomplice. As soon, therefore, as I received a letter from him—of which, since you know so much, you may have heard—I left Santo Domingo for Cuba, and thence came here, determined to discover if such a person as Henri de Marsillac really existed. I was speedily assured on all sides that he did not exist, that no one of the name was known in Louisiana, and that your family alone represented the De Marsillacs of the past. It seemed then my duty to inform some representative of your family of what had been done in Hayti. To my inquiries as to how this could best be accomplished, I was informed that you would soon be in New Orleans, and that I could make my communication to you. This I was resolved to do until I heard from Mr. Varigny that you did not desire to receive any communication on the subject. Such a decision relieved me at once from all responsibility in the matter ; and from that time to this I have had no intention of approaching or addressing you on the subject. But to-night"—he paused a moment— " to-night I read, or thought I read, in your eyes an apprehension. And this I felt bound to dissipate. I felt bound to tell you that you have nothing to fear from me."

" What could I have to fear from you, Mr. Atherton ?" asked Diane proudly, her crowned head lifted high.

"That you alone can answer," replied Atherton. "Believe me I have no desire to press any inquiry into your mystery, or even to speculate why none of your friends know of the existence of the man who found the treasure of your ancestor. I am only glad to see that a part at least of that treasure has come into rightful hands"—he looked directly at the diamonds—"and I have no intention of taking any one into my confidence with regard to what I accidentally witnessed and knew. I fancied that you might like to have this assurance, which is my excuse for touching upon the subject."

She was again silent for a moment before answering, and then she said :

"I do not deny that I am glad to be assured that you will not continue to make inquiries which can only annoy and embarrass us. Nobody but ourselves—nobody at all—was, or is, concerned in the finding of what you call the treasure of our ancestor. Have we not, then, a perfect right to maintain any mystery that we like regarding it? That mystery conceals nothing wrong—so much I assure you—and has but one drawback of which I know : its seeming ingratitude towards yourself."

"That," he said, "is of no importance at all. In any inquiry which I have made, nothing was further from my mind than any thought of myself."

"I have no doubt of it," she replied earnestly ; "but the fact remains that this apparent ingratitude has been a matter of great concern to all of us, and a positive grief to one. I should like you to believe this."

"Do not press my powers of credulity too far, Miss Prévost," he said quietly. "Since you assure me that the mystery hides nothing wrong, it is difficult for a plain man to see a reason for its existence, and quite impossible for him to believe in regret on the part of any one for conduct which had no necessity to justify it."

"I did not say *that!*" cried she quickly. "I did not say there was no necessity to justify it—for there is such a necessity. I only said that it concealed nothing wrong, and that we have a right to preserve a mystery if we like about our own affairs."

"It is a right which I, for one, have not the least intention of challenging," he replied gravely. "If you will allow me to repeat my apologies for having ever touched upon the subject at all, and my earnest assurance that I shall not do so again, we will consider it closed. There is, however, one thing which I should like you to do for me, in acknowledgment, let us say, of the small part I played in recovering the jewels which at present adorn you ; and that is"—to her great surprise he drew a ring from his finger—"to give this, as I suppose you are able to do, to the person who called himself Henri de Marsillac ; saying from me that, since the friendship of which it was to be a token has evidently no longer an existence on his side, I, on my side, must decline so keep his trinket longer."

Diane, who had evidently never heard of the ring before, stared at it in helpless dismay.

"Did he give you that?" she asked. "Was it one of the jewels you found?"

"It was one of those jewels. To gratify him I consented to keep it as a remembrance of an adventure which I now wish to forget. Will you, therefore, oblige me so far as to return it to him ?"

"I cannot—I dare not !" said Diane, shrinking back from the ring which he offered. "O Mr. Atherton, don't ask it of me ! It—you don't know—it would break his heart."

Atherton smiled incredulously. " Will you try the effect ?" he said dryly. " I have little faith in broken hearts."

" I think you have but little faith in anything," answered Diane with sudden spirit. " You certainly have not any in a—person who deserves better thoughts from you."

" How has he proved that he deserves them ? By desertion, by silence, by utter lack of faith in me—but this is folly ! What" (sternly) " have I to do with your mystery or your jewels ! Take the ring, Miss Prévost. It is yours, if those diamonds which you wear are yours."

" It is *not* mine," said Diane, putting her hands behind her ; " and I will not take it. If the person who gave you that had given you all the jewels, including the diamonds which I wear, he would have been clearly within his right ; since but for him and but for you they would never perhaps have seen the light, and certainly never have been beheld by us. Nothing will induce me to take that ring from you, Mr. Atherton ; so it is useless to offer it to me."

" You refuse absolutely to deliver it—with my message ?"

" I refuse absolutely."

" Then you will force me to discover the whereabouts of this Henri de Marsillac for myself."

" If that is a threat," said Diane, " I have nothing to reply further than that it is somewhat out of keeping with your assurances of a moment or two ago."

" You are right," he said, suddenly recollecting himself. " It is out of keeping with them, and was but an expression of irritation. You will perhaps acknowledge that I have some cause to be irritated."

" Yes," replied Diane, with unexpected candor. " I do acknowledge it. You have great cause to be irritated, and to judge harshly ; but if you would believe——"

" You have already perceived that I am a person of little faith, Miss Prévost," he interposed. " Don't, therefore, try that faith by asking me to believe impossible things. And, to prevent further rudeness on my part, here, I think, comes some one in search of you. It will not do for the queen of the evening to disappear, even for a short time."

CHAPTER VI.

IT was Varigny who entered, and whose glance around the room showed that he came in search of some one. When he caught sight of Diane, it was at once apparent of whom he was in search ; and when he saw Atherton, it was as plainly perceptible that he had not known who her companion would prove to be. He looked surprised, and paused abruptly. An instinct told him that these two people—unable at first to banish all traces of earnestness from their faces—had not been talking ball-room platitudes ; and mingled with the sense of intrusion which every one, save the most hopelessly obtuse, feels under such circumstances, was a pang of jealousy so keen that it made him for an instant forget good manners. Only for an instant, however. His pause was only momentary, and he then came forward with quite perfect courtesy.

" I was told that I might find you here," he said, addressing Diane ; " and, since this is our dance, you will pardon me for seeking you. I hope that I do not interrupt——"

" Nothing of more importance than a conversation in which everything has been said that there is the least necessity to say," answered Diane, rising. " I have thanked

Mr. Atherton for his kind intentions towards us—at least, if I have not thanked you before, let me do so now," she added, turning to that gentleman. "Believe that we deeply appreciate *all* your kindness."

Perhaps it was her queenly appearance which lent a queenly grace to these words; but the smile with which she uttered them war that smile of Diane's which all her life had laid hearts low before her, and the memory of its sweetness remained with Atherton like a perfume after she had taken Varigny's arm and moved away.

But it was natural that its sweetness seemed less irresisti-ble to the man to whom it was not addressed. Varigny had indeed often before seen such smiles bestowed by Diane upon others; but he had never before been conscious of the anger which now burned within him like a flame. "*All* your kindness !" What did that mean? What was meant to be understood under that comprehensive emphasis? What part had Atherton played in the doings of the myste-rious De Marsillac which resulted in the payment of Madame Prévost's debt? For the first time a flash of the jealous suspicion with which he regarded the unknown man was directed towards Atherton; for the first time he re-membered the wealth of the latter and his reticence con-cerning all the details of his acquaintance with De Marsil-lac. These suspicions necessarily took no definite form; but they were enough to feed the fire within him, and to provoke resentment more from the very fact of their vague-ness, which was in itself an offence; for why should this stranger be admitted to Diane's confidence in a matter from which her oldest friends were excluded?

Occupied with these thoughts, he hardly knew how silent he was as they walked down the corridor towards the ball-room; and had nearly reached the door of this apartment

when he suddenly felt how impossible it was to enter and
join the flying throng of dancers, while his mind was so
disturbed and his heart so sore.

"You have sat out one dance," he said abruptly, turning to Diane. "Will you give a few minutes from another
to me? I should like, if I may be permitted, to ask you a
question."

"I am not at all anxious to dance," Diane replied quietly. "As I told Mr. Atherton, my train very much interferes with my pleasure in dancing. It is one of the penal-
ties of royal state."

"Then we will take another turn," said Varigny, facing
around as he spoke to walk again down the length of the
corridor. The waves of music rising and falling in the ball-
room had, like a spell of enchantment, summoned all but a
few couples lingering here and there in shaded recesses;
and the long vista of the gallery, with its palm-lined walls,
its glistening floor, along which stretched a broad strip of
crimson carpet, and its fanciful lamps, was at this moment
entirely deserted.

Diane felt her heart beating quickly as they turned.
What did Adrien wish to say? Would he explain the
change that had come over him? She still felt a little resentful of this change, yet was conscious that only a few
words were necessary to sweep away all resentment in a
flood of tender and exquisite emotion. After a moment's
pause Adrien spoke—very stiffly.

"The question which I wish to ask," he said, "is briefly
this: Do you think it wise to admit to your confidence an
entire stranger, at the same time that you refuse to explain
to your friends a mystery which this stranger has, by his
inquiries, made notorious?"

The tone in which this question was uttered, even more

than the words themselves, so much astonished Diane that for a moment she was unable to reply. It was absolutely her first intimation, not only that Varigny had given a thought to the subject of which Octave alone had spoken to her, but that any injurious misconception might arise in the mind of any one from the mystery to which he alluded. He saw her surprise ; and, since she did not reply, went on in a gentler tone :

"Is it possible you have not considered this ? Is it possible you have not reflected that both the mystery and the confidence are likely to afford food for such gossip as—as I cannot bear that you should incur ?"

" No," said Diane, startled by the tone of the last words, " I have not thought of it. It has not occurred to me that a matter which concerns only ourselves—I mean my own family—can be of interest to others. We have certainly a right to preserve reticence about our own affairs."

"A right—yes. No one questions that. But do you know the world so little as to imagine that it gossips only of matters into which it has a right to inquire ? On the contrary, it is in the things which do *not* concern it that it takes the deepest interest, and to which it gives its worst interpretations."

" But what interpretation could possibly be given to that of which you speak ?" she asked, pausing to regard him with astonished eyes.

He shrugged his shoulders impatiently.

" How can I tell ?" he answered. " But you may surely see for yourself what a morsel it is for gossip to roll upon its tongue. This man Atherton comes here a stranger (no one knowing anything of him except his reputation for wealth), and inquires on all sides for a non-existent person —a De Marsillac, of Louisiana, whom he says that he met.

He talks of some mysterious transaction in which this person has been engaged, which is connected with the payment of your mother's indebtedness, and he expresses a desire to see you as soon as you arrive, to give information on some point deeply affecting your interest——"

" I have told him," interposed Diane, " that his information is unnecessary ; that we are perfectly aware of everything which he wished to tell ; and that we endorse all the actions and statements of the—person called De Marsillac whom he met."

" And do you think that this will satisfy the world ? Do you really imagine that it is possible to maintain secrecy on such a point without giving rise to gossip which your friends can neither answer nor resent ? Even if you have not given Mr. Atherton your full confidence, he certainly knows far more than any of us of this matter, in which figure an unknown man and a large sum of money."

Diane's astonishment now began to give way to indignation. She could hardly believe that this was Adrien Varigny speaking to her so coldly, almost sternly. " An unknown man and a large sum of money !" Even more offensive than the words was the manner in which they were uttered. She had too little knowledge of the world to be aware how far he was in the right, and the anger which it was so difficult to rouse in her began to stir.

" Do I understand," she said, meeting his glance with a fire in her own which he had never seen before, " that you mean to imply that there is anything in our reticence on these points which the world would have a right to censure ?"

" I think," he answered, " that such reticence is unwise, and certainly uncalled for, if there is not anything in the facts which would demand censure."

"You are kind enough to qualify your last words with an 'if,' " said she proudly. "It seems that it is rather from our friends than from the world that we have to expect harsh judgment if we do not satisfy their curiosity."

Varigny started as if he had been stung. Indeed had a humming-bird suddenly developed the stinging power of a wasp, he could not have been more astonished than by these words from Diane.

"Is it in this manner that you interpret what I have said?" he asked, in a tone of the deepest surprise rather than of offence. "Then, indeed, I must apologize for having spoken at all. Believe me I have no curiosity on the subject of your mystery—none. I have felt an interest and concern at seeing you put yourself in a false position, which I fancied our old friendship warranted. But I shall not need to be informed of my mistake again. Let me take you back to the ball-room."

"One moment," said Diane, who felt as if something choked her. "Since you are evidently right in saying that the world, including one's friends, has only unjust suspicion and censorious comment for whatever it does not fully understand, I must tell you, for the sake of others if not for my own, that in what you are pleased to call our mystery there is no wrong involved; nor anything that concerns any one but ourselves."

"There you are mistaken," he replied impulsively, speaking as he had not the instant before had the remotest intention of doing. "Whatever concerns you concerns me, Diane. You know that I love you; and, knowing this, you might undersand how bitter it is to me that you should withhold your confidence from me, and that a stranger should know more of what affects your interest than I do."

How often it occurs that the good gift which would fill our hearts with delight and gratitude did it come at the moment when we are longing for it, is delayed by fate, or by the fault or infirmity of others, until that moment is past, and another has come in which it loses half—nay, sometimes all—its sweetness and value ! Such was the case now with Diane. Had these words been spoken by Varigny even so short a time before as when they turned from the ball-room door, they would have filled her with happiness ; but now, angered, indignant, resentful of unjust censure and suspicion, she could only feel that they made the attitude of the speaker more unpardonable. Her pulses were throbbing with excitement ; a conflict of feeling, in which it was impossible to say what emotion was strongest, possessed her, as she lifted her proud young head like the queen she looked.

"And do you call *that* a reason for what you have said to me ?" she asked in a low, vibrant tone. "It seems to me that it rather makes it worse. If you—loved me, you would have faith in me. You would not, you could not, think of suspecting anything wrong in a mere reticence about our own affairs. I do not believe in a love which has no trust."

"In other words, you know nothing of love," answered Varigny. "If you did, you would understand that it demands as well as gives trust. And do you trust me ? Will you tell me who this unknown man is, and how he is so closely connected with you that you answer for his acts as if they were your own ?"

"Will I tell you—when you ask me in such a tone as this ? No. I should despise myself if I did."

"Then that is enough. I am answered. If I am not worthy of your confidence, I am not worthy of anything else."

"And if I am not worthy of faith, I am worthy of nothing."

They had ceased walking ; Diane had dropped his arm, and they stood facing each other like two duellists, forgetful of their surroundings in the excitement of the moment, when suddenly, with a loud, final clash, the music ceased, and an immediate rush from the ball-room of dancers, eager for the cooler air of the corridor, ensued. Varigny instantly offered his arm again.

"I think," he observed in his usual manner, "that this is all we have to say. Forgive me for detaining you so long. And, now that our dance is over, allow me to take you back to your court."

CHAPTER VII.

"ADRIEN," said Octave, "what is the reason that Diane is talking of going home at once, when she came with the intention of spending several weeks here ?"

Adrien, whom she had arrested on his way out of the house, stood drawing on his gloves and did not look at her.

"How should I know ?" he answered. "Mardi Gras is over, and Miss Prévost probably finds herself dull. The ashes received in church this morning have seemed to lie rather heavily on the spirits of everybody to-day ; although, for my part, I consider them very appropriate. *Memento homo quia pulvis es, et in pulverem reverteris ;* only it is not necessary to wait until one is dust one's self to see other things resolved into ashes."

"A very good frame of mind for *Mercredi des Cendres*," said Octave, regarding him keenly ; "but so unusual on your part as to rouse suspicion. You don't usually find the ashes so appropriate to the end of the Carnival. Something has happened. Come in here and tell me about it."

Despite a little resistance on his part, she drew him into the small sitting-room at the end of the suite of reception-rooms, which was her favorite retreat ; and there forced him into a chair.

" Now," said she, sitting down opposite him, " tell me what occurred between Diane and yourself last night. Of course I knew as soon as I saw your face and hers that something had occurred."

" I was really not aware that I had such a tell-tale countenance," he replied, flushing slightly. " But you are right. Something did occur which there is no reason to conceal. Miss Prévost was kind enough to tell me that she had no belief in my love and no confidence in myself."

" Adrien ! It is impossible ! Diane could never have said that. You must have misunderstood her."

" If you know more of the matter than I do, there is no need to question me," he answered irritably. " I am telling you—in substance—exactly what was said."

" But how did such a thing come to be said ? What drew it out ? Tell me" (impatiently) ; " for I am sure you have been stupid."

" If I was stupid, it was not for lack of sufficient explicitness on her part. To begin at the beginning, I found her with Atherton when I went to claim a dance for which she was engaged to me ; and they had the air of people who were engrossed in very important conversation. When I apologized for interrupting them, she said that they had finished what it was ' necessary ' they should say ; and then turning to Atherton, she thanked him with emphasis for *all* his kindness, before moving away with me."

" Well ?"—as he paused at this point.

" Well, you may imagine that this brought to my mind very forcibly the singular mystery which seems to connect Atherton and the Prévosts with some unknown person whose very existence Diane declines to explain. It has seemed to me an inexplicable mystery ever since I first heard of it—more inexplicable and more serious from its connection with money—and her tone towards this man, whom she had just met for the first time, absolutely confounded me. I found it impossible to refrain from speaking—from telling her that she was making a mistake, which the world would hold very serious, in admitting this stranger to a confidence which she withheld from her oldest friends. To this she replied that they (her family) had a right to preserve what degree of reticence they chose with regard to their private affairs ; and added that it appeared to be from their friends, rather than from the world, that they had to expect harsh judgment if they failed to satisfy their (our) curiosity."

" O Adrien ! that does not sound like Diane."

" Nothing that she said sounded like Diane. Some influence seems to have changed her utterly. I am sorry to say that when she declared that their mystery concerned no one but themselves, I was foolish enough to lose my head and reply that it concerned *me*, since I loved her."

" And then ?"

" Then she said that she had no belief in a love which showed no trust. I replied that love demanded as well as gave trust, and that if she cared for me she would not withhold her confidence regarding this mysterious man who seemed so nearly connected with her family affairs. In short, Octave, it was a deadlock. She demanded a blind faith in proof of *my* love, and I asked confidence as a proof of *hers*. Neither of us received what we asked, and so—*voilà tout !*"

"But it is impossible that this can be the end. You were both angry—I am sure of it—you both asked too much. But especially you were in the wrong. Why did you tell Diane in such a manner that you loved her ? Why did you make your love a claim to force her confidence ? Of course she resented your lack of trust. Any woman would have done so. And yet you *know* that this mystery conceals nothing wrong."

"I know nothing of the kind. How can I possibly know it ? I only know that people, unless they are absolute idiots, do not make mysteries of things which there is no reason to conceal. But, right or wrong, the fact remains that Diane does not love me, or she would give me her confidence."

"If you had asked for it properly, I am sure that she would have given it."

He shrugged his shoulders as he rose from his seat.

"I don't know what would be your idea of asking properly," he said ; "but of this I am sure, that I shall never ask in any manner again. Miss Prévost can hereafter have as many mysteries as she likes, and confide in whom she likes, without the least interference from me. And if she is intending to go away in order to avoid me, pray let her know that such a step is unnecessary, since I am on the point of leaving the city myself. There are matters requir-ing attention on the plantation, and I shall go there to-morrow."

"O Adrien, you will not be so foolish !"

But Adrien was already gone beyond the reach of remon-strance.

Octave remained silent and motionless for several minutes after his departure, until at last her meditation bore fruit in two words. "*Quelle bêtise!*" she murmured; and was on the point of leaving the room when the door opened and Diane entered.

But what a different Diane from the brilliant queen of last night's ball! She looked pale; her eyes were heavy, her movements languid; and as she sat down on a low couch and sank back on the cushions with which it was piled, there was little to remind one of the Psyche-like maiden who seemed usually to brighten the world by merely condescending to exist in it.

Octave looked at her keenly as she resumed her own seat.

"You are quite a picture of 'After the Carnival,' Diane," she remarked. "I never saw you used up by a ball before. You look as if, like Adrien, you are in a frame of mind to have found the ashes very appropriate to-day."

"Yes," said Diane a little listlessly: "I am used up. Evidently gayety does not agree with me. As I told you this morning, Octave, I think I must go home. I am too much of a country mouse to enjoy dissipation."

"But there is no need to run away from dissipation, now that the *Carême* is here. We shall be quiet enough after this, never fear. You did not look very much like a country mouse last night. It has been long since Rex has had such a beautiful queen, or such a magnificent one either. What superb diamonds those were that you wore! Every one noticed them."

"They are family jewels," answered Diane quietly. "They belonged to my great great-grandmother."

"I thought they must be family jewels, because the setting is evidently old. I wonder you have not had them reset. They would gain so much in brilliancy."

"Perhaps we may have them reset some day. Until now we have had many more important things to think of."

"I wonder," said Octave again—and she suddenly sat erect with the energy of her thought—"that you did not buy your release from Burnham with those jewels, instead of taking into consideration the sacrifice of yourself. They must be nearly, if not quite, valuable enough to have paid the debt."

"But we did not have them then," said Diane without reflection.

"Oh! I thought you said they belonged to your great-great-grandmother."

"So I did"—blushing suddenly; "but, all the same, they have only lately come into our possession."

"Ah!"

Octave could hardly restrain the further questions which burned, as it were, upon her tongue. But she remembered that she touched the skirt of a mystery which was already making so much trouble, and she forbore. More and more, however, did this mystery torment and puzzle her. What could be the meaning of it? Was it only folly, or was there really something very strange—anything wrong was impossible—at the bottom of it? She said to herself that lasting misapprehensions often result from lack of plain-speaking, and she was determined that she would try if a little of this plain-speaking could not sweep away the misunderstanding between her brother and her friend.

"Diane," she said suddenly, "you will be angry perhaps, but I cannot help it. I must tell you that I have heard from Adrien what occurred between you and him last night, and that I am very sorry."

Diane started, for she was not expecting this, and looked

at her with eyes in which there was nothing of anger, but only a pained wistfulness.

"Perhaps I am sorry, too, Octave," she replied simply. "But that does not help the matter."

"Oh, yes, it does—it must, Diane!" cried Octave eagerly. "If you are sorry, everything is possible; for I assure you that *he* is sorry too. And out of two sorrows joy should come."

"Not necessarily—not unless there is more than mere sorrow in the case."

"And there *is* more—there is love. Can you deny it? I know that he loves you, and I believe that you love him."

"There is no such thing as love without faith," said Diane proudly. "I would not believe any man who declared in the same breath that he loved and that he distrusted me. What he calls love is a sentiment not worthy of the name."

"Diane, Diane," said Octave warningly, "don't be so foolish as to ask what men are not capable of giving. *We* give the kind of faith you ask, but *they* do not. Their love is always jealous. And it is not just to say that Adrien distrusts you. He is only deeply wounded that you will not give him the confidence which you give a stranger."

"What stranger?"

"Mr. Atherton."

"You are mistaken. I have given him no confidence. He knows no more than any one else, except that he has met the—person called De Marsillac."

"And who is that person, Diane? See, I am bold enough to ask the question which is in the mind of every one. I am bold enough to tell you that you cannot maintain this mystery; that it is a folly and a mistake, since the world always puts the worst possible construction on what is concealed."

" You have learned your lesson well, Octave. That is just what your brother said to me last night ; and I tell you now what I told him then : that the world has nothing to do with a reticence which we choose to maintain on our private affairs ; and that while I would willingly give confidence to those who trust me, I will never satisfy the curiosity of those who make such confidence a condition of trust."

" O Diane ! if you spoke to Adrien in that manner, it is no wonder he was hurt."

" And how else should I have spoken to him ?" asked Diane, with the same air of pride. " Should I violate the confidence of others in order to satisfy Adrien that a matter in which my mother—mind, *my mother !*—is concerned is altogether honorable ? I do not think you appreciate how deeply offensive his doubts are."

" Again you are unjust. I am sure he has never thought of such doubts as you suggest. Can't you understand—will you not understand—that he is simply wounded that you do not think him worthy of your trust ? And I will not deny that he is also jealous of this unknown man who seems to have done so much for you."

Diane's gesture seemed to signify perfect indifference on the last point ; and, after waiting a moment for reply, Octave pleadingly went on :

" Diane, it is a little thing to ask after all our friendship : tell me who this man is."

Diane looked at her pale and resolute.

" Octave," she said gravely, " I would tell you in a moment, if it were not that to tell you is the same as telling your brother, and that I cannot do. It would be to say that I accept his love without his trust, and to this I will never condescend.''

'' You are throwing away his happiness and your own by such foolish obstinacy.''

'' And what is he doing? The first demand was on his side. He did not ask my love, and leave me to give my confidence as a natural result of giving *that* ; but, on the contrary, he made the confidence a condition of deigning to offer his love at all.''

'' Diane !''

'' That is an exact statement of the case, Octave. And now, if you please, we will say no more about it.''

She rose as she spoke and left the room ; while Octave, clasping her hands, lifted her eyes towards the ceiling and cried again in heartfelt tones :

'' *Quelle bêtise !*''

CHAPTER VIII.

'' I wonder why I am staying here ?''

It was Atherton who made this remark to himself, as he sat in his pleasant sitting-room in the Hotel Royal, near a bright coal fire, and looked out through a window beside him at the quaint, red-tiled roofs of the ancient buildings, with their green-painted iron balconies, across the narrow street. He liked his quarters ; and the old French city had laid her fascination upon him, as she lays it upon all who are able to appreciate what is antique, picturesque, and as far as possible removed from the crudity and color-lessness of ordinary American life. But it was certain that this was not the climate recommended to him by the doctors who had ordered him to the West Indies. Although nothing can be more charming than the winter climate of New Orleans when the weather is fine, nothing can be more disagreeable when, as often happens, it is bad. And very bad it chanced to be at present. The sky at which he gazed was of a cheerless gray, lowering over the perspective of roofs and chimneys ; and it was not necessary to venture forth to be aware that the atmosphere was of a most penetrating dampness. A greater contrast could not be imagined to the brightness of the day preceding—the day of uproarious Carnival gayety ; but such changes are an established feature of the New Orleans climate.

It was natural that the change should have depressed Atherton, especially when taken in connection with other things. He had just finished reading a letter from his father urging him to return to the tropics—to Cuba, Jamaica, Santo Domingo—anywhere he liked so that he quitted at once a climate so likely to do him harm. And while he had little disposition to set forth again upon a round of travel without interest or occupation, he told himself that he had as little inclination to remain where he was. In fact, a sense of disappointment altgether disproportioned to the cause that roused it weighed upon him. He had come here for two purposes—to trace out the mystery of the boy who had accepted his help and then so ungratefully vanished, and to warn the people whose inheritance he had assisted to place in the hands of one who was possibly a robber and an impostor. And he had failed in both objects. He had not traced the boy—the mystery surrounding him was as deep as ever ; and he had found his warning to the descendants of Henri de Marsillac altogether unnecessary. The treasure had passed into their hands—he had ocular proof of that in the diamonds which the night before had flashed upon Diane's neck—and he occupied in their eyes the unenviable position of one who officiously meddled with what did not concern him.

Yes, there was no doubt of it, there was nothing whatever to keep him here. Even Diane—he would be quite frank with himself—even Diane had disappointed him. His curiosity to see her had been excited by the certainty that she was indeed the Diane of whom he and the boy had talked as they went upon their treasure-quest ; the beautiful maiden ready for self-sacrifice, whose ransom they were seeking. He had said many fanciful things of her then, and some of them returned to his mind when he found that there was really such a person. He had gone to see her, expecting he hardly knew what, but chiefly perhaps to find one who would remind him of the boy he had lost : to see in feminine guise the charming face, the beautiful eyes, the frank lips that had so entered into his heart that even indignation could not cast them out. And he found Diane totally different. Beautiful, yes—beautiful in the style which had been described to him—but totally unlike the picture he had made for himself of what she would be, and hence to him a disappointment.

So he, too, had his share of those ashes of *Mercredi des Cendres* which Adrien Varigny found so appropriate, and liked the taste of them as little as any other son of man. Life indeed seemed very tasteless altogether, as it stretched before him in immediate perspective. What was he to do with himself ? Where was he to find an interest to occupy the existence which for some time he must spend in seeking for health, or in at least averting disease ? The question carried his mind back to the pleasure he had taken in the adventure in search of the buried treasure ; but it was too much to hope for anything like that again. If he could only find the boy, forgive him his foolish mystery, his fare-well, and take him as a companion, he might find idling tolerable—nay, more than tolerable with one so sympa-thetic, receptive, and attractive. But plainly this was not to be hoped for either ; although he never strolled through the narrow, dark streets and passages, like bits of old Paris, without looking to see the lithe young figure and pic-turesque face emerge from some shadowy court or archway.

Thoughts of this kind led him to put out his hand and take up a large portfolio lying on a table near, which con-tained the photographs he had made in Hayti. Turning them over, he found one which represented the spot at Millefleurs where the treasure had been found—that green, enclosed circle of the garden, in the centre of which stood the old sun-dial. And by the side of the sun-dial, with one hand laid upon it, was the figure of the boy, whom he had insisted on photographing. As he looked at the picture he recalled what a degree of insistence had been necessary to induce him to allow himself to be taken, and his reluctance appeared very significant in the light of later events. " He did not want to leave anything by means of which he might be identified," Atherton said to himself, with an intelli-gence in which he had been lacking at the time. " I re-member now that, making an excuse of the sunshine, he even drew his hat low upon his brow, so as to shade his face deeply. But he did not succeed in rendering the picture unrecognizable. It is dark, but it is *he*. There is no mis-taking it."

He looked at it intently, full of the recollections which it aroused, and with his yearning towards the original—the strong affection he had conceived for him—hardly lessened by this evident proof that his disappearance was premedi-tated even then. It was still in his hand when a knock at the door was followed by the entrance of a servant with a card.

"Mr. Varigny," he said, reading it. "Show him up."

Five minutes later the two men had shaken hands and were seated before the leaping brightness of the fire.

"I am very glad to find you in," said Varigny; "for, since I understood you to say that you would not be much longer here, I might not else have had the pleasure of seeing you again, as I myself am leaving the city to-morrow."

"I shall certainly not be here more than a few days longer, if so much as that," Atherton replied. "If your absence will be long, you would not therefore be likely to find me on your return."

"I shall probably be absent several weeks," said the other; and then a momentary silence fell.

It was broken by Atherton, who, glancing out at the gray sky and roofs glistening with dampness, remarked:

"The heavens seem doing penance to-day for the brightness with which they gilded the gay foolery of yesterday. It is fortunate that *this* is not Mardi Gras."

"Oddly enough, we almost invariably have bright weather for Mardi Gras," answered Varigny. "But our climate can be occasionally what Englishmen call 'beastly,' and to-day merits the term. I really don't wonder you are thinking of departure. You must regret the tropical sunshine you lately quitted?"

"One fine day here makes one unable to regret anything," said Atherton. "But I believe this excessive variableness of climate is just what the doctors want me to guard against. So I must turn my face elsewhere, although where I have not yet determined."

"You are not thinking of returning to the West Indies?"

"I really don't know—I haven't decided at all. There is unfortunately nothing to force me to choose one place more than another ; and I cannot at this moment think of any place with sufficient attractions to tempt me."

"My knowledge of the West Indies is limited to Cuba," said Varigny ; "but I am told that some of the other islands are even more attractive."

"The gem of the West Indies is undoubtedly the island of Santo Domingo," returned Atherton. "Nature has done absolutely everything for it, but man has so cursed it that it is the saddest spot I know."

"Were you in the French portion, now called Hayti ?"

"I left that part of the island only a few weeks ago."

There was again a moment's silence ; and then Varigny, with an apparent carelessness which was belied by the nervous grasp of his slender hand upon the rim of the hat which he held, observed :

"I have always felt a particular interest in that island, because we have among us a good many of the descendants of those who fled from it at the time of the insurrection of the slaves. Some of our best friends—the Prévosts, for example—are, on one side at least, 'San Dominguiais.'"

"The mysterious De Marsillac whom I met," said Atherton quietly, "was there to visit the old estate of his family ; and I accompanied him on the expedition. There" —he tossed over the photographs beside him, and selecting one, handed it to Varigny—"is a picture of the place as it appears to-day."

Varigny received the photograph eagerly and looked at it with interest.

"It seems still a very handsome house," he remarked ; "but is apparently unoccupied."

"It is a ruin," Atherton answered. "It has been a

magnificent house, but what you see is merely a shell. Within those walls there are only roofless chambers filled with rich tropical vegetation. The grounds surrounding it are of great extent, and must once have been of extreme beauty, but they are now an overgrown wilderness."

"You have no other views of the place, I suppose?"

"Yes, here is the best photograph I made—a view of the superb avenue of palms which leads from the gates to the house. And here"—after a perceptible pause—"is a view of a certain spot on one of the terraces of the garden."

When Varigny, laying down the picture of the avenue with an expression of admiration, took up the last photograph offered, Atherton, who was watching him closely, saw an immediate increase of interest in his manner.

"Whom does this figure represent?" he asked quickly.

"That," said Atherton, "is the young man who called himself De Marsillac, and whom I accompanied there."

Varigny did not speak, but he rose at once and carried the picture to the window. Then followed silence in the room for the space of two or three minutes. Atherton, sitting motionless, looked at the fire, and said to himself that whatever revelation came—and he had an instinct of some impending revelation—it would not be of his seeking. Accident alone had led to his showing this picture ; and if the intense observation which his friend was bestowing upon it resulted in a discovery of the identity of the bearer of an extinct name, this result would have no interest for him beyond the natural gratification of his curiosity.

When, however, Varigny presently turned and came back to the fire, he was conscious of a distinct sense of disappointment ; for plainly his curiosity was not to be gratified. And yet there had been a revelation. There was not in his mind a shade of doubt of that. The young Creole preserved unmoved the quiet composure of his manner, but he could not control the paleness of his face, nor the glow in his eyes—that enlargement of the pupils so significant of strong mental emotion.

" It seems," he said, in a voice which he strove to render careless, but in which Atherton detected the strain of effort, " that this—person was very young."

" A mere youth," Atherton replied : " not more than nineteen or twenty years old."

" And"—was there a note of suspicion here ?—" you saw no reason to suspect him of being anything but what he declared himself while you were with him ?"

" Certainly not. No suspicion entered my mind. Why should it have done so ? He seemed a boy of a particularly high type, with all the frankness of nature one usually associates with boyhood, and much more than the ordinary degree of refinement. His attractive qualities were very great. It is difficult for me to believe that he was in any sense an impostor."

" An impostor, no," said Varigny thoughtfully. " I don't think he was that ; in fact, we have Miss Prévost's word for it that he was not."

" And yet every one is agreed there is no De Marsillac living."

" *Male* De Marsillac, no—at least not that we are aware of. But the family have naturally a claim to know more of the subject than others can ; and, since they endorse this—boy, we have no right to challenge his pretensions."

" I have not thought of doing so," said Atherton stiffly. " It is not a matter which concerns me in the least."

" Pardon me," returned the other quickly. " In saying ' *we* have no right ' I was merely using a form of speech. I am well aware of the reticence you have observed on this subject ; and, as a friend of the family, I thank you for it. And now may I beg a favor ? Will you lend me this photograph for a few hours ?"

There was a pause. Atherton looked keenly at the young man who, full of irrepressible eagerness, stood before him. A sudden disinclination to do anything, or to allow anything to be done, which could in any way harm the boy who had been his companion in distant Hayti made itself felt with an intensity for which he was unprepared.

" Mr. Varigny," he replied at length, " I have just said that this matter does not concern me in the least. But I am concerned to keep a pledge which I gave to Miss Prévost last night : that, so long as her family chose to maintain this mystery, I would do nothing to interfere with it."

" Did Miss Prévost ask for this pledge ?" inquired Varigny anxiously.

" No. It was altogether voluntary on my part. Having seemed to interfere in their affairs, I felt bound to explain why I had done so, and also to assure her that she had no further interference to anticipate from me."

" And she said——"

" If I remember rightly, that she did not deny she was glad to hear it. Therefore I am doubly bound—by my voluntary assurance and by her expressed desire—to do nothing to dissipate a mystery which, however singular it may appear to us, it is the wish of the family to maintain. This being so, I should not perhaps have showed you that photograph—which was taken, I may tell you, against the strongly expressed wish of the original ; and I hope you will not misunderstand me when I say that I cannot allow you to carry it away."

" Do you think it possible that I would use it to affect any one injuriously ?"

" I cannot imagine that you would—at least consciously. But do you not see that I am bound to maintain discretion on my part, without regard to what yours might be ?"

" If you knew me better, you would not hesitate to trust me."

" If you were my own brother, Mr. Varigny, I could not violate my pledge for you. I greatly fear, indeed, from your eagerness, that I have violated it already, though unintentionally—that you recognize the picture."

" No : it is impossible to say that I recognize it. I am only struck by a likeness so strong that I cannot account for it ; and if I repeat my request that you will let me carry the photograph away for an hour, it is only that I may show it to my sister, under pledge of secrecy if you desire. Believe me"—with great earnestness, as Atherton still hesitated—" I would put my hand into the fire before I would do anything to injure or annoy Miss Prévost or any of her family. But to obtain a little light on this mystery is very important to me ; and *I* am not pledged to respect it."

" Casuistry, as far as I am concerned, I am afraid," said Atherton, smiling. " But be it so. I cannot refuse to trust you. Take the photograph, and do not misunderstand me when I say that in the use you make of it my honor is concerned as well as your own."

" I shall remember," answered the other gravely.

CHAPTER IX.

So it came to pass that Octave, still seated where Diane had left her, meditating on human folly in general, and that of the two persons in whom she was immediately interested in particular, was very much surprised by the speedy return of her brother ; and still further surprised by the unusual excitement of his manner.

"What is the matter?" she asked quickly, as soon as she saw him.

He replied by drawing the photograph from his pocket and handing it to her.

"Octave," he said, "here is a likeness of the unknown De Marsillac. Look at it and tell me if you have ever seen the face before."

Still more surprised, but with an interest equalling her surprise, Octave received the photograph, and, like himself, at once carried it to a window for the benefit of all the light available on so dark a day. A minute passed ; then, without turning her eyes from the picture, she said :

"I think that papa keeps a magnifying-glass on his writing-table. Go and bring it to me."

Her brother left the room, and in a moment later returned with a glass in his hand. She took it eagerly and held it over the photographed face, regarding it intently for some time longer. Finally looking up, her eyes full of startled astonishment and incredulity, she exclaimed :

"Adrien, if Yvonne Prévost had a twin brother, I should say that this was he !"

"But Yvonne Prévost has no twin brother—no brother of any kind," said Varigny.

"That is true—but what a likeness ! Viola and Sebastian were not more alike."

"Viola and Cesario, perhaps you mean."

"*Adrien!* Do you think——"

"I don't know what to think, Octave. It was for that reason I brought this picture to you, though Atherton was very loath to let me have it. He was sorry for having showed it to me ; for it seems that the person represented was very averse to being photographed ; and he had, moreover, promised Diane to do nothing more touching the mystery in which they choose to envelop the identity of the so-called De Marsillac. Therefore I am pledged to show the picture to no one but yourself, and you are pledged to secrecy regarding it.''

" I shall certainly not *talk* of it," said Octave with an emphasis which seemed to indicate that she might, however, do something besides talk. " But I don't understand —did Mr. Atherton himself take this photograph ?''

" Certainly. It represents a scene in the gardens of the old De Marsillac estate in Hayti, where he went with that —person.''

" Why did they go there ?''

" I cannot tell you. He gave no explanation. He has several other views of the place, but this is the only one in which the figure enters.''

Octave looked at the figure again silently for a moment, regarded it again through the magnifying-glass, and then observed meditatively :

" And the person was reluctant to be photographed ?''

" Exceedingly reluctant, Atherton says ; and, therefore, he has scruples about showing the picture, joined to scruples about breaking his promise to Diane.''

" Diane, then, talked to him on the subject ?''

" Did I not tell you that I found them in earnest conversation last night ? 1 never doubted that they were talking on this subject. But it is evident that she did not give him her confidence. He is as ignorant of anything concerning the identity of the mysterious De Marsillac as when he first began his inquiries ; but has given a pledge to her to proceed no further with these inquiries.''

"There is certainly something exceedingly strange about the whole matter," said Octave. "I never heard of anything like it before. The question of who is this De Marsillac is almost equalled in mystery by the other questions that arise —as, for example, what was he doing in Hayti at the old family estate? Why did Mr. Atherton begin his inquiries by saying that the Prévosts had suffered some injury or loss by him? And, most wonderful of all, where did the money to pay Madame Prévost's debt come from? And where did Diane obtain diamonds fit for a queen?"

Varigny nodded gloomily.

"I saw them," he said.

"Saw them!—the diamonds! Why, you would have had to be blind not to have seen them. They are superb, and would be twice as effective if properly set. The setting is very old, and bears out her assertion that they belonged to her several times great-grandmother, and have only lately come into her possession."

"By what means?"

"That is part of the mystery. She is absolutely reticent about the means. And such secretiveness is something so new in Diane that I cannot understand it. This picture, however, makes one thing certain, Adrien: you have no rival to fear in this boy."

"It was never a question of a rival in my mind," said Adrien haughtily. "It was a question of Diane's confidence."

"And Diane thinks that it is a question of *your* confidence, and so there you are—at a deadlock! *Eh bien*, I shall now take hold of the mystery and turn it inside out."

"Octave," observed Adrien warningly, "remember I promised Atherton that no use would be made of this photograph."

"Here is the photograph," said Octave, promptly returning it to him. "Take it back to Mr. Atherton at once, so that he may be quite sure I make no use of it. But you did not promise that I should not use the knowledge it has given me; and in that respect I shall act according to my best judgment."

"What are you going to do?"

"I shall not tell you. If you don't know you can't object. Only try and behave to Diane as if your relations were not hopelessly strained; and don't forsake the world for the plantation for a day or two yet. Now go."

But notwithstanding the gesture of dismissal which accompanied these words, Varigny lingered.

"Octave," he said again, "take care how you touch this thing. I am beginning to believe that there is very good reason for the reticence of the Prévosts."

"Go!" said Octave more imperatively still. "I don't ask assistance and I don't need advice. Go!"

He hesitated yet a little longer, regarding her doubtfully the while; and then, with a significant movement of the shoulders, left the room.

Thus left with a free hand, Octave hardly waited for the door to close before she flew to her writing-desk—a pretty, silver-decked affair in the brightest corner of the room—and dashed off the following letter, without giving herself time for reflection or hesitation :

"My dear Yvonne : Knowing the position you hold in your family—more as if you were its head than one of its younger members—I do not think I can do better than to appeal to you for assistance in a matter which concerns us both equally—since it touches the happiness of *my* brother and of *your* sister—and of which I suspect you will never hear from Diane.

"I am sure you believe with me that Adrien and herself were made for each other, and that they have both been aware of it for some time. When Diane came to us for her present visit, I was charmed to think that the romance would no doubt reach its natural conclusion, and give us the gratification of beholding the course of true love for once run smooth. But, instead of this, misunderstandings have arisen—or, to be strictly accurate, one misunderstanding has arisen, of so serious a nature that I fear it will prove an insurmountable obstacle to their happiness unless it can be removed. And for this reason I address you, hoping that it may be possible for you to assist in removing it.

"Briefly, then. I wonder if Diane has mentioned to you that a certain Mr. Atherton has been here for several weeks, inquiring on all sides for a mysterious young man named De Marsillac, whom he met in the West Indies, and had reason to suppose came from Louisiana. Naturally, every one whom he met assured him that there is no such De Marsillac, and that your family alone have any right to represent the name, as far as Louisiana is concerned. Then this gentleman, who seems to have never properly laid to heart the golden rule of minding one's own business, expressed great concern lest your interests should in some manner suffer from the doings of the De Marsillac whom he knew, and declared that he possessed important information which must be communicated to one of the Prévosts. Diane's arrival seemed to occur opportunely to gratify him ; but, to the surprise of every one, Diane declined to receive either himself or his communication ; declared she stood in no need of information ; knew the mysterious De Marsillac, endorsed his doings, and, in short, would hear nothing about him. One might have supposed the matter would end here, but no. The persevering Atherton was presented to her at the Rex ball (oh, if you could have seen how *perfectly beautiful* she was that night !) ; and, it is to be presumed, at once opened his budget. At all events, Adrien found them deep in conversation ; and, seizing the first opportunity offered him afterwards, proceeded, with a man's delightful tact, to reproach Diane for giving her confidence to a stranger, while withholding it from himself. This, I may say in passing, was unjust ; for Diane had given no confidence to the troublesome Atherton, his knowledge being just what it was originally—neither more nor less. But who expects reason from a jealous man ? And Adrien is very jealous—comprehensively jealous—of the unknown De Marsillac and everything connected with him. You can fancy *his* point of view : ' Diane cares nothing for me if she withholds her confidence from me ; has unexplained connection with an unknown man who masqueraded under a name to which he had no right, and concerning whose relation to her family and herself she positively refuses to say anything.' Then fancy Diane's point of view : ' If Adrien loved me, he would trust me. He would not demand my confidence in this manner ; he would be willing that I should give or withhold it as seemed best to me ; but, whichever I did he would never, never forget himself so far as to imagine that I could be in the wrong.' Then follow high sentiments, injured dignity, resentment, and final alienation on both sides.

" This is how the matter stands at present. Neither will yield an inch. I am astonished at Diane ; for she is always so gentle and seems so easily influenced, but in this matter she will not be influenced at all. I am sure she is unhappy, but she refuses even to tell *me* anything about this De Marsillac who is the cause of all the trouble ; and she talks of leaving us in a day or two. Of course Adrien is miserable, but obstinate as a mule.

" Now, Yvonne, dear Yvonne, you must know as well as Diane does all about this person. Cannot *you* clear up the mystery in which he and his doings are enveloped, and let these two foolish people be happy ? Mr. Atherton has told Adrien that nothing will induce *him* to make any further inquiries or take a further step of any kind in the matter ; so there is no revelation to be looked for there, and the only hope is in you—in your common-sense and courage. Surely there is nothing in this matter which demands concealment ; and, if not, for the sake of Diane's happiness, such concealment should be ended. I appeal to you because I am certain that Diane will never tell you at what a cost to herself she is keeping faith with some one, and you ought to know it. Don't think that I interfere in what does not concern me, but let me hear from you ; and believe me

" Ever yours,   OCTAVE."

The ink was hardly dry upon this impulsive letter when it was mailed ; and Octave then spent twenty-four hours in growing alternately hot and cold with varying hope and fear, until at last a telegraphic message was put into her hand. She opened it and read :

" Expect me to-morrow.

" YVONNE."

CHAPTER X.

"Dear Mr. Atherton : Will you take a cup of tea with me at five o'clock this afternoon ? An old friend of yours wishes to have the pleasure of renewing acquaintance with you.   Pray don't fail to come.

"Sincerely yours,

"Octave Varigny."

"Now, what does that mean ?" said Atherton to himself, when, returning to his room after an absence of several hours, he found this note on his table. "I am very certain that I don't care for a cup of tea with Miss Varigny, and still less to meet any old friend whom she has possibly discovered.   Unless indeed——"

He paused as a sudden thought flashed across his mind. It seemed incredible, and yet—after all, perhaps it was better to go. To ignore a lady's invitation was not very courteous ; it was too late to send an excuse ; and this was as good a way as another of making his adieux, since he had decided to leave New Orleans the next day. He glanced at his watch. A quarter to five. He had barely time to keep the appointment ; and, now that he was aware how narrowly he had escaped missing it altogether, he became suddenly conscious that he would not have missed it for anything.

It was a little after five when he rang the door-bell of the Varigny house, and was shown into a drawing-room, where a group were assembled, composed of the entire Varigny family and Diane Prévost. As he entered Octave came forward to meet him.

"O Mr. Atherton," she cried, "how good of you to be so punctual! I feared, since my note had to be left, that you might not receive it in time ; and if you had not come I should have been so disappointed."

"Fancy, then, what my disappointment would have been," replied Atherton. "But I am rather a lucky man, so I returned to my hotel barely in time to find your note and present myself at the hour you designated."

"That *was* lucky," said she approvingly. "Now come and I will give you a cup of tea as soon as your greetings are over."

There was no lack of cordiality in the manner of any of the group, but Atherton felt something more than cordiality in that of Octave when he came to the tea-table, by the side of which she had seated herself, for his promised cup of tea. Her eyes seemed at once full of warm approval and bright significance as they rested on him, while he was well aware that his own expressed an unspoken question. It was a question which she lost no time in answering.

"You must have been surprised by my summons," she said, as he sat down in a low chair beside her, fragrant, steaming cup in hand. "But I thought the hint of an old friend would be sufficient to bring you."

"Do you think," he remarked, not unmindful of the obligations of gallantry, "that anything more than your kind invitation was necessary to bring me? Yet I must confess to some curiosity concerning the old friend. I am unable to imagine who it can be."

"Are you indeed?" she asked with evident surprise. "Why, I fancied you would guess at once."

"It is hardly possible," he said, looking at her intently, "that it can be——"

"One whom you fancied mysteriously lost? Why not?

To the fairies Determination and Good Will all things are possible."

" I begin to believe that you are the embodiment of those fairies," said he. " But tell me——"

" No," she interrupted quickly ; " I can tell you nothing. In fact, I have only time to speak to the assembled company before your—*our* friend arrives."

She sprang lightly to her feet and stood erect—a charming figure, full of animation and enjoyment of the situation, tapping with a spoon against the delicate china of her teacup to attract attention. Every one looked at her, her father and mother smiling as at the gay nonsense of a child ; Diane with surprise, and Adrien with distinct apprehension. He alone divined—and feared—the subject on which she was about to speak.

" Since it is in compliance with my request that you are all gathered here at this special moment," the clear young voice began, " I wish to tell you for what purpose I have made the request. Every one present is aware that we have heard much lately of a certain unknown person called De Marsillac" (Diane perceptibly started) ; " and some of us are also aware that the mystery surrounding this person has been of a nature to produce many—ah—misunderstandings. This being so, it seems well that the mystery should be ended ; and, therefore, I have been requested by the person in question, Monsieur Henri de Marsillac——"

" Octave !" It was an exclamation from Diane which thus stopped the speaker at the very point and peroration of her address ; and Diane sprang to *her* feet with a haste and energy foreign to her usual movements. " I forbid you to go on !" she cried. " You have no right——"

" Pardon me," returned Octave ; " I *have* a right. I speak, as I have already said, by the request of——"

"It is impossible—it cannot be true!" interposed Diane passionately. "And if it is true, I will not permit it."

"Diane," said the other quietly, "you have no right to interfere."

"I have every right," answered Diane, with the same strange passionateness. "It is you who have no right to interfere—as you have interfered, as you know that you have interfered!"

"I interfered no further than to tell the person most concerned that this mystery was causing trouble——"

"To whom?" inquired Diane, lifting her head proudly. "Who besides ourselves was concerned in our mystery —if you choose to call it a mystery? I call it merely a reserve which we had a right to maintain about what concerned ourselves alone. Do you imagine," cried the girl, with a sudden lightning flash of her eyes upon Varigny, "that *I* was troubled, or that I would condescend to gratify curiosity, reward distrust——"

Up to this instant the rest of the group had sat motionless; listening, astonished, and uncomprehending, to the dialogue between the two who understood each other. But the last words, together with Diane's scornful tone, were understood by another, and suddenly Varigny rose.

"Diane," he said, coming to her side, "you cannot think that I had anything to do with this?"

Diane gave him another lightning glance.

"How do I know?" she asked. "One who has no faith, no confidence, might well take any means——"

"Say no more," he interposed quietly. "Let me only show you once for all whether or not I have confidence." He took her hand. "Come with me to the library," he said. "We will leave Octave to give or withhold as she pleases revelations which I agree with you in thinking that she has no right to make."

"She has no right," repeated Diane ; "and I will not permit them to be made."

"I never intended to make any revelations," said Octave. "I leave that for one whom you cannot deny has such a right ; one who has promised to be here ; one"—as the sound of a carriage driving up to the door was heard— "who *is* here."

"Come !" said Varigny again, in an imperative tone, to Diane. "For myself, I will know nothing which you do not wish to tell me—neither now nor at any other time."

He led her as he spoke from the room—not into the hall, where there was now a sound of some one being admitted, but through a curtain-hung archway at the lower end of the apartment into a room beyond, whence it was evident that they quickly passed, since the sound of a closing door was heard just as the door of the drawing-room opened and a servant's voice announced :

"M. de Marsillac."

It is impossible adequately to describe the thrill which was felt by those whose expectation and interest had been so curiously and unexpectedly heightened by Diane's protest and by the withdrawal of herself and Varigny, when that name was heard, and when there entered a slender, graceful youth, with deer-like head and easy, buoyant step, carrying his hat in his hand.

Madame Varigny sat motionless, gazing at him intently ; the Colonel put up his *pince-nez* to see more clearly ; Octave stood still, with the air of one who enjoys a scene which has been carefully prepared ; and it was Atherton who, putting down his teacup with a haste which almost upset it, rose and went forward impulsively.

"Henri!" he cried, extending his hand with a gesture of welcome. "I thought that I had lost you forever."

"Can you ever forgive the manner in which I treated you, Mr. Atherton?" asked the well-remembered voice, as the equally well-remembered eyes looked up at him wistful and appealing. "I assure you I have not been able to forgive myself."

"You must have had a very strong reason for acting in such a manner," said Atherton, regarding him with a delight that surprised himself, and conscious that for the pleasure of this meeting he was ready to forgive anything.

"A very strong reason, yes," the other replied in a low tone. "You shall judge for yourself how strong."

He gave the hand which held his own a quick, nervous pressure, then dropped it; and, passing Atherton by, went directly to Madame Varigny, who still sat motionless, with an expression of mingled astonishment and incredulity upon her countenance.

"Does not Madame Varigny know me?" he asked, pausing before her.

"Yes," she answered gravely, almost sternly. "You are Yvonne; and this is a kind of acting which I confess myself altogether unable to appreciate."

"Yvonne!" cried Colonel Varigny.

He made a quick stride forward, and taking hold of the slender young figure, turned it around, with the face towards the light. The boy—to use the term once more—did not shrink from his scrutiny. The graceful head was thrown slightly back, as that of one who has no cause for shame; and the frank brown eyes met unwaveringly those keenly bent upon them.

The Colonel murmured a French oath under his white mustache.

"It *is* Yvonne!" he said then. "But who could have imagined it? My dear, what is the meaning of this?"

"That is what I have come to tell you," answered Yvonne.

She did not glance towards Atherton as she spoke. It was only Octave who observed how his astonishment had the effect of causing a complete physical collapse. He absolutely dropped into the nearest chair, as if the surprise had been a veritable blow. Meanwhile Yvonne, taking Colonel Varigny's hand in hers, drew him back to where his wife sat.

"I see," she said, in clear, sweet tones, that were distinctly audible to every ear, "that Madame Varigny disapproves of me, and she is quite right. Nothing but the most extreme necessity would justify my assuming this dress and doing what I have done. If I had nothing more to justify me than a daring spirit, a love of adventure, or even a desire for fortune, I could neither hold myself excused nor ask any one else to excuse me. But I had much more. And I have come to tell you, because you are all my friends"—and here for an instant her glance rested on Atherton—"what induced me to undertake a venture so wild and a risk so great. But where"—she turned to Octave—"are Diane and your brother?"

"They left the room as you entered it," answered Octave, who felt keenly how much her dramatic scene lacked completeness by the absence of the two persons for whose benefit it had primarily been arranged. "Diane resents what she calls my interference, and vehemently objects to any revelation on your part; while Adrien thought the eleventh hour not too late to display a chivalrous confidence, by refusing to hear anything she did not sanction."

"It does not matter," said Yvonne. "He will know

everything from Diane instead of from me, that is all.   She will feel at liberty to speak now ; and will speak more willingly because he has given, even late, this proof of confidence.   You were right in thinking that she was bound by a pledge of secrecy before ; and bound, no doubt, by her own pride also."

"And is it possible," said Colonel Varigny solemnly, putting on his *pince-nez* again to regard the speaker, " that you are the De Marsillac of whom we have heard so much, who was in the West Indies with this—this gentleman here?"

"He can bear witness that I am," replied Yvonne, with another momentary glance towards Atherton.   "No one could know better ; for without his assistance I should have failed in all I went to do.   But let me tell you my story from the beginning.   I want to end all mystery and misunderstanding, and induce Madame Varigny, as I hope I shall, to look at me more kindly."

"I do not mean to look at you unkindly, Yvonne," said Madame Varigny ; " but you cannot expect me to pretend to approve a thing which fills me with horror.   That you, a French girl, brought up as *our* daughters are, should have put on man's dress and gone alone to the West Indies——"

"It is true," said Yvonne, as the lady paused in a manner which said more than any words.   "It is, on the face of it, a dreadful thing that I, a French girl as you say, brought up as only French girls are, should have put on man's dress and gone alone to the West Indies.   I acknowledge it, and I felt it—ah, you can never guess how much ! But there was one thing even more dreadful, and that was *not* to go."

"Tell us what you mean, my dear," said Colonel Varigny gently.

Yvonne looked at him gratefully. To plead a cause to unsympathetic auditors is very difficult, and she saw that she had no sympathy to expect from Madame Varigny until her case was fully proved—if even then. But here was an auditor who was prepared to judge kindly. Yvonne was proudly conscious that there was nothing in her conduct, except its unconventionality, which needed condoning; but, still, she had a sense of comfort in addressing this listener, who stood ready to sympathize rather than condemn.

"I am anxious to tell you what I mean," she said. "To be brief, then. I am sure you know of my mother's pecuniary embarrassments. We never talked of them to our friends, but they were very great. Year by year the burden of our difficulties grew heavier and the problem of life harder. Every sacrifice that could be made was made, every self-denial practised. With the plantation I did all that could be done without command of money——"

Colonel Varigny nodded.

"You did well," he said emphatically. "No man could have done better. It was not without reason they called you on Bayou Tèche ' the man of the family.' "

"I suppose," Yvonne went on, "that from filling so many of what are usually a man's duties, I came to have a man's thoughts, as far as the family were concerned. I had a knowledge of our affairs which no one else possessed, not even Diane, because mamma consulted me about everything; and I had a sense of responsibility towards the others, and a passionate longing to do something to remove the weight of our troubles from my mother and to improve our almost hopeless situation. I always said to myself that if ever a chance arose by which I could do something, no matter how hard, to gain those ends, I would do it at any cost. And I meant what I said."

Those looking at her and listening to her were of the opinion that she had fully proved that she meant what she said.

" Of course you understand," she continued, " that the great trouble was debt—debt which we could not pay, struggle as we might. And the worst debt of all was one for which the plantation—all that we had for our support —was mortgaged to a man without mercy. You know him. His name is Burnham and he is the son of my grandfather's overseer."

" I know him," said Colonel Varigny, this time grimly. " Every one knows him. He is, as you say, without mercy."

" Well, you can fancy what it was to be indebted to such a man, and to have the debt always hanging over us. Last November he came to my mother and told her that the debt must be paid, or the mortgage would be foreclosed. He offered her, however, one alternative, and that was to accept his son as a husband for Diane."

" Yvonne !" cried Madame Varigny, and " Yvonne !" gasped the Colonel ; while both added in a breath, " Impossible !"

" It sounds like an old-fashioned melodrama, does it not ?" said Yvonne. " But it is true, nevertheless. Diane, our Diane—think of it !—had been chosen by this low-born usurer as the wife of his son ; on the condition of which marriage he would graciously leave my mother in possession of her home during her life. My mother had but one impulse—to reject the proposal at once and let him do his worst. But he insisted that she should take time for consideration, and that Diane should be consulted. We consulted her, never thinking it more than a mere form ; but, to our horror, Diane declared that she would marry the man. She said that it was the only thing she could do to relieve my mother of troubles she had heretofore witnessed helplessly, and that she was resolved to do it. Neither argument nor remonstrance had any effect upon her ; for, gentle as she is, Diane can be very obstinate——"

" There is not a doubt of that," observed Octave.

" The only concession we could gain was that she would take no step to let the Burnhams know her resolve for three months ; and I promised her—I think, indeed, I took a solemn oath—that within that time I would, by God's help, obtain the means to pay the debt, and so release her from what she held to be the necessity to sacrifice herself. When I made this promise I had no idea how I should keep it ; but a few hours later God—as I truly believe—showed me the way. I found in an old desk some papers relating to the estates which my great-great-grandfather lost in Santo Domingo ; and there among those papers, never seen by any one until I discovered it, was a paper written by Henri de Marsillac, telling his family that on the night of the insurrection of the slaves, having need to fly for his life, he had buried in the garden a large sum of money which he had then in his possession, and indicating the exact spot where it was to be found. Was it not natural to believe that the money thus buried still remained undis-turbed where he had placed it ?"

" There was at least a strong possibility that it might be so," replied Colonel Varigny, at whom she looked. " A probability strong enough to justify you in sending some one to search——"

" Ah !" she interposed quickly, " but where was that some one to be found ? We have not a man belonging to us. There was no friend of whom we could ask so great a service ; and to send any agent save the most trust-worthy would have been madness. I knew all this perfectly, and I never thought of but one thing—to go my-self."

"Yvonne, Yvonne!" murmured Madame Varigny, as if in late remonstrance.

"I told my mother so," said Yvonne, turning her beautiful, wistful eyes upon the last speaker; "and she declared it was impossible, asking how could a girl go alone and unprotected on such an errand. And then it was that, like an inspiration, the thought came to me of *this*"—she made a gesture indicating her masculine attire. "I said that if I could not go as a girl I could go as a boy. I had always felt as if I *were* a boy, and I knew that the dress would be a complete disguise and protection. Indeed— think of it for a moment!—how could I have gone other- wise? Who was there to accompany me, who to protect me? I am not speaking only of conventionality, of the *convenances* which a French girl is brought up so strictly to respect. It was more than a question of a chaperon : it was a question of absolute danger—such danger as no girl could dare alone." She turned and for the first time ad- dressed her most silent auditor. "Mr. Atherton," she said, "will *you* tell them whether or not I could have done what I did as a girl?"

As if this were the appeal for which he had been waiting, Atherton rose and came forward to her side.

"No," he answered, "you could not. This revelation," he went on, addressing Madame Varigny, ' is a greater astonishment to me than to you ; but, with my knowledge of what it was that was undertaken, what difficulties sur- rounded, and what absolute peril had to be risked in order to accomplish it, I emphatically endorse all that has been said. It was not possible for any girl, no matter how brave, to have undertaken it."

·'And yet," said Madame Varigny, smiling in spite of herself, " it was a girl who did undertake it."

Atherton cast a confused glance upon the figure by his side.

" So I am told," he said ; " but even yet it is difficult for me to believe it—difficult to credit that the boy who bore himself so bravely even for a boy, through scenes which I shudder to recall, was, after all, a girl. I do not know what judgment you may have for such a deed," he added, looking around the little circle ; " but to me it seems nothing less than heroic."

" And so it was !" exclaimed Colonel Varigny, bringing his hand down with emphasis upon the mantel-shelf, by which he stood. " I never heard of anything so brave in all my life. And you succeeded, Yvonne—you succeeded ?"

Yvonne made a gesture of her hand towards Atherton.

" Thanks to him, yes," she answered. " I found the money which freed my mother and Diane ; but I could never have found it without his aid. And do you not think now," she added, addressing still wistfully Madame Varigny, " that there is something to be said for me—that I had reason enough to justify even such a step ?"

Madame Varigny's answer was to rise and take her in her arms.

" My dear," she said, " Mr. Atherton is right : it was nothing less than heroic. I admire and love you with all my heart. But, all the same, we must not allow this to be known by the world, which respects conventionalities more than heroic deeds. You will now come and lay aside this dress forever ; and Mr. Atherton"—she looked at him with a smile so warm that it was like sunshine—" must dine with us this evening, in order that he may forget Henri de Marsillac, and meet—Miss Prévost."

CHAPTER XI.

" Forget Henri de Marsillac, and meet—Miss Prévost.''
These words had not once ceased to echo through Atherton's mind, like a refrain of which he hardly understood the meaning, during the interval of time which elapsed between his departure from the Varigny house and his return there, in accordance with Madame Varigny's invitation, for dinner.   Forget the boy whom he had taken into his heart, against whom his indignation had been so deeply stirred, and yet whom he had never ceased to regard with affection, and find instead—a young lady !   The thought was bewildering ; and not less bewildering was his attempt to read-just his mental attitude towards the person whose identity had so suddenly and completely changed.   He was conscious chiefly of a mingled sense of exasperation and admiration —exasperation that the boy who had taken so deep a hold of his fancy was vanished out of existence, had never indeed existed at all ; and admiration for the girl whose daring had been equal to such a task, and whose courage never failed in its execution.

Looking back on the past, he found himself indeed lost in wonder at the manner in which she had sustained her part without faltering—sustained it so completely as not to excite his suspicion in the faintest degree.   Never had he for a moment thought of his companion as anything but a boy, delicate, imaginative, fanciful perhaps, but altogether virile.   And lo ! all the time that companion had been a girl.   And not a girl who had been brought up without the restraints and protections that in another day were deemed essential for girlhood, who had been thrown upon the world and forced to acquire independence of habit and thought ; but a girl who came out of the heart of a country and a race where old traditions are still in force, where conventionalities are not relaxed, and the steps of a maiden of good birth are still hedged with restrictions. A girl who had never gone beyond the shelter of her home unprotected ; who, despite her dauntless courage, knew no more of the world than a child, and shrank from all knowledge of its rude reality as only a woman so constituted and so trained can shrink ; yet who, putting aside all shrinking and all fear, took a step from which the boldest of the New Womanhood might draw back, and passed unscathed as Una through the perils which encompassed her venture.

Thinking over it all, the heart of the man thrilled with admiration, wonder, and yet exasperation, too. How great must have been the power of love and the rare quality of self-forgetfulness which could nerve such a woman to such an undertaking ! How truly heroic was the deed—and yet how mad ! What if she had been discovered ! What if she had not met himself ! What if he had been murdered on the night when death passed so near to them in the remote Haytian mountains ! How mad it was, and yet— there could be no question—how heroic !

It was in a frame of mind made up of these sentiments that he returned to the Varigny house, and was shown into the drawing-room, where the revelation of the afternoon had been made ; and where, instead of long shafts of sunlight, there now reigned a soft glow of lamplight and fire-light. In the first moment of his entrance the room seemed to him empty—waiting, in its luxurious spaciousness, its air of a transplanted Parisian interior, for the life that was to fill it—when suddenly a figure arose from a shaded corner and came towards him.

He paused, holding his breath. Was ever transformation so complete, and was ever likeness so great? No, he had not lost the boy whom he had known and loved. Here was the same face, identical and unchanged, that had smiled upon him through all their journeyings; the same eyes that had met his so frankly and so kindly a hundred times, although it was a young lady, clad in shimmering silk and cloud-like lace, who bore this well-remembered head upon her slender neck, and extended to him the hand he had once declared too small for any practical purpose, but which now proved that it was not too small to give a grasp of warmest friendship.

"It is not 'Miss Prévost,'" she said, answering his thoughts as if they had been spoken; "it is 'Henri de Marsillac' to you, Mr. Atherton, always—always!"

"But what if I prefer Miss Prévost?" he said, with a sudden rush of feeling which seemed to clear away all bewilderment and all conflicting sentiment. "Henri de Marsillac was a delightful boy, and how much I have grieved for his loss I can never tell you; but Miss Prévost"—he paused a moment—"is all that he was and more besides. For what would have been merely daring in him takes the higher name of heroism in her."

"Thank you!" she said softly. "I have often wondered what you would think if you knew the truth. I have wondered if you would be horror-struck, disgusted perhaps; or if you would think that the necessity justified the deed, as it seemed to me that it did."

"I not only think that it justified the deed," he answered, "but I can hardly credit my own good fortune in having met a woman capable of such a deed. Do you remember what I said to you once—on the terrace of Millefleurs—about the type of woman I had always dreamed of?

I little thought that I was speaking to one who fulfilled the type, as well as bore the name which suggested it.''

"I remember," she said. "Your words comforted me at the time ; and made me hope that, if some day you should learn the truth, you would not judge too hardly one whom you had helped so kindly.''

"And yet," said he, almost sternly, "you went out of my life without a word of explanation ; you cast me aside like a tool you had used, and for which your use was over ; you were content never to see or hear of me again——"

"No, no !'' she cried, her eyes filling with tears. "I was not content. It seemed a necessity, but it almost broke my heart. I have been wretched ever since, with the sense of my ingratitude—so wretched that all pleasure in my success was obliterated. I cannot tell you what I have thought, what I have felt ; but I can tell you that the necessity to speak, to explain the mystery at last, made me happier than I have been since we parted.''

"But it was not for me you spoke at last. It was for your sister, whose happiness this mystery menaced——"

"In learning that, I learned also for the first time of your presence here. To serve the other purpose, would not a few words to Adrien Varigny have sufficed ? But I heard that you were here ; and I could not but come, to give, even so late, the confidence you had won a hundred times over.''

"And for which I am a hundred times grateful,'' he replied. "It has not come a moment too soon. I was going away to-morrow, going to a life of lonely wandering, going to try and banish forever from my mind the boy I had grown to love. But now life takes another color and meaning. I have recovered all that I lost, together with much more, that my heart divined, though I was too dull to understand. But I understand now. And you, too, Yvonne—for I cannot but call you by the name that seems made for you—you, too, understand ; is it not so ? We were friends and comrades when we were together, but has not separation taught us that we are something more ? Has it not made you feel, as it has surely made me, that our meeting was no chance, and that we have need of each other ?''

She gave him one quick, radiant glance from moisture-dimmed eyes, as he took her hand again.

" But I thought it was to be Diane," she murmured ; " and I have grieved to think that you would be—disappointed."

He laughed as he bent to kiss the hand he held.

" It was only to be Diane," he replied, " because I dreamed of her as Yvonne. The disappointment came when I found she was not Yvonne. But now I have Yvonne herself."

" Have you ?" said Yvonne.   " I am not sure of that. For, after all, what do you know of her ? It is Henri de Marsillac whom you want."

" It is *you*," he answered, " whatever you choose to call yourself. Yes, I want Henri de Marsillac, my friend, my companion, the boy who took such lodging in my heart that not even anger availed to cast him out. But, still more, I want Yvonne, the lady of my dreams, with the courage of a man and the heart of a woman ; tender, heroic, daring—ah, words are too poor to say what I think of her and how much I want her !"

" But," she said, " can you ever forget that I masqueraded in boy's attire——"

" I can never wish to forget it," he answered indignantly. " Forget the deed which does you so much honor, through which I knew you, for which I love you ! Ah, Yvonne, this is folly ! My heart is yours—has been yours all along by some subtle instinct of its own, although I did not know it. Tell me if you will take it now—if you will give me back my lost companion—if you will make my life worth living by sharing it with me ?''

The brave lady of his dreams would have had '' no cunning to be strange'' when wooed by one to whose suit her heart responded, and neither had Yvonne. As simple and direct now as in every action of her life, her frank eyes met his, lovelier than ever in the light which filled them, as she said :

'' It would make me happy to share your life—I have known that ever since we parted. I have missed you every day, every hour. But you—I have just heard from Diane what would have almost broken my heart had I heard it earlier : that you were so angry with me, so determined to cast even my memory out of your life, that you wanted to send back to me the one poor little token of me which you possessed—the ring I gave you.''

'' Yes,'' he admitted, '' I did want to send it back ; for I was furiously angry with you. But should I have been angry if I had not cared for you so much ? Have you yet to learn how near akin sometimes are anger and love ? As for the ring, I will wear it even in my grave if you will let me give you another—a ruby it shall also be, to tell you what love is by the deep fire in its heart.''

'' Give me what you please,'' she said simply. '' I can promise that nothing will ever make me desire to send it back to *you*—no, not if you went away to-morrow and never returned.''

'' There is not much danger of such departure on my part now,'' he laughed. '' When I go you shall go with me, Yvonne ; and we will sail around the world, as I once suggested that we should—do you remember ?"

Yvonne suddenly started.

"Oh, what a selfish wretch I am !" she said, as if to herself. "I told you then, and it is as true now, that they could not do without me at home."

"They must learn to do without you," said he, with triumphant selfishness. "I need you more than they do ; for no one could take your place with me, while with them it may be filled. And I will take care, Yvonne, that it is filled while we are putting a girdle around the earth."

The opening of the door at this moment prevented reply. It was Octave who entered ; and towards her Atherton, turning, led Yvonne.

"Mademoiselle," he said, "since you have kindly played the part of those fairies, Determination and Good Will, of which you spoke a little while ago, and have by your act ended a mystery which threatened the happiness of more than two, it is fitting that you should be the first to hear of the immediate consequence of what you have done."

"I have already heard of one immediate consequence, which amply repays me for my efforts," answered Octave ; "but if it is possible that there can be another——"

She paused and looked inquiringly at Yvonne ; but it was Atherton who replied :

"Can a good fairy doubt what is the end ? We heard this afternoon the story of a girl's high-hearted daring. Let me add the sequel of a man's appreciation. Miss Prévost is good enough to believe that in the journey which we made together we learned enough of each other to venture the longer journey of life also together."

"Yvonne !—is it indeed so ?" cried Octave, flinging her arms impulsively around the slender form. "Oh, how delightful ! how romantic ! how perfectly appropriate ! This is better than I ever hoped or dreamed. It is what should be ; it makes everything proper and right, and ends the story fitly. But how did you find time to fall in love with each other while you were searching for that treasure ?"

"It was then we learned to know each other," answered Yvonne. "Who does one know half so well as the person with whom one has shared adventure and danger ?"

"I must take your word for that," said Octave ; "because I have never shared adventure and danger with anybody, and I fear there is not the slightest hope that I ever shall. O Yvonne, are there no more treasures to be found by another girl, who would almost die of pleasure if Fate would grant her such an adventure and such a romance ?"

"There is some silver plate which was left behind," replied Yvonne, smiling ; "but I would hardly advise your going to seek it. You see, you might not meet another paladin. I doubt if there is another to be found."

"I doubt it also," said Octave. "Well, one must not be envious. You were made to do brave deeds, and it is right that romance should crown heroism. Mr. Atherton," turning to that gentleman, "I acknowledge that you are a paladin and deserve your reward ; but I hope that you fitly appreciate what you have won in winning our Yvonne."

"I think," he replied, "that I do appreciate it ; but my life, not my words, must prove my assertion. Meanwhile she has, once for all, resigned her position as the man of the family in my favor——"

"Ah, no !" cried Octave. "You are too late in applying for the position. It is already taken. Yvonne, have you not told him ? Does he not know that Adrien has already been accepted to fill that place ?"

"I am delighted to hear what you intimate," replied

Atherton, smiling; "but I must deny that any one save the person who has already filled the position can accept a substitute for herself."

"Here he comes," said Octave, turning around as the door again opened. "Now you can settle it between you."

"There is nothing to settle," said Atherton, as Varigny came forward. "I offer my warmest congratulations to one who has won so fair a bride as Mademoiselle Diane; but I must still contend that the position which Yvonne has held, Yvonne can alone bestow—together with herself."

THE END.

THE UNIVERSITY SERIES

STORIES OF COLLEGE LIFE

I. Harvard Stories. Sketches of the Undergraduate. By W. K. Post. Fifteenth edition, 12mo, paper, 50 cts. ; cloth $1 00

" The undergraduate who haunts the classic shades of Cambridge has often been sketched, but never on the whole with so much piquancy and fidelity to truth as by Mr. Post."—*Boston Beacon.*

II. Yale Yarns. By J. S. Wood. Fifth edition. Illustrated, 12mo $1 00

" College days are regarded by most educated men as the cream of their lives, sweet with excellent flavor. They are not dull and tame, even to the most devoted student, and this is a volume filled with the pure cream of such existence, and many ' a college joke to cure the dumps' is given. It is a bright, realistic picture of college life, told in an easy conversational, or descriptive style, and cannot fail to genuinely interest the reader who has the slightest appreciation of humor. The volume is illustrated and is just the book for an idle or lonely hour."—*Los Angeles Times.*

III. The Babe, B.A. Stories of Life at Cambridge University. By Edward F. Benson. Illustrated 12mo $1 00

" Distinctly lifelike and entertaining. . . . There is possibly an oversupply of the dialect but this dialect is assuredly clever while irresponsible and is irradiated with ingeniously misapplied quotations and with easy paradox. . . . The local color is undeniably good." —*London Athenæum.*

IV. A Princetonian. A Story of Undergraduate Life at the College of New Jersey. By James Barnes. Illustrated, 12mo $1 25

" Mr. Barnes is a loyal son of the College of New Jersey, with the cleverness and zeal to write this story of undergraduate life in the college, following his successful use of the pen in earlier books, " For King and Country," " Midshipman Farragut," etc. . . . There is enough of fiction in the story to give true liveliness to its fact. . . . Mr. Barnes's literary style is humorous and vivid."—*Boston Transcript.*

G. P. PUTNAM'S SONS,

NEW YORK.　　　　　　　　LONDON.

Works by Anna Katharine Green

I.—THE LEAVENWORTH CASE. A Lawyer's Story. 4to, paper, 20 cents; 16°, paper, 50 cents; cloth . \$1 00

" She has worked up a *cause célèbre* with a fertility of device and ingenuity of treatment hardly second to Wilkie Collins or Edgar Allan Poe."—*Christian Union.*

II.—BEHIND CLOSED DOORS. 16°, paper, 50 cents; cloth \$1 00

" . . . She has never succeeded better in baffling the reader." —*Boston Christian Register.*

III.—THE SWORD OF DAMOCLES. A Story of New York Life. 16°, paper, 50 cents; cloth . . . \$1 00

" 'The Sword of Damocles' is a book of great power, which far surpasses either of its predecessors from her pen, and places her high among American writers. The plot is complicated, and is managed adroitly. . . . In the delineation of characters she has shown both delicacy and vigor."—*Congregationalist.*

IV.—X. Y. Z.; A Detective Story. 16°, paper . 25 cents

" Well written and extremely exciting and captivating. . . . She is a perfect genius in the construction of a plot."—*N. Y. Commercial Advertiser.*

V.—HAND AND RING. In quarto, paper, 20 cents; 16°, paper, illustrated, 50 cents; cloth \$1 00

" It is a tribute to the author's genius that she never tires and never loses her readers. . . . It moves on clean and healthy. . . . It is worked out powerfully and skilfully."—*N. Y. Independent.*

VI. —A STRANGE DISAPPEARANCE. In quarto, paper, 20 cents; 16°, paper, 50 cents; cloth . . . \$1 00

" A most ingenious and absorbingly interesting story. The readers are held spell-bound until the last page."—*Cincinnati Commercial.*

VII.—THE MILL MYSTERY. 16°, paper, 50 cents; cloth \$1 00

" Shows the author's skill in the manufacture of entirely new and original complications, and as the central figure is a fresh and charming girl, the reader is absorbed and thrilled and wrought up to the last degree in following her fortunes to their triumphant sequel."— *Commercial Advertiser.*

VIII.—7 TO 12—A DETECTIVE STORY. Square 16°, paper . . . . 25 cts.

G. P. PUTNAM'S SONS, NEW YORK AND LONDON.

Works by Anna Katharine Green

IX.—THE OLD STONE HOUSE, AND OTHER STORIES. 16°, paper, 40 cents ; cloth . . . 75 cents

" It is a bundle of quite cleverly constructed pieces of fiction, with which an idle hour may be pleasantly passed."—*N. Y. Independent.*

X.—CYNTHIA WAKEHAM'S MONEY. With frontispiece. 16°, paper, 50 cents ; cloth $1 00

" ' Cynthia Wakeham's Money ' is a story notable even among the many vigorous works of Anna Katharine Green."—*New York Sun.*

XI.—MARKED "PERSONAL." 16°, paper, 50 cents ; cloth $1 00

" The ingenious plot is built up with all the skill of the writer of ' The Leavenworth Case ' to the very last-chapter, which contains the surprising solutions of several mysteries."

XII.—MISS HURD ; An Enigma. 16°, paper, 50 cents ; cloth $1 00

" A strong and interesting novel in an entirely new field of romance."

XIII.—THE DOCTOR, HIS WIFE, AND THE CLOCK. 32°, limp cloth . . . . 50 cents

" The story is entertainingly told. . . ."—*Cincinnati Tribune.*

XIV.—DR. IZARD. 16°, paper, 50 cents ; cloth . . $1 00

" Those who have read her other books will not need to be urged to read this ; they will be eager to do so, and we assure them a very interesting story."—*Boston Times.*

XV.—THAT AFFAIR NEXT DOOR. 16°, paper, 50 cts. ; cloth $1 00

" The success of ' That Affair Next Door,' Anna Katharine Green's latest novel, is something almost unprecedented. ' That Affair Next Door,' with its startling ingenuity, its sustained interest, and its wonderful plot, shows that the author's hand has not lost its cunning, but has gained as the years go by."—*Buffalo Inquirer.*

THE DEFENCE OF THE BRIDE, AND OTHER POEMS. 16°, cloth $1 00

" It is long since any volume by a wholly new poet has been marked by a single poem so strong and concentrated as ' The King's Musketeers ' in ' The Defence of the Bride, and Other Poems.' It tells its story tersely and powerfully. . . ."—*The Nation.*

RISIFI'S DAUGHTER. A Drama. 16°, cloth . . $1 00

" Both in its conception and its expression, it is a thing of beauty and of power."—*Boston Christian Register.*

G. P. PUTNAM'S SONS, NEW YORK AND LONDON.

www.ingramcontent.com/pod-product-compliance
Lightning Source LLC
Chambersburg PA
CBHW031146120726
47905CB00006B/1840